THE SHACKLED SERPENT

K.M. LISTER

To anyone who has a heart full of stories.
Dream them. Write them. Share them.
They deserve to be heard.

And to me,
YOU DID IT!

This book contains content that might not be suitable for
some readers, including, but not limited to, depictions of:

Grief
Profanity
Graphic violence
Torture
Explicit sexual content
Death

PRONUNCIATION GUIDE

Characters:

Maeve Wyndell: Mayv Win-dell
Arden Wyndell: Ar-din Win-dell
Livinia Wyndell: Liv-in-yuh Win-dell
Ottilie Ashbrook: Aw-tuh-lee Ash-brook
Drustan Bennett: Droo-stin Ben-it
Jerik Flint: Jair-ick Flint
Andrina Verral: An-dree-nuh Vair-ull
Kayd Glynvyre: Kayd Glen-vy-er
Madam Prea: Ma-dum Pray-uh
Osmar Glynvyre: Os-mar Glen-vy-er
Sir Halton: Sir Hal-tin
Niam Myradove: Nee-um Me-ruh-dov
Alta Myradove: All-tuh Me-ruh-dov
Aila Glynvyre: Ay-luh Glen-vy-er
Amsden Verral: Ams-din Vair-ull

Locations:

Galfei Thalor: Gal-FAY THUH-lore
Terakeld: Tair-UH-keld
Phandolus: Fan-DOL-us
Fiermoor: FEAR-more
Amphitea: AM-fih-TEE-uh
Nythfaedell: Nith-FAY-dell
Rutherglen: ROO-thur-glen
Ardorein: AR-dor-RAIN
Lokaep: Lo-cape
Orolen: Or-UH-lin
Holmfirth: Holm-firth
Crullfeld: Cruel-feld
Derlow Grove: Der-low Grove

Other:

Spiicrete: Spy-CREET
Nukorynn: Noo-KOR-rin
Amithydia: Am-ih-THAY-dee-uh
Ryllikaar: Ray-lih-KARR
Hathil: Hawth-EEL

OROLEN
NYTHFAEDELL
NORTH WESTERN DISTRICT
PHANDOLUS
RUTHERGLEN
ARDOREL
FIERMOOR
CRUITFIELD

Galfei Thalor
Lokaer
Secret Spring
Serpent Hill
Derlow Grove
Terakeld
North Eastern District
Royal Docks
The Unlighted Sea
Central District
Southern District
Amphitea
Eastern Docks
Holmfirth

PART I:
A CONTENDER

1

Deafening. That's the best way to describe the silence that wholly surrounds me—in my family's dusty dwelling, in the barren alleyways of Terakeld, even in my heart. The hush is suffocating, ever present.

I shouldn't exaggerate. Mother used to say it was impolite.

"Maeve Wyndell," she'd say, *"nothing good comes from exaggerating. You must speak the truth. Only the truth."*

The truth is, I can hear the tedious drip from the faucet we haven't fixed since winter. I can hear Father's deep breathing as he stares at the floor and refuses to utter a word. I can hear my heartbeat pick up as I ruminate over what's to come in just mere hours: *the trials.*

My hands begin to tremble against the top of the tottering table in the corner of our home. Dread fills me deep to the core. I see the trials for what they are: a way for the kingdoms to remind us—the humans of Galfei Thalor—that we are inferior to those who reign above us. Those who think otherwise are simply too ignorant to see it.

The callouses littering my palms snag on the wood of the table as I wring my fingers together. My teeth dig into my lower lip, and sweat beads along my brow.

The story of how the trials began is taught to us in school, drilled into young, impressionable minds for generations. Our teachers and Elders say the four kingdoms came together to bring prosperity to our lands after the Last War. They say they saved us from the dangerous lives our kind used to live. To show our thanks, we are to serve one of Galfei Thalor's four kingdoms for ten rotations. Thus came the trials, introduced to determine who we belong to.

Our time spent as servants is supposed to bring us honor. We are meant to believe that it is our sole purpose in life and that nothing will bring us more fulfillment. I don't buy it. Nine rotations ago, those rose-colored lenses that blinded me from the truth shattered into nothing. Nine rotations ago, Mother was killed, and it was the kingdoms' fault.

The heel of my boot taps insistently against the chipped floor of our home. Another sound interrupting the silence. The dread that sits deep in my stomach turns into a pulsing sorrow before twining together with a brewing white-hot rage. Mother is dead. The kingdoms tore our family apart. And soon, I will be shipped off to bow before those whose hands are stained with her blood. How my brother, Arden, left for his trials five rotations ago with eagerness in his eyes is beyond me.

I glance up at the only family I have left in Terakeld. My father is sitting in his old rocking chair before the small cracked hearth we use to keep warm in the winter. Worn animal hides surround the structure, each fur strewn across the floor. Our hearth was once what breathed life into our home. Now, it only conjures up memories of happier days filled with laughter and love. Mother humming as she cooked supper. Arden and I playing tag in our single room home. Father reading to us as we settled in for the night. All of it echoes against the bare walls and musty furniture. A life lived long ago.

The back of my hand swipes across my forehead, the skin now glistening with sweat. It's the first day of the summer season, and the heat is already leaking through the cracks in our walls. Like our empty hearth, there are no flames in the shell of the man who sits before it now. I hate what he's become: a shadow of the loving father he used to be. That father I long for is dead.

After Mother died, he simply stopped—stopped eating, stopped walking, stopped providing for Arden and me. My brother—only sixteen at the time—took evening shifts in the fields after school, so we wouldn't starve. Perhaps that is why he was ready for his servitude once he came of age. He wouldn't have to carry the burden of this family any longer.

"Father?" My eyes focus back on his sunken, sweat-slicked face.

He says nothing. He doesn't move a muscle. My jaw clenches, and my teeth grind together as I hold in a scream. For once, I can admit I want him to acknowledge me. I want him to say something. I want him . . . No, I *need* him. I have needed my father since the day we burned my mother's body behind our home, and yet, he abandoned us, shutting us out and becoming nothing more than an empty vessel.

My wooden chair scrapes against the cracked floor as I abruptly stand up. He doesn't even flinch. My stomach knots, and tears well in my eyes before I force them back. What I need now is to get out of here, to clear my head before my life changes forever.

"Father, the trials are today."

Nothing but silence.

My eyes sweep over his motionless body, then move across the open room that is our home. The dull floors blend into the chipped wooden walls. The singular window—near the door and stained with grime—casts a sliver of mid-morning light into our already-dim dwelling. My cot sits directly below the window, and Father's is perpendicular against the wall. After Arden left for his trials, we burned his cot during that first winter to keep warm. Before it turned to ash, his cot was along the back wall near the basin. Now, there's nothing but dust settling in the empty spot he once occupied.

"I am going to tend to some things before meeting the others in The Square this evening. We leave for our trials just before dusk. I would like for you to be there to see me off." I look at him once more. A part of me hopes he'll turn his head, look into my eyes for the first time in nine rotations, and say something, anything. My name, possibly. It's been so long since he uttered it out loud.

I miss the sound of his voice, but I am only met with more silence.

My eyes drop to my dirty boots, and I release the hopeful breath I was foolishly holding. The huff of air—soft and barely audible on any other day—pierces the silence around me, twining with the faint sound of the dripping faucet.

Suffocating. Ever present.

Without a word, I dig my nails into the skin of my palms and walk out of the only home I have ever known.

2

Heavy breaths leave my lungs with every crunch of gravel beneath my feet. I weave my way through the dirty streets of the Central District, where I live, toward Terakeld's Towne Square.

Looking around, I take it all in. The small cabins that line the narrow pathways with little to no room in between. Some stacked atop one another with rickety ladders leading to crooked windows used as doors. The soot-covered trees and shrubs with wilted leaves and broken branches, yearning for water that rarely comes. The dirty puddles that barely cover the bottom of each well on every street corner. Rotted buckets sit nearby, waiting to be filled once again.

Home. My heart seizes. It isn't much. It isn't great. But it's mine.

Heavy boots stomp against the ground behind me. Stepping to the side and turning toward the noise, I spot them—an impenetrable unit dressed in copper armor. *Guards.* Guards who patrol the streets of Terakeld and stand tall atop the buildings with batons in their hands and swords at their sides.

"Move," the commander at the front of the pack barks at me, as if I wasn't already to the side. His golden eyes brand me to my spot, and the thin gills on the side of his bronze neck quiver in disgust. He leads a unit of merfolk stationed here to make sure we comply.

My mouth clenches tight, and my eyes drift to the side. The less eye contact, the better. In the distance, I see a wave of gold flash behind a building. An elven unit marching to the east.

Home. Held hostage by the kingdoms and their guards under the guise of safety.

I swallow against the lump in my throat. *Don't cry, Maeve. Don't cry. They don't deserve your tears.*

The merfolk unit's loud march grows quieter and quieter the longer I stand, frozen, with my back against the side of a gray shack, and my head tilted to the sky. Perhaps if I stare at the sun long enough, my eyes will burn away.

I harshly press the heels of my palms against my eyes to stop the tears threatening to escape. "Get a hold of yourself," I mumble, wiping away the tracks of moisture left behind with shaking hands.

When my eyes open again, the world seems brighter. A type of bright that stings my irises. It's a welcome feeling—a distraction that pulls my thoughts away from the painful ache in my chest.

Moments pass as I gather myself once more and push away from the wall. Inhaling a deep breath, my lungs fill to the brink with warm Terakeld air. I let it out and take a step forward.

Towne Square is the core of Terakeld, the place where our land comes to life. Normally, people from all four districts mill about their everyday lives—some go to the jobs they acquired after their servitude, while others waste away in the tavern.

Today is different.

"Open your eyes, people!" screams a man with red splotches littering his face and an angry vein pulsing across his forehead as he struggles against the grips of our Elders. "Don't let them continue doing this!"

I slow my steps as I approach the crowd beginning to gather around him. Many sneer at the man, yell profanities, and spit on the soil where that group of merfolk guards accompanying the Elders force him onto his knees.

"Traitor!" one woman hisses loudly enough for all to hear.

Others—quiet and somber—try to smooth their wrinkled brows and lift their downturned lips. Grave expressions masked by indifference.

The guards force the man's left hand above his head, and the Elders stand, stone-faced, nearby. An ear-splitting click thunders against my skull as his wrist is shackled to the scarred, wooden post protruding out of the ground, his bare back facing outward.

He struggles to get free. "You'll see! You'll all see!"

The defiance in his eyes and the sweat gleaming against his alabaster skin makes bile rise into the back of my throat. My body freezes, and my vision begins to blur, morphing the present and past together into a muddy haze.

The man's rugged physique transforms into soft curves. The image of ash-brown waves that match my own flashes before my eyes, flinging to the sides as a woman thrashes against the chains bolted to the post.

I try to stop that painful memory from rushing in. I try to stop the stale scent of copper that has stung my nostrils since that day, nine rotations ago, from suffocating me. I try to stop it, but it's no use. The memory successfully crawls its way out of a deep, dark corner of my mind, and everything shifts.

Everything shifts . . .

Everything . . .

It had been a dreary winter day. Four days before the new rotation, to be exact. Onlookers bundled in coats and scarves filled every inch of Towne Square. Parted mouths hung open as eyes widened in horror at the sight in front of them.

Father and Arden stood off to the side next to me. Red-skinned tiefling guards surrounded us, their barbed tails flicking against the ground in anticipation.

And in the heart of The Square stood a stone fountain and statue of a regal elf, a ghost-like changeling, a horned tiefling, and a merman in aquatic form sprouting from the water, looming over my half-naked mother. Goose bumps covered her bare, olive skin, and her chest rapidly rose and fell—a white cloud of fog falling from her shivering lips—as she pulled at her bonds.

"Thank you all for gathering here today." The Chief of Elders's voice ricocheted around the open area. "These are unprecedented times. Lies are spreading across our community. A small group of traitors led by this woman—Livinia Wyndell—are weaving a web of deceit and destruction.

"She claims the kingdoms are oppressing us, making us work in unfair conditions. We all know this is false. She is nothing more than an angry woman who is sick—in body, mind, and soul."

A wall of heads crowded around us had nodded in agreement. They looked down on Mother and murmured under their breaths. They were people Mother grew up with, people who were welcomed into our home for supper. And they had turned their backs on her before my eyes, when she never turned her back on them.

I wanted to run to Mother. I wanted to scream at the Elders and guards and anyone who would listen that she was only sick because of her servitude assignment. The tiefling mines damaged her lungs. She had the right to be angry. She had the right to speak out, so no other would meet the same fate she had. Even when her illness made standing too difficult for her, she still stood up for what was right. But what was right led her here.

Father's fingers had painfully dug into my shoulder, forcing me to stand still, as if he knew what I yearned to do, what my body screamed at me to do.

"Let this be a lesson to any who stand by this woman. Speak lies about our kingdoms and face the consequences," the Chief of Elders said, the leather whip creaking under his firm grip as he turned toward my mother. "Look upon the kingdoms' fountain, Livinia. Look at your Gods as you receive your punishment and ask the kingdoms for forgiveness."

Mother's head had lifted upward toward the fountain stationed behind the whipping post. Her eyes hardened, and a snarl ripped through her gritted teeth. Then she turned to me. Her gray-green eyes—the same eyes that look back at me when I stare into the mirror—pierced my soul.

"Know the truth, Maeve. Embrace the truth. Speak the truth." It had been a whisper, meant only for me. Tears welled into the corners of my eyes.

In her last act of defiance, Mother dropped her gaze to the ground, refusing to look at the fountain.

The crack of the whip had screamed across the cold Terakeld air. The sound made me flinch, grating against my bones and cementing itself into my soul. Father's grip had tightened with each lash. Strike after strike after strike, the Chief of Elders sent the whip into Mother's flesh. Blood pooled around her limp body, but she didn't make a sound except for the long, drawn-out breaths she released in the seconds before the whip, once again, split open her skin and muscles.

More lashings, and those breaths became weak.

More lashings, and those breaths stopped completely.

I rapidly blink my eyes and shake my head to banish the horrid memory, and the sight of blood coating Mother's broken and open back disappears. The man's smooth, pale flesh replaces it in an instant.

Mother died chained to that very post, and Father, Arden, and I were forced to watch.

We changed that day. Arden turned cold. Only I was allowed to see his rare moments of vulnerability. Gone was the glee that coated his every word. Father not only changed from the suffocating grief that came with losing a lover and life partner, but in his silence, I could see the guilt eating him alive. He stood by while his wife did the right thing. He stood by while she died.

And me? I've clung to my mother's last words. The little girl who believed in our kingdoms and all the good they've done for us died the day her mother did.

That day, something changed in Terakeld, too. No longer were we a community. Instead, Terakeld split in two: those who believe in Mother and her movement—like this man, whose second wrist is being forced into the rusted shackle—and those who don't. They call themselves kingdom loyalists. They look down on anyone who sympathizes with the movement. They spit on the few brave souls who actually speak out.

"Please!" The man's voice is hoarse now. His head swivels around, looking for anyone to help. "Gallus! Ester! Aileen!"

Three known sympathizers. My eyes shift, easily finding them in the crowd. Their gazes are hard, and their mouths are pressed firmly in tight white lines. None of them utter a word. The only reason they aren't chained to the whipping post as well is because they've kept their mouths shut. It's the smart thing to do. It's what I do. Speaking out is useless. Nothing will change the world we live in.

"Quiet, Vlad. Do not drag others into your mess. You did this to yourself." Elder Payne, the current Chief of Elders, speaks to the man whose head now hangs low in defeat. Elder Payne's scarred fingers twitch around the leather whip—the same leather whip that took Mother's life . . . the same leather whip that took dozens of others since.

The wrinkled man turns back to the crowd and raises his voice. "Speaking falsities about our glorious kingdoms is a punishable offense. We know that. They know that, and yet they continue to do so."

The four other Elders in their pristine robes stand around the man. Two on either side of the whipping post, as still as the stone fountain's statue behind them.

Elder Payne continues. "Why spread lies about our gracious kingdoms when we all know they have given so much to our kind? It's disgraceful. It's humiliating . . ."

I begin to push my way through the growing crowd. My boots scuff against the ground, and plumes of dust waft behind me. I don't want to see another life lost. I *can't*. As I clear the gathering and head toward the market on the opposite side of The Square, a crack cuts through the taut, warm air. The man's guttural scream follows a second later.

3

MY STEPS QUICKEN, TRYING to get as far away from the man's screams as possible. The smells of meats, sweets, and fresh leathers fill my senses as I approach the marketplace.

Despite the sharp cracks of the whip and that man's screams distorting into moans in the near distance, life is going on as usual in the market. It's bustling with people. Couples are browsing different selections of textiles. Merchants are organizing their stock. Children are enjoying their first day of summer break by playing tag between the stands and carts.

One girl, who looks only a few rotations younger than me, is holding a basket of ripened fruits and pleading with the graying merchant at the produce stand. My steps slow as I walk past the two.

"Please, Mr. Hankin, I can help with anything you need," the young girl begs, the words leaving her lips in haste. Her eyes are wide and wild, desperation oozing off her. "My brother leaves for his trials today, and Gran is too old to work as a spinster now. The extra money could really help."

The corners of my mouth fall as I think about the mortal children having to work before completing their trials. It shouldn't have to happen, but it does. After one's ten rotations of servitude, they're expected to start a life in

14

Terakeld . . . To get a job to keep our land running and start a family so the kingdoms continue to have servants for generations to come.

Sometimes, it doesn't work out like that.

Suddenly, I'm hyperaware of the rough callouses on my hands and the thin white scars that dance along my fingertips. The fields are no place for a child to work, and yet I took Arden's position when he left. I was only fifteen at the time.

Shaking my head, I turn toward the cheese stand just up ahead. The crunching of gravel beneath my boots drowns out the produce merchant's reply.

"Hello, Maeve!" the cheese merchant, an older woman with round eyes, calls out as I approach her stand. Her voice is kind, her cadence lilting with every word.

"Hello, Ms. Beverlye." I nod before browsing the cheese selection before me. She's laid out several options today.

I reach into the pocket sewn onto my brown cropped linen pants and pull out two dull brass coins. It's the last of what I made working in the fields.

Pointing to a large wheel of white cheese speckled with spices, I say, "Just two small wedges, please."

"Of course, dear!" Ms. Beverlye exclaims. Another crack of the whip snaps in the distance. My body reacts, flinching slightly. It's enough for the cheese merchant to notice. "I'm sorry you must witness such violence before you go to your trials. But you know those abhorrent, ungrateful rebels . . . they get what they deserve."

My gut tightens, and my fingers curl. Mother didn't deserve it. None of them did. The woman doesn't notice how quiet I've become.

"The kingdoms could easily squash it, but a rebellion as minuscule as this doesn't deserve the time of day—"

"Maeve, over here!" A silent exhale rushes past my lips at the interruption.

Quickly turning my head in the direction of the sound, I feel warmth flood my body. My best friend, Ottilie Ashbrook, with bouncing curls of copper and a smile that lights up her bright honey-brown eyes, bounds toward me as she waves above the crowd. She is the most beautiful person I've ever had the pleasure of meeting. The pure kindness in her heart gives me hope for the future. I can't help but grin at the sight of her.

"I thought I'd find you here." The freckles that dust the top of her rich, clay-colored nose bunch together as she beams at me. "Hello, Ms. Beverlye," she addresses the merchant.

"Hello, dear! Are you ready for today? The trials are such an important time for any young mortal." The older woman's fingers delicately remove a knife from its holder and begin cutting two small wedges off the wheel of cheese.

A brush of red dances along Ottilie's cheeks. "I can't believe today is the day! We've been told about the wonders of the kingdoms and servitude our whole lives, and now we'll finally get to experience it."

Her giggle flutters around the cheese stand, and she's bouncing on her toes, as if she can't wait to be shipped off somewhere else . . . away from her home, away from her family, away from me.

Ms. Beverlye's smile broadens at seeing her so excited to serve.

The merchant gracefully rips a piece of white linen cloth and begins wrapping the wedges as she asks, "Which kingdom are you hoping chooses you? Perhaps you'll spend your time in Amphitea with the merfolk just like your father or in Phandolus with the changelings like your mother. Speaking of your parents, are they around? I have a wheel of their favorite cheese whenever they're ready."

My eyes shift downward. My boots are stark against the ashen ground. I know exactly where Ottilie's parents are. Her hesitation tells me she knows I know as well.

"They're in The Square . . . spectating." Another crack of the whip. From the corner of my eye, I can see Ottilie's head turn toward me. Just slightly. Enough for me to know how regretful she feels.

"Good for them," Ms. Beverlye chirps. It's like she completely forgot what happened to Mother. It's like she was never friends with her. "If I could, I would—"

"But to answer your other question," Ottilie interrupts the merchant, much to my relief. "If I could choose any kingdom, I'd want to go wherever Maeve goes." At this, I lift my head and send my friend a soft smile. "So, Fiermoor, since we all know she'll get chosen by the tieflings. Just like everyone else in her family. But if I don't get that lucky, I'd love the elves to choose me. I've heard Nythfaedell is breathtaking."

I tune out Ms. Beverlye's response as polite applause erupts from the center of Towne Square. The whipping is over. That man—that *rebel*—is no more. He will never take another breath. He will never spend a clear morning roaming Terakeld. He will never speak his truth again.

"Know the truth, Maeve. Embrace the truth. Speak the truth."

But the truth will do nothing. Nothing will change. *Nothing*.

Terakeld seems to always be at its loudest after a whipping. The birds begin to chirp again. The clock tower connected to Towne Hall rings with the number of lashes the rebel received. People talk animatedly, as if someone isn't hanging from a bloody post, limp and open for all to see. It's a rush of noises all at once, barreling into each of us.

Through the chaos, my ears perk up as I hear a deep chuckle mixed with high-pitched giggles—a father laughing with his children. The sound makes me think of the man I left motionless in our home. A shiver creeps down my spine like a trickle of water at the thought of him not moving from that very spot. Will he starve? Will he wither away into nothing? Once I'm back from servitude, will the first sight I see be his bones scattered across our floor?

"Here you go, dear." Ms. Beverlye's voice pulls my attention back toward her and Ottilie. She places a small bundle of cloth on her stand's counter.

"Thank you, Ms. Beverlye," I say. My next words leave my mouth before I can reel them back. "While I'm gone, will you look out for Father? I know you two grew up together, being in the same trial group and all. After Mother . . . I'm worried. I'm worried about what will happen to him once I'm away."

The woman's eyes soften. There's pity behind them. It gives me solace that she at least remembers her old friend. "Oh, child. There's no need to be worried. Of course, I will keep watch over him," she coos. "Now, now. Chin up! There's no need to be sad on your big day!"

Ottilie's hand wraps around my own and squeezes it gently. My chest eases, a weight lifted by the merchant's reassurance.

I take a deep breath and nod at the woman, who is now beaming. "Thank you." I mean it. Father won't keel over and die. She will watch him. She will . . .

"To the meadow?" Ottilie smiles. Another squeeze to my hand.

I smile back. "To the meadow."

Picking up the cloth-wrapped pieces of cheese, I stuff them in my only pocket and make my way out of the market with my best friend in tow.

Tall golden grass tickles our shins, and a small breeze cools the sweat pooling down our necks. The sun is at its highest point now, blazing down on us as we look across the meadow. An oasis, away from the dust and grime, on the outer edge of Terakeld.

In the distance, the dark-blue river gushes by, each wave sparkling with every movement. The tall majestic Moon Elm tree sways near its bank. The tree's sage-green leaves move with the wind, and as they do, silver glints off the surface. Shining metallic colors dance along the branches like a performance meant only for us.

"It's always so beautiful here," Ottilie sighs before bounding toward the great tree.

I nod and bite my lip as memories flood my senses like they do every time I come here. Arden pushing me into the river before jumping in himself. Mother picking me up so I could pluck the dainty spring flowers from the Moon Elm branches to liven up our home. Father hugging me close as we dug into breads, fruits, and nuts for lunch. I sear them into my mind to take with me. Moments in time to think back on while I'm away.

"Maeve?" Ottilie's voice rings out across the sparse flowers scattered along the grass, pulling me away from happier times. She jogs toward me, grabbing my hand again and hauling me toward the Moon Elm.

Sitting upon the lush grass, I settle against the large rough trunk and take out the cheese I bought from Ms. Beverlye. Ottilie plops down next to me with a sigh. Her legs cross as her face turns toward me.

"I know today is hard for you . . ." Her words trail off as my shoulders tense. A scoff slips through the barrier of my tightly pressed lips. She continues as if she didn't hear it. "Maeve, this is your chance to start anew. You're going to get to live in one of the beautiful kingdoms, meet new people, and—"

"Be forced to provide for creatures who seemingly have everything and despise our kind."

"You're lucky no one is around to hear you talk like that." The words come out clipped. Ottilie's brows furrow, and I can see the conflict she feels in her glazed eyes. She knows my truth, she knows how I feel, and she supports me, like the best friend she is. But her and her family are loyalists, and she still sees the kingdoms as saviors to our kind. We're opposites through and through, yet our friendship simply *works.* "What happened to your mother is not going to happen to you."

I turn my head away from her, facing the river once again. Her gaze is persistent, pinning me in place and burning into the side of my face. The salty tears I've been struggling to keep at bay all day spring up once again. A wayward tear breaches my lash line, and her soft thumb rises and wipes it away.

"I know you don't think anything good can come from the next ten rotations, but I have faith."

"In what?" I question with more bite in my tone than intended. "The kingdoms?"

She doesn't waver at the harshness of my voice. "In you." She leaves no room for debate. A small smile flickers across my features, and the line between my eyebrows smooths out. She has so much—*too* much—faith in me. "Do you remember, before everything went to shit—your mother, the whippings, Arden leaving—we would come down here? We'd pretend we were merfolk, swimming in the river's current. Do you remember that?"

A laugh, light and breathy, rushes out as I nod.

Ottilie sends me a dazzling smile. Mischief laces around it. She reaches down into the pocket of her navy pants and takes out a stone-blue ribbon, placing it in my hand. My eyes go wide at the feel of the fabric. *Silk.* How she could have come by anything made of silk, I have no idea. The textile can only be found in Amphitea, the kingdom of the merfolk. Perhaps her father kept a piece of his servitude with him.

I'm at a loss for words.

Thankfully, Ottilie fills the silence. "I'm still hoping we get assigned the same kingdom, but if not, this is just something to remember me by."

She watches me admire the small strip of silk. I notice her silence, and I admonish myself for not thinking to give her anything. I look up at her, and I know she sees the panic in my eyes because a giggle escapes her lips. "Don't even think about feeling bad. I'm just a softy, and we both know you aren't."

I chortle, short and loud. She's right. She's always right.

Before I can properly thank her, she seizes the ribbon from my palm and forces my body away from the Moon Elm tree, with my back to her chest. Grabbing strands from the topmost layer of my hair, Ottilie ties a neat bow around them, patting down fly-aways as she goes. A beat later, she sighs, marveling at my new addition. Arms engulf my shoulders tightly from behind.

My throat tightens—feeling as if someone is wrapping their hands around my esophagus—as I hold in a sob. I can't put into words how much I value this gesture.

"Thank you," I whisper. The words are cracked. It's all I can muster. Ottilie squeezes me close one last time before letting go.

"Now, don't you go soft on me, Wyndell," Ottilie chides, as I turn back to rest against the tree trunk with a rare, genuine smile.

I unwrap the cloth around the pieces of cheese. Handing one of the small wedges to Ottilie, she takes it, kindly returning a smile and touching hers to mine. "Cheers," she whispers, then takes a bite.

A beat of silence passes as she chews. Then, she releases a drawn-out breath. "I'm scared, too, you know."

My head whips around at the sound of her wavering voice. Chewing on her lower lip, she's now facing the river, eyes glossed over and brows furrowed.

"Of what?" I whisper.

"The trials . . . Life after the trials, really. So much can change in ten rotations. I don't . . . What if we don't know who the other is when we come back? I can't lose my best friend."

Her words shove a knife into my chest, wedging open my heart. "We will always be best friends, Ottilie. Nothing—not the trials, not the kingdoms, not ten rotations apart—will come between us."

The corners of her lips lift slightly. Her head falls onto my shoulder, resting in the silence that falls between us. Minutes pass. Birds chirp above us, and the grass sways around us. It's peaceful. It's serene. Nothing like the heavy, weighted silence I felt in my home earlier today.

But something gnaws at my mind like an insistent mouse burrowing in my brain.

"What do you think the trials are like?" The words slip out. That simple question has been weighing heavy on my heart for days now.

"I don't know. They don't teach us that in school," Ottilie says simply, as if that were that.

"But why?" I push. "Why doesn't anyone talk about it? Not even the rebels speak about the trials themselves, just their servitude."

A deep sigh. Exasperation wafts off Ottilie. "I don't know, Maeve. Just trust the Elders. Trust the kingdoms. They know what's best for us."

Ottilie—so blind, so conditioned.

I don't have the heart to argue with her. Not when these are the last moments we'll have before everything changes. So, I bottle up the worry that's eating away at my soul and the sadness I feel for having to leave my home, and I enjoy the meadow for all that it is.

Beauty. Peace. Tranquility. *Home.*

4

M Y EYES SHIFT BEHIND my eyelids, moving back and forth to the sounds of the meadow and rushing river. Despite not seeing the world around me, I know it's time. The warm summer air is cooling just enough to raise the hairs on my arms.

Blinking, I open my eyes and stare up at the bright, blue sky between the Moon Elm's silver-green leaves. The sun is beginning to dip. I long to stay in this bliss for the rest of my life.

"Are you ready?" Ottilie's voice fractures the tranquil quiet around us.

I turn my head toward her, the grass scratching at my cheek. She's sprawled out on her back. Her honey-brown eyes meet mine, anxious excitement shining brightly within them. A tentative smile grazes her freckled lips.

"No," I mumble. Weight creeps in around my chest. The hours we spent in the meadow weren't enough, knowing that the next time I'll see it, everything could be different. My time here in my oasis with Ottilie could never be enough.

"We're already cutting it close. It'll take us an hour or so to get back to The Square. Come on, Wyndell." Ottilie sits up, brushing off the stray pieces of grass that stick to her tunic. As she stands, she runs her fingers over her corkscrew curls. "Need to look presentable for the ceremony," she hums and extends her hand toward me.

My body screams at me while I stare at her dainty fingers. My bones bang together, and my blood turns to lead, begging me to ignore her gesture. But it's Ottilie. I would follow her to the ends of the world.

Reaching out my hand, my fingers curl around Ottilie's as she pulls me up. My head feels foggy, and my limbs become heavy once I'm standing. Even as I walk out of the meadow, arm-in-arm with my best friend—the constant light in my dreary life—everything in my entire being is yearning to stop.

Don't go to The Square. Don't complete your trials, it seems to say.

I want to listen more than I can put into words. My body—*my soul*—knows how much I don't want to do this. *Don't go. Don't go.*

Dong! The bell tower rings out, signaling the five-minute warning before the trial ceremony begins. We're just in time.

Our journey out of the meadow and through the Northwestern District—where Ottilie lives—was a blur. It's like I have no recollection of it whatsoever.

Several guards are lined up along the border of Towne Square. Some are covered in copper armor, others in gold. Merfolk and elves. The people of Terakeld are beginning to gather around a makeshift stage in front of the fountain and whipping post still coated in mostly dry crimson, with a handful of wet streaks running along the wood. They murmur to one another and greet their neighbors as they approach.

Near the stage, guards are dressed in silver armor. The changelings. My eyes sweep past them, never looking at them for too long. They look more ghost-like than being with their frost-white hair, light gray—almost white—skin, and icy blue irises that blend into the whites of their eyes. Each guard's hand is firmly holding the pommel of their swords, ready for anything.

Surrounding the five Terakeld Elders off to the side are large muscular beasts with leathery red skin, ram horns protruding out of their foreheads, and barbed tails caressing the ground. The tieflings. Armor made of Spiicrete—a rare bronze-and-maroon crystal only found in the mines of Fiermoor—cover their bulky frames. Nearly as impenetrable as it is strong, Spiicrete can slice through anything—even elven gold. It's the only mineral able to penetrate it.

My eyes turn cold. *My mother fell ill because of that armor. She died for it.*

"Hey," Ottilie says softly, pulling my attention toward her. Her hand perches atop my shoulder, and her eyes soften, like she knows what plagues my mind. I smile back reassuringly. "I need to go find Ma and Pa. One last goodbye before we take off. Will you be okay by yourself?"

I nod and let her go. A few moments later, a high-pitched squeal echoes across The Square. She's found them.

Now alone, without the comfort she provides, I gently push my way through the crowded bodies, staring at the dirt-covered ground and mumbling apologies whenever I bump into someone too hard. I reach the group of other contenders. What a horrendous title the kingdoms gave us . . . contenders. We're not competing to achieve some glorious goal. We're being forced to give up our freedom. We're being forced to give up *everything*.

Boisterous laughter rings out from the center of a group of boys.

"I'm telling you. I'm bound to be a soldier for whatever kingdom chooses me." That raspy voice—a voice I know all too well—pulls at my attention like an invisible string. My eyes land on Drustan Bennett. "I'm hoping for the tieflings. I know I would thrive in the ranks of their warriors."

He shakes out his shaggy black hair and throws a sly wink in my direction, quickly enough so the others don't see. Drustan Bennett—with his crooked smile and marsh-green eyes. His muscles flex under my gaze.

If it were any other day, I'd ogle each ripple beneath his tight tunic and send him the look. A secret look he has seen several times in the past. Those muscles would quiver above me as he claimed me against the scratchy, hay-covered floor of the abandoned barn just north of here. But it's not just any other day, and his excitement grates against my eardrums. So, I peel my stare away from him.

There are nine of us who will complete our trials this rotation. We come of age when we turn twenty, and once that happens, we must serve. I still remember my twentieth birthday. Late autumn air barreled into me as Ottilie barged through the rotting door of my home. She saved up enough coin for two slices of lemon cake with raspberry filling and sang me "Happy Birthday" as Father sat—silent as ever—before the pathetic pile of wood I gathered burning in the hearth. A pleasant moment with my best friend clouded by the dread wrapping around my gut, knowing what was to come.

We get twenty rotations in Terakeld. Twenty rotations with family and friends and as much freedom as the Elders and guards allow. I know that if it were up to the kingdoms, they probably would have taken us right out of our mother's wombs, still wet with fluid . . . our eyes barely open. And our Elders would have let them.

"I wouldn't be surprised if no kingdom chose you, Flint," Drustan prods at the youngest of the contenders. The other boys laugh loudly in response.

Jerik Flint turned twenty not more than a week ago. He doesn't look the youngest, with his broad back and stubble. He's quiet . . . reserved. He ignores Drustan's jab, hunched over and staring at his feet. My hand yearns to be placed on his shoulder, giving him the comfort he so desperately needs.

Dong! A second ring of the bell tower fills The Square. The ceremony is starting. Elder Payne corrals us into a line like unsuspecting cattle going to the slaughter. I notice we're in the order of surnames. Ottilie is first. I am last.

We make the short climb up the rickety stairs onto the worn, wooden platform. We're forced to turn and face the crowd.

"Welcome all to this rotation's trials!" Elder Payne waves his hands above his head and gestures toward the crowd. "These nine men and women before you will soon embark on a journey that will change their lives forever. A journey that is the core of who we are as a people, as mortals of Galfei Thalor. They will help our kingdoms, and in doing so, they will help provide for us all . . ."

I skim the crowd for Father. Several people are smiling wide as the Chief of Elders continues to recite his speech. Their backs are straight, and their chins are high. Standing front and center are Ottilie's parents, proud tears welling in their eyes. Their bright smiles speak for themselves; they're delighted to see their daughter off to serve one of the kingdoms.

A handful of others have blank expressions on their faces. One brave woman is outwardly scowling, her teeth bared for all to see. I recognize her from Mother's whipping. She was on the opposite side of Towne Square that day, far enough away, so no one would notice her. But I did, and I remember the moment her knees hit the dusty ground, and she sobbed into her hands. It was the same moment Mother stopped breathing.

There have been a handful of times when I've seen her around Terakeld, whispering with known rebels or strolling through the market, only approaching carts owned by sympathizers. Each time, I'd want to speak with her. Each time, I'd stop myself, never having the courage.

Her vibrant greenish blue eyes snap from Elder Payne to me. And she stares—stares and stares like she knows me. Her expression turns sad, and her teeth dig into her bottom lip, trying to stop it from wobbling. I realize then she does know me. I am the daughter of her late leader, and I am being shipped away to a life of servitude.

"One thousand twenty-seven rotations ago, the course of our race changed forevermore," Elder Payne's voice echoes across the open area. The four remaining Elders are lined up at the front of the stage. They're stoic, standing as still as statues. No emotions on their faces. No warmth in their rigid bodies. Just as they were at today's whipping. "Our ancestors—savages, *killers*—revolted against the kingdoms despite their generosity. They let us live among them. They let us work and roam, and yet, that wasn't enough for our kind."

A small huff shoots out of my nostrils. My toes tap restlessly inside my boot. We all know how the Last War came to be. There's no need to recite it again.

Elder Payne continues. "Mortals pillaged and slaughtered those living peacefully within the kingdoms. Thus, the Last War began. Our kingdoms came together to end the mutiny, and on the other side of war, the four kings ascended into the sky, becoming loving Gods that watch over our world. They guided our kingdoms' new rulers to bring our people out of the trenches and into civilization. For that, we thank them and the kingdoms who so generously gave us another chance at life. The elves, for they raised a piece of the sea floor from its sandy depths and gave us a home. The changelings, for they . . ."

Elder Payne's words become nothing more than a distant buzzing in my ear, like a gnat looking for a place to land. It's the same speech he gave during Arden's trial ceremony, the only one I've been to since Mother died.

That day, I had to force Father out of his rocking chair and drag him on stumbling feet all the way to Towne Square. Arden's eyes never left mine during the entirety of the ceremony. A rare softness meant only for me shined behind his glinting gaze—his excitement to leave clashing with his brotherly love. There was a tether between us then; it felt like we were the only ones in The Square. Every single person, including Father, who sat on a bench in the back of the crowd and stared into nothing, was forgotten in those moments.

Father. Scanning my eyes across the gatherers, I see no sight of him. I *asked* him to be here. I *asked.* Maybe he's just late. Yes, that's it. He'll shuffle into The Square any moment now, with Ms. Beverlye to guide him. She said she'd watch over him. I keep my eyes trained on the buildings of the Central District, hoping to see him emerge. Any moment now . . .

Two of the Elders leave their respective spots in front and walk around the stage toward the fountain. I feel eyes on me—studying me—as a hot gaze singes against my cheek. Without looking, I know it's Ottilie checking in on how I'm doing. I know she knows Father isn't here. I know she knows how much I wanted him to show without even voicing it to her.

Swallowing down nothing but the saliva coating my throat, I slightly turn my head to the left. All the other contenders are a blur except for her. Ottilie's round eyes—just beyond Drustan's puffed out chest—meet mine.

They're full of sympathy, full of *pity*.

My heart falters, forcing the breath from my lungs.

The two Elders return from the fountain. Each ascending the steps on either side of the stage and holding clay bowls carved with scenes from the Last War. The one closest to me brings the bowl to my lips. The other does the same to Ottilie.

The Waters of Genesis from the kingdoms' fountain is given to all contenders. It's said to be a blessing from the Gods and Galfei Thalor's rulers. A blessing that we are ready to serve. To me, it's nothing but stale water—murky with algae and drops of rebel blood.

The Elders make their way down the line until the last contender takes a sip, then they descend the stage steps and get back in position with the others.

Thunderous claps echo across Towne Square, signaling the end of the ceremony. Elder Payne bows deeply for the crowd, then turns around and politely claps for each of us. It's over. The ceremony is over, and Father didn't show. I should have known better. I continue to hold out hope that he'll change, drastically improve, and remember that he still has a daughter and a son who—despite everything—love him. I need to stop this useless wishful thinking.

The four Elders in front of the stage walk toward the steps and motion for us to follow. The other contenders wave goodbye to their loved ones. I stay silent. No one is here for me.

A warm, phantom brush glides down the slope of my neck. My breath hitches, and tears spring into the corner of my eyes. I don't know how, but I know it's her. It *feels* like her.

Mother.

I've never felt anything like this. Nine rotations have passed, and she's never made herself known to me. Why now?

The presence gently nudges against my shoulder, propelling my feet to move.

Go forward, Maeve. I am with you, she seems to say.

Something in my chest eases and tightens all at once. Knowing I am not alone, I follow the line of contenders to The Unlighted Sea.

5

THE UNLIGHTED SEA IS like a dark, inky serpent wrapped around Ter-akeld, constricting and suffocating. Splashes of bright oranges and reds reflect off its near-black waves. The sun's final farewell until it rises again come dawn.

No one speaks as we navigate the rocky terrain of Terakeld's eastern coast. Three skiffs moving with the tide ominously await our arrival.

Three of the Elders move toward the skiffs, one for each. The fourth raises his voice above the billowing breeze and pounding waves. "Three of you in each skiff. Do not disrupt the order in which you have been placed. You"—he points to Ottilie, Drustan, and one other—"in that skiff over there."

He proceeds to direct the rest of us to the proper boats before stepping aside and nodding to the three Elders-turned-helmsmen. "May you have good fortune, contenders," the Elder yells. His deep-set eyes scan each of us as we sit in the docked skiffs. "Make our kingdoms proud!"

The shrill sound of the skiffs scraping against the sandy shore of the island pierces through the wind in my ears. Wrinkled hands wave us forward, ushering us out of the boats and guiding us inland.

We are a uniformed line of contenders, like soldiers entering battle. Our feet march in sync up a slight incline. One step. *Thump.* Two steps. *Thump.* A constant drumbeat against the ground. A death march toward a life in chains.

After hearing about the island in school, I was expecting . . . *something.* Something more than a barren rock jutting out of the sea. It's dull and gray, just like Terakeld. We walk through two straight lines of copper, gold, silver, and Spiicrete—guards standing at attention. Scattered among the merfolk, elves, changelings, and tieflings are mortals in matching armor. *Servants to the king-doms.*

As the ground flattens out, the lines of guards unfurl, creating a circle around an open area. They surround us, ensuring we do what we're told. Lit torch-es—held by the mortal guards—flicker in the breeze and cast an ominous glow upon us.

Splashes of vibrant colors cut through the drab landscape. Four tents—one for each kingdom—stand tall against the dark red-and-purple sky.

Gold posts carved with vines hold the deep green fabric of the tent farthest to the left. Seated within are two tall males with golden crowns atop their long auburn hair and pointed brown ears. The elves of Nythfaedell. Raw, undiluted power radiates off them, flowing through us as we quietly stand here in a line. The older of the two—the king, it would seem—softly nods toward us. The other doesn't move a muscle. He only stares down upon us like we're nothing but ants.

Next to Nythfaedell's tent is Amphitea's. Light-blue embroidered shells atop the purple fabric shimmer under the torch light. A lanky bronze-skinned woman with deep purple hair and a crown of coral laid against her forehead is lounging on a cushioned chaise underneath. Shimmering pearls and jewels draped around her ankles shine just beneath the hem of her sheer blue dress. She looks sharply at each of us.

The tieflings radiate menacing intimidation. The King and Queen of Fiermoor are standing—unlike the other rulers—under the deep bloodred tent that seems to seep into shades of black. They're warriors first, monarchs second. The king's large muscular arms are across his Spiicrete-covered chest. His nearly black horns are heavily scarred, and the point of the left is broken off and jagged. The queen has a grace to her—despite her chain mail gown—that the king doesn't. Sharp edges hidden beneath her soft features. These two chose my family as slaves. Mother, chosen to work in the mines. Father, chosen to transport the mine workers to their stations. And Arden . . .

I wonder what Arden was chosen for. The letter the Elders send to contenders' families only reveals the kingdom they will serve. For all I know, he could be here right now, hidden beneath Spiicrete, holding a torch to light our way.

Tearing my eyes away from the beastly rulers, they land on the changelings—the leaders of Phandolus. There are three of them, all unnerving under my gaze. The blue and silver of their tent is nothing more than an afterthought. Two slightly older changelings with haughty expressions and refined attire perch atop small thrones under the awning. Their daunting eyes study us, as if they're memorizing our features, so they can shed their skin and shift as night falls.

Standing beside them is another. She's slightly younger and paying no attention to us. Her gaze—icy daggers as sharp as the jewel-encrusted crown atop her head—is glaring to the side toward the elves. Her pale upper lip curls, and her eyes narrow. *The princess.*

I rip my gaze away from the phantom-like beings and look around the open area before us. A table of various weapons is near the changeling's tent. Three massive crates are opposite that next to the elves'. In front of the merfolk's tent is a bright branching red coral, unnaturally sprouting from the earth as if it came from the sea below.

Before I can mull over what any of this means, my world turns black as a blindfold is tied securely around my head.

"Welcome, contenders!" someone declares with a melodic voice. One of the queens. "We are elated to begin this rotation's trials. You will complete four tasks—one chosen by each kingdom. If you refuse to take part, you *will* be sentenced to death. If you refuse the kingdom who has chosen you, you *will* be sentenced to death."

The voice pauses, allowing that to sink in. *Sentenced to death.* This is barbaric. This is—

"The order of each task is as follows: Nythfaedell, Amphitea, Fiermoor, and Phandolus. Let us begin."

I hear the Elder who eliminated my sight walk toward the other end of the line toward Ottilie. His boots crunch against the barren ground, the only sound penetrating the dense tension surrounding us. A moment of nothing before I hear my best friend's timid footsteps walk forward. She's first. I can hear her gait gradually turn more confident as she grows farther away. I can picture her giving the rulers her most charming smile, putting on a show for her kingdoms.

Suddenly, metal grinds against metal. My taut body flinches, and my heart drops at the sound of heavy paws pounding against the ground. One of the crates. Whatever is inside is now free. A loud screech—shrill like an eagle—fills the air. My ears ring, and my already-closed eyes squeeze tighter. Fast footsteps hit the ground. Ottilie is running. Toward the creature? Away from it?

My heartbeat begins to quicken. My fingers twitch at my sides, yearning to rip my blindfold off just to see what's happening. Ottilie grunts, and a handful of rare curses slip through her teeth. Screeches and stomps fill the air around us in response. I shift on my feet, willing myself to stay calm.

It sounds worse than it is, Maeve. Everything sounds worse when you can't see. The struggle between Ottilie and the creature seems to last a lifetime. I bite the inside of my cheek. *Please, just stop.*

Then, as if the universe was listening, it does. It goes quiet except for that sickening crunch of metal against metal. It's excruciating. Is that it? Is that the first trial? Is it over?

No one speaks for a while. I hear clanking and crushing coming from the left. Something starts to boil as the liquid's bubbles begin popping in the air. Minutes pass—long minutes that feel unending.

Fuck this blindfold.

Finally, I hear Ottilie's steps again. They stop for a brief moment, then continue toward the right.

"That's all?" Ottilie's meek voice is soft. She sounds farther away, closer to the tents now.

"Go on," a feminine, sultry voice says. The elves' trial must be over. Amphitea is second. The voice must belong to the merfolk queen. I can hear the faux kindness leaking between her teeth.

The sound of Ottilie's footsteps coming closer makes my heart skip. A beat of silence, then I hear her fall to the ground. She coughs and coughs, like there's something stuck in her throat. A wet, gurgling sound that makes my skin prickle. A rough, dragging sound against the dry earth makes my toes curl. Never have I heard anything so awful in my life. I swear I even hear a faint, broken "help" flit away from her lips.

I press my nails into my palms. *Don't let your mind run wild,* I tell myself. *Ottilie is fine. She has to be fine.*

Long minutes pass, and the sounds are getting worse. Finally, a deep inhale pierces the air, putting an end to those horrible noises that will haunt my dreams from here on out. Ottilie's boots scrape against the ground as I hear her get back on her feet. Her breathing is labored—deep and ragged—but she's breathing. *Thank Gods she's breathing.*

After a few moments, Ottilie's breath evens out. Then, she speaks again. It's so good to hear her voice. "I don't understand—"

A faint click comes from one of the tents—the tieflings. Then, as if the world was ablaze, an intense lick of heat warms my skin. Sweat beads along my neck and drips down my spine. Fire crackles against the summer air. *Fire.*

"Whoa," Ottilie squeaks out. I can hear her walking toward the contenders again. This time, she's closer to me. I long to lift my blindfold up to take a peek. Just a peek. Something to let her know that I'm here for her.

Ottilie lets out a loud breath, like she's preparing herself for something. One step. A sharp hiss. Then, a cry—so broken that my heart clenches—bursts out of her.

My hand flies to my blindfold, ready to rip it off.

Don't. It's Mother again—that warm presence that is so new and comforting. Her voice rings through me, just as gentle as I remember. My fingers shake as they grip onto the edges of the one thing standing between me and my best friend. *Don't. Nothing good will come if you take that off,* she says.

Reluctantly, my hand falls to my side. Behind my eyelids, it burns. Unshed tears, full of frustration, wait to fall.

Another cry slices across the air around us. My blood turns to ice despite the heat of the flames. And that smell . . . seared, rancid beef. *Burnt skin.* The scent sticks to my nostrils, making me gag.

I hate these trials. I hate not knowing if she's all right. I hate this.

I hear a few more stumbling steps, then Ottilie lets out a victorious cry. Slowly, the heat dwindles away.

There is a stillness to the air as I hear Ottilie make her way toward the last tent. The changeling's tent. A long silence is shattered by a bellow so loud my eyes snap open beneath the blindfold. Swift footsteps run across the open area.

"Oh Gods," Ottilie utters. She sounds terrified.

Laughs—high and low, raspy and smooth—ring across the area before a hoarse scream that sends shivers down my spine drowns it out. Then iron clashes loudly. It's like a crack of thunder, over and over again . . . clash after clash.

The weapons on the table. She's fighting. Ottilie is fighting someone. She's never lifted a weapon in her life. The closest she's come to such a thing was when she begged Arden to play pretend guards, and they used sticks found on the ground.

Oh Gods.

A heavy thump hits the ground. The musky scent of dust pluming from the impact makes me choke. Then stillness. Nothing but silent stillness.

"The first trials are complete," the voice of an Elder resonates behind us.

It's done. I let out the breath I was holding, my lungs seizing now that new air fills them. Ottilie did it. She completed her trials. The corners of my mouth tick up. *She did it.*

Drustan is next. It takes longer than expected before I finally hear his confident footsteps approach the center of the training grounds. Drustan's first trial begins almost immediately, with that gut-wrenching scrape as a crate opens. Instead of a piercing screech from the creature Ottilie faced, slithering scratches against the ground before a roar nearly bursts my eardrums. Much of the rest is the same: painful coughing that makes my skin crawl, the cracking of fire and heat singeing my skin, and the blows of weapons and wild cheers. Then a bell rings, high-pitched and light.

I can't say how long I've been standing in this very spot. My feet ache, and my skin's cold. The only reprieve from the involuntary shivers that rack my body, from both the air and the nerves I'm trying to conceal, are the dimly lit torches surrounding us and the burst of fire in the third trial.

With a thump, the eighth round of trials ends. Silence ensues. No bell is rung.

Out of the eight contenders who have gone, only five chimes were rung.

Why bells? What do they mean? My mind begins to race with possibilities. But they're cut off as I hear the footsteps of an Elder approach me from behind.

I'm the only one left. I'm next.

6

MY LASHES FLUTTER, BLINKING rapidly as soon as I feel the fabric covering my eyes fall to the ground. It takes a moment for my sight to adjust. The sun is completely below the horizon now, and the sky covers us in a blanket as dark as the sea. Torch lights dance along the open area and against the kingdoms' tents, battling for dominance against the swath of night.

The Elder behind me is already retreating to stand with the other two, who are observing from the side. The other contenders are nowhere to be seen. Each step he takes pounds against my skull. The farther he gets, the heavier I feel. My stomach, my blood, turns to stone, filling with dread.

Time's up. There's nothing I can do now. It's my turn to complete the trials.

Nythfaedell is first. My throat tightens, and I force myself to swallow around it. A deep exhale, and I take my first step. One right after the other until I'm facing the two elven royals. There's a guard in gold armor I didn't notice before—another elf, from the looks of it, with his high cheekbones and ethereal, glowing skin—standing tall behind them.

No one utters a word. My weight shifts from foot to foot.

Then, the elven king raises his hand, lifting a miniature flag with Nyth-faedell's crest. It's an elegant shield, with two snakes wrapped in flowers twining around the border, a miniature dragon perched atop it, and tall trees in the background. It's something I would never have noticed before, and under the flickering flames around us, it looks as if the snakes are slithering together. It's almost hypnotic.

The looming guard steps forward. He looks bored. As his armored arm extends toward me, he finally looks up. Our gazes connect for a brief moment. His eyes flash—his pupils swallowing the deep hazel of his irises—and his nostrils flare. Each of his features contort against one another. Brows furrow. Lips part. Nose scrunches. He must really despise us mortals.

My hand harshly snatches the piece of parchment hanging limply between his fingers, and my body turns away from him. I hear him take several steps back, stumbling toward his spot behind the royals, as I read the elegant penmanship inked across the page.

Three creatures await you, but only one will greet you. Collect what's needed and create a brew. Stir and stir, time is true. Heal or kill, it is up to you.

Griffin- one feather   Two-headed Wyrm- one scale   Unicorn- one horn shaving

One of the crates screeches open. The parchment drops out of my hand as my head whips around to see the creature chosen for me. A beautiful white unicorn steps out and shakes its mane before looking at me intently. My mouth drops open, and my eyes widen. The creature is unlike anything I've ever seen—majestic and breathtaking and intimidating all at once. Two jagged marks along its horn shine under the torch lights. My heart clenches at the sight.

Sweeping my eyes to the table near its crate, my vision zeroes in on a serrated knife. I can see the realization creep into its earthy-brown eyes as it watches my every move. Another mortal sent to harm it. I falter for a second, frozen in place.

I don't want to do this. I shouldn't *have* to do this.

Then, those three words hit me in my gut, the threat that lies beneath these trials. *Sentenced to death.* I will be sentenced to death if I refuse.

"I'm sorry," I whisper into the air, hoping the unicorn understands the regret I feel.

I make for the knife, pumping my arms and legs as fast as I can. Adrenaline courses through my veins. The unicorn brays loudly in response and charges. Veering to the side, I dodge the creature. My boots slip on the gravel, and I fall. Plumes of dust from the ground waft around me, lodging into my nose and throat. My knees and palms scrape against the ground, stinging as I scramble back up onto my feet and quickly snatch the blade from the table.

Pounding hooves against the hard ground echo behind me. Turning toward the sound, my eyes lock onto the unicorn's. Weariness flashes across them as it gets closer to me. I swear I feel the creature fight itself—its instinct to protect itself—as if it doesn't want to charge at me or skewer me. I jump out of the way, flinging my body to the side, barely missing the tip of its horn. Before I fall again, I catch myself with a few stumbling steps. It was so close, close enough to touch if I'd reached my hand out to the side.

That's it. The idea barrels into me—fast and focused. I gulp down enough air to fill my lungs to the brink as I watch the creature shake its head and turn around to face me again. I position myself in a ready stance. The unicorn charges, and I stick the knife between my teeth. This time, I wait as long as I can before making my move. Heavy hooves pound. My breath catches in my throat.

Just a little bit farther . . . Come on . . . Almost there . . .

Smoothly stepping to the side, I manage to grip onto its thick white mane, using it as momentum. If I had waited a second longer, I'd have a horn protruding out of my back, its pearlescent color covered in blood. It trumpets out harshly as my leg swings onto its back, and I pull myself up with shaking arms. The unicorn races to the other side of the grounds. My fists tighten around its mane, and my thighs clench down on its sides as I'm thrown side to side atop its back before it races back again toward the elves. It's frantic. It's scared.

"It's okay," I mumble roughly around the knife between my teeth. Finding my balance as the unicorn slows down into a trot, I lift my right hand from where it was gripping and remove the weapon from my mouth. The unicorn stomps a hoof, and its muscles tense, as if he senses the blade is now in my hand. With my other hand, I slowly run my fingers against its silky, smooth fur. "It's okay."

Once the creature stops moving completely, I close my eyes and silently lay against its neck for a moment to catch my breath. Its coat smells of jasmine and something I don't recognize or entirely understand. The unicorn relaxes under the weight of my chest, its deep breaths moving my body with it.

After a moment, I hesitantly sit back up and lean over to scrape off a long single piece of the majestic horn. The unicorn tenses again as I do but stays still.

"I'm so sorry," I whisper into its ear, the muscle at its base twitching in response.

My lips curve into a soft smile as I ungracefully dismount the being and pat its side before guiding it back toward its crate. Once inside, it turns and stares deeply into my eyes, as if it's thanking me for simply caring.

Boom! The crate shuts, sealing me off from the unicorn and bringing me back to the reality I must face. The trials. My eyes drop to the ground. That poor creature . . . just another thing the kingdoms use. I can feel eyes from the elven tent searing into my back. I don't glance their way. I don't care to know what they're thinking.

Keep moving. The faster you finish this task, the faster you finish your trials.

With bated breath, I make my way to the table next to the crates and wonder what the purpose of this trial is. Four sleek golden bowls litter the table. Each has a small amount of ingredients in them. Thankfully, they're labeled: barley,

Night Vine, elven gold flakes, and water from The Unlighted Sea. There are remnants of other ingredients smeared across the table, as if the other contenders were rushed and spilled them. A black smudge in the corner looks like charcoal. Off to the side is an orange leaf broken in half. Neither of which are included in my ingredients.

A small chuckle breaks through the barrier of my lips as realization hits. Different ingredients for the different creatures. Everything I need is laid out before me, waiting to be dumped into the potion. Unicorn horn, barley, Night Vine, elven gold, and seawater. I can't help but wonder what ingredients the other contenders worked with.

Shaking my head free from the thought, I chuck the strip of horn into a waiting mortar. The other components—sans the seawater—follow. My hand twists the pestle, crushing each ingredient together into a fine powder.

"Think, Maeve. What's the test? Why make an elixir?" I mumble under my breath. "Think, think, think."

The trial instructions said, *Stir and stir, time is true. Heal or kill, it is up to you.*

Then it dawns on me. Time. That's the answer. When Terakeld's apothecary visited school to speak about how the kingdoms taught humans healing methods to survive after the Last War, they always said it takes time to heal. Destruction comes easy. Helping takes patience.

Placing the mortar of dry ingredients onto a stack of hot coals, I add the seawater. Cracks and sizzles fill the silent air as the concoction begins to boil.

A healing elixir is ideal. Perhaps the elves would find it in their cold, cold hearts to give it to the unicorn once I'm done. But time isn't on my side. It's late and dark, and if I remember correctly from the apothecary, a healing potion would take at least ten more minutes. I don't have ten more minutes; I want to leave my trials behind as quickly as possible. So, I create the opposite: a brew that will stop the hearts of those who drink it.

A few moments pass. Deceivingly sweet and inviting dark-gray smoke glides out of the mortar into the cool atmosphere, and I know it's done. Another thing the apothecary said: the deadliest mixes are often the sweetest.

Using the bottom of my tunic as a barrier between my skin and the mortar, I quickly place it atop a small table next to the elven king, who leans over and inspects my creation. He's hard to read; I can't tell what he's thinking as he does. Once he's done, he looks toward me. With a drawn-out breath, he nods.

My muscles relax. I didn't even realize how stiff I was. My first trial is done.

Movement from the merfolks' tent catches my attention. The queen is rapidly waving around her small flag, demanding I hurry. A guard with gills peeking out just below his copper helm meets me at the front of the tent and hands me another piece of parchment without so much as looking at me. I unravel it.

From the depths of The Unlighted Sea, a coral sprouts through the earth. Approach its stony branches and break off a piece.

My eyebrows knit together as I stare at the instructions. That's it? When I look up at the queen, she simply smiles at me. She waves her hand out in front of her. *Go,* she seems to order.

I slowly turn around and walk to the middle of the open area. There's a single white line I didn't notice before drawn into the dirt. It's just in front of where we all lined up before being blindfolded.

Now facing the coral, I look closely at it. It's nothing special, merely a thick, central stump that leads down into the dark shadows of the hole it sprouted from. I can't help but wonder if it's still attached to the seafloor below the island. Nine red branches sprout from the stump, but eight of them are merely stubs now, broken off from the others before me. One last untouched branch sticks out of the right side.

Looking up from the small tree-like structure toward the tents, I see the rulers watching me, unmoving and with no emotion. I can feel the Elders' gaze at my back and the guards surrounding the grounds from all sides. The merfolk queen nods once more, urging me to move.

Pain engulfs me as soon as I cross the line. My knees buckle. I collapse onto the ground, gasping for air. It feels as though my lungs are magickally filling up with water. Truthfully, I believe they are. Saltwater tinges the back of my throat as my lungs constrict. The air I try to gulp down clashes against it.

Bracing myself against the ground, I timidly try to stand up, but the agony is too much. My knees buckle again. I want to scream, but the only sound that comes out is a sickening gurgle. My eyes nearly bug out of my skull, and tears stream down my cheeks. I can't breathe. I can't . . .

I think of Ottilie and her near-silent cry for help. A cry I so desperately want to mimic. But deep inside me, something holds me back. Something stops the word from breaching and shoves it back down despite my brain screaming for anyone to stop this pain. Nine rotations ago, Mother refused to give the Elders and, in turn, the kingdoms the satisfaction of her cries as she was whipped. They didn't deserve to hear her pain then, and they don't deserve to hear my pain now, no matter how frightened and powerless I feel.

I muster up as much strength as I can, and the slow, excruciating crawl toward the coral begins. My limbs are leaden. My head throbs. My vision blurs. My lungs burn. So much pain. It would be easier if I just gave up, allowing the water in my lungs to consume me.

About halfway to the coral, my limbs start to slow down, and my crawl comes to a stop. Black spots start to obstruct my vision. I can feel my heartbeat beginning to slow. I desperately want to close my eyes and succumb to the darkness. It'd be so easy. So easy . . .

Pressure builds in my smoldering chest, and a wheeze slips through my constricting throat. As if that wheeze were a dam, saltwater spills from my lips as coughs rack through my body, and relief floods my senses. I take a deep breath. Air—glorious air—fills my lungs.

Thank Gods.

The relief, however, is short-lived. My lungs scream at me, and I swallow a sob as I feel the water trickle back into my lungs. Clawing at the earth, my nails grip into the dry soil, and my knees shuffle against the ground, causing my pants to rip. I wince as a stinging sensation erupts across my left kneecap. I focus on it, clinging onto the pain for dear life. A tether to reality. Blood dribbles down my shin and pools into my boot. The warm, sticky liquid reassures me of my beating heart. I am still alive, even though I feel as if Death is breathing down my neck.

One excruciating tug against the ground, and I wheeze. Another excruciating tug closer to the coral, and water sloshes in the bottom of my throat. Finally, my body slowly drags itself forward, and the coral comes within reach. The heaviness in my arms makes it difficult to lift them. My hand barely touches the red invertebrate before falling limply to the ground.

Don't give up.

Gathering all the energy I have left in my body, I force my arm toward the coral again. The stony branch scratches my skin—the sting, another reminder that I'm alive—as my fingers firmly grip around it. I pull down, snapping it off.

My body collapses lamely next to the coral, and the branch rolls out of my hand. With my head turned to the side and my cheek pressed against the dusty ground, water gushes out of my mouth. A split second later, my chest begins to move, pressing into the earth. It's labored at first—my lungs burning with each movement—but then the pain eases. I savor the feel of air in my lungs again, ignoring the eyes searing through my skull as the kingdoms watch.

A test to see how I'll do underwater. I couldn't imagine living a life like that. *Don't pick me once this is over. Please, don't pick me.*

Laying there a moment too long for the merfolk queen, she clears her throat. There's no compassion in the sound. She's annoyed, as if my almost dying is an inconvenience to her time.

A strained exhale blows through my nostrils. My shaky limbs push up against the ground, and my feet plant themselves into the earth as I stand. The weight of my body makes my knees buckle slightly, and my legs tremble.

She seems pleased with my willingness to obey her wishes as the gleam in her eyes shines vaingloriously. The slight nod of her head signals the second trial is complete.

Without waiting for the tieflings to wave their flag, I turn my back on her and stomp toward the red-and-black tent. The King of Fiermoor lifts his black eyebrow as I approach, and his queen's stare is unwavering at his side. No guard is with them. They forego their flag altogether, and the king hands me the now-dreaded piece of parchment.

With a knitted brow, I read the parchment a few more times, then look at the King and Queen of Fiermoor. The queen reveals a Spiicrete canister from behind her back. As she opens the lid, tendrils of flames float past me like dancing threads of smoldering red-and-orange silk. My head turns, following the stream of heat, and my eyes widen at the sight before me. The coils of fire delicately knit together, creating tall thin panels of flames. Each panel spins in different directions.

A burning maze . . . A test to see who can withstand the heat of Fiermoor.

My steps are measured as I approach the flaming cluster of panels, and my skin tingles under the waves of boiling heat. Each panel rotation is timed perfectly, only leaving enough space to pass through every few seconds. That rancid smell of burnt flesh from the other eight contenders—*from Ottilie*—floods to the front of my mind. Making it through this course without being singed seems impossible.

Standing at the maze's opening, I see the tiefling king and queen studying me through the panels. The left side of the king's mouth ticks upward, forming a slight smirk, like he's imagining the screams that will rip from my throat when my skin melts off the bone. Even if my skin is charred, and my nerve endings are seared, I will grit my teeth to ensure no sound of despair is heard.

Still grateful for the air in my lungs, I release a steady exhale to steel off my nerves and charge into the fiery maze. One step in, and the heat is unbearable. My eyes burn under the black smoke. The crackling of the fire echoes throughout my ears, and ash begins to creep into my lungs.

Rapidly, my body moves before my brain knows what it's doing. As the panels spin in different directions, it's hard to determine which way to go. There isn't a clear path, so I let my legs move for me. Never stopping. Never overthinking. Only gliding my way through this dangerous dance. Each dodge and sidestep is a chance to burn under the blaze.

A quick move to my left, and I avoid a ferocious flaming panel. However, the maneuver leaves my right side vulnerable. The knob of my shoulder bubbles and sizzles, melting away before my eyes. A choked sob sticks to the back of my smoke-coated throat and is drowned out by the roaring blaze surrounding me. My arm goes limp. A sharp throb travels from my shoulder to my fingertips. *Fuck.*

My teeth bite down on my tongue to silence the whimpers attempting to escape. The metallic taste of blood coats my gums and pools along my already-cracked lips. I gag at the smell of my burnt flesh and blood-coated mouth.

Not far now.

My opposite hand grips and supports my hanging limb, and my feet advance me through the inferno before my left shoulder meets the same fate as my right.

Through the panels in front of me, I can see how close I am. My legs move faster, twisting and turning through the flames. Once my body breaches the last of the panels, my knees hit the ground. I keel over, my hands gripping the dusty soil in front of me as I greedily take in as much clean air as my lungs can take. The heat on my back dulls as the ropes of flames pass by my slumped body and back into the canister. The tiefling king simply nods in my direction, then glances at the final tent, whose flag is already raised.

My weak body quivers. I wince under my seizing lungs and charred shoulder as I slowly gain my footing. A sense of unease flushes over my skin as I stumble toward the three ghostly changelings waiting to give me my last trial. I fight the urge to look away.

The princess—whose attention is now off the elves—stalks toward me like a wild feline approaching its prey. Her long white hair swishes in time with her hips, and she extends the piece of parchment toward me. I pluck it from her dainty fingers, the black paint coating her nails flashing against the torches' flickering lights.

Ferociously thudding against my chest cavity, my heart feels like it will burst out at any moment as I read the last trial I must complete.

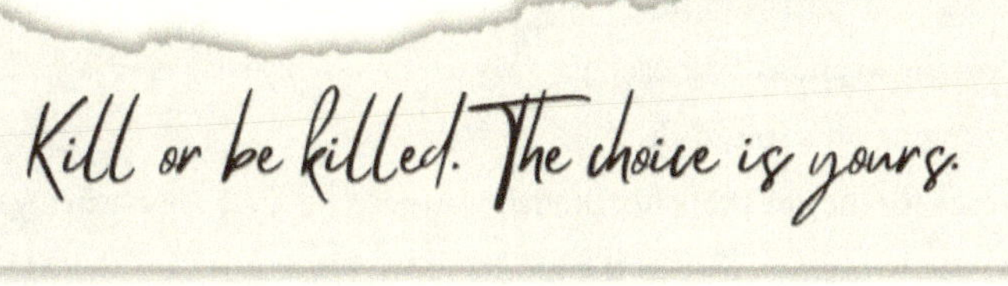

7

T HE HAIRS ALONG MY arms rise. My hands begin to shake.

My eyes stay trained on the trial's instructions.

Kill or be killed. The choice is yours.

Amused laughter pierces my eardrums. It's high-pitched and condescending. Pulling my gaze away from the parchment, I'm met with piercing pale blue—nearly white—irises gleaming down at me. As the changeling princess looms tall, her smile twists into something sinister, revealing her too-white teeth, even under the darkness of night.

Her smile suddenly drops when I stay planted in place. She flicks her head sharply toward the table of weapons to her left, urging me to get moving. Her white eyebrow raises in challenge.

The violent *thump thump, thump thump* of my heart can be heard in my ears as I approach the table, drowning out all other sounds. Bile rises into my throat at the sight. Swords and knives are covered in blood; they didn't even bother to clean the weapons after each use. My eyes suddenly snag on a jagged strip of flesh hanging off a spiked club.

I reach for the one thing not drenched in gore: an ax. It's heavy in my shaking hand, nearly plummeting to the ground once it's dragged off the edge of the table. My burnt shoulder shoots sharp pain down into the fingers wrapped around the ax's hilt from the weight. No wonder no other contender chose it.

Gravel crunches on the other side of the open area. Turning around, I see two guards in silver armor face me, with swords gleaming at their waists. I tighten my grip around the ax's hilt. My eyes dart frantically, looking for a way out. I don't want to kill. I don't want to die. The guards take another step closer—still near the far side of the grounds—and my eyes snap toward them. That's when I notice it. Their skin isn't a ghoulish white, and their eyes are separated by splashes of green and brown. Mortal guards—servants who have no choice but to kill or be killed, much like me.

Groans float out of the tents, and the leaders within gesture wildly at my hesitation.

"Don't keep us waiting. We don't like to wait . . ." Amphitea's queen adds to the moans. The end of her sentence trails off into a giggle as she picks at her pointed nails.

The younger elf—the Prince of Nythfaedell—leans forward in his chair. "Go on, little mortal." Excitement glimmers in his eyes. "Rip the throats out of these measly, insignificant men. They mean nothing to us. We can always get more. Maybe the changelings will replace one of them with you." His laugh grates against my ears. The elven king turns his head toward the prince as a deep line forms between his brows, while the other royals join in like a pack of wild dogs.

My eyes widen, and my stomach churns. Weight crushes against my lungs in realization, a heaviness similar to how it felt when they were filled with seawater. These trials don't mean a damn thing. They aren't tests. They aren't anything. This—*all of this*—is just for the rulers' amusement. Those who rule over my fate are simply watching a show, and I am the unfortunate fool who knows none of the lines.

Do they even care about obtaining servants? Or is this merely a way to toy with those they think lesser of? I'm standing here, grounded to the earth below my boots, like a deer frozen in fear at the sight of a hunter. Staring at these rulers drowning in silks and jewels and trying to wrap my mind around the truth. Mother was right. They really are monsters.

The changeling princess nods toward the two guards, and a primal scream tears through the air.

My head snaps to the side. One of the guards charges toward me with his sword raised, ready to give the killing blow. I stumble away from the princess and the echoing laughs of the other rulers. I back away until I feel a wall of cold stop me. A tiefling guard stands tall behind me, locked in formation around the trial grounds. Two mortal guards holding torches are on either side of him, staring blankly ahead.

"Kill or be killed, mortal." The tiefling's yellowing teeth peek out behind his lips as he smiles menacingly. Then his giant hand pushes me back toward the center of the open area, toward the charging human.

The guard is almost upon me now. His eyes are hard, determination swirling within his green irises. He swings his blade and slams it down toward me. I scramble backward, falling to the ground. He strikes again. I narrowly miss his sword as I roll to the side. The burn on my shoulder screams as dirt wedges into the open wound.

Kill or be killed.

The ax in my hand drags against the ground as I clamber away from him, causing plumes of dust to whirl around us. He stalks toward me.

"I'm not dying today," he growls, his upper lip curling with each syllable.

An arc of silver flashes against the night sky as he brings his sword over his head and slams it down upon me again. I can't dodge him this time.

Kill or be killed.

I lift the heavy ax and shield myself with it. The handle blocks the sword's blade, and a crack forms along the wood from the impact. My shoulder burns, and my knuckles turn white from trying to keep him away. The muscles in my back ache as I struggle to stay upright on the ground and keep his blade away from me. The guard pushes down harder with his sword. My arms shake under the weight. Swiftly, one of his gloved hands clasps onto the end of my ax.

Kill or be killed.

"Give up," the guard hisses.

His hand pushes down harder, using his body weight against my searing shoulder. My eyes squeeze shut, and I grit my teeth together. *I'm about to die.*

My right arm buckles against the pressure, and I fall onto my back. The momentum rams the knob of my ax into the ground. I can feel my left arm extend upward from the shift in weight. A sickening squelch and then warmth.

My eyes snap open.

The blade of my ax is wedged into the guard's neck, his blood spilling onto my face and chest. The guard drops his weapon and falls to the side, the dust sticking to the crimson coating his neck. Trembling fingers graze the oozing gash. He tries to say something, but nothing comes out. With fearful, wide eyes, he stares into my soul.

I frantically scoot away from him, fleeing from what I've done. I watch as the life fades from his eyes.

Kill or be killed.

Pounding steps hit the ground. Closer and closer, they come. The second guard storms toward me. My fingers grip the dirt on the ground as I get back onto my shaking feet. As he swings his sword, I throw the dirt into his face.

"Bitch!" his hiss echoes between the two of us. The guard staggers backward as his sword arm continues its path.

I flinch away, but the tip of his blade slices across my left cheek. I feel blood ooze from the gash, mixing with the other guard's coating my skin. While the man vigorously rubs at his eyes, I stand still.

"Go on!" someone yells in the one of the tents. "Attack him! Make it exciting!"

My fingers lift to my bloody cheek and touch the torn flesh.

Kill or be killed.

My mother's presence glides over the cut and pushes at my fingers. *Fight, Maeve,* she says. *You will die if you don't. Live to see another day. Fight!*

My grip tightens around the handle of the ax, and I lift it. The guard's red, splotchy eyes finally open, and he laughs as he takes me in. There's something about it that makes my skin crawl.

"What are you going to do, Maeve Wyndell?" he taunts.

I falter, and he laughs again. Someone from the direction of the tents yells out, screaming at one of us to do something.

The guard lowers his voice so only I can hear and leans toward me, completely unfazed by my fighting stance. "That's right, I know you. I know your family. I know your lying bitch of a mother. I was fourteen when I watched her die like the rebel filth she was."

A deep, raging fire erupts within the depths of my entire being. Fury wraps itself around my veins like a ribbon, pumping flaming heat throughout them.

Kill or be killed.

I release the ax. The sound it makes as it crashes to the ground is no more than a muted thud. My hands whip forward and grip onto the bottom of his silver helm. His eyes widen as I violently rip it off his head and strike him across the face.

Kill or be killed.

I hit him anywhere I can reach until he falls to the ground and shuffles away from me. I don't let him get away, rushing toward him in a flurry of swinging arms and claws.

Kill or be killed.

Dazed from a hit to his skull that reverberated down to my bones, he tries to fight me off as I straddle his waist.

My mother was not a liar. This trial is proof of that. How dare he speak so ill of her?

I bring the helm down onto his face. Over and over again as crimson coats the silver. I lose count of how many times I hear the nauseating cracks of bones breaking. The piece of armor feels heavy, like it's telling me to stop . . . like it *knows* I should stop, but I can't.

Kill or be killed.

Everything is a blur. His features cave in after each blow. Blood splatters against my flesh. I don't even realize I'm screaming until I have the urge to take a deep breath.

That's what stops me. Not the sight of his bludgeoned head beneath my body, but my need for air. I let the helm fall to my side, and I stare at the massacre I caused.

Kill or be killed.

Kill or be killed.

Kill or be killed.

8

"T HE FINAL TRIALS ARE complete!" one of the Elders yells out, his voice ringing against my skull.

I manage to crawl off the mangled corpse before unloading the contents of my stomach onto the ground. My body convulses as the wedge of cheese I shared with Ottilie floats among my bile. The adrenaline that was previously rushing through my veins suddenly dissipates. I squeeze my eyes shut, refusing to look at what I've just done, and retch once more.

The violent heaves begin to cease, and the shaking in my limbs becomes no more than a twitch. Heaviness weighs down my head, while a painful throb beats against my temples. Finally, my eyes flutter open as I hear what sounds like something being dragged nearby. Another mortal guard in silver armor pulls the legs of the first man I killed away from the center of the grounds and behind the changeling's tent.

Movement to my left pulls my attention away from the way his head lulls limply to the side. Under the flickering torch flames, I narrow in on two of the Elders near the pathway to the beach in the distance. They're fiddling with heaps of white cloth on the ground. My brain clashes with my eyes, working to understand what I'm looking at, until I see a bare, limp hand fall from underneath the sea of white.

Dead bodies. Contenders' bodies. My eyes widen in horror at the thought of the other contenders never finishing their trials, their lives senselessly cut short.

She's fine. She's fine. She has to be fine.

My eyes strain as I try to look closer at the hand under the night sky. "Please," I whisper in desperation. "Please, let Ottilie be safe."

There was no bell once her trials were over, and I have yet to hear one ring for me. *She's fine.* I am alive. Here I am—broken and bloody—but alive. *She's fine.*

An Elder moves to pick up the body. The white fabric shifts slightly and reveals the top of the contender's head. My stomach drops. *No.*

A lump forms in the back of my throat, holding back a sob that's fighting to rip free. Time stills, mocking me as I see what I so desperately wish wasn't true. The sound of the summer's night breeze and the crashing sea waves in the distance are drowned out, becoming nothing more than a distant buzz. My body—*my soul*—goes numb. All that's left is my muffled breathing and thumping heart.

Ottilie's corkscrew hair bounces with every step the Elder takes. He's taking her away. Away from me. I want to run to her—to take her from that man who doesn't care about the life she lived. I command my body to get up and scoop her from his arms. I command my body to hold her and cry and scream and curse the kingdoms, who are quietly watching me at this very moment. I command my body to *do something*. But my body stays where it is, completely numb from the loss of the only light in my life.

The words I spoke to her among the meadow's flowers and Moon Elm tree haunt me. *Nothing—not the trials, not the kingdoms, not ten rotations apart—will come between us.* I lied.

No tears are shed. A black void replaces the cavity where my heart once was. Every second I stare at my dead friend, what little life and love and happiness I tightly held onto drains from my body. I feel numb. I feel nothing. I *am* nothing without Ottilie.

Is this how Father feels?

A high-pitched ring breaks through the hush that has fallen upon the open grounds. My head swivels around sharply toward the sound. The nearly glowing eyes of the changeling princess meet mine. Her hand is still raised, holding the silver bell, and a smile that makes my empty stomach churn forms across her white lips.

From that look alone, I know I am hers. The words of the elven prince hit me in the chest as the lingering rings of the bell echo across the island.

"Maybe the changelings will replace one of them with you," he said.

Fast and sure footsteps approach me from behind. A sharp pinch pricks the side of my neck. The shock halts me for a moment, my body tensing . . . completely frozen. Then I feel a needle glide out of my skin, and the pain begins. My skin prickles, and my muscles become weak. It feels like acid is slowly soaking into my nerves. The burn makes me sweat, yet my bones feel brittle, like frost is coating the marrow within.

A gravelly voice rumbles near my ear. "You will see your father and brother again, Maeve Wyndell, so long as you do what you are told and speak not of the trials which took place. We preserve our traditions through silence. Do not make the same mistake as your mother."

I try to place the voice. It's one of the Elders, but I'm not sure who. I can't seem to remember their names or what they look like or why we're here, for that matter.

"Congratulations, everyone," someone declares. Sitting on my knees before a body covered in gore, my body wobbles uncontrollably as I look for who spoke. A group of creatures are gathered around each other. Three have white skin, two have nightmarish horns, and one glows, as if her skin is made of gold.

What are those things? What am I? Who am I?

Black spots obstruct my vision. A haze clouds my thoughts. Everything spins.

Two beings with pointed ears don't join the others. They sit under a green tent, talking among themselves. The younger one looks angry. Why is he so angry?

I feel my body slump over, but I can't stop it.

A third creature with golden armor steps forward toward the open grounds, toward me—whoever I am—but stops himself. He looks like he's fighting an inner battle.

The ground is cold and hard underneath my cheek. When did I get down here?

Another voice can be heard in the distance. They're muttering something I can't quite place. With each word, the voice becomes louder. A chant becoming clearer and clearer until it's as though the words are encroaching upon me, suffocating me with sorrow.

I can feel my lips moving in time with the beat. Is that my voice? I can't tell.

Ottilie . . . Mother . . . Father . . . Arden.

Who are they?

Everything goes black.

9

Darkness comes and goes. The stars above blur together, forming swirls in the deep, night sky. I'm rocking back and forth, back and forth. The sound of water crashes to my side. Cool mist coats my clothes, sticking to my skin and making me feel like I can't breathe. Nausea racks my body, and I heave to my side. A phantom sits beside me, white as morning haze. It glances down at me and sneers. My vision goes dark once again.

I'm thrown to the ground. Grime clouds around me and gets stuck in my throat. Coughs erupt from my lungs, and my body aches under each movement. My eyelids are heavy, struggling to stay open.

What happened?

A sharp click pierces the air. My leg feels heavy, as if something is weighing it down. I think someone else is here with me. There's shuffling somewhere nearby, but I can't tell.

Where am I?

A single sliver of light barely illuminating wherever I am begins to disappear. Darkness creeps in before a door slams shut, the sound echoing against the walls surrounding me.

I try to stay awake, but I can already feel hazy sleep drifting in around me, engulfing me like a shadow. I try to . . .

Sleep. That sounds nice.

My already-heavy eyes shut. Sleep sounds really nice.

"No. No, no, no. Please!" a frantic, deep voice ricochets around me.

Slumber fades away, disappearing as if it were dust. The light tingle of groggy wakefulness begins to thrum in my veins, and I blink my eyes open. Or, at least, I think I do. All I see is darkness. A black void surrounding me. My body is leaden, and my mind is fuzzy.

"Up. Now!" another deep, gritty voice—different from the one that woke me—yells.

I hear iron clash together and something large drag against the ground. The sound sends a shiver down my spine, eerily reminding me of home, of Towne Square, just before a whipping is about to take place when a rebel is dragged toward that Gods awful post.

Before I can think too closely on it, I feel my consciousness begin to slip away once more . . .

A pearlescent horn flashes by, close enough to see multicolored sparkles glinting against the murky torch lights. A loud bray, and it flashes by again.

"I'm sorry."

My voice carries itself across the open grounds and toward the unicorn, who is no longer running but staring at me instead, as if it knows I mean it.

My fingers curl around something hard. Looking down, I see a jagged strip of the same pearlescent color. My eyes snap up, but the unicorn is gone.

Heal or kill, it is up to you.

That phrase repeats itself over and over again like a chant in the distance.

Heal or kill, it is up to you.

Heal or kill.

Kill.

Kill or be killed. The choice is yours.

"You did this to us," gravelly voices hiss behind me.

After spinning around, I gasp and fall backward onto the ground. Standing before me are two guards. One's neck is split open so deep I can see the white of his spine, blood spewing onto the ground. The other . . . I can barely look at him. His face is disfigured, caved in completely. He has no eyes, no teeth, no nose, nothing.

"You did this to us."

I lurch forward. My body shoots up into a sitting position, my chest heaves violently as the image of those men disappears into the darkness around me. Sweat trickles along my spine, and strands of hair stick to the back of my neck. There is no light wherever I am. It's cold and clammy. The only sounds are the breaths escaping my lungs.

I blink several times. My sight begins to adjust to the darkness. I'm in a small room. Bare walls made up of large stones cemented together. A wooden door with several locks and no windows. An impenetrable box. A cell.

I look down toward the hard, dusty ground that makes up the floor, and I see it: an iron shackle is locked around my ankle and chained to the floor. A prisoner, a *slave*.

Cold, pale blue eyes flash in my mind. Those eyes—so sinister, so proud. The changeling princess. *The trials.* She chose me. The changelings chose me, which means I'm in Phandolus.

I try to remember what happened before she rang that silver bell. And after. How did I get here? It's fuzzy, with massive blank spots warping my memory.

Shit. I squeeze my eyes shut tightly and shake my head, trying to remember. Why can't I remember?

"Calm down," I croak out, my dry vocal cords rubbing against each other. The words are loud in the empty cell.

My hands begin to shake. I silently inhale as I fist my hands, forcing them to stop, and I open my eyes again. To my right, a bucket full of water sits near the wall. My barren throat begs for me to take a sip.

I shift my body toward the bucket. The chain rattles against the ground, and what feels like fire pierces through my right shoulder.

"Agh!" I yelp, the sound getting caught in the back of my throat from the pulsing pain.

An angry red burn covers the knob of my shoulder. My skin is blistered, and pus oozes around it. I gag at the sight.

"What the hell?" Shaking fingers touch the burn, and a hiss slips through my teeth. I know I got this from the trials. I must've, but I can't remember how. Why can't I remember?

Despite my charred shoulder barking in protest, I slowly scoot toward the bucket of water, and my dirty hands plunge into it. My hands lift toward my lips in the shape of a makeshift bowl.

Rejuvenation. Pure, unadulterated rejuvenation. That's what I feel as soon as the room temperature liquid touches my tongue.

"Okay, Maeve. Think," I mumble around a mouthful of water. "Which trial caused the burn? What do you remember?"

Another greedy gulp of water. My dream blinks across my vision.

The unicorn. I remember the unicorn and scraping a piece of its horn off. I remember making a potion with it. That was the elves' trial. The first trial. Yes, I remember that. The King and Prince of Nythfaedell. The guard in his golden armor. The other crates and the table of ingredients.

Good.

More slurps loudly fill the empty cell, and I splash some water onto my face. My left cheek stings as soon as the water touches it.

My hands pause under the water at the feeling. Another flash of my dream. A sword slicing toward me. The feel of blood seeping down my cheek. So much blood . . . not all of it mine.

The guards. I remember them, too. The guards I brutally murdered. The guards who had to kill or be killed, just like me. Just like Ottilie.

Still submerged under the water, my hands begin to shake violently. Water splashes onto the ground.

Ottilie.

She's gone, killed by the guards the changelings sent after her.

A harsh, dry sob rips out of my throat, and tears gather just behind my eyes. They don't fall, as if my body is unwilling to let them. Some sort of defense mechanism, despite my heart feeling as if it's breaking into a million little shards—jagged and sharp enough to slice through my chest.

I remember the numbness I felt when I first saw her limp body being carried away. I try to get that feeling back, reaching deep into my soul and demanding that void of nothingness.

Please, grant me this. I can't feel this pain, this loss. It's too much.

My broken heart only clenches in response before its beats falter from my next thought.

Lifting my hands out of the bucket, I fling water off my fingertips as they reach for the back of my head. The silky, smooth ribbon brushing against my skin sends waves of relief throughout my body. Ottilie's parting gift is still there, tightly wound around my hair, unwavering, like our friendship.

That invisible dam holding my tears at bay breaks—like my body reached its tipping point from the feel of the silk and couldn't hold it in any longer. I bring my damp hands to my eyes and cry into them. I cry for Ottilie. I cry for the life she will never get to live. I cry for the unicorn I hurt. I cry for the guards I killed. I cry for the time that has somehow been stolen from me.

What else happened at the trials? Did I see any of the other bodies? Was Drustan one of them? How did I get this burn? Why can't I remember anything?

My face contorts, and frustration boils the blood in my veins. Leaning my back against the wall, I sit, silently racking my brain for anything I might be able to remember as my tears begin to slow. It doesn't work. The rest is blank.

10

TIME TICKS BY SLOWLY. Or, at least, I think it does. The darkness of the cell is unchanging.

My head leans back against the wall. I feel the ribbon Ottilie gave me snag on one of the stones. I untie it and slide it out of my hair to inspect. It's duller now, with soot coating the beautiful blue color, and one of the ends is slightly frayed.

A sigh of relief. It could be worse.

As I knot the ribbon around my hair once more, the door slams against the stone wall and a bright light streams into the cell. It's blinding.

I push myself close to the wall as much as I can, hoping I blend in. My heart rapidly pounds against my ribcage as a hulking guard stomps inside, dragging someone by their collar.

The changeling doesn't look my way. He simply throws the person down onto the ground, and I swear I hear the crack of a bone on impact. The guard chains them up before stomping back out of the cell.

I don't have enough time to see who it is. Just as my eyes begin to adjust to the light, the guard slams the door closed so hard it rattles on its hinges. Darkness engulfs us once again.

I can just make out the outline of whomever it is. They're hunched over against the back wall of the cell. Nothing can be heard except for their sniffles and my unsure breaths.

I stare at them for a few minutes as my vision adjusts to the dark once again.

"Um, hello?" My voice is shaky. I don't know what else to say. The figure curls in on themself even more. They're facing away from me. "Are—are you all right?"

Slowly, they turn around. I'm met with wide, tear-filled brown eyes. It's Jerik Flint. The youngest of the contenders is sitting before me, chained to the ground, beaten and bloodied. His long, blond hair is matted, covered in dirt and blood. His lip is split open and his left eye is swollen shut. He has cuts on his arms, and his legs are purple and black. The right side of his clothes are charred and tattered, with pale muscles peeking through each rip.

He wrings his thick fingers together. He's unsure—of me, of our circumstances . . . I'm not sure which. He keeps his uneasy eyes on me like a skittish fox in the meadow.

"Jerik." His name on my lips is hesitant, each syllable a drawl. His eyes widen just slightly, like he's surprised I know his name, as if we didn't have classes together since we were little. Then, as if my concern overrides all hesitancy, my questions rush out: "Jerik, what happened? Who did this to you?"

He opens his mouth, but no words come out.

I crawl toward him and drag the bucket of water with me, despite the pain shooting through my body. I get as close as I can before the chain around my ankle snags taut. This is as far as I'm allowed. I rip the bottom of my tunic and dip it in the water. His eyes widen even more. He's terrified. I'm terrified, too. I barely know him. I should be worried about myself, but this is the right thing to do. So, I lift the damp cloth and raise my eyebrows. He gives me a hesitant nod.

Placing the cloth against a deep gash along his forearm, I ask what happened again. Jerik only hisses in response, and I chastise myself for prying. "I'm sorry, you don't have—"

"Don't . . ."

Jerik's voice is rough. He swallows around nothing and tries again. "Don't let them take you out of this cell, Maeve."

My hand pauses just above the cut. "What?"

Jerik repeats what he said but with more conviction this time. "You're safer here."

I set the piece of fabric down across the lip of the bucket and stare at him. "What did they do to you?" I growl out, my words sounding like they belong to someone else.

Jerik shakes his head, grimacing in pain. "No . . . no. The changelings didn't do this. They—the other servants did." Large tears break through his lash line and roll down his bloody cheeks, following wet tracks that have yet to dry.

With a long, defeated sigh, he furrows his brows. "I was taken to my assignment. A real shitty one. Literally. I'm a stable boy. For the next ten rotations, I'm going to be shoveling shit," he scoffs. "The guard gruffly introduced me to the other stable boys. As soon as he left, they jumped me . . . I-I made sure not to make a sound in front of them. I know they wouldn't have stopped if I did. Once they were done, they picked me up and slapped me on the back like nothing happened. They told me it's some sort of welcoming initiation."

Jerik gulps and grits his teeth, attempting to reign in his emotions. "They told me that I will . . . that I'll be excited to join in on the fun once next rotation's contenders come. I-I don't think I will. I could never. It was horrible, Maeve."

He continues on. Every detail about his assignment and the guard coming to pick him up without a second glance rushes out. Each sentence is interrupted by a sob. I can do nothing but stare as he reveals it all to me. The speed of Jerik's voice increases, and his breathing becomes shallower, like it's getting harder and harder to get the words out. He's rambling, hysterical now. Panic at what happened and what is to come is overtaking him . . .

"Why did I get this assignment?" Jerik blurts out. "Was I not good enough for anything else?"

The breath in my throat catches, and my eyes widen.

"Jerik." My hand squeezes the only part of his knee that's not bruised, and I lower my head to meet his downcast stare. "Don't say that. Your worth does not come from the assignment you are given. Not even the best assignment Phandolus has to offer will be good enough for you . . . for any of us. Do you hear me? They do not deserve to have us . . . to *use* us."

Jerik's eyes widen and flit toward the closed cell door. His strong jaw hangs slack, and his throat bobs. They're blasphemous words—words that would have me chained to the whipping post if I were back in Terakeld. Perhaps here as well. But he needs to understand.

Silence falls over us before he whispers, "You can't say those things, Maeve."

"I know," I mutter as my shoulders fall.

11

D AYS GO BY, AND no one comes for me. Each morning, Jerik is taken to the stable. Each evening, he's chained up once again. And each day, I'm left alone, sitting in the same dark cell. It's like they're waiting—waiting to see how long it takes for me to break under the isolation.

The changeling guard that picks up Jerik leaves me two small loaves of bread to last me the day. Sometimes, they're fresh, their soft bites melting in my mouth. On those days, I feel less like a caged animal. But sometimes, the bread is hard and moldy, with every bite feeling as if I'm swallowing stone. On those days, I don't eat.

I wonder if today will be one of those days. I wonder what meals Jerik gets when he's at the stable.

Turning my head to the side, I look over at the man chained beside me. He begins to sit up, pulling on the hem of his tunic to wipe away the sleep from his face. A part of me doesn't want him to leave for the stable today. A part of me wishes he'd stay with me, even though that would deprive him of the real world—the fresh air—on the outside.

His companionship—the silent presence that warms the cell when he's here—gives me solace in this lonely life I'm living.

The door's hinges creak loudly as it swings open, pulling me out of my thoughts. My head swings toward it, eyes squinting against the light of the hallway before they can adjust. Jerik sends me a kind smile as he prepares to get up. There's a promise in his eyes when he does. He'll be back. But he stops mid-crouch when he notices a different guard is at the door. Standing next to him—refined and domineering—is the changeling princess.

An elegant, royal-blue gown drapes over each curve of her body, and her silver jewel-encrusted crown creates shapes of light against the dark walls. Her chin is high, but her icy eyes are on me. She sends me a smile. At first glance, it looks like any other. Kind, even. But then I notice the way her painted lips twist together. Malevolence hides behind it.

You belong to me, she seems to say without words.

I brace myself to be dragged out of the cell, just as Jerik had been before he was first taken to the stable, when I was in and out of consciousness. Or jerked around and yanked by his collar on stumbling feet each day since. Instead, the guard simply walks toward me, unlocks the shackle around my ankle, and takes back his place next to the princess.

My eyes zero in on the iron chain lying limply next to my newly freed foot. The skin just above my boot is red and raw. The princess impatiently clears her throat, drawing my attention away from the thing that once held me prisoner.

"Up." Her voice sounds like it's coated in honey yet still has the sting of a bee.

She quickly turns her back on me and walks through the cell's door. I hesitate for a split second until the guard looming by the threshold sneers at my frozen body and juts his head to the side. A silent order to follow his princess.

Walking toward the lit doorway, I look back at Jerik, whose stunned frame has been motionless since he laid eyes on the royal. Deep rivets line his forehead as he watches me leave. There's fear there—fear for me, and I can't help but think there's lingering fear for himself as well—twirling under his shock. I can only imagine what he's thinking. Perhaps he's wondering why I'm not being dragged out. Or perhaps he's worried I'll come back beaten and bloodied, just as he had on his first day. I want to give him comfort, even if it's only a sliver of what he's given me when he's not away, but the door slams shut behind me before I can wave goodbye.

The flow of the changeling princess's silk skirts guides us through a narrow pathway. Her heels click against the stone ground, disrupting the stagnant air around us. Mounted torches illuminate the hallway. Wooden doors—identical to the one I've been staring at for days—line its walls. My eyes dart to each one I pass, and my fingers twitch at my side.

The hallway ends, and a stone staircase looms ahead. The princess climbs each step with grace. Her dress looks like a rushing waterfall cascading down into a dark-gray lagoon. I hesitate again. I'm about to leave the cells. I'm about—

The guard roughly nudges me forward. Another silent order.

Step-by-slow-step, the dim cold fades behind me as light and warmth begin to replace it. Gooseflesh erupts across my skin, and I pick up scents of flowers and perfumes. My nose is bombarded by the smells after only being used to the damp dirt of the cell.

I step into a grand hallway filled with charcoal art and crystal statues. The princess leads us to the right, where it opens into a massive foyer.

The black marble floors shine, as if they were made of liquid as dark as coal, and the white veins laced throughout look like they are moving, pulsing under my feet. Intricate scenes of war and victory are painted into the domed ceiling of the foyer. Changelings armed with silver swords. Tieflings and merfolk following changelings' orders. Golden weapons scattered across the ground. I don't know this war. I don't see any humans depicted in the paintings. It must be a tale from many, many rotations ago. Suspended in the air and interrupting the story the paintings tell, is a chandelier of black metal branches with crystals so clear it looks as if nothing is there at all.

The princess strides onward. The guard bumps me from behind, nudging me forward and pulling my attention from the ceiling. I see another hallway opposite us that's identical to the one we just emerged from. On my left, there are massive, almond-shaped double doors, and to my right, two grand staircases peek out of imposing white marble arches. Colorful flowers twine around the luxurious stone rails. The only color in the vast foyer.

A chill brushes against my cheek as we venture farther into the space and pass a shrouded alcove between the staircases. Against the back wall, another set of double doors are ajar.

As we pass, I strain my neck to peek inside. A black stone throne sits in front of a long dark-blue-and-silver tapestry against the center of a black wall. Stone steps covered in vines lead up to the solid black rock of the throne. They wind their way up the armrests and around the edges of its pointed back, stopping on either side of a massive silver crystal that gleams beneath the flickering chandelier. No one is perched atop the blue cushioned seat, despite the voices just beyond the throne room's threshold.

I tear my eyes away. That throne room . . . It doesn't feel right. Pulsing. Raging. Nothing good has come out of the countless meetings held there. I can feel it.

The princess guides me toward the start of the second staircase. We begin to ascend, and the guard is on my heels, making sure I have nowhere else to go. At the top, a large mural hangs in a silver frame with an iridescent sheen. "House Verral" is etched into the bottom of the frame. It's a family portrait. The changeling King and Queen of Phandolus stand tall, proud of their leadership. The queen is holding two babies wrapped in white furs that nearly blend into their skin.

"Walk," the guard behind me grunts out, pulling me away from the painting.

We continue down the hallway to the left until we reach a curved black door at the far end of it. The guard hurries forward, roughly pushing past me, and opens the door for the princess. She saunters in. A beat later, I follow.

My eyes widen slightly as they scan the room. I'm in her chambers. White furs are strewn across the black marble floor. The furniture atop the hides are dreamy shades of blue and gray. A door on the far side is ajar, and I see the corner of a lavish bed. Fire inside a hearth warms the room despite the heat of summer.

My eyes idly sweep across a full-length mirror that stands tall against the wall before snapping back to my reflection. My cheeks are sunken in from the lack of food. Dark circles stain the skin just below my eyes. The cut on my cheek is red around its edges and scabbed over completely. It's deep and jagged, bound to leave a scar.

A muscle in my jaw tenses. I rarely gazed into my reflection back in Terakeld, but when I did, I used to see my mother on the other side—smooth olive skin, bright gray-green eyes, and wavy ash-brown hair. When I was younger, Father always said I was the spitting image of her. It was something I was proud of and held onto dearly after she passed. Now, as I look at my reflection, it's not her that I see. Any trace of her disappeared when the sharp blade of that guard's silver sword slit my skin open, barely missing my eye.

"It's a pity," the changeling princess coos as she walks toward a regal sky-blue chaise and lounges across it. My head turns, following the sound of her voice. "You were so pretty before my guard gave you that."

Her gaze dips to the scab. It burns under her stare. I can see the amusement behind her features. My teeth grind together.

"Is there anything else I can get you, Princess Andrina?" the guard, now at my side, asks before I can open my mouth.

Princess Andrina Verral. I should have known the name of the one who stands before me. Our teachers taught us the names and ages of each living royal, but my mind always drifted during those lessons. I hated learning about families that use and discard us. So, I never cared to learn.

Without looking at him, Princess Andrina shakes her head in dismissal. The guard bows deeply before walking out of the sitting area and closing the door behind him.

Now alone, no one moves. I stare at her. She stares at me. The only sound is the popping of wood beneath the flames. It's a standoff. We are two predators, carefully calculating the other's next move.

I take the opportunity to look at her . . . *really* look at her. Her long white hair nearly reaches her hips and looks as soft as the silk ribbon Ottilie gifted me. It slightly curls at the end, and petite blue flowers are woven through each strand. Her eyes are the same unnerving color as the rest of the changelings'—frigid ice glinting over a lake—but the dark powder tinting her eyelids makes them pop. It's almost hard to look away. Her cheekbones are prominently high, and her chin points downward. She's stunning. I hate the thought as soon as it enters my mind.

Princess Andrina barks out a high-pitched laugh, shattering the silence.

"I have been waiting for someone like you," she says, clearly pleased. "You, Maeve Wyndell, are defiant."

My name sounds wrong as it rolls off her tongue.

"I can see the hatred you harbor for the kingdoms. Although you hide it well, you're burning with it. Charred to the core." Andrina stands up gracefully and begins circling me with swaying hips and mischievous eyes. "There's something vicious lurking within you. You have anger and resentment that the other contenders did not have. I saw it as you bashed that mortal's head in with his own helm. I want it. I *need* it. It's why I rang the bell for you. It was my decision and mine alone, and now, you will serve *me*."

She halts her stalking steps in front of me. She's so close I can feel her cool breath on my skin. "Your assignment is to kill. You will kill whomever I tell you to *whenever* I tell you to . . . in the name of Phandolus, of course."

Spinning sickness tilts the world around me. My stomach turns to lead and drops into my gut. *An assassin.* That's what I'm to be for the next ten rotations. A killer tied to a leash that the changeling princess holds. I'm not a killer, though. I *can't* be. I don't *want* to be. And yet . . . I've already taken two lives.

Warmth suddenly envelopes me. Mother's presence wraps around me, holding me close. I breathe in the feeling of her, willing my heartbeat to slow.

Then I feel something else. It feels like pure light.

No. It can't be.

Ottilie's presence twines around Mother's. Warmth and light mixing together. A sob wedges itself into the back of my throat. I can feel my knees wanting to buckle, to fall on the floor and wail in front of the princess. My lower lip wobbles.

The princess laughs loudly. "Chin up, Maeve. You look good covered in blood." She smiles down at me with a glint in her eyes, not knowing the truth behind the emotion I feel that I'm sure is written across my features.

My fingers curl, and my nails dig into my skin as I stare back at the Princess of Phandolus. Ottilie is dead because of *her*. Deep down in my gut, a fire begins brewing. That feeling of light—*of Ottilie*—pulses around me, thrumming against my skin and stoking the flame.

You were right, Wyndell, Ottilie seems to say. *Nothing will come between us. Not even death.*

You shouldn't be dead in the first place, I want to scream. *You should be laughing and smiling and dancing and stealing my pieces of cheese. You should be* breathing*!*

"Now"—Princess Andrina's voice cuts through the room—"you will train with three of my personal guards of my choosing. You will share meals with them, too. I need you fit before sending you off on your assignments . . ."

She begins listing off the skills I'll be learning and the exercises I'll be doing. I can barely make out the words forming on her lips. I'm unmoving as I watch her talk.

It should have been me, not Ottilie. It should have been Andrina or the merfolk queen or the elven prince. Any one of those foul creatures. Anyone but her.

"I look forward to your services, Maeve Wyndell," Andrina says, sauntering over to the closed door and rapping her knuckles across the wood. It swings open. The guard bows to the princess and stands, ready to take me back to the darkness of my cell.

My steps are slow, yet my mind races. The grasp of unrelenting ice digs into my soul. The kingdoms and their *meaningless* trials are the reason no one will feel the warm embrace of Ottilie's hugs or hear the light fluttering of her giggles as she plays with the younger kids in Towne Square. They killed her. They deserve to know what it feels like to lose someone they love.

Suddenly, resolution overcomes me. That brewing fire erupts. I will get justice for Ottilie. I will happily obey Princess Andrina's orders to kill. No one in these Godsforsaken kingdoms is safe. They killed Ottilie, so I will kill them all.

Just as I am about to cross the threshold, Princess Andrina's pale arm shoots out like a cobra striking its prey. Her grip is vise-like, and her sharp, painted nails dig into my skin, halting my next step. She leans in closely.

"You are not to speak of this conversation or your servitude assignment with anyone other than myself." Her voice is as soft as a whisper with a poisonous bite. "If you so much as utter a word, I will rip your throat out and do the same to your brother and father."

12

"WELL, WHAT HAPPENED?" JERIK turns to me as soon as his ankle is shackled and the guard closes the cell door at the end of the day.

Staring blankly at the wall opposite me, my back rests against the rough stones. I've been in this very position since I got back from Princess Andrina's chambers. I don't turn to look at him, but I feel his stare burning against my skin.

I can't tell him the truth. I can't tell him I'm going to be an assassin for the changeling princess. I can't tell him that I'm looking forward to hurting the kingdoms like they've hurt me. I can't—

"Maeve," Jerik calls out, interrupting my racing thoughts. Finally, I face him. His eyes roam over my body, looking for any signs of blood or bruises . . . Any signs that I was *initiated,* just as he was. "What assignment did you get?"

I open my mouth, but nothing comes out. The words feel stuck, glued to my esophagus.

Images of Father and Arden flash before my eyes. Empty eyes. Mouths open wide. Blood spilling out of their necks. Andrina's threat rings against my skull over and over again.

"Maeve?" Jerik asks again. This time, my name stretches with uncertainty.

"Chambermaid for the princess." The words are out before I can even process what I'm saying.

Jerik nods as he takes me in. "Hey, that's better than a stable boy. You'll get to be in the palace, at least."

"Yeah . . ." My voice sounds distant. I can't shake the anger that has been boiling beneath my flesh since settling on the idea of getting justice for Ottilie.

And that fire is laced with fear . . . Fear for my family's safety. Those images continue to streak across my vision. My fingers fidget. My thumb presses down against them, popping each knuckle. I can feel my chest tighten and my heartbeat speed up.

"Can I . . ." The words trail off. Jerik's brows furrow together, waiting for me to speak. My mouth closes, and I squeeze my eyes tightly. A long exhale then, "Can I sleep next to you tonight?"

I open my eyes and take Jerik in. His eyes are slightly wider now, and his brows are raised. My gut twists. I shouldn't have asked.

"I just meant—"

"Of course, you can, Maeve." Jerik's soft voice interrupts me.

He shifts closer to me until his chain snags tight, and he lies down on his side. I do the same, facing him. My hands are folded underneath my head, and my knees are bent just enough to touch his.

The corner of his mouth hesitantly ticks up, and I get lost in the swirling shades of brown that make up his eyes until they flutter closed. Silence surrounds us, and I use this time to study him. His blond eyelashes rest against the tops of his cheeks. His lips part slightly as sleepy breaths glide past. A vein in his neck pulses languidly in time with his heartbeat. He's handsome, achingly so.

"Jerik," I whisper. He hums in response. "Do you remember the trials?"

His eyes open and lock onto mine. "Bits and pieces," he tells me, shaking his head. "I remember my lungs filling with water and a maze of burning panels."

"I don't remember that," I rasp out. The burn on my right shoulder flares up, scorching under nothing, as if it remembers getting seared by the very panels Jerik speaks of.

"They were the merfolk and tiefling's trials, I believe. I don't remember the other two, though . . . and nothing after the bell rang." Jerik's arm reaches over and lightly trails around the charred edges of my dirty tunic and the blistered skin of my shoulder. Chills erupt in its wake.

"I remember them." My eyes drop to the ground. "It's better if you don't."

A beat of silence passes between us before he says, "Tell me." His voice is firm, sure. My eyes snap up and connect with his. "I want to remember it all."

So, I tell him everything I can remember, and he tells me.

Water splashes against the ground as Jerik washes off his face before another day of work at the stable. I try to move toward the bucket without wincing. My muscles scream at me from combat training yesterday, and the cut on my stomach from weapons training the day before throbs with each shift of my body.

I grit my teeth together so Jerik doesn't notice. My heart clenches, and my chest feels heavy from the lengths I need to go to keep the truth from him. I hate the lies I'm forced to tell, so he doesn't suspect I'm doing anything other than changing the princess's bedding and drawing her baths.

Now at the bucket, I plunge my hands and drink a few handfuls of water as Jerik wets his hair. A light hum rumbles from his chest. I can't put the tune together, but it's nice—soft and melodic. If I close my eyes and simply listen, I can pretend I'm not chained to the floor. I could be anywhere in the world. I could be in the meadow.

"What's the thing you miss most about Terakeld?" I ask him.

Jerik faces me, wet strands of hair flicking pebbles of water onto my skin from the movement. He looks at me as he contemplates his answer, but before he can say it, a different voice rings out.

"Terakeld is a shithole, just like its inhabitants."

Jerik and I start. My body jerks away from the bucket. Jerik nearly falls over.

From the darkest corner of the cell, a changeling I don't recognize appears. How we didn't notice his moon-white skin, I don't know. He's dressed in a uniform similar to the other guards, but instead of dark blue and silver, black cloaks his body.

He turns to face me. "Princess Andrina needs you, Maeve Wyndell. She says it's urgent."

I'm frozen to my spot. I don't move a single muscle as this unknown guard unlocks my shackle. I don't move as he stands over me. From the corner of my eye, I can see Jerik's head swiveling from me to him.

The guard notices, too. "The princess likes keeping her *chambermaids* on their toes. Only the best for the future ruler of Phandolus," he explains to Jerik before gripping me by my arms, pulling me to my feet, and ushering me out of the cell.

"Lighter! Swift on your toes!" the guard in black yells as I balance atop a wooden beam tucked in the tall pine trees behind the palace.

I nearly fall as his demands reach me from several meters below. I try to ignore him as I continue the obstacle course. I'm nearly done. All that's left is a jump across a large gap between two planks of wood and the climb down the tree.

More demands. More yelling. If anything, he's being louder than me, drowning out each stumble and grunt I make. Finally, I hop onto the damp soil. It squishes under my boots. At that, he rolls his eyes.

"You are to be an assassin, mortal," the changeling chides. His nasally voice grates against my skin. "You cannot be making the amount of noise you are now. I was in your cell for several minutes, and you didn't even realize I was there. That's the level of silence you are expected to achieve."

The guard takes in my heaving chest and disheveled hair. Sweat glides down the side of my face, and I can feel my cheeks burning red. He grimaces at the sight.

"Now, there's a mile-long trail that starts just beyond those trees." The stealth guard points his boney finger toward a group of trees bunched together. "You will run it. If I hear so much as a branch snap or a rock rolling, you will do it again. Over and over, until you get it right."

13

A HISS SILENTLY SLIPS through my teeth as I adjust my weight against the cell wall next to Jerik. Three weeks have passed since my first training session, and I'm still sore after each one. Combat training. Weapons training. Stealth training. An endless loop spent in the presences of those three grating guards—one for each type of lesson.

The guard who trained me in combat put me through the ringer today. It hurts to walk, sit, *breathe*. I can already feel several bruises beginning to form along my ribs, and my knuckles are swollen and red.

For once, I'm thankful for the dim cell. Jerik doesn't notice how beat up I am when I'm cloaked by darkness. My eyes shut as I will away the pain throbbing across my body.

"My sister." Jerik's voice softly interrupts the silence.

Turning my head toward him and blinking away the blur, I study him. The hand holding a sharp rock he snuck from the stable pauses in his lap. Half of his beard is trimmed; all that's left is light-brown stubble.

"I'm sorry?" I shift my body to face him.

"You asked me what I miss most about Terakeld." He looks at me for a breath longer than normal and then returns to his task, bringing the rock up to his cheek and scraping downward.

I forgot I asked him that. It's been weeks.

"I miss my sister the most. We did everything together. She's my best friend. Leaving her behind for my trials . . . I'm worried about her, Maeve." He finishes the last stroke of his rock and breathes out a long sigh. "She's already so stressed about helping Gran make ends meet now that I'm away. She got a job in the market the day we left."

Realization hits me then. That girl who begged for a job at the fruit stand was Jerik's sister. I should have seen the resemblance—their dirty-blond hair, straight noses, and deep brown eyes. I should have known, but Jerik was always just a blur in my mind—someone who was there, who I had classes with, who I would see walking around the market, whose Gran is a known kingdom loyalist. My family, Ottilie, even my trysts with Drustan, shoved the sweet man before me into the background of my life. Someone I didn't care about enough to take notice of. My heart seizes at the thought.

"She'll be okay." I reach over and grab his hand. My fingers lace between his, and I squeeze. I try to pour everything into that simple gesture.

He looks down at our hands and then slowly glides his eyes back to mine. They sear into me with an emotion that I can't describe. I think I see timid gratitude twining around the depths of his irises. He squeezes back.

The corners of his mouth tick upward. A soft smile that I want to burn into my memory forever.

"What about you?" His thumb idly rubs circles along the top of my hand. "What do you miss the most about home?"

I open my mouth to answer. I hesitate and close my lips again. I want to say Arden, but it's been five rotations since I last saw him. I'm used to his absence. I want to say Father, but he hasn't been the father I need since I was eleven.

After a moment of Jerik's eyes roaming across my face, I answer, "The meadow." His light-brown eyebrows lift slightly. "You know," I add quickly, "the one by the Northwestern District."

Jerik's head nods. "I know the meadow. I just wasn't expecting that to be your answer. Did you go there a lot?"

My head bobs, and my throat tightens around nothing. All the times I played with Arden, lounged with Mother and Father, and swam with Ottilie hit me in the chest. Tears spring against my eyes.

"It's my . . ." I choke on the words, like each syllable is digging its claws into my tongue, resisting to be set free. I force them out. "It's my favorite place in the world. My best memories are there. With my family . . . with Ottilie." Her name cracks as it rolls off my tongue, and several tears escape.

Jerik tugs on my hand, bringing it closer to him. "Why did you . . ." His words trail off.

My head dips toward the ground. I focus on the small wet spots on the ground as another tear adds to them. I can't look at him. I don't want him to see me like this.

"Maeve." He clutches onto my fingers, trying to get my attention. "What happened to Ottilie?"

Back and forth, my head shakes. A soft brush of light glides against my cheeks—Ottilie, trying to wipe away the wet tracks falling down my face.

"Maeve—"

"She's gone." A sob rips out of my throat.

Finally, my eyes meet his. Through the water pooling along my lashes and blurring my vision, I can see it begin to dawn on him. His face pales. Gravity pulls his jaw open.

"What do you mean?" A timid question I can tell he already knows the answer to.

"Kill or be killed," I answer, dejected and broken, with a hint of venom.

The warmth from Jerik's hand instantly evaporates as he lets go of me and runs his fingers through his hair. Absolute horror twists around his features. His eyes dart from side to side. His mouth opens and closes like a fish out of water.

"My mother was right. About everything," I mumble, fighting against the tears leaking out. Blond hair swooshes around. Red-rimmed eyes bore into me. "They were all right. Every single soul that was lost on the whipping post. They were right."

The white around Jerik's irises gleam under the darkness. A stray teardrop rolls down his cheek. He blinks, trying to gain his composure, but doesn't say anything. Facing away from him, I stare into the void that makes up the other side of the cell.

Grief. Pain. Anger. It all slams into me.

"If more people listened to my mother and those who followed her . . . If more people didn't hide the truth behind ignorant lies of gracious kingdoms and honorable servitude, Ottilie would still be alive. If I had spoken up . . ." I inhale deeply, my breath shuddering.

Grief. Pain. Anger. I'm in a trance.

I don't even realize what I'm saying. I vaguely hear the sound of chains rattling together as more words slip through my lips. "There are more of us who think like they do, who believe in the truth only the rebels are brave enough to speak out loud. Neighbors. Merchants. There aren't many of us, but we're there. Hiding behind cowardice. Our hands are stained with Ottilie's blood, just as much as the kingdoms'. If only we'd used our voices."

Large warm hands engulf my cheeks and turn my head. Jerik's wide, terror-stricken eyes pull me back to the present. "Maeve," he whispers, urgency lacing his voice. His thumbs wipe away the remnants of tears. "Do not ever speak those words out loud again. They're dangerous. You don't know who is listening and who could use them against you. Do you understand?"

Tears well again, but I nod in response.

"Okay, good. Come on, let's get some rest." Jerik gently lays me down against the dirt-covered ground before settling behind me. Our chained ankles touch, and his arm wraps around my waist.

Restless sleep pulls me under.

"Get up, mortal!" The guard training me in combat looms above me with a snide leer as I lie on my back, struggling to breathe.

My lungs seize around nothing, all air gone. My sternum aches from where the bottom of his boot kicked me. Two months of training, and I'm still no closer to where I need to be when it comes to combat. I'm excelling at stealth and weapons training just fine, but there's something about hand-to-hand fighting that I can't grasp.

The changeling strolls away from where I lie, his footsteps echoing against the walls of the training room, and waits. My eyes stay trained to the ceiling for a quick moment before rolling onto my side and hoisting my body off the stone ground. I glance at the table of knives and daggers that sits to my right. Long swords are mounted onto the wall above it. He wouldn't be so smug if I were wielding one of those.

"Stop stalling," he barks. "Perhaps you need some more motivation."

Before my eyes, life flows through the guard's colorless skin, making it a beautiful pale ivory and the light blues of his irises turn the same brown as the soil outside. Dirty-blond strands begin to form at the roots of his cropped bone-white hair and work their way down, growing as it does. His crooked nose from the brawling rings the guards use to let off steam straightens, and the scar that runs down through his bottom lip to his collarbone disappears. Jerik Flint stares back at me. But he's off. His smile doesn't hold any kindness in it. His eyes don't soften when he looks into mine.

"If you do your job correctly, you won't need to resort to combat whatsoever," the guard grumbles. The gravelly voice doesn't match the skin he's wearing.

It's like nails scratching against metal. "But it's better to be prepared. Now, pin me down, and you may go."

With eyes alight and teeth bared, the fight begins.

14

THE SLOW, DEEP BREATHS of slumber shallow out as sleep evades me. Before I even open my eyes, I feel it. Something is different . . . Something is *off*.

My gut twists at the feeling. The air is charged with a crackling current. A current that will shock me if I make the wrong move. A current that knows something is about to shift.

Jerik's arm tightens around my waist like he can feel it, too, even though he's sleeping soundly.

Even deep in slumber, he grounds me. When I'm lying with him after grueling days of training, no longer do I feel that anger warping my being. He allows me to forget—forget that we're chained to the floor. He eases something deep within me.

Twisting around as quietly as I can, I turn to face him. Subconsciously, he notices the movement and pulls me closer. My eyes roam over his face. I feel the urge to run a finger over the stubble covering his cheek and the curve of his strong jawline. He looks so relaxed without the burden of our servitude. So handsome.

Waking up next to him each morning makes my stomach flutter, like butter-flies bursting to get out. Safe. Comforting. Seen. That's how I feel when we're like this before he has to go to the stable and I have to train.

Fleeting thoughts of a life after servitude slam into my mind . . . A life with him . . . A life without trials. I imagine waking up next to him in a quaint Central District cabin. Instead of the cold cell ground, we're lying on a cot big enough for the both of us. I imagine long walks along the river and frolicking hand in hand through the meadow. I imagine sharing stories and truths from our time in servitude over warm tea before a roaring hearth. Truths that I will finally be able to reveal without my father's and brother's lives hanging in the balance.

The imaginary life I just conjured up should scare me, but it doesn't. As I gaze at him sleeping soundly, I know our time together has spurred feelings I'm unused to. Feelings that not even Drustan could elicit from me as our moans filled the air and the rough floor of that abandoned barn dug into my hands and knees.

Perhaps these feelings surfaced in the face of trauma, leaning on him when no one else can seem to endure the weight of what we went through. Perhaps my feelings are true, and they evolved as I got to know him. I'm not sure. What I do know—with a certainty I've never felt before—is, I don't care.

I like him. A gentle trickle of Ottilie's presence runs down my spine.

"I like him, too," I whisper to the spirit of my best friend.

"Hmm," Jerik moans. His lips softly smack together, and he begins to stir.

I hold my breath and stay still, wanting to give him a few extra moments of peaceful rest before the day begins. A sharp inhale, and his eyes flutter open.

"Hi," he mumbles around the sleep lacing his voice. A soft smile graces his lips.

"Hi," I whisper.

Jerik untangles himself from me and sits up. I follow, pulling the bucket of water toward us. Now that I'm not wrapped in his embrace, that feeling of *knowing* returns. Something is different. My hands begin to tremble as I dip them into the water to splash my face. Jerik immediately notices.

He plunges his hands under the ripples of the water and pulls mine out with his. "What's wrong?" He uses his tunic to pat our hands dry and grips onto my fingers to stop the trembling.

"I don't know. I just feel off. Something's—"

The door opens wide, its hinges creaking harshly. Like every morning before, whichever guard is tasked to train me that day comes to pick me up. It seems like, today, I'll be doing weapon's training. However, unlike every morning before, the guard is early. Dread cements itself deep in my gut. Today is different.

As the changeling guard stomps toward me, he notices Jerik holding my hands.

"Well, isn't this sweet? Princess Andrina will love to hear about this. She doesn't like her *chambermaids* being distracted." My shackle slides to the side as soon as it's unlocked. "Up, mortal," the guard orders.

My journey to the cell's opening is sluggish as I force my feet to drag against the dusty ground. I send a quick glance to the sweet man still chained to the floor. He's watching me with eyes that hold an intensity that I've yet to see from him. I can tell he feels the shift about to occur by his constricting muscles beneath his tunic, resisting the urge to stand.

I halt my steps as I stare into his round brown eyes. One hug . . . Just one hug . . .

"Now, mortal!" I flinch at the booming yell near the door.

My lower lip wobbles, and wet silver gathers in the corner of my eyes. Jerik's smile—kind and warm and reassuring—gives me the courage to put one foot in front of the other. With a tentative wave, he bids me farewell just as the sound of the door's iron lock slides into place. A sense of finality claws itself into my soul. Swallowing down a pathetic whimper, I follow the guard away from Jerik and the cell I've learned to call home.

Each step is an effort. My feet feel as if they're being weighed down by concrete blocks. Hesitancy grips hold of me when we turn right out of the dungeons instead of left, where the training room is. We're heading toward the foyer, toward Andrina.

The foyer is quiet except for the sound of our boots against the marble floor. The doors to the throne room are closed now. It's too early for servants to begin their day's work. The smell of eggs and roasted ham wafts through the emptiness from the royal chefs preparing breakfast.

As the guard leads me toward the second set of stairs, my ears perk up at the sound of a quiet sniffle. Standing motionless before the large family portrait at the stairs' landing is a changeling in an elegant gown. Her ice-white hair is braided in a coronet, and a grand crown covered in blue jewels rests atop it. The Queen of Phandolus.

We begin to ascend the steps. The queen hears us and straightens her spine, wiping away a stray tear as she turns around. Her posture is regal, her expression anything but.

"Your Majesty." The guard bows his head.

I follow suit. "Your Majesty," I murmur.

As she passes us and descends the stairs, she doesn't even glance our way. The queen looks haunted, like it's too much effort to fully hide the emotions consuming her.

Once the queen is far enough away, I ask the guard in front of me, "What's wrong with her?" It's a blunt question, a question I'm sure no one asks aloud and lives to see the day. Thankfully, the guard doesn't skewer me on the spot.

"The queen never got over the loss of her son. Not even her mate can fill the void in her heart," the guard mumbles, pushing me down the hall so hard my feet stumble.

There was once a changeling prince. My eyes idly roam over the family portrait. I'm sure our teachers gave a lesson on what happened in our classes, but like then, I can't bring myself to care as I'm ushered toward Andrina's chambers.

Before crossing the threshold to the princess's sitting area, the guard peels right and escorts me through a different door. I step into a bedchamber much smaller than the princess's royal suite. Inside, Andrina is circling a bed in the center of the room. Her long lanky fingers run over the gray silk and multicolored furs that lay atop it. A large window on the far side of the room casts the rising morning light across the floors. The snowcapped mountains gleam in the distance.

Against the wall, a vanity made of beautiful onyx stone shimmers with purple-and-blue hues. In place of powders and lip stains, a variety of weapons lay atop it. Steal knives and daggers of all sizes with silver accents glint in daylight's arrival. A long sword with a jagged blade takes up the full length of the table, and several darts with tips coated in a mysterious black film are off to the side. *Poison.*

"Do you miss sleeping on a bed, Maeve?" she questions. Her tone bites with condescension, taunting me.

The princess doesn't give me time to reply. Not that I would have, anyway. With feline grace, her heels click as she approaches a wardrobe made of that same onyx stone, with two jagged mountains in front of a large, pointed snowflake and a crown of stars carved into it. She opens its doors, revealing rows of dark-colored clothes.

"It is time for you to start going on assignments. I will need you close. This"—she spreads her pale arms out wide, gesturing toward the room—"is yours. All that you need to do your job is in this room. You will still have meals with my guards, but if you require anything that needs to be brought up to your new chamber, my personal servants will help."

Princess Andrina cocks her head toward the wardrobe. I know what she is saying without her even moving her bloodred-tinted lips. *Get dressed. Now.*

I nimbly run my fingers against the clothes that are neatly hung. The fabrics are soft—linens, silks, wools, even some textiles I have no name for. I've never felt anything so luxurious.

A completed outfit, most likely picked out by the princess herself, is hanging from a hook on the inside of one of the doors. A loose, long-sleeved tunic and plain pants make up the basics. Both are solid black. A sleeveless, hooded vest hangs behind the other pieces. It's a beautiful shade of wine. The only color in the ensemble.

Princess Andrina scoops up a dark leather corset belt and long leather gloves and places them onto the bed. Both are covered in straps and buckles that I'm positive have no purpose other than enhancing the look of the outfit as a whole. Dark leather boots are also placed upon the bed.

I begin to undress. My body shrinks slightly under the princess's cold, scrutinizing eyes.

"You are to kill the Duke of Ardorein in Fiermoor," she declares, watching for any reaction. My arms pause above my head for a split second before regaining my composure and removing my tattered top completely.

This is it. This is what I've been waiting for, training for. My first shot at justice. A wave of exhilaration barrels into me. I feel Mother and Ottilie twine up my legs and settle against my chest, letting me know they're here.

This is for you, I think as clearly as I can. I hope they understand.

"What did this duke do?" I ask as I pull the clean black tunic over my head and tuck it into my new pants. The clothes fit perfectly.

"Do not question me or my methods of picking those who must perish, stupid mortal." The words are a sharp hiss.

My eyes harden. Moments pass, and neither of us say a word. Then that disturbing smile of hers returns.

"Now . . ." The princess pauses, daring me to interrupt as she plucks a small piece of rolled parchment from her bodice. Unraveling it, I realize it's a miniature map of Galfei Thalor. She points toward a section of land that juts up from Fiermoor and continues. "Ardorein is a northern territory in Fiermoor, so you will not have to travel far. It is directly across The Unlighted Sea from the small village of Rutherglen." She points to an area near the southeastern shore of Phandolus. "The tiefling duke is a sloth, so this should be an easy first assignment. Something to simply get your toes wet."

Andrina rolls the map up once more, placing it back in her bodice, and leads me over to the vanity full of weapons as I finish securing the last buckle on the belt. "Combat should not be an issue. He won't fight back, which is a good thing. My guards tell me that's your weakest skill."

I glare at her reflection in an oval mirror mounted above the vanity before shifting my eyes away and taking in my appearance. A raised, pink scar is the only thing left of the cut just below my eye. The darkness of the outfit brings out the color of my irises. They don't look as muddy and dull. The gray-green swirls complement the black fabric covering my skin.

"When you come back, we will continue your training. Not all victims will be as placid when you take their life. Go on. Take your pick." Princess Andrina's eyes dart down toward the weapons before she steps behind me, her reflection completely concealed by mine. She combs her fingers through my hair, and I clench my jaw at the feeling. The ribbon Ottilie gifted me falls to the floor. A blast of fire from deep within me surges at the sight. How dare she.

"You won't be needing that tattered thing any longer," she huffs and comes back into view. A primal urge to rip her fingers out of my hair and break each bone twists my soul, startling me. Instead, I reach for a black leather strap next to the knives and daggers, meant to wrap around my thigh. Next to that is a brown leather scabbard for bigger weapons. Fastening the buckles on both and picking out my weapons keeps my mind off the roar of anger that thrashes in my blood.

Ottilie's light tries to soothe me. It doesn't work. Even when she was alive, there were times even she couldn't calm my raging emotions.

Three small knives and two darts slide easily into the thigh holster. I sheath the sword and a larger dagger into their respective holders—the sword across my back and the dagger at my right hip. I drop a thin silver tube into my boot meant for the poisoned darts just in case.

"A coachman is waiting for you at the back entrance of the castle. He will take you as close to Rutherglen as he can. From there, you must find your own way to Fiermoor." The princess leers at my reflection. "Speak not a word of this to anyone. Now, go."

She turns around, her gown bustling behind her, and walks toward the window. With her back to me, I quickly pick up the ribbon at my feet. It's hastily stuffed into a small pocket sewn into my pants, and I walk out of my new bedchamber.

15

T HE WHEELS OF THE carriage grind to a halt at a dead-end on the edge of a dense forest. Without a second glance, the coachman snaps his reins as soon as my feet touch the ground. The horses turn around, beginning their journey back to the castle and abandoning me in this unfamiliar place.

I force away the nervous knot in my stomach that made itself known on the ride here as my feet mindlessly move me through the thicket of tall pine trees in the direction the carriage was previously going. Rutherglen must be that way.

I sidestep leaves and branches that cover the mossy ground, the stealth guard's training ingrained in me now. It smells like it just rained—musky and fresh—yet the vegetation is bone dry. Shrill chirps from the high branches of the tall pine trees and breaking twigs in the brush from unseen critters fill my ears. It's peaceful here.

As beams of sunlight begin to seep through the thinning branches, my hands move to the hood at my back and gently pull the material over my head. It rests just above my eyebrows, with its shadow concealing my features.

A small seaside village is just ahead—Rutherglen. Light-gray—nearly white—translucent-like figures move between the salt-worn buildings, greeting one another with neighborly waves and hugs. The sounds of a lute carry across the wind from another part of the village, mixing with the giggles of children with milky-white hair and alabaster skin chasing one another through the alley-ways. They remind me of the children I saw running around the market before the trials. They remind me of Ottilie and me.

My features twist as I force myself to look away.

Ottilie is dead. Remember that, Maeve. She is dead because of the kingdoms. The kingdoms must pay.

My steps are soft, nearly soundless against the ground, as I approach the village. I slink through the buildings and use hidden nooks that help me go unseen. The shadows I hide in when a changeling rounds the corner are cool against my skin.

Once I clear the curving pathways and reach a sunless alley, my cautious steps turn into a confident stride as I approach the town's small worn docks. Waves crash against the shore. The Unlighted Sea is more active here than the coastline of Terakeld. A handful of boats bob in the waves, anchored to dark wooden posts. A lone changeling helmsman stands silently next to one.

Slipping my fingers into a pouch hanging off my corset belt, I run my fingers over the pile of silver Phandolus coins Andrina's coachman gave me. The helmsman eyes me suspiciously as I approach.

"I have a job for you if you want it," I call out. His eyes narrow.

"Here." I drop two more silver coins into the changeling's hand, adding to the four I've already given him. "Wait for me to return. And make sure you aren't seen—"

"You think I don't know that, mortal?" The helmsman lifts his eyebrow at me. "Crossing the kingdoms' borders? The secrecy? Whatever you're doing, I don't want to know about it. But for an extra coin, I'll deny I ever saw you if someone comes asking."

The helmsman's lips curl upward in a greedy smile as I drop another coin in his waiting palm. He pockets it and drags his boat behind the black sandy dunes of Ardorein's shore for cover. Then I begin my trek in the direction of the duke's manor.

As The Unlighted Sea grows farther away and the sand beneath my boots turns to hard, black rock, the scent of salt in the air transitions to a heavy smog that sticks to my lungs. It's hot and humid, and what sounds like fire ominously crackling deep below the ground surrounds me.

There is no grass, no dirt. Nothing other than rugged boulders piled into clusters, large spires jutting out of the ground and steam rising through cracks across the land. There seems to be no life, no homes, nothing. A dreadful place, barren and dark, despite the midday sun.

Finally, in the distance, I see a building. The first structure I've seen since arriving. It's a large manor—the duke's manor. It's just beyond a thin bridge with black stone arches at each end. My footfalls cautiously slow, and I stop near a boulder, crouching low.

A blur of red to my left catches my eye. A tall muscular tiefling seems to have materialized from one of the looming spires. He walks toward another spire and stands at the base of it with an arm crossed over his chest. I watch him for a moment—his red skin popping against the inky setting—before another blur of red materializes in front of him.

My eyes strain, trying to understand what's happening. Then it hits me. I swivel my head around toward the several spires I walked past. Some have cavities carved into them. Doors—they're doors. And the spires themselves are the tieflings' homes.

My heart rate increases, and my hands turn clammy. I'm a fool, a damned fool. I should've been careful. I should've been more observant. I could've been caught. All those rotations of not paying attention in class are coming back to bite me in the ass. I should have known that the tieflings of Fiermoor mostly live in the spires. I should have known.

Pressing my body closer to the boulder, I stay like that—slowing my pounding heart and getting my bearings—until I no longer can. I need to keep moving. I need to get closer.

Edging my way toward the bridge, I slink behind boulders and steer clear of the spire homes. Every few minutes, I stop. I hide. I wait. I decide it's safe enough, and I move again. It's tedious but necessary.

"*Take your time,*" I remind myself of what the guard who trains me in stealth always says. "*You are an assassin, a killer cloaked in shadows. There is no need to rush unless your life is at risk.*"

By the time I reach the bridge, the sun is farther west. Steamy waters of The Unlighted Sea churn far beneath the thin walkway, the opaque liquid mixing with the fiery depths of Fiermoor.

"This is no different from the wooden planks high in the Phandolus trees," I whisper under my breath as I cross the bridge. I mastered that after a handful of training sessions. I will master this bridge.

The steam from below rushes past me and sticks to my clothes, turning them damp as I cross. The sheer force of it makes my legs wobble.

Don't look down.

I quickly find my balance again and quicken my steps. My feet dart toward a cluster of smaller spires as soon as I cross the bridge's second arch. From there, I watch. I wait.

Dusk is beginning to blanket Ardorein. Lanterns around the manor begin to flicker on, one by one. Dome-shaped roofs stand stark against the purple-and-orange sky, with iron chimneys releasing smoke into the air.

I see a handful of tieflings in capes and dresses through the manor's windows. The occasional mortal in ragged uniforms passes by as well. Servants of the duke. One walks past, and the thundering in my heart swallows all sounds around me. I swear it's Arden. The way the servant walks with long strides, taut shoulders, and the way his dark-brown hair flops against his forehead makes me nearly scream out my brother's name. But with a quick shake of my head, I realize it's not him.

Horse hooves clop behind me, drawing nearer. A carriage races past. Clouds of black dust plume in its wake. Skidding to a stop in front of the manor, a brooding tiefling emerges from the carriage, wearing a dark-gray doublet and loose pants that stop at his knees.

One of the guards standing at attention near the grand entrance greets the tiefling. "Welcome back, Your Grace."

There he is. The Duke of Ardorein.

I track the duke's movements. He approaches the tiefling guard, yells at a mortal servant for taking too long to open the manor's doors, and scoffs as he crosses the threshold. The arrogant way he holds himself makes my fists tighten.

Soon, he will be dead.

When I first found out I would be Princess Andrina's personal executioner, I denied being a killer. But now, as I stare at the duke, I feel no apprehensiveness about taking this creature's life. Nerves? Sure. Determination? Definitely. But no second-guessing.

Waiting for the veil of darkness to come, my knees ache as I stay crouched. My eyes sweep the exterior of the manor, adjusting to the quickly dimming light, until I see the duke open a second-story window on the far-left corner of the building. He savors the evening for a moment, his eyes fluttering closed, his lungs filling with the smog-filled Fiermoor air. I'll grant him this brief moment of peace before he dies.

Finally, the plum sky turns as black as the land around me. My nerves thrum just beneath my flesh as I slip toward the open window. I grip the patchwork stone wall and begin to climb. My nails crack against each jagged stone, and pebbles of blood drip down my fingers.

Under my straining grip, I pull my body through the open window and slither against the wall into a shadowy corner, assessing the room. It's large, with an opulent bed of wine-red silk and ebony furs sitting in the middle. Scented candles of smoke and berries flicker on a bedside table. My silent steps pull me to a barely open door, and through the small opening, I see the duke's head disappear with a splash past the edge of a luxurious Spiicrete bath that glitters under the sconces welded to the walls.

After slipping into the bathing chamber, I watch the duke's blurry red outline lie motionless under the water from the lip of the tub. His eyes are closed. He looks at peace.

The thought of Jerik worms its way into my mind. I wonder what he'd think of me if he saw me now, standing over a tiefling and readying myself to take his life. But as fast as that thought comes, it disappears. The yearning I feel to get justice outweighs anything else.

Unclipping a small knife from my thigh holster, I ready myself. My grip tightens on the blade's hilt as the duke breaches the water. Not a second later, my left arm wraps around his horned head, and my right arm slashes the knife across his throat.

The power that surges through me while it cuts deep enough to hit his spinal cord comes directly from my core, tearing through my flesh as it breaks free. So much power in that simple movement. It's intoxicating. It's thrilling.

His body goes rigid, and his pupils flicker in fear. Thick crimson blood seeps from the deep slit into the opaque water. Wet gasps and violent splashes fill the quietness of the bathroom.

Drops of blood drip down the knife in my shaking hand that's pumping with adrenaline. I stand still—Mother and Ottilie silently with me—as I watch the tiefling struggle to live, to survive his fatal wound. Their presence thrums beneath my skin.

For you, I think silently.

I take one last look at the dying duke—the corner of my mouth ticking up—and leave the manor.

When I am above The Unlighted Sea—halfway across the dark bridge—a shrill shriek pierces the air. Pride hits me in the gut.

16

S ITTING AT THE VANITY in my new bedchambers, I idly move my hand back and forth. Light-red drops of water drip down my forearm as the wet piece of cloth cleans off the tiefling duke's dried blood that coats my knife.

My hands pause, and a small puddle of watery blood near the hilt of the weapon gathers when I stop. Something in me is shifting. I felt it as soon as the blade ripped through the creature's neck, and now, as I ruminate on what I did, it's even more palpable.

I liked killing that tiefling. I liked knowing that—despite taking orders from the changeling princess—I'm doing something that makes an impact. No longer am I merely going through the motions of life, of sitting by while others speak out against the kingdoms. I'm doing *something*. It's a powerful feeling. A welcomed one.

A caw screeches near my window, and my head snaps toward the sound. The knife plummets to the floor, barely missing my bare foot. An eagle of some kind swoops by and heads toward the tall mountains in the distance as the dark reds and purples of another day's end paints the horizon and reflects off the snowcapped tops. A few stars glitter in the rapidly darkening sky just outside my window.

With a sigh, I bend over and pick up the knife from the floor before wiping it off with a dry piece of linen and placing it on the vanity with the other weapons. When I got back to Phandolus earlier this morning, the first thing I did was dump the blades and darts onto the table before collapsing into the soft, clean bed minutes later. Slumber overtook me until a couple of hours ago.

I needed the rest. My brain—completely muddled after the spike of adrenaline disappeared once I reached Fiermoor's beach—was too tired to think about anything other than sleep on my journey back. The changeling helmsman must've noticed because he didn't say a word. And the trudge back to the palace was excruciating; I caught myself wanting to stop and sleep in thickets of bushes several times.

But now, my racing thoughts can't seem to stop. I repeatedly go over everything—every detail—from my assignment: traveling to Rutherglen, the boat ride to Fiermoor, the walk to the duke's manor. Everything I did right. Everything I did wrong.

Roughly opening the drawer of the vanity, I retrieve a piece of parchment, a quill, and a small inkpot before sitting on the floor. Hunched over, I quickly scribble everything I want to improve before my next assignment, starting with learning as much as I can about the other kingdoms. Never again will I be caught off guard like I was with the spire homes. Geography. Topography. Where important leaders and courtiers live. All of it.

Once I have a list I'm happy with, I fold it up and stuff it under my pillow so I can give it to whichever guard I'm sure will retrieve me in the morning. A request to be trained in these weaker areas. Then I shuck off the clothes I didn't bother changing out of before, pull on a black tunic from the wardrobe, and climb into bed.

Closing my eyes, I try to slow my thoughts and force tiredness upon me. I need to sleep, despite having slept all day. Training will be brutal if I don't.

I toss and turn; nothing works. Sleep evades me, and my racing mind won't cease. The image of the tiefling duke lying in his bloody bath water. The excitement I felt when I slashed his neck open. The anticipation for training tomorrow so I can master the things I need to improve. Sleep isn't an option, it seems.

With a huff, I turn onto my back and open my eyes, staring at the marble ceiling above me. Only then do I allow the blond-haired man, chained to the floor beneath the palace I'm in, to enter my thoughts. I wonder what he's thinking. I wonder what he would say if I told him what I'd done. I wonder if he'd look at me any differently knowing that I enjoyed spilling the tiefling's blood.

Wringing my fingers together atop my stomach, I think it over.

He'd understand. He has to understand . . .

17

T HE MIDDAY SUN BEATS down on me as I trek along the northern shore of
Fiermoor, toward the Eastern Docks. Spouts of steam bursting from the
ground cause beads of sweat to roll down my neck, pooling at the dip between
my collar bones. The only relief is the occasional gust of sea breeze that cools my
skin.

My bones hum in anticipation, tightening my joints as if it's urging me
faster. A week after I killed the Duke of Ardorein, Andrina gave me my second
assignment. The Queen of Amphitea's royal advisor is next to die.

A rush of adrenaline burst through my body at the news, despite her saying
that this kill won't be as easy as the first. She said the advisor is always with his
queen. I didn't care. After that first kill, I felt powerful, and I liked it.

I'm finally doing something to stand up against the kingdoms, just like
Mother did nine rotations ago. This is for her. This is for Ottilie. Justice is sweet,
and I don't think I'll tire of it.

A ship's horn blares nearby. The Eastern Docks are just ahead. I adjust my
hood, pulling it tighter over my eyes as I approach. Several tieflings happily greet
each other as they spend their day on the docks, their chatter mixing with the
crashing waves against the rocky shore.

Weaving my way through the towering beings, their conversations die down as they notice me. I feel their stares burning against my cloaked skin, roaming up my body from my boots to my hood.

"What is one of her kind doing here?" one tiefling with maroon skin whispers to another.

Another hisses, "Look at that thing, thinking it's better than us."

A tiefling in a black corseted dress that shows off her muscular light-red legs tracks me with her slate eyes as I walk past. "Selfish elves should stay in Nythfaedell," she spits in my direction.

I don't allow my steps to falter, but the muscle in my jaw tenses at the accusation. They think I'm an elf, since my round ears are hidden beneath my hood. Let them think that. Better that than a rogue mortal who has left her servitude station. Thankfully, the tieflings seem to go about their business as soon as I pass them—forgetting me as quickly as they were to chastise me.

Near the edge of the berth, I notice large wooden barrels. They're being loaded onto a trade boat. *Firestone Mining* is inked onto the side of the ship in bold black script. Stamped onto the barrels, large red words catch my eye. *Warning: Spiicrete inside. Handle with care.*

My breath seems to snag at my windpipe as a small barely audible squeak escapes. The tiefling mining operation. This barrel—these crystals . . . This is what took Mother away from me.

Just beneath the warning, I see it. The world quiets around me. Two small lines shaped like waves are stamped over an inky conch shell. I zero in on three words etched in elegant penmanship. *Export to Amphitea.* My eyes burn into the text as if they could brand the words there themselves. My way to the merfolk, to my next kill.

The dockworkers heave the last of the Spiicrete barrels up the ship's ramp before bounding toward a stack of crates in front of a different ship, waiting to be loaded. The ramp is left open. No dockworker, no guard, no ship captain stands by.

A single breath in, and I slink toward the ship. The sloshing sea drowns out the sound of my boots lightly clicking against the ramp. As soon as I board—crouching low so no one sees me—loud laughter and gruff voices come up behind me. The ship's crew is coming back.

Silently rushing toward an open trapdoor near the ship's helm, I descend the steps just as the crew's loud boots stomp onto the main deck. Damp darkness surrounds me, and the smell of musky wood invades my nostrils. Only a sliver of warm light flickers in the corner, where a lantern swings with the movements of the waves. The cargo hold is nearly full of barrels of Spiicrete. I tuck myself behind the highest stack of barrels as the trapdoor closes above me.

"May we have fair winds and following seas!" a voice booms from above. Yells and cheers follow, then the ship lurches away from the dock.

My breath catches in my throat, and my eyes snap open as the ship jerks to a halt. The rock of the waves must've lulled me to sleep. Light floods into the cargo hold while the sailors descend the steps and rummage around the barrels in the back. Retreating from my hiding spot, I keep one eye on the crewmembers as I sneak up the cargo hold stairs and off the ship.

We've arrived on a crescent-shaped beach covered in bone-white sand. The taste of warm salt graces my lips as I inhale deeply while taking refuge between two large boulders tucked along the edge of the sand and water.

Crouching low, I wait for the trade ship's crew to unload the cargo and clear the beach. It takes longer than I'd like. By the time the ship is no more than a speck on the horizon, the sun's bite against my skin is rapidly dimming into a slight brush of warmth instead. Finally, I stand, knees cracking from the movement, and make my way inland.

The white sand beach transforms under my boots into bare light-gray rock that reminds me of a cloud holding onto a summer shower that's not quite ready to release the water onto the earth below. I trek in the direction of the palace—a mental image of the maps I've been studying guiding my way—and take in the world of the merfolk around me. On land, it doesn't look like much. Pockets of hot springs break up the seemingly endless barren rock, steam whimsically floating up into the sky. So unlike Fiermoor, where it erupts, releasing pent-up pressure, as if the land couldn't handle holding it in any longer.

Melodic humming as sweet as honey dripping down a bee's hive flutters from my left. Two women holding hands walk toward a pool of crystal-clear water. They're both naked. Long, flowing, pink hair glides down the ivory back of the one on the left. The other is curvier, with short hair made up of orange corkscrew curls and skin like Ottilie's.

Just as their toes dip into the water's ripples, flesh transforms into scales. Two shimmering tails replace their once-bare legs. A deep green tail with shades of light blue and silver laced throughout it flicks upward before diving out of sight. The other—as gold as the elven guard's armor on the day of our trials—follows a second later.

Laughter—high and low—and excited splashes of water waft out of a cave to my right. The sounds of merfolk enjoying their afternoon.

Keep moving, Maeve.

The Amphitea palace comes into view after several minutes. It's smaller than what I imagined, similar in size to the duke's manor in Fiermoor. The architecture, however, is spellbinding, akin to the jewel-like tails I briefly encountered. Beautiful white stone stands out against the rocky terrain. Sections of the walls are covered by bright-colored coral—inching its way up like ivy—and tall spiral spires loom over the rest of the palace.

Just beyond the palace are three long rectangular buildings of the same white stone jutting out of the ground. Men and women in faded blue-and-purple uniforms—some covered in loose sand that falls off the fabric with each step—emerge from shadowed arches in front of each building. Their bodies are hunched over. White plumes of dust and sediment cloud around their ankles as their feet drag against the rock. Mortal servants of Amphitea.

My head turns sharply away from the sight as my heart clenches. Squaring my shoulders and digging my nails into my calloused palms, I slip into the palace past the sparse guards roaming the outskirts of the grounds. The halls, decorated by colorful shells and hanging spheres of pastel underwater plants, are empty. Every corner, every walkway. There's no sign of life in the palace.

That is, until a group of voices flutter through the deserted passageways. A breath of air I didn't realize I was holding rushes out of my lungs, and my shoulders relax. Knowing I can now get caught somehow makes me feel more comfortable, more in my element. The idea that I might be discovered sends a thrill through my veins that I didn't know I needed until I tasted it.

I follow the voices with a deadly quiet—a hunter stalking its prey—until waves slopping against stone drown it out. A corridor of steps to my left leads down into a hallway filled with seawater. Schools of fish swim past the steps, following the shimmering blue tail of a merman.

Of course the palace goes down, deep into the depths of The Unlighted Sea. The map I studied didn't depict that, but it makes sense. I should've known. A hiss of a curse slips through the slits between my teeth.

"Come on, you bastard . . . Where are you?" I whisper, barely audible. There's an edge to it, impatience cutting through each word. If this advisor is below the waves . . . I don't even want to imagine what Princess Andrina will do if I fail. Would Father and Arden still be safe?

A shiver slices through my spine as my search for the advisor continues. Just follow the voices. Follow the voices and hope that the queen is among them. Wherever she is, her advisor will be as well. Then figure it out from there.

Two slightly ajar copper doors shining against its white stone frame come into view. The source of the voices is just beyond the threshold. There is a nook concealed off to the side in a sliver of darkness. I creep toward it and settle in the shade. Through the crack near its hinges, I see a table surrounded by several merfolk sitting in the center of the room. Seated on a copper and coral throne at the head of the table is the queen, adorned with a dew-covered coral crown atop her forehead. A crown fit for the ruler of Amphitea.

Those in the room have serious looks on their faces. The queen is scowling as she looks down at some sort of document lying on top of the table. My eyes lock onto the green-haired man behind her, who's taking notes on a strip of seaweed and whispering into her ear.

There you are.

Carefully, my pointer finger and thumb pluck out a poisoned dart as my other hand reaches into my boot, removing the silver pipe that was tucked away. They feel heavy in my hands, burning my skin, like they're calling me, begging me to use them.

My chest twinges at the thought. The shift inside me spreads like a black blanket, inching its way to cover me completely. Death calls to me. Death begs me to take as many lives as possible.

Warmth and light twine around my fingertips. Mother and Ottilie, always with me. It feels like they're fighting against that shift. In an instant, the thought disappears. I'm doing this for them. They *want* me to hurt the kingdoms in their name.

"You are dismissed," the merfolk queen orders.

My body presses closer to the wall. The others exit the war room, gliding past me without so much of an inkling that they're being watched. Stuck in their untouchable world without a shred of fear that it could all end. Today, I will shatter that mindset of theirs.

The queen lingers behind. She and the green-haired advisor quietly mutter to each other for a moment longer. My ears strain as I try to decipher what is being said.

"Tomorrow, we will contact the Lady of Crullfeld. There, we will reassess, but our partnership with the tieflings is of the utmost importance," the queen says as her advisor scribbles each word down.

A generous bow from the merman. Then the queen turns heel and strides out of the room, flanked by two guards I didn't see before. The advisor mills about the area, tidying up and finishing his notes. My eyes never leave him; each step is monitored, each stroke of his pen under my keen stare.

I prudently insert the dart into the tube, careful not to prick myself, and bring it to my lips. My gaze zeroes in on his neck, just above the gills that quiver as he writes something down. Just like the targets in weapons training. A beat of silence, then a rush of air leaves my lungs, sending the dart flying through the crack between the door and the frame. The point of the dart hits its intended mark.

The advisor chokes down his shock with a weak gasp and pulls out the dart. The vibrant purple of his eyes churn with confusion. A muted thump as he drops the dart, then the louder thud of his body hitting the floor reverberates through the empty room. Quick, sharp pants fill the silence soon after as the poison seeps into his veins. Inky black lines spiderweb out from where the dart lodged itself into his neck. Frothy white foam dribbles out of his mouth and down his neck.

"Please," he rasps out, trying to call someone for help. However, he knows there is no hope. I can see it in his eyes.

As I watch him convulse and writhe against the floor, I can't help but not be satisfied. I drop the tube back into my boot and vow to never use it again.

From now on, my hands will do the killing. I want to feel the power I first felt when I killed the tiefling duke again. I won't let a feeble projectile have all the fun.

18

There's something intoxicating about pinching one's string of life taut and deciding when to snip it in half.

Every few days, Princess Andrina orders me to kill another on her long list of enemies. Dozens of deaths are now on my hands, stained with blood, despite the absence of crimson coating them. From elven lords to tiefling generals, I've traveled all over Galfei Thalor, doing her bidding. Sometimes it's a simple journey down the hall. It's a strange euphoria, slicing open the chalky skin of those I pass every day. Their names never known, but their unearthly changeling faces recognizable. It sets my nerve endings alight.

An old me—a version I do not know anymore—would feel ill at the thought of relishing in the fact that I wield Death's scythe against those who hurt me and my own. But now . . . I guess it's a good thing that version of me is no more.

Standing in front of the small oval mirror in my bedchamber, I search for that girl. Perhaps she's still there, hidden beneath the embers blistering my very being. I don't recognize who stands before me. She's stronger—leaner—with a glint in her eye that reveals just how dangerous she is.

I like what I see: a new Maeve coming to fruition, unflinching under my gaze. My olive skin isn't so dull anymore. My hair isn't tangled together from dirt and dust. I can't help the curve of my lips and think that I am blossoming into

114

someone I have always meant to be. Confident. Strong. A fighter ready to take on the flames and do what she must for those who've been burned.

Dressed in simple linen pants, a loose tunic, and knee-high boots that make me look like nothing more than a mortal servant, I turn from my reflection and exit my chambers. For the first time since moving out of the cell, no obligations burden me. No orders from Princess Andrina. No training sessions with her guards. Today, I can sneak around the grounds and get some fresh air. Today, I intend to visit Jerik at the stable.

My teeth dig into my bottom lip, attempting to stop my full, uncalculated smile from forming at the thought of the brown-eyed man. But my anticipation breaks through, and my darkened soul seems to sing at the feeling.

Jerik. It's been about a month since I left him. I miss him so much, a small part of the old me lingering in my hardened state.

I keep to the walls of the hallways, portraying nothing more than a servant on her way to fulfill her duties, before exiting the stone palace. The air is beginning to cool as the summer season dwindles away. Soon, autumn will be upon us. Nonetheless, the brisk air is not enough to warrant a coat but enough to flush my cheeks as I journey across the palace grounds.

Tall pine trees. Snowcapped mountains. Lush green grass. Structures that tower over me and seem to have a sheen to them that no building in Terakeld has. Their homes—the kingdoms are magnificent. Phandolus, especially. Bitterness coats my tongue as if I said those words out loud.

My steps grow faster once I spot the palace stable. It's just ahead, near the edge of the forest. The excitement I feel begins to gain control of my body.

Jerik. A sigh draws out of my lungs. I get to see Jerik again.

My impatient steps falter . . . I left him alone in that damp, cold cell. My gut throbs with guilt, and my steps slow. While this man I care deeply for is chained to the floor with nothing but a bucket of water, I have been resting in silken sheets and eating more cheeses and breads than I've ever seen in all my rotations.

My throat dries, as barren as a desert. I hope he's okay. I hope he knows I didn't want to leave him.

A loud bray in the distance brings me back from my racing thoughts. My head shakes violently, and my march down to the stable begins again.

The stable is stout, bare, and uninspiring. The massive structure is made of plain dark wood. It looks peculiarly out of place, like a mucky stain on a pristine marble counter—an eyesore that distracts from the beauty surrounding it. Large cutouts across the sides of the stable for the stallions and mares to get fresh air when confined in their stalls allow me to take a swift look inside. Large beady eyes stare back at me, though, blocking my view. The creature's long slimy tongue finds my cheek, leaving a wet streak in its wake.

"Get out of my way," I mumble to the horse, wiping its saliva with the back of my sleeve.

With a huff, I walk away from the placid beast and along the edge of the stable, until two large, wooden doors come into view. One is slightly ajar, and I quietly approach it.

Jerik. There he is. An unbidden grin breaks through, my features lighting up at the sight of him. His long blond hair rests just past his shoulders. His shirt, cleaner than when I saw him last, stretches across his broad back.

Rays of sunshine peek through several cracks in the stable's ceiling and hit the profile of his face, transforming him from a stable boy servant to the most beautiful man I've ever laid my eyes upon. His straight nose and long eyelashes shine under the light. Breathtaking, truly breathtaking.

Those dreams I experienced while lying in Jerik's arms before I was taken away flash before my eyes as I take him in. Hopefully, ten rotations from now—when this is all over—I won't be so tainted by death that it can become a reality. Jerik Flint could be my future beyond the gore-soaked life I live.

"Hi, stranger," I call out. My voice is more air than sound. Never once in my life have I heard something like that come out of my mouth. It slightly surprises me, leaving a burning blush blazing across my cheeks and nose.

My smile abruptly falls just as Jerik turns away from the rake in his hand and the pile of hay around his feet. His pinched brow relaxes, and his concentrated grimace transforms in a way I imagine I looked like just mere moments ago. He seems happy to see me. Yet, I don't feel that same joy any longer.

Cuts and bruises cover the half of his face that was shielded from me seconds ago. He looks worse than when he got his assignment—when he was *inducted* into his position. Murky shades of yellow, green, and purple litter his skin, replacing the perfect pale I've dreamed of for weeks.

A sharp inhale cuts through my teeth. "What in all of Galfei Thalor happened to you?" My shriek—loud enough to stir the horses confined in their stalls—draws attention from the others in the stable.

Jerik's soft smile fades into a grim line. His eyes sweep slightly to the side—a gesture so small I almost miss it—where a group of other stable boys are now huddled together, snickering. A wave of sickness washes over me, and I glare violently at them, cutting daggers. Those simmering flames deep down flicker as I take them in. They take joy in hurting him because he's new. I can see it in the gleam in their eyes as they glance between us.

Flashes of red flare in front of my vision. I feel a rage inside me that is normally reserved toward the rulers of the kingdoms when I look at them. Beating each and every one of those stable boys into a slushy pulp crosses my mind. I could do it, and—my eyes shift to Jerik, his strong frame caving in on himself—I would enjoy it.

A split second of horror thrashes through my veins before it disappears completely. I bite the inside of my cheek, reminding myself to slow my breath and unfurl my fist. I cannot unleash myself upon these mortals. They're *mortals.* They can't know who I am. *He* can't know who I am.

My attention turns fully toward Jerik. He's unsure and . . . Is that embarrassment? Slow sadness seeps into my bones, my nerves. A few steps forward, and we are standing face-to-face. He doesn't meet my eyes, doesn't move a single muscle.

"Jerik." His name is a tentative whisper.

His brows furrow as he shuts his eyes. The muscle in his jaw twitches as he grinds his molars against each other. He remains silent, with his fists curling at his sides. Only our breaths mingle in the space between us.

"Let's go for a walk," I offer softly. My fingers itch to touch him, to gently grab his hand and guide him out of the stable far away from those vile men. His mumbled words halt any notion of reaching out.

"I can't stop. Not until the day is over." The words are broken, some without sound at all, as he attempts to deceive prying ears.

Keeping my voice the same volume as his, I reassure him, "It's okay. I promise."

I won't let anything happen to him. And if we get caught by the guard tasked with taking him back to the cell, I'll take care of that, too. The knife I hid in my waistband presses into my skin as if responding to the silent promise.

My right hand reaches forward and caresses his thick fingers—featherlight and caring—before threading them together. His skin is warm against my own, and a suppressed shiver dances down my spine. It reminds me of the hearth in our home in Terakeld. *He* could be my home. With a slight squeeze around his hand, I send him a smile to let him know that I mean it and lead him away from his world of abuse . . . if only for just this moment.

As soon as I guide him through the stable doors, our steps stop. His shoulders relax, and a deep sigh releases from his lungs. Away from prying eyes and the vicious snickers, his burdens seep out of his pores. His head is bowed, and his eyes are closed. I yearn to rub away the wrinkle between his brows, but instead I give him the time he needs, the time he deserves.

After a moment, he slowly opens his rich brown eyes. They glitter with unshed tears that he quickly reigns in, hoping I don't notice. I don't let him know that I do. Another breath. Then another. Then his head cocks to the side. He stares at our hands intertwined together, my thumb rubbing small circles across his skin. There's a burning weight to his gaze. Heat rises from the tips of my fingers all the way up to my cheekbones. I hope the color of my skin remains the same.

A beat later, his eyes slowly move up my arm and meet mine. He smirks. One corner of his chapped lips quirks up, and his teeth glint against the sun. Jerik Flint actually smirks and looks good while doing it, despite the cuts and bruises. If I could, I'd stare at the sight for the rest of my life. It makes my heart beat rapidly.

"You're insatiable!" I say, my laugh echoing against the trees as I shove him away.

He stumbles to the side, his own deep rumble of a laugh mixing with my own. Our mirth slows to joyful sighs until our breaths are the only thing that is heard between us. We stand there, studying each other. One, two, three beats later, I'm lunging into his arms. My arms wrap around his neck, while his snake around my waist.

The weight of his body against mine grounds me. Jerik, always grounding me, even when he doesn't mean to.

"Who would've thought you'd miss little old me?" he muses. It sounds like the air in his lungs was sucked out of him—happy and relieved.

"Shut up and let me have this," I mumble into his neck. My breath bounces back against his skin into my face. His large hand around my waist squeezes my flesh tighter. If only he knew how much I needed this.

Peeling myself from his grip, we break apart. As he smiles widely at me, he winces slightly as his lower lip cracks, blood beading to the surface. I use the sleeve of my tunic to wipe it clean.

"What are you doing here?" he asks, his eyes roaming my body, searching for any sign that I'm hurt. My stomach flutters as he does so.

I want so fiercely to tell him that I couldn't stand one more day without being in his presence, that my entire being was aching to see him . . . That I had the day off from learning how to hone my deadly skills. Instead, I do what I've been forced to do since becoming his friend: lie.

"I bargained with another chambermaid to get the day off. I'll take over her duties for the next few days if she covers me today." I pause. "She was more than happy to oblige."

I try to hide a grimace, schooling my face into a nonchalant calm. I hate lying to him, but I know I have to. To keep him safe. To keep me safe. To keep that imaginary future I yearn for safe. He seems to buy it.

"Come on," I exhale as I reach my hand out to him once more. "The others can shovel your section of shit while you're gone."

I'm positive they won't. They'll leave his piles untouched. I think he knows it, too, because he chuckles and shakes his head at me as if I said the most outlandish thing. The sight makes my lips tug farther up toward the sky. I only said it to make him feel better, my desperation to spend time with him clinging to the sound of his laugh. I'm happy it worked.

With a squeeze, his fingers embrace my own, and I lead him away from the stable and into the forest. Not far from the tree line—close enough to still spot the brown shabby wood of the horses' home—is a creek. That's where I take him.

One night, a few kills ago, while I was lurking through the palace halls on my way to cut a changeling courtier's chest open, I overheard a palace servant talking about it. Apparently, it's where she experienced the touch of a lover for the first time. My stomach turned to lead when she spoke of how romantic it was despite its fleeting nature in between her shifts. Her *shifts*. A special moment, an important life milestone, tainted by the hands of the kingdoms. The thought makes me ill.

As we approach the running water, I understand why she chose this place for a moment she will always remember. The area surrounding the creek is quiet and peaceful. Rushing water and chirping birds are the only sounds around. The water sparkles under the light beaming through the tree branches, as if twinkling fairies are gliding across the stream in a dance. The moss coating the ground is damp from the early morning mist, and the dew along its green surface is beginning to drip into the rich soil below.

Shucking off my boots and rolling my pants to my knees, I tentatively dip my feet into the clear water. The cold chills me to my bones, so unlike the pleasant water of the meadow, but it's refreshing all the same. Jerik joins me and hisses when the water envelopes his battered feet. Once settled, I turn to him, unsure of what to say now that I am here.

"How are . . ." The words trail off into nothing. A beat later, I ask, "Are you okay?"

I take in the evidence of his beatings. The darkest purple over his left eye is still fresh.

"I'm okay." He must see the worry in my eyes. His hand reaches over and rests on my thigh. "Really."

I nod, trusting what he is saying, *trusting him*. I wish he could trust me.

"It's just how the stable works, but I would give anything to have a different assignment. One where I'm not looking over my shoulder." Jerik pauses as he takes me in. "What about you, Maeve? You just disappeared on me. I asked about you to anyone who would listen, but it's like no one knows who you are. No one knows you exist."

Good. No one should. That means I'm doing my job right.

I sigh out loud. It's driven by the dread deep within me, knowing I must lie once again.

"Princess Andrina makes sure her chambermaids are just that—*hers*. We answer to her and no one else. I wouldn't be surprised if the king and queen have no idea I'm even a resident in their palace." I try to look bored, relaxing my muscles and shrugging my shoulders, like my servitude assignment is dull, when, in truth, it makes my blood sing.

He nods. It's easy—so horrifyingly easy—to deceive him. A part of me yearns for it to get even easier, just so I won't have to feel this insistent ache in my stomach each time I do. I know it won't.

Our conversation flows easily after that. No more talking about the stable. No more talking about the deception I've threaded together in front of his very eyes. We are whole now that we're together, leaning on one another. It feels like only minutes have gone by when Jerik says he should get back. I dread having to say goodbye to him. If I could, I'd stay here—in this unknown forest—forever. With him.

"So soon?" I ask, lifting my feet from the stream and shaking them dry before slowly fastening my boots back on. My wilting emotion is evident in my absurdly whiny tone.

He nods as he does the same and begins to walk toward the line of trees. I follow him. Each step is heavier than the last, wanting to drag out our time, even for a few seconds.

"The Head Groom will be wondering where I am. Everyone has been on edge lately because of the . . . *Shackled Serpent.*" Those last two words are barely above a whisper. His voice is low, and his eyes dart to the side to see if anyone is around.

What is he talking about?

Jerik turns his head at my silence. The look on my face makes him chuckle. "You're telling me you heard of this hideaway creek, but you haven't heard of the Serpent?" The crease in my brow becomes deeper as I attempt to understand. With a sigh, he continues. "The others and I heard the Head Groom talking about it with some other changelings. Apparently, the nobility of the kingdoms are dealing with an assassin problem."

My steps falter, and my eyes slightly widen.

"I know. It's scary stuff." He moves aside hanging branches for me as we make our way back. "It sounds like all four kingdoms are worried. Whomever is responsible, there are dozens of deaths on their hands. I couldn't imagine a more vile person."

At those words, my windpipe closes harshly, and my heart shatters.

As we breach the forest and walk toward the stable, his voice lowers slightly. "It's not just the kingdoms who are scared, though. Tales about the murderer are beginning to take life. Stories are making their rounds from royal revels to the cells they keep us in. I've even heard the rebellion in Terakeld is gaining traction, thinking this killer is one of them. We need to be careful. *You* need to be careful, Maeve. We don't know who they'll target next."

A sharp ringing in my ears blocks out everything. I can't even comprehend the worry he has for me. A sizzle of pride simmers deep within my gut knowing that those who hurt me are hurting just as much. They're scared, and I like that. But there's a small knot forming in my chest that I can't ignore. The kingdoms aren't the only ones frightened: Jerik is, too.

My voice remains low, shaking slightly. "Wh—why . . . Why do they call whomever it is the Shackled Serpent?"

"I heard it's because they slither around unnoticed when they're on the hunt." He chews on his bottom lip with furrowed brows, shaking off a shiver as he stares into the distance. "One servant told me the evil inside the assassin's heart is concealed so thoroughly, they could be hidden in broad daylight. There's also a rumor that whoever is spilling blood across Galfei Thalor was once a servant to one of the kingdoms, getting back for the ten rotations they had to serve."

The giant doors of the stable arrive too soon. I'm silent for what feels like a moment too long. The rumors aren't far off. After a moment to shake off my intruding thoughts, I pretend to be shocked. My mouth opens wide, forming an O, and my eyes match it. Jerik wraps his arm around my shoulders and squeezes, pouring as much comfort as he can into the gesture. I feel like a sham, as conniving as Andrina herself.

I twist in his embrace and hug him tightly, hoping he can ground me as he always does. My arms wrap around his neck. Firm, unyielding. I don't want to say goodbye. Not yet.

Pulling away just enough to look at him, my eyes flicker down to his lips. A kiss to hold us over . . .

If he notices the gesture, he doesn't utter a word. Instead, I lunge into him again, crushing his lungs beneath me. I don't want to let go. I don't know when I will see him next. Minutes pass before there's a silent squeeze on my hip, and we part. Then I watch him enter the stable to begin his work again.

While I stand outside of the stable, as still as the statue in front of the palace, two words ring against my skull: *Shackled Serpent. Shackled Serpent. Shackled Serpent.*

I can't help the thrill that laces around my bones and slithers up my body. There are tales about me, working their way through the kingdoms. I am deadly and dangerous . . . I am to be feared.

Quickly turning on my heel, I begin the journey back to my bedchamber. A slow, creeping smile forms along my lips. I am the Shackled Serpent. May those who rule above us sleep with one eye open.

19

A DEEP, COOL HAZE surrounds me as I stand in the middle of the palace grounds. They're empty and still. There's no sign of life here. No mice rustling through the grass. No morning breeze flowing through my hair. No horses neighing. *Nothing*. My breathing is all I hear.

In the distance, the stable is shrouded by fog. The wooden structure looks worn, the colors muted. If I wasn't looking for it, I would have missed it, completely blending into the bland shades of the normally vibrant forest surrounding it. The aroma of the wet wood travels through the stale air and stings my nostrils. It's musky and earthy and sticks to my throat. It makes me want to gag.

My feet move forward on their own accord. I don't even hear my footfalls against the brush. All there is is me, the hollow nothingness, and muffled breaths thrumming through my eardrums.

Closer and closer, I approach the stable. Hardy laughs pierce through the dull drone that fills my head, pushing at its boundaries and seeing if the pressure can crack through. Sticking my head through the cracked stable doors, I spot them. A group of men—stable boys—lounge on stacks of hay. Glass cups meet their lips as dark liquid sloshes against its barriers. They seem so happy, so carefree. Their smiles are genuine. They look like boys I could have befriended in Terakeld long ago.

Pale skin—bruised and battered—flashes before my eyes, and the shame that laced Jerik's eyes when I saw what they did to him pounds against my vision. Blood rises to the edges of my skin, turning it flush as my upper lip curls.

"What do we have here?" I purr, sauntering toward them.

Their eyes go wide. One boy with black hair freezes as he takes me in, his cup motionless against his chin. Another—whose head is shaved, no more than stubble protruding through his dark skin—hops off the tallest stack of hay and sizes me up. A predatory smirk forms where it was taut with confusion just mere seconds ago.

"You here to make things more interesting?" he coos. His eyes roam up and down my body, taking all of me in, as if I were sprawled naked over his bed. I can tell he's their leader, the one who calls the shots in the group. He'll die first.

I let him come close. I let his dirty fingers dance up my arms and over my collarbones. I let him think he has me, and when his lips draw nearer and his breath hitches, that's when I unleash my true self upon him.

As fast as a summer's lightning strike, my dagger materializes into my hand, and I plunge it deep into his gut. Ripping up to his chin, he splits in two like a fresh melon ready to devour. Gore and guts spill out of him onto the floor as he collapses into a heap of nothing but bone and skin. The others stare in horror before guttural screams tear out of their throats.

Now the fun begins.

A feral, toothy smile contorts my features, and the others cringe away from me as I leisurely approach. The dagger in my hand twirls around my fingers as I calculate how I want to end each of them.

The first to run is a redheaded boy. He's next.

I snatch my hand out at him before he can get away. His back faces me as he attempts to wriggle out of my clasped grip.

"Don't struggle," I hum as I pull his body flush against mine. The other boys are frozen in fear as they watch their friend's last moments alive. "Or do. I don't care. Either way, you die today."

Small bumps form across the skin on the back of his neck where my breath caresses it as I speak his death sentence. His chest rapidly rises and falls. My right hand lifts slowly enough to make him squirm more so than he already is. A whimper slips through his quivering lips. The sound brings me a dark wild sense of joy. A slight pause to leave him guessing and then my blade slowly tears across his throat.

A feeling—light and airy—rushes over me. Nostalgia. *Just like the Duke of Ardorein.*

The copper stench of his blood floods the stable, coating my hand and flowing down his chest. I don't register the thump that resonates against the ground when I drop his body.

Who's next?

I cut one of the boys' Achilles tendon, deeming him immobile, before I snap his neck. I spar with one of them for fun—giving him a false sense of hope—before stomping his skull into the ground. I tie up the last boy, the boy with raven-black hair, to a post and cut his skin open one slit at a time until he's sobbing for me to stop.

Slowly, so he feels every second of brutal pain, I push my dagger through the bottom of his chin up into his head. Crimson blood gushes out of his eye sockets, and the sound he makes is like music to my ears.

Looking around, I take in the carnage and can't stop the joyous laughs that burst throughout my body. They deserved it.

A hand grips my ankle, causing me to jump back slightly. I look down at the body of the first stable boy I've slaughtered. But instead of his deep, dark skin, pale ivory is in its place. Looking up at me with blood flooding out of his mouth is Jerik.

My eyes snap open as a long deep gasp heaves from my lungs. Sleep escapes me as my lungs fill to the brim. The pitch-black darkness engulfing my bedchamber silently judges me for what my mind conjured up. The silence of my room roars around me, screaming "*killer*" and "*monster*." As my breaths even out, I don't shy away from those words. I let them wash over me, judging me.

I feel the faint brush of light and warmth against my hand. It's dim, barely even a whisper, against my skin, as if I'm losing my grip on Mother and Ottilie. Like my connection with them—my humanity—is dimming as well. I feel it drain from my entire being. It feels like the darkness that tainted my soul after killing those mortal guards is spreading, surrounding me entirely . . . unable to be relinquished.

The thick silent air is right. I am a killer and a monster because, as I lay here, cloaked under the night sky, I don't feel chained to guilt or regret for the lives I've taken. I feel calm. I feel liberated.

PART II:
A KILLER

20

A CHILL IN THE air seeps through my clothes and wraps around my bones. As I look out my chamber's window, the warm cup of tea resting against my palms does little to heat my skin as the change in seasons begins to sweep over Phandolus.

Flashes of last night's dream— the dream that's so terrible, *should* be so terrible—reverberates throughout my consciousness. Every subtle sweep of my gaze across the tops of the dewy pine trees and snowcapped mountains is interrupted by an image of mutilated stable boys sprawled among blood and shit and hay.

I want to get rid of those images. I want to feel remorse for ever creating such thoughts. But just like last night, as I laid in the darkness that matches my soul, I can't. My heartbeat doesn't quicken. My skin doesn't turn clammy in terror when those snippets seeped in crimson blink into existence, obstructing my view. A part of me feels empty, lost under the hand-crafted killer I've become. I was fine with it. I relished in it before I knew how much I've tainted myself.

Killing mortals and loving it. That's something I never thought I'd think of so fondly, but I would happily gut those stable boys for what they did to Jerik.

Biting my bottom lip, I yearn for the comforting caresses of Mother and Ottilie. But they don't show. *Please, show.*

The door to my room bursts open. My head snaps to the side, and the jerk of my body causes the tea in my cup to spill over its edges and onto my hand.

Andrina strolls over the threshold with a wicked gleam in her eye. "Good"—her hands clap together—"you're up!"

In lieu of greeting her, I merely move from my spot at my window and retrieve the piece of ripped cloth I use to clean my weapons laying on my vanity. I dry my hands as she continues without noticing the minor disruption she caused.

"I have a new assignment for you." She pauses.

My heartbeat ticks up slightly, the cloth pausing over my wet fingers. Unbidden, that darkness in me sings at the princess's announcement.

Lifting my head, I look back up at her; however, I don't say anything. How can I when my mind keeps straying to the dream I had? It feels like a fight is happening inside me. Much of my soul—dark and inky from the killer within—battles for dominance over what little part of me cares. That part begs to see Jerik again, so he can ground me and bring me back to who I used to be. The other part of me—much stronger—yearns to show those other stable boys just how deadly their taunts toward him could be.

Her eyes narrow as she looks at me. Stubborn annoyance accentuates each syllable as she hisses, "Be grateful, mortal. It would do you well to show some respect."

She's waiting for me to thank her, to grovel at her feet for giving me another opportunity to kill, I realize. Never—no matter how many assignments she gives me, no matter how much closer she gets me to what I really want—will I ever grovel before her.

When I don't, she scowls and rolls her eyes. The growl that rumbles in the back of her throat makes my teeth clench.

"I want Prince Kayd Glynvyre of Nythfaedell dead." Her eyes roam up and down my body, taking in every inch of my figure—my entire being—and judging what's there.

My eyes bulge at the news. That familiar thrum of anticipation beneath my skin ramps up. Finally, I'll get my hands on a royal family member. I can already feel his warm elven blood coating my hands. It's thrilling to think about. I'll need to be careful on this assignment. Killing a royal is *big*. And now, with my reputation known across Galfei Thalor, the palace's guards are sure to be on high alert. It will be a challenge, but one I'm eager to tackle. Struggling to conceal my grin, I dig my teeth into my bottom lip.

"And the captain of his personal guard." Andrina picks at her painted nails.

My smirk drops, and my eyebrows knit together. I can't help but wonder out loud, "A guard?"

Andrina nods without glancing up from her fingers. I've killed several beings since becoming an assassin. Dukes, advisors, lords, ladies, even generals . . . A guard seems . . . mundane.

"Yes . . . a *guard*," the changeling princess coos before looking back up at me. Her laugh echoes through my bedchamber as she takes in my furrowed brows and downturned lips. "Spies are powerful tools, Maeve . . . and what I've learned about that guard needs to be corrected."

Corrected. It's a vague answer. A nonanswer, really, but I'm not surprised. Andrina once told me to not ask about the reasons she sends me away to do her bidding. And truthfully, I couldn't care less. If the death of this guard hurts the royal family of Nythfaedell . . . good.

With a curt nod, I lunge for the cloak that's draped atop my bed. The elven kingdom is waiting for me. Princess Andrina's cold white hand harshly grips my arm, halting my movements. Her nails dig into my skin, where blood pools under the sleeve of my tunic.

"You will wait until the midday feast in the Great Hall before leaving for this assignment. My mother and father have invited guests from the other three kingdoms to discuss business . . . Representatives, courtiers of the *lesser* crowns. I don't want you taking the long route to Nythfaedell. The prince and his guard must die *tonight*."

On past assignments, I've had to travel through the tiefling and merfolk territories to get to the land of the elves, avoiding the bridge that connects it and Phandolus. Andrina once told me it's because the elves are cowards, afraid of the "*superior race*" and are known to use magick to make the sea between their land and the changeling's deadly and impossible to cross.

During my research, I learned that it's the only direct route used by royals, advisors, and courtiers of each kingdom when on business. It can only be crossed by those approved by the highest ruler of each land: the kings.

Andrina continues. "While the representatives are dining with my family, you will sneak onto the elves' carriage. That is how you get across the bridge. That is how you get to the prince and his guard." Her grip on my arm ceases, and she gives me a nod. She snaps her fingers, and a mortal chambermaid comes in with a platter of fresh breads, meats, cheeses, and fruits, setting it down on my bed and scurrying off. "Eat. I don't want you blacking out before you get there. You're no good to me if you can't do your job."

The halls are empty as I creep around the corners toward the back entrance of the palace. The outdoor grounds are empty as well, while servants and courtiers attend to the midday meal.

Out in front of the palace, coachmen are stationed outside the entrance near their respective carriages. They look bored, twiddling their fingers and scuffing their boots along the gravel as they wait for the feast to end.

Hidden behind a handful of shrubs, I press myself closer to its leaves. It's hard to conceal myself in the open on a clear day such as this. Peeking over the plant, my eyes narrow in on the deep green carriage with gold accents—the colors of the elves—and notice there are no guards standing at attention nearby.

Perfect.

The palace's entryway doors creak loudly on its hinges as a human servant strides through them. The elven, tiefling, and merfolk coachmen meet her near the steps. I shallow my breathing as I strain to hear what she says.

"Your respective passengers will be out shortly." Faux confidence shields the meek tremble to her voice. The coachmen either don't notice it or don't care. "It will only be a few more minutes."

Now's my chance. While the coachmen are distracted, I let out a long, silent exhale and swiftly rush to the carriage. Barely a sound is heard beneath my feet, as if I were merely the wind drifting around the browning leaves scattered across the ground. Crouching down low enough to see the bottom of the carriage, relief floods my senses despite the adrenaline that pumps through my veins and makes my hands shake. Multiple metal bars crisscross one another, with just enough room to hook my limbs around.

A couple of the coachmen huff loudly, barely concealing their boredom—or perhaps annoyance—and begin to turn back toward their carriages.

"Thank you," one of them says kindly as I hear the servant rush back up the steps and through the doors.

My heart pounds against my rib cage, and I shimmy my body between the front and back wheels of the elves' carriage. The rocks on the ground dig into my back, and my nose burns from the mud and soot that sticks to its underside. I hold in a cough slowly crawling up my throat. My nostrils burn from the effort to keep it down. Looping my arms around two vertical bars and weaving my legs through two others, I use all my strength to haul my body up, my back hovering slightly above the ground. Not a minute later, chatter from the kingdoms' several representatives flood the open area.

I wince as the carriage shifts from the weight of the elves as they enter it and prepare for their journey home. My arms are already burning, the pain traveling from my limbs to my core. To relieve some of the tension in my shaking muscles, I dig the bottom of my boots against another bar and push.

Just then, the carriage jerks. We're off to Nythfaedell.

As the horses pick up speed and we weave our way through Phandolus, I squeeze my eyes closed, willing the ache overcoming my body to disappear. Over hills and through the woods, it feels like we're crawling, despite the rocky path below me speeding by. The sweat on my arms pools at the crease of my elbows, and my body begins to shake.

"Do. Not. Give. Up," I grit out between clenched teeth and will myself to stay strong, unafraid of anyone hearing me over the rushing wind and creaking carriage wheels. Tears bead in the corners of my eyes, and a sob sits in the back of my throat, waiting to be released.

Hold. On. Maeve.

Hours must have passed. It's hard to keep track of time when my body is struggling to hang on and the only thing I see is the ground beneath me when I crane my neck to the side.

The rocky path begins to shift. Pale gravel turns into a coal-black stone, so smooth I can see a wavy reflection of the carriage's wheels spinning within it. A distorted image of myself, shrouded in the darkness of the bridge we must be on, stares back at me.

The image begins to blur into nothing. My heart leaps to my throat. The rash waves of The Unlighted Sea are below me now, churning the deep-colored water together and creating frothy white ripples. My arm muscles spasm as I automatically grip tighter onto the carriage and squeeze my eyes shut.

Breathe. I need to breathe. We're still on the bridge. I can see the map I studied behind my eyelids. The way the dark shading of the bridge closest to Phandolus gradually fades into no shading whatsoever. *It's just the change in stone.*

The carriage jerks as it hits a ridge in the road. Slowly, my eyelids slip open, and my head turns back toward the sea below. The bridge—now a beautiful, nearly transparent stone with streaks of rainbow glimmering off it—guides us toward the elven territory.

A large splash in the water draws my attention away from the peculiar over-pass. Below me, just feet away, is a behemoth of a creature.

"Oh!" A breathy gasp slips through my lips and catches on the wind.

A silver eye with a thin black slit down the middle snaps open and stares at me intently. I begin to laugh under my breath, unable to stop myself at the sight. A giant serpent glides through the waves. Dark shades of green and purple sheen across its scales with every movement, slithering up and down.

My heart seizes. I wish Ottilie could see this. She would've loved to gaze at such a majestic creature. She always had an affinity for the grand, magickal lands the kingdoms seemed to be.

Ottilie, if you're here, you'd never guess what I'm looking at. I adjust my grip on the metal bar below the carriage and stare down at the serpent, waiting for that familiar light to press against my heart or twine around my arm.

Nothing. Nothing comes.

My chest deflates, and tears pebble behind my eyes. Where is she? Why can't I feel her?

Deep down, I know why, but I refuse to say it out loud despite the heavy shadow looming over my soul.

Come back, Ottilie.

As if it knows what I'm feeling, the serpent shifts its body—keeping up with the carriage—and lifts its head farther out of the water, coming as close to the invisible bridge as it can. Looking into its eyes, I can see—no, *feel*—the emotions of the creature. There is no longing or trepidation, only bliss and a fulfilling sense of freedom. A feeling I can't help but think it wants me to experience, too.

We peer into each other's souls, entranced by the sight before each of us, until its long black tongue flickers out of its mouth and senses something nearby. This seraphic beast, which I have been deemed to represent, gives me one last look and dives deep into the water, leaving me with nothing but a tightening in my chest and tears flying into the wind. If only I were as free as the monster in the waves.

One day, I vow. *One day, I will be.*

Sundown comes and goes before the carriage grinds to a halt. It's pitch black outside now, mostly likely in the middle of the night. Or perhaps a few hours before dawn.

My body spasms and convulses a few inches above the ground as I wait for the elven representatives and coachman to exit the carriage and trudge toward the palace doors. As soon as I hear them slam shut, I release my grip on the carriage. My back hits the ground with a hard thump, and a silent sob rips out of my throat. For a moment, I let myself feel the pain winding through my body. I lean into it, my muscles feeling like lead and sludge at the same time.

My shaking hands rise toward my face and wipe the dirt from my cheeks. Wet tracks run down them from the tears that have started to fall a couple hours ago, mixing with the grainy sediment from the road and wheels. I want so badly to stab Andrina as soon as I get back for making me take this route to Nythfaedell.

I allow myself a few moments of stillness to catch my breath and rest my limbs before I have to keep moving. After several attempts, my body shuffles out from under the carriage. Once in the open air and away from the soot, a pungent smell punctures my senses—the same smell that seems to engulf me each time I'm here. Even when I arrived on the shores of Nythfaedell for the first time to kill a count in the west, I felt like I knew that smell. Now, as I lay here with heaving lungs, I still can't put my finger on what it is.

It makes me feel safe. Just as night's dark blanket over this kingdom does. There's something about Nythfaedell that feels different from the other kingdoms—lighter and not so deadly. My muscles tense, and my heartbeat picks up at that feeling. Things that don't feel like threats usually are. I can't let my guard down.

Ignoring the protests and screams from my bones, I crawl toward a glowing neon flower bush potted at the corner of the palace's drive to examine my surroundings. Even under the night sky, the palace is breathtaking. Most of the structure shimmers against the starlight, likely some type of quartz. Patches of dark, dull voids—several windows and massive arched doors—are scattered among the glittering walls.

No guards are along the perimeter, but surely, they're there.

Pressing my body closer to the bush, I blend into the cloak of darkness the night provides. A thrilling streak of anticipation courses through my veins, alleviating the aching pulse in my muscles from the thought of infiltrating the palace right under the noses of those who live here.

To my right, glowing Night Vine laced with iridescent flowers creep up the curved tower and lead to a small open archway. Climb that, slide through the window, and I'm in.

Scaling the vines is hard. Thorns prick my palms, and the scent of those otherworldly flowers makes me lightheaded. My arms scream—hating me for the abuse they've endured today—and my mind begs me to rest for a few hours. But in a few hours, the sun will rise, and I will no longer have the upper hand as the palace sleeps.

I bite my bottom lip to stop any noises from escaping as my trembling hands finally grip the window's opening. Quietly pulling myself through, I land in the tower with more grace than I thought I could conjure in the state I'm in.

The tower is nothing more than a lookout. A single wooden chair sits near the open window, and winding stairs lead downward. Next to the chair is a half-eaten platter of bread and jam. Someone was here not too long ago but left before I arrived. If I didn't know any better, I'd think the Gods are looking out for me, as if they, too, want the elven prince dead.

Keep moving before the lookout comes back, I chastise myself.

Only allowing the tips of my toes to touch the ground, I silently descend the stairs. Keeping my back glued to the wall while my heart rapidly pounds against my chest, I enter the white-and-gold hallways of the palace. The corridors have a certain elegance that is welcoming. It seems to wrap around the palace entirely, feeling as if a cool autumn breeze is caressing my body, swaddling me in reassurance and safety. Similar to the cloak of night outside.

I know it's dangerous. That welcoming embrace that I yearn to lean into is nothing but a venomous spider luring its kill. So, I keep moving. I move despite my eyes drifting to the warm-toned paintings on the walls, urging me to get trapped in their web. I move despite the empty halls that make the hairs on the back of my neck rise.

The palace is a labyrinth of turns and dead-ends and locked doors. I don't know which way to go, which way is correct. If only I found layouts of it during my research.

Hiding within the cool shadows behind a tall marble statue of an elven warrior, I spot a servant bowing low at the threshold of two massive golden double doors. She's holding a used cup of tea. As she unknowingly passes me and walks down the hall, I begin to follow her, keeping to the corners and shadows. Hopefully, she can lead me to where I need to be.

After winding through several hallways, she enters a plain, wooden door and closes it before I can slip through. *Shit.*

I lean my ear against what I assume is the door to the servants' quarters. My ears strain to listen as someone begins to speak.

"Madam Prea, King Osmar is awake and getting ready for his ride to the surrounding villages this afternoon."

King Osmar. The elven king. My eyes widen, and my jaw drops. I was so close to the crown, so close to causing true hurt in this kingdom. I could go back . . .

A regal voice—older, more wise, but so, so tired all at once—responds. "Good. I will send word to the Head Groom to get his horses ready. You are dismissed for your morning kitchen duties."

My mind automatically drifts to Jerik, working under Phandolus's Head Groom. I wonder if he's ever had to wake before the sun rises to prepare the changeling king's steeds.

Shaking my head and focusing back on the task at hand, I press my ear back to the door and hear movement around the room.

A different voice pipes up. "Madam." It's high-pitched and unsure. "I am assigned to the East Wing this morning to wake Prince Kayd in a few hours. This will be my first time. Is there anything I should be aware of before serving him?"

My attention narrows in on what she said. *The East Wing.* That's where the sleeping prince is, and the guard shouldn't be too far away. That poor girl, who I can tell just wants to do her job well, is unknowingly leading a wolf to a lamb for slaughter.

"Wake him with a warm cup of tea—not too hot—and a pastry from the kitchen," the older voice says. "He will expect you to dress him, and once you do, stand silently off to the side until he leaves for the training grounds to watch his guards. Do not speak a word to him unless you're greeting him or he asks you something directly."

My eyes roll into the back of my head. This Prince Kayd really is as foul as he made himself out to be at the trials.

"Thank you, Madam Prea," that squeaky voice speaks out again.

Quickly peeling myself away from the servants' quarters before anyone spots me, I make for what I assume is the direction of the East Wing. My steps are rushed yet quiet, as if I'm not even touching the ground. Lost from my earlier wandering through the labyrinth-like hallways, and with no immediate windows along the pathways to track my direction with the stars, I am slow to find the correct part of the palace.

The entrance to Prince Kayd Glynvyre's chambers isn't hard to miss. Like his father's, it's shrouded in elven gold with carvings of tree branches and leaves adorning it. The only difference between the two is the single door staring back at me instead of the much grander double doors the servant exited.

Peeking my head around the corner, I see no guard stationed outside of the prince's rooms. Interesting. Perhaps I'll have to find another way to the captain of his guard.

Gooseflesh erupts across my arms as I take a step closer. Then another. My head swivels around, making sure I'm not missing anything. That sickly sweet, alluring sensation this kingdom emits forms a pit in my stomach. The sooner I'm out of here and on my way back to Phandolus, the better.

My palm rests atop the golden doorknob. Even *that* seems to draw me in, whispering an invitation to twist it open. One silent breath to steady the anticipation pounding under my skin, and I'm pushing the door open and slinking into the chamber's darkness.

Simmering embers in a hearth and the moonlight beaming through a large round window are the only sources of light in the room. My eyes begin to adjust, and I can make out a sitting area and a desk covered in scattered pieces of paper. To my right is an open door leading into a bath chamber. With my back to the wall—so no one can sneak up behind me—I make my way to the left, where a small nook sits. Inside the nook is an archway that leads to none other than the prince himself, slumbering peacefully in bed.

There are no windows, and the dull light from the sitting area does not reach this far, but I can make out the shape of his bed. It's large and luxurious—everything I'd expect for a prince. A wardrobe sits opposite of it and large swords—gleaming despite the lack of light—hang against the wall. I didn't even need to bring my own weapons. It would've made the ride here easier without the extra weight.

One silent step closer. I pause. Then another. I pause again.

As I slither to his side, a malicious smile creeps onto my face. This is it. The elf prince will die tonight, and I will gladly watch as the blood seeps out of his body just as he watched Ottilie's.

My hand delicately unsheathes the dagger strapped to my side. I pull it out, then lifting it high above my head, to plunge into his chest. For a split second, I still. I'm frozen in place as I stare at the hateful prince. His words during my last trial reverberate through my skull: "*Maybe the changelings will replace one of them with you.*"

Blistering flames lick up my veins and into my heart. I hope he wakes and sees me—the mortal he taunted before the last trial—as I pierce his heart. I hope he remembers what he said. I hope he's just as scared as I was when I had to fight off those two guards.

I slash the dagger down toward him.

"Agh!" Strong, unrelenting arms wrap around my body from behind, stopping me mere centimeters before I can sink the killing blow. My dagger loudly clanks to the ground as frantic yells and pounding boots flood the chambers. I struggle against the fierce hold keeping me from fleeing. I kick and claw, panic setting in. I barely notice the prince bolting out of bed and lighting the candle atop a table in the corner of the room.

Andrina was right, I think to myself as I try to wrestle off the guards now swarming me. My grunts and the guards' shouts fill the silence that once was. *Combat has always been my weakest skill.*

I can't let them take me. I won't let them take me. I fight harder than I've ever fought in my life. It takes two guards to wrangle me away from the side of the bed and into the sitting area.

No. No, no, no.

It takes another to stop my feet from flailing around but not before my heel connects with a nose.

No, no, nonononono.

My frantic movements only stop as the pummel of a sword connects with my temple, turning my world black.

21

A SOUL-CHILLING DARKNESS SURROUNDS me, seeping into the marrow of my bones. My eyes flutter open, and that void doesn't dissipate. Grogginess fogs my brain. The dryness in my mouth and throat feels like sandpaper. My head throbs, a steady, sharp pulse pounding against my skull like a drumbeat.

Lifting my hand to rub my temple, I feel my wrist snag on something tight. I try again and again until the skin on my wrists is raw from whatever is tethering me to this old, creaking chair.

"No," I whisper. "No, no, no, no." My broken words begin to slur together. Panic seizes my body, my senses chugging into overdrive.

As my bleary eyes begin to adjust, my head swivels from side to side, surveying where I am. It's a bare room, similar to my old cell in Phandolus. But this time, there are no chains fettered to my ankles. This time, rope binds them to the chair's legs.

My breathing becomes sharp. My chest constricts, getting tighter, as if the walls are caving in and crushing my body.

I've been captured. I . . . Realization dawns on me. *They're going to kill me.*

I frantically tug harder at my restraints, not caring if I rub my skin down to the bone. I need to get out of here. A thought crosses my mind. A thought I don't want to admit, because once I do, I'll feel weak. I will no longer feel like the feared assassin that makes the kingdoms quake. I'll feel like the contender being forced to stand blindfolded while her best friend fought for her life. But I can't help it. I'm . . . I'm scared. I'm—

"That's not going to help."

My spasming muscles ripple to a halt. My body tenses at the voice behind me, rough yet regal at the same time. I've heard that voice before. An elf with flawless brown skin and long auburn hair circles around the chair and stops before me.

Prince Kayd Glynvyre.

He towers over me. His long muscular arms cross over his broad chest, anger radiating off his looming body.

A black tunic with gold embroidery drapes easily over his torso. The gold diadem twisted into branches rests atop his forehead just above his left eyebrow, which is cleaved by a thin white scar. The golden jewelry adorning his long pointed ears shimmer despite the darkness of the room.

I meet his piercing eyes as they bore into me. There is nothing but disdain swirling within his forest-green irises. He's looking at me as if I'm nothing but a smudge of dust under his boot. To him, I probably am.

Don't let him see you scared. Don't let him know how weak you feel tied up to this chair. Don't let him know who you truly are.

"So"—the prince sighs as his long slender finger plucks a speck of invisible dust off his shoulder—"you're the one who's terrorizing our kingdoms. The one who has everyone talking." His eyes roam down my tethered body. "*The Shackled Serpent.*"

My breath catches in my throat. I can feel my eyes widen just slightly. His lips curl up into an amused smile.

"Oh, yes. I know who you are. Sure, there are plenty of hitmen hired to take out cheating lovers and debtors, but no one other than the infamous Shackled Serpent would be stupid enough to try to take a royal's life. Looks like you were. Didn't work out so well for you now, did it?" The elf sneers at me with a twinkle in his eye. "You really thought killing me would be that easy? Ever since talks of the deadly assassin emerged, we've been ready. Security has been upped, and my personal guards, though hidden, are on standby every night."

He pauses when I don't say anything and barks a booming laugh in my face.

"I can't believe such a little thing like you has every kingdom up in arms. You are nothing but an insignificant, mortal *girl*." His lips curl on the last word, as if he doesn't like the taste of it, like the very sound is poison in his mouth. Then Prince Kayd laughs again.

Anger and disgust burrow deep in my chest and begin to simmer silently as I stare at the prince. He's arrogant and prideful. I can already tell that he's everything I hate about the kingdoms.

"Laugh all you want, *Prince*. I'm the thing creatures like you have nightmares about." I lean forward, baring my teeth and getting as close as I can before the ropes stop me. If I weren't trapped, I would rip out his tongue right here and now with no remorse, then present it to the king, before ripping out his.

The prince's pink tongue glides along his bottom lip as his laugh gradually dies down. His eyes harden, and he hisses through his teeth, "Who are you working for?"

He doesn't remember me from the trials. Huh. It wasn't long ago, only a few months.

My gaze stays locked on his, and I refuse to utter a word. His green eyes snap down to the only movement noticeable on my face: my lips. They turn upward in a supercilious way that lights a raging fire behind his cracking facade. Exactly like I hoped.

I will not talk. I will not break. Too much hangs in the balance. The elves will kill me once I give them what they want, and I want to get back to Phandolus, back to Jerik.

"Answer me!" Prince Kayd roars. The booming timbre of his voice makes my eardrums ring and my heart stop for a second. "I am the Prince of Nythfaedell. I demand you answer me, mortal!"

And then it comes. I can't help it. It starts with the quivering of my lips, then the dam breaks completely. Hysterical laughter disrupts the tense quiet in the cell.

"You—" I gasp for air between my tittering, and a drop of joyous liquid runs down my cheek. "You don't hold any power over me. You're not *my* prince."

The elf's jaw ticks to the side, and his nostrils flare. His slim hand strikes me across the cheek—fast and powerful. A burning wake is left in its path. I can feel the blood rising closer to my skin. If I could bring my hand to it, I know it would be hot to the touch. Unwelcomed tears form just behind my lash line, my eyes burning from the sting.

Slowly—tantalizingly slow—Prince Kayd bends down before me. His fury-filled eyes bore into mine. I can smell the rage seeping off him. My nostrils begin to burn, but I don't let it show. Instead, I bite my lip to look as if I'm holding back more laughter, wanting it to cease.

Seething, the prince grits out, "Who. Sent. You?"

Long moments pass between us. No one speaks. No one moves. It's a stand-off to see who has the power, and although I'm the one tied up, I can't help but think that I hold all the cards.

With a manic smile—displaying all the anger I harbor toward the kingdoms, anger now directed at this elven prince—I rock my head backward, then slam it forward. My forehead collides with Prince Kayd's nose.

"Mortal bitch!"

Glints of light—blurry and spinning—obstruct my view. Nausea hits me, and it takes all my effort to swallow it down. Despite the training I received from the combat guard in Phandolus, I'm still unable to execute this move without feeling ill. Prince Kayd stumbles back, his hand covering his nose, as blood drips through his jewel-ladened fingers.

He reaches behind his back, near the top of his pants. Something glints in his other hand, but my eyes stay trained on his piercing green ones that remain locked onto me. Bringing it at eye level, the prince reveals what he now holds. A dagger, *my* dagger. He's grinning now. Blood cakes the ridges of his teeth as he smiles darkly at me. It's a frightening sight.

"Now," he drawls, "let's try this again."

The cuts—*the stinging cuts*—begin.

Days go by. I'm not sure how many. Time was lost to me—falling away into an endless chasm—as soon as my skin was sliced open for the first time. Since then, I have yet to go long without beatings and mutilations from the prince. Slick, fresh blood coats the crusty, dry layers from days-old cuts. The strong scent of copper is suffocating, thick, and nauseating. I can taste it, the metallic tang coating my throat and making it hard to swallow.

My head is heavy, hanging low. I'm too exhausted to lift it. The sight of the dirty bucket of water at my feet makes my lungs heave, and my throat snap shut. Memories of a black cloth draped over my face and water pouring on it slam into my mind. The rise and fall of my chest come quick and fast, like my body is searching for air that's already there.

Inhaling as much air as I can through my nose, I try to calm myself and stop my body from reacting to those memories. The heaving and shaking slows to a dull thrum, and the hysterical fog in my brain clears. I don't think I can handle . . . No, I don't think I can *survive* another day of this. My eyes begin to burn, and I suck the tears back deep into my skull.

I will not cry. I will not cry. I will not cry.

The door behind me creaks open. I tense at the familiar gait of Prince Kayd as he enters the cell, wincing at the pain that shoots across my flesh from the movement. A second set of steps follow closely behind, drowned out by a quick, sharp intake of breath I know doesn't belong to the prince.

My head stays limp, the muscles in my neck seizing when I try to lift it, as the prince and his guest get closer to the broken body that holds my soul. Two pairs of boots stop in front of me. I close my eyes. I feel broken . . . I am . . . No, I am *not* broken. I am not . . .

"Are you going to cooperate today, mortal?" Prince Kayd sneers.

The muscles in my neck quiver as I slowly lift my head, my gaze traveling up from the toes of their boots. I don't answer the prince. Instead, my eyes shift to the other elf standing next to him. I'm met with those same hazel eyes I encountered at the trials—the ones tucked inside that gold guard's helm. He must be the captain of the prince's guard. His stare is unrelenting, fury wafting off him as his eyes roam my body. His figure is completely rigid and motionless.

"Do you like what you see, elf?" I growl at him, with a hate-filled leer.

His eyes widen slightly, and a muscle ticks in his sharp jaw. I can see his fists curling from my peripheral vision.

My gaze travels up the strand of dark-brown hair partially falling over his right eye. It's short on the sides and longer on top, a handsome cut that I can't help but think Jerik would look good with. He's slightly taller than the prince, only by an inch or two, and his black tunic stretches tightly over his lean shoulders. Where the prince's beauty is forceful and unattainable, this guard's is simple yet breathtaking.

"Kayd." The guard's voice is low, but there's an edge to it. As he speaks, he doesn't waver under my stare, penetrating me behind the cuts and bruises. "I'm in charge of your prisoners, just as Sir Raimond oversees the king's. When you sent word that the assassin was captured, I didn't authorize torture."

A rough scoff bursts through the prince's lips as his head swivels sharply to look at the other elf. "I'm the prince. I can do whatever I want. Remember your rank." From my peripheral vision, I can see Prince Kayd turn back to me. "Who sent you?"

Like every time before this, I don't answer. This time, not even giving the prince the courtesy of looking at him.

Suddenly, my eyes squeeze shut, and my body slumps over as Kayd's fist connects with my gut.

"Kayd!" the other elf barks.

Before I can catch my breath, the prince unsheathes my dagger and jabs it into my shoulder just below my collarbone. Faster than I can comprehend, he rips it out of my flesh and punches me a second time.

Something inside me breaks, snaps like a flimsy twig beneath a boot. A sob that feels like I've been holding in for days rips from my raw throat and breaks through my tightly closed lips.

"The changelings!" My voice is hoarse as I blurt out the information I've been fighting so hard to keep in. I don't need to look at the two elves to know victorious grins must be twisting their features. The words continue to pour out as unrelenting tears cascade down my cheeks. "Princess . . . Princess Andrina. She claimed me after the trials. Her guards trained me. And . . . and she turned me into her personal assassin."

I'm panting as soon as the words stop. The rush of blood flows out of my newest wound and pools at my waist. Finally, I open my eyes again and look up. Prince Kayd's upper lip begins twitching, and his eyes narrow. Hate simmers out of him. It's intense and terrifying. It feels as if he detests Andrina more than he does me.

Swiftly—faster than my brain can process—the prince moves himself and the guard to a corner of the room.

"Why would she want a personal killer?" the prince inquires. Their hushed discussion flits throughout the small room.

"You two do know I can hear you, right? There's no need to act like I can't." My voice comes out strong despite the tears rolling down my cheeks.

A deep, warning growl vibrates from the prince's throat.

"She's cruel, Kayd," the guard sighs, ignoring me completely. His voice is deep and husky, almost a purr that caresses each nerve in my body without even trying. "Nothing is off the table when it comes to getting what she wants, and we both know the lengths she'll go to get it. Power is everything to her." His eyes glaze over for a split second before they clear, as if it never happened. Kayd seems to notice, too.

I watch as they have a quick, silent conversation before the prince marches out of the cell. The guard hesitates for a moment, his eyes flitting to me, then toward the direction his prince went. With a drawn-out sigh, he squeezes his eyes shut tightly before crossing the room and shutting the door behind him.

The quiet returns. The *drip, drip, drip* of my seeping blood is the only disruption in the void of nothingness.

I take a deep breath, my gashes screaming at the movement. I close my eyes, yearning for some relief from the excruciating agony, and will away my thoughts.

22

"**W**AKE UP."

My body flinches violently as I'm pulled from my pitch-black slumber. The ropes tied around my limbs keep me from falling over. I wince at my stinging, raw wrists. Pus and blood ooze audibly at the movement. I cannot stop the groan from rumbling deep in my throat. The pain is almost too much to bear.

Bleary-eyed, I look up to find the prince's captain towering over me. His dark-brown brows are furrowed, and his eyes roam over me, pausing over the worst cuts and gashes littering my flesh. He surveys each one before he kneels in front of me.

A pregnant pause passes, and no words are exchanged. Neither of us move. I don't breathe. It's as if he's studying me, scrutinizing me. I stare back with sharp precision despite my tear-stained face, which his eyes dip toward, taking in the dried streaks.

With shaking hands, he reaches for the ropes tied to my feet. His slender, beige fingers begin to untie my restraints. I try to get away from him, my upper body thrashing, my partially bound feet pushing against the floor. Anything to get an inch away from the elf.

He's going to kill me. I've told them what they needed to know.

His hands halt as his gaze snaps toward my face. His eyebrows rise as his eyes widen, and his lips part, slightly tilted down. Before I can even blink, his features twist around each other, creating a deep-rooted scowl, as if I imagined what I saw before.

"Stop," he snarls coldly. The guard drops his gaze and doesn't look back at me while he continues to untie my bindings. "Stop moving. You cannot serve Nythfaedell tied up in this reeking cell."

I stop my pathetic attempt at an escape and freeze. My stomach turns to cement, and icy dread begins to infiltrate my lungs, my soul. "I don't serve the elves," I rasp out.

"You do now." Even with his head tilted down, concentrating on a particularly bothersome knot, I can see the hardness in his eyes. There is unwavering resolve in his features.

I stay as still as stone until my wrists are free of those coarse ropes. The stinging along my skin is cooled by the damp cell air. But the sight . . . Bile rises to the back of my throat. The jagged red skin glints in the scarce light. I can see bits of bone peeking out from where the rope dug too deep. I stare and stare at it, hoping—*wishing*—that my skin will mend itself together again.

He stands up, back straight, as if there is no one other than his role as a guard inside. "Up."

My hesitation is brief, unnoticed in the half of a breath it lasts. I get up slowly. My body is worn, the pain nearly making me black out. I force my knees not to buckle and grind my teeth together to stop the scream boiling deep down in my chest. The guard just stands by and watches me struggle as I get on my wobbly feet.

Once he can see I'm somewhat stable, he brushes past me and begins walking away. Toward the open door.

The door. Realization hits me as I turn away from the bland stone wall I've been staring at for who knows how long.

Then I really hesitate.

This could be it, my way out. If I could just get past the guard's towering form, I could make a run for it. I could do what I do best and slink into the shadows, escaping this horrid kingdom. I could do it. I know I could.

"Now, now, *Serpent*," the guard drawls with just a hint of distaste as he spits out my alias. He turns back around to face me. It's like he knows what I was scheming, like he *feels* my internal hesitation, as if it were a part of him.

His left eyebrow raises, daring me to do something. That single irritating expression sets a fire roaring deep within.

"Even if you did get past me, what are you going to do? That foul changeling princess most likely thinks you're dead. It's been days since you arrived here, days since she sent you off. And it must be known to her and her court that Prince Kayd is still breathing. You *failed*." His lips slightly curve upward.

He seeps confidence and arrogance.

"You're the captain of Prince Kayd's guard, are you not?" I stay standing, pushing my shoulders back and lifting my chin, as if I'm not a broken mess of cuts and gashes. My eyes are daggers piercing the elf.

A soft chortle escapes his sneer as he looks me up and down. "Yes."

"I don't get it," I hum.

"Get what, Serpent?" The words grate through his perfect teeth.

"Why I was sent to kill you, too. Prince Kayd? That, I understand. He's powerful, *important*. But you?" Despite the state I'm in, I manage to project as much boldness as I can and look him up and down, studying him as he did me while I was tied to the chair. "I don't get it."

His eyes flash in shock, almost as briefly as the previous expression I thought I imagined, before he composes himself once again. "Then, it looks like you failed twice. Like I said, don't try it. Andrina has forgotten you . . . moved on from an insignificant mortal such as yourself. I'm sure she's already forgotten your name. We always do."

I can't help but think he's wrong. Princess Andrina's investment in me wouldn't just go away, not with the way she made sure I was trained or the way her sinister smile would light up when I came back from an assignment. Definitely not with the way she made sure I would do it, threatening the lives of my family.

A sharp intake of breath as realization strikes me like a slap to the face. My body almost gives out at the sudden panic I feel for Father and Arden. This is the first time they've crossed my mind in weeks. My eyes widen just a fraction.

Now that I haven't returned to Phandolus, what will happen to them? The princess' initial threat rings through my ears and bounces against my skull. Those horrid images of my family's throats torn out, their blood seeping into the dusty Terakeld ground, begin to materialize.

"Take me to Prince Kayd." The demanding words tumble out without restraint. "I must talk with him."

The guard raises his eyebrow again. It's edged this time. Not a challenge but a warning. "You're in no position to make orders, *mortal*. You will see him when he pleases." The sound of his voice grinds out through the ridges in his teeth, rumbling around me and vibrating my bones.

I stomp across the cell, wincing with every step and willing away the black spots clouding my vision. I halt inches away from where he stands. My chest puffs out, and my chin lifts as I stare him down defiantly. I'm close enough to smell him. Pine and spice mix with the copper scent of my spilled blood. The guard's hazel eyes bore into me, flicking from one side of my face to the other.

"If you do not take me to him, I will kill you when you least expect it. Do you understand, *guard*? Perhaps you'll be bathing just as the Duke of Ardorein was, or maybe I'll plunge my dagger into your heart while you sleep. You would die how your precious prince should have." The venom in my voice slithers out, calm and deadly. It's the voice reserved only for my next victims.

"Or maybe I'll let you live, keep you alive so you live the rest of your days looking over your shoulder, wondering when I'll strike." A smile fit for Princess Andrina graces my lips before disappearing abruptly. "Take me to him. *Now*."

Before I can blink, the room spins. I'm slammed to a stop against a stone wall, so hard that I'm surprised it doesn't crack beneath the pure force of it. My body screams in protest, and my eyes widen in alarm. Quickly, though, I steel off my features to feign indifference. His clothed forearm crushes my windpipe as he holds me still. Solid muscles flex under his skin. It pushes harder and harder until I can barely breathe, and my eyes begin to bulge.

The guard's nostrils flare. Through my increasingly blurry vision, I see him trying to restrain himself. His chest heaves against mine, cool breath brushing against my lips. I can imagine all the ways he's debating on ripping my very flesh apart with his bare hands.

His rough voice dips dangerously low, like embers idly burning in a hearth, as he utters, "You do not make commands here. You are nothing but an inconvenient speck of dust in our world. If you do not follow me, I will drag you by your hair to your new chambers. Now, move."

His forearm pushes once more against my windpipe as he steps back from me and walks out of the cell.

23

T HE CHAMBERS THE GUARD leads me to are beautiful. I'm lost for words as I drag my tired feet across the threshold of what he says will be my new home.

The white stone walls of the small sitting area are adorned with a cornice of gold tree branches, delicately meeting the edges of the tall ceiling. The floor is a deep brown wood. White and tan furs are scattered across it with what looks like care and precision. A beige chaise with embossed legs and a matching chair are positioned before a gold hearth that's already burning against the brisk air of early autumn. There is no window in this room, yet there is still natural light somehow cascading throughout it.

A half-opened wooden door with beautifully painted branches that match the golden cornice is along the opposite wall. I crane my head to the side, trying to see inside, before the door to my right—also painted—swings open. Out comes a small group of servants, no more than four, all human. Following them is a tall elegant elf. Her dress is the same color as the uniforms the others wear but instead of simplicity . . . it screams extravagance. Graceful white lace trims the edges of her long bell sleeves and high collar. Silken skirts flow divinely to the ground like a cascading early morning mist rolling down a hill.

Her beauty radiates brightly in the chamber's sitting room, almost as if her skin is glowing. Compared to the dull and dirty skin of the human servants beside her, she looks like she bathes herself in the sun's rays. The mortal's heads are bowed, and their hair is tangled like they don't even own brushes, but instead swiftly used their fingers to look as presentable as possible in the presence of elven royalty. Ire heats my skin at the unjust cruelty toward those of us who had the unfortunate luck of being born mortal.

"Sir Halton." The female elf curtsies deeply with a bowed head. My body stiffens ever so slightly. *Halton*. Something seems off about that name. It doesn't suit the foul creature that hides behind those cold hazel eyes for some reason, but I can't put my finger on why that is. She continues. "We have it from here."

Her regal voice—the same voice I heard in the servants' quarters the night I got captured—lingers in the air between them. There is tension there, between the guard and her. Perhaps it's because she's older than him. I can tell by the gray-white hair braided atop her head and the faint wrinkles at the corners of her purple eyes.

The kingdoms' creatures can live much longer than mortals. I've heard elves live the longest, spanning several hundred rotations, while tieflings, changelings, and merfolk usually pass once they near three or four hundred. I wonder how much older she is than him. I wonder how she feels having to bow to him.

"Madam Prea," he remarks after a taut pause, respectful and calm. Through the corner of my eyes, I see him tilting his head down toward her. Then he turns toward me, gaining my full attention. Tightly—and with none of the charm he just used—he declares, "The prince will see you when he deems fit," and exits through the door we came in.

The mortal chambermaids begin undressing me, roughly removing the scraps of fabric hanging by a thread before the guard, Halton, even closes the door. Strips of my top flitter to the ground. I look down at my aching body in silence. Nausea rushes into me at the sight of how mangled it is. Purple, green, and yellow splotches of flesh make me want to gag. I look like a corpse that has been rotting in the sun. The fresh blood pumping out of the deeper gashes reassures me I'm still alive.

The overseeing elf, Madam Prea, circles my now naked body. She takes in everything—the blood and gashes and bruises—with scrutiny in her purple eyes, as if I had any say in the state I'm currently in. My muscles tense as her gaze drags slowly along my exposed skin.

Her long bony fingers reach out toward where I stand, almost touching me. Without thinking, I retreat, taking a small step back just out of her reach.

Her left eyebrow raises at me. "You cannot meet Prince Kayd in such a state." Her voice holds authority that makes me want to immediately bob my head and agree. However, I don't move. I don't come closer to her outstretched hand.

The sharpness in Madam Prea's stare softens at my hesitation. That unnerves me even more, and the hairs on the back of my neck rise. I don't know her. I don't trust her. But the caution and pain glazing over her features causes my breath to release from my lungs. It looks as if she cares about a mortal she doesn't even know. Why would she care about me?

Madam Prea gives me time, saying nothing. Only that softened gaze looks at me. I take a hesitant step toward her, then another until she's right in front of me.

"I'm just going to use my magick to heal you. Will you let me do that?" Her soft smile is tentative.

I take another moment to assess her. There is a kindness to her that I am unused to. She reminds me of Mother. With a subtle nod, unsuspecting tears burn my eyes. It takes everything in me to stop my knees from buckling. If Madam Prea notices, she doesn't show it.

The subtlest of touches caress my damaged flesh. A featherlight sensation, like trickles of lukewarm water gliding along gooseflesh, works its way from her fingertips and slowly weaves my ripped skin cells back together. *Magick.*

It only takes a few minutes. In that time, it looks as if no harm came to me at all. No cuts. No scabs. The repulsive, discolored flesh is gone, and in its place is fresh olive. Life flows just underneath, more so than I've seen in several rotations. A tint of pink rushes over my body. I feel good. Better than good, like I slept fully for the first time since Mother died . . . like I can rip apart my enemies without breaking a sweat.

Madam Prea's right hand moves toward the scar underneath my eye, while her left hand aims for the puckered skin at my shoulder. Gone is the serenity I felt. I freeze before straightening my spine and stepping away from her once again.

"Not those," I say, my voice hoarse.

The ugly reminders of the trials seem to burn as the elf observes them. I can see the questions forming in her mind, questions she is too polite to ask. In truth, I need the scars. I need them to remember who I am—who I was when I left Terakeld . . . who I was before I became the Shackled Serpent.

Madam Prea only nods, then signals the others to attend to me.

I'm led into the room where the servants appeared from only minutes ago—my new bathroom. My jaw drops slightly in awe. Beautiful white-and-gold marble glitters below my feet. A large gold mirror leans against the far corner, and a luxurious golden basin is stationed against one of the walls. But none of that is the cause for how breathless I am. The bath is otherworldly. I have never seen anything like it. Carved into the floor, three small steps lead down into the steaming water that's waiting for me. Perfumes and soaps line the edges, and serene candles are lit at each corner.

Madam Prea urges me forward, and I tentatively take a step down. A meek sob slips through my quivering lips as the water envelops my foot, then my entire body, while I slowly sink farther into its soothing warmth. I cherish the moments the chambermaids give me. My deep breaths fill my lungs, and my eyes close. I can't help the content smile that spreads shyly across my face. After those torturous days, tied up in that cell, it feels like a boulder has been lifted off my chest.

I let a single tear fall before I feel the servant's hands upon my body. They begin their work, scrubbing the dirt and dried blood away from my newly healed skin in silence. One girl is delicately working a brush through my hair, careful of the matted strands and blood caked against my scalp.

Too soon—my bath is over too soon. I want to protest as the water begins to drain. I want to plead for a few more moments concealed by the steam that curls off my skin. But as I look down and see the red-tinted water from my blood, any thoughts of staying disappear. My stomach churns at the sight, and I get out.

Water glides down my bare legs once I retreat from the bath, gathering in a puddle on the marble floor. I'm unsure of what to do. I see no linen to dry myself. The chambermaids are of no help, leaving me there, clueless and alone. A shuddering breath to gather my wits and then my feet are moving in the direction they left.

One step across the threshold into the sitting room halts me. I look down at my naked body. Not a single drop of water graces my skin anymore. Only my hair is slightly damp. My head whips around to stare at the door now behind me. Nothing is amiss about it, and yet . . .

"Welcome to Nythfaedell, girl," Madam Prea's voice rings out beyond my line of sight. I turn back to look at her. She's standing in the sitting room closer to the other door. From this angle, I can see a bed inside. "We elves have magick . . . unlike the other races of Galfei Thalor. It's all around us. It's in everything we do. It's who we are. This palace—each stone and walkway—is laced with the magick of our people." She looks pointedly at the door behind me. Sliding her gaze back to me, she nods and turns around.

Magick. It's everywhere here. It's . . . That's what I smell throughout these lands. No other kingdom has a scent like it. Whimsical and otherworldly. *It's magick.*

"Wait!" I call out, my bare feet pattering against the ground, until I'm next to Madam Prea at the door's threshold. "Elves are the only ones with magick?"

Madam Prea's brows furrow together. "Of course, we are."

"Then . . ." My words trail off. Maybe Jerik didn't remember the merfolk and tiefling trials correctly. If they don't have magick, then there is no way our lungs could have filled with seawater and burning panels could have materialized into thin air. "During the trials, other kingdoms . . . It's—it's like they used magick for their tasks."

A short sigh slips through the barrier of the older elf's lips. Her eyes are kind as she takes me in. "For the trials—for that one day each rotation—the elven kingdom siphons off our magick to any kingdom that wishes to use it."

"Why would you do that?" The words are a whisper.

Madam Prea's lips purse at the corners. "It's been that way since the end of the Last War."

She ends the conversation by entering the room. Without a word, I follow.

The human maids are standing in my new bedchamber, waiting for my arrival. The room is bare except for the vast bed in the center. White wooden posters protrude from the corners, and draped across each of them is a sheer white fabric canopy, creating a secluded spot for me to slumber.

The servants begin shifting on their feet as they wait expectantly for something I'm not sure of. However, their eyes avoid me. Some are looking down at the floor or my feet. Others are glancing around the room.

My eyes widen. Here I am, gaping at my new bed with absolutely nothing on. I'm bare for all to see. Embarrassment tints my cheeks pink. Not at my body being on display but because I don't know how to proceed. I feel incompetent.

"Um . . ." I trail off. The touch of Madam Prea appears once more on my shoulder. It's a feeling I can't help but cherish despite my mind screaming at me not to, screaming at me that I should despise her because of what she is.

She announces, "Girls, our guest needs to be dressed." My head turns to face her profile. I wonder if she knows my name or who I am. I can feel my heart drop slightly at the thought of her knowing what a ghastly being I am. That feeling shocks me even more. "She is not accustomed to our way of living. Remember, she is like you. In Terakeld, you do not ask to be dressed. So, she does not ask, either."

The others nod to the elf in charge and fully look at me. Then they begin rustling around the room. As they retrieve clothing from a wardrobe I didn't see at first, hidden in a far corner, Madam Prea speaks aloud once more with authority.

"After today, she will decide whether she would like to utilize you all for dressing or if she would like to dress herself each day."

I'm stunned into stillness. *A choice.* I have not had the luxury to choose anything in so long. Not since before Arden and I were forced to grow up far faster than we should've, when our family of four turned to three.

And why am I any different from these mortal servants? Why do I get to live in luxurious chambers and be waited on? Why do I get a choice when they don't? It was like this in Phandolus as well, living above the dungeons that hold the servants' cells. Although, I was next door to Andrina so she could keep me close. Here? I didn't see Kayd's door on my journey from the cell. I'm not close—or at least not as close as Andrina wanted.

Madam Prea shakes her head and says under her breath, "Do not refuse the kindness Prince Kayd has given you. No good will come from it." As if reading the emotions swirling around my head.

I look at her as she stares into my soul. There's a sense of silent pleading across her features. Nodding, the elf sends me a small smile, her nude-painted lips curving toward the ceiling, as she turns back to watch over the chambermaids. My gaze follows.

Laying upon the lush silk bedding is a gown. It's a soft sage-green color with what looks like a simple floor-length skirt and puffed sleeves. My body goes taut, and before I can object, the fabric is being pulled over my head.

I haven't worn a gown since I was a child, since the day we burned Mother's body. After that, there was no one around to sew the garments for me, and we didn't have enough coin to buy one. I ended up donning Arden's old tunics, and Ottilie gave me a few pairs of pants in the past. Hiding my scowl with a bite of my tongue, I say nothing.

As if she can sense my displeasure, Madam Prea pipes in, "You may have a choice in who dresses you, girl, but when going before the Prince of Nythfaedell, you will look the part."

I do not reply. I simply stand there as the chambermaids fasten the corseted top—all breath wretched out of me—and wrap a tan-and-white floral belt around my waist as an accessory. Before I know it, they are ushering me out of the room and back into the bathroom, where that floor-length mirror awaits.

The gown is beautiful. The color truly accentuates my eyes and skin tone, but it's just not me. Perhaps if I grew up in different circumstances, I'd appreciate the way the dress flows over my figure. I put on a kind smile as I look into the reflection at the group of mortal girls beaming around me like I'm the most stunning being in the world. They take pride in their work, and I don't want to dim that.

With a flick of her wrist, Madam Prea dismisses the swooning girls, and I hear them swiftly exit my chambers. We are left in silence as the door shuts. I watch the female approach me. Her fingers move deftly in my damp hair. Madam Prea begins braiding the right side of my hair, from the top of my scalp to the ends near my shoulder blades, letting the silence grow between us. I think of how kind she is. I think of how much she reminds me of Mother.

"Do you know why I'm here?" My voice is as soft as the gown draped over my body. I'm not sure I want her answer.

"What is your name?" the elf asks instead of answering.

Don't tell her. The less the elves know, the better, says a part of me scrambling to take hold of the situation—to survive.

Ignoring it, I answer, "Maeve Wyndell."

Madam Prea nods with a sad smile. "Well, Maeve Wyndell, I know you are important to the prince . . . and I know you came from a different kingdom," the elf explains slowly so I can process it all. "I also know you're dangerous."

My heart involuntarily clenches, the blood in my veins chilling. She's right, of course, but her words hit me harder than I would have ever expected. Madam Prea fastens the one braid and begins on the other.

"That's all I know. No details were given to me." A sigh. "I was cautioned to be wary of you, girl. But when I look into your eyes, all I see is darkness that's shielding a broken mortal who doesn't know where she belongs."

My throat bobs. I shift my eyes away, breaking our eye contact. She fastens the second braid and waves her hand over her work. Tiny white flowers materialize and weave themselves throughout my ashy-brown strands. It's beautiful, and it reminds me of Andrina. Madam Prea exits my chambers without another word.

As I stare at my reflection, I know the elf's words ring true. Terakeld is home, but I never felt like I truly belonged. Not since Mother. Phandolus is a place where I was reforged into something *other*. A cruelness fit for changelings seeped into my mortal heart, creating an unnatural blend of both. There, in that kingdom, I still didn't belong. Not really. And here, in Nythfaedell . . . in a land I don't know, there is uncertainty surrounding my place.

My soul is tainted from all the blood I've spilled, the anger cementing itself into my heart is the darkness Madam Prea sees. She's right. I am broken. I am alone. I don't belong.

My mind shifts to Ottilie, the reason for the justice I seek. She would hate who I've become. But she's not here to endure a life without her best friend. I am. And it's as painful as the blistering burn on my shoulder festering in the days following her death.

Ottilie . . .

Briskly, my feet begin to move. I run to the sitting room and sigh in relief when I see my shredded clothes still in a pile. My knees slam into the hard floor, and I rummage through the strips of bloodied fabric. My frantic search comes to a halt when I spot it. There, nestled in a ruined pocket of my pants, is the stone-blue silk ribbon I never part with. A reminder of simpler days in Terakeld. A symbol of the strength I need to keep going, keep killing, keep obeying.

In this ridiculous gown, I pad toward the chair before the fire. The crackling of the wood as it burns is the only sound in my chambers. I barely move a muscle, but my mind is racing. As I think about the darkness twining around the monster I've become, I clutch the ribbon tightly against my chest and let the silent tears fall.

The hissing fire is merely glowing embers when the guard, Halton, returns. He's dressed in a new outfit, and from the dampness of his hair, it looks like he just removed himself from his bath.

"Prince Kayd—" the elf stops mid-sentence and looks down at where I sit. His hazel eyes take in the gown I'm donning and the flowers in my hair. His jaw clenches, and his nostrils flare slightly. A sharp inhale, then he continues. "He will be pleased to see you like this."

I don't respond. I don't move. I only stare at him as he stands in the doorway, my upper lip curling and my eyes narrowing dangerously.

Halton clears his throat. "Prince Kayd is ready for you, Serpent."

He stands still—back straight, face hard—and waits. As I stand, a tingling sensation—thousands of pinpricks from disuse—shoots up my legs, but I ignore it and walk toward the door Halton's stationed at. With a nod, he pivots and guides me out into the halls of the elven palace.

Each step is unbearable. The speed at which we walk causes my feet to snag on the skirts of my gown. The puffy sleeves continue to ride up, digging into my underarms. If I could rip the fabric free of my body and approach the prince in only my underthings, I would. The thought of it—the guard's shocked and furious features—sends a jolt of joy through my body. Instead, I tug at the tightness of the sleeves in search of some relief.

Halton throws a menacing scowl in my direction after a particularly loud huff as I attempt to adjust the corset that's constricting my lungs.

"Stop," he orders with a grunt. When I don't, he shakes his head in exasperation and proceeds to ignore me the rest of the way.

We arrive at double ivory doors that are ajar, causing the golden crest carved in the middle to split. There, Prince Kayd is waiting. He's seated in a grand, deep green chair. Not quite a throne but close. I wouldn't be surprised if his court bows before it.

Instead of white-and-golden walls like the halls, they're a warm beige. Dark, wooden beams connect with the ceiling. A plush chaise and two large chairs sit empty except for the pillows and furs draped over them. It's cozy . . . cozier than the other rooms I've seen in the palace so far. A table against the right wall is filled with fruits, cheeses, breads, and wine; to my left, a large window takes up almost the entire wall. Through it is the perfect view of Nythfaedell's land.

Nightfall is already here. A ribbon of relief simmers in my veins after not knowing the time of day while I was held captive. The sky is a brilliant bright purple, similar to the color of Madam Prea's otherworldly eyes, with swirls of midnight blue. Stars are just now beginning to blink into existence. Massive trees are filled with glowing lights strung through the branches, and luminescent bugs buzz around each bulb in brilliant neon hues.

"Stunning, isn't it?"

My gaze pulls away from the beauty before me and locks on the creature who relentlessly carved into me, like a savage ripping into meat for the first time. My nostrils flare at the sight of him. His evil smirk forms in reply.

The silence is heavy between us, my rage colliding with his amusement. I will not be the one to break. I will not be the one . . .

"What do you want, mortal? Halton here says you *demanded* to see me. Demand away." Leisurely, he waves his hand dismissively and leans back in his chair, with one of his legs bending, so the bottom of his foot rests on top of it and his arm drapes over his knee. His eyebrow is raised, waiting. A complete, condescending ass.

I square my shoulders, my spine straightening. With a lifted chin, I say, "You need me."

He barks out a loud laugh. I continue as if he didn't.

"If you didn't, you would have killed me the second I revealed who sent me. You want me to work for you, serve you . . . *kill* for you. I will. But . . ." I pause, taking in the prince before me. No longer are his shoulders relaxed. He removes himself from his lounging position and leans forward, his elbows resting on top of his knees. "Only *if* Nythfaedell swears to protect my father in Terakeld and my brother in Fiermoor."

"She threatened their lives, didn't she?" A snicker flutters out of his smirk as he shakes his head. "Typical Andrina."

Halton approaches Kayd, with brows tucked in farther together and his arms locked behind his back. The two quietly discuss my proposition and the logistics of protecting two mortals they care nothing for and have no connection to. Abruptly, Kayd halts their conversation, stands up, and walks toward me. Unwavering, I stand and hold his gaze as he stops no more than an arm's length away.

"I will provide protection for your father in Terakeld. My guards stationed there will keep a close eye on him. However, I refuse to do so for your brother. He's in enemy territory. He serves the tieflings. They will be his only protectors."

The thought of leaving Arden at the mercy of those horned creatures makes my gut twist. I'm positive they wouldn't care if they found a mortal servant bleeding from his throat. They didn't care about Mother's illness. Why would they care about him?

I chew on my bottom lip as I contemplate my options . . . or lack thereof. Arden is strong. He's quick-witted and brave. He would be able to hold his own. Father, on the other hand, can't. He can't even pull himself away from the cottage to eat. He needs this. He needs to stay safe from that cruel princess and her legion of guards.

I nod slowly. "Deal," I whisper and extend my hand.

He bares his teeth in a sickening smile and clasps my palm in his. My gut churns at the feel of his skin on mine. His grip is tight and hot, like he's searing our bargain into my skin—into my soul.

"It is agreed, then, Shackled Serpent." He releases my hand and turns on his heel. From over his shoulder, he demands my leave. "You may go."

24

F IVE DAYS. FIVE WHOLE days since I've made my deal with Prince Kayd. Five whole days since I was last tortured. Five whole days and not a single word about my first assignment for the elves.

I should be raw from the trauma I experienced during those days I spent in that cell, beaten to a pulp. I should be tormented from the pain and damaged beyond the stab wounds. But . . . I'm not. Only anger thrums beneath my skin. That same anger I felt when my own blade sliced open my skin. That's all there is. Anger. Only anger.

While that white-hot feeling fuels me inside, my body is restless. It's used to constant training, constant traveling, constant killing. No number of push-ups and sit-ups and no amount of pacing before my hearth and wandering the palace grounds can combat the yearning I feel to get back to my goal. Now that my father's safety is taken care of, my mind has drifted from him yet again. I'm a horrible daughter. I know it. My heart knows it. But my body doesn't seem to care.

An early autumn morning breeze ruffles through the ends of my hair—each strand tickling my collarbones—as I barge through the palace doors toward the back of the grounds. Instead of looming snowcapped mountains and dark pine woods of the changelings' realm, I'm surrounded by tall, welcoming birch forests. Glowing butterflies fly up toward the tree houses in the distance, where young elves can be heard laughing. Nythfaedell is beautiful. Even more beautiful than Phandolus.

Here, I have just a smidge more freedom than with the changelings. The prince has given me free rein of the palace grounds. I can explore. I can walk along the many gravel pathways and marvel at the art in the hallways. No longer am I glued to the one ordering me to kill, hidden in my chambers, and having to resort to sneaking around.

My feet take me toward the Crystal Lake Garden, a place that has become an oasis for me over the past few days. In order to get there, though, I must pass the prince's training grounds. The king's training grounds—full of older, more experienced elves—is on the opposite side of the property.

Pointedly ignoring and tuning out the clashing swords and grunts of pain as I approach the sparring guards, I think of the exotic flowers lining the Crystal Lake Garden's clear, glimmering water. When I'm there, I feel like I'm the same girl I was back in Terakeld. It's peaceful and reminds me of my meadow. The quiet—sans the water lapping against the banks and the buzz of insects flying around—brings me relief. I feel no prying eyes watching me while I'm there.

During my time here, I've noticed several guards keeping their eyes on me as I walk the palace grounds. Others, I can only feel. They lurk in the shadows, like wraiths ready to attack. I assume Halton is too important to be given such an assignment—keeping tabs on me to make sure I don't slaughter anyone without permission. But if he is, I have yet to see him. The image of a lurking shadow with hazel eyes pops into my head, and a shiver trails up my spine.

I pick up speed, my feet crunching through the perfectly cut grass as fast as I can. Peace is waiting for me in the form of that garden.

Prince Kayd's men pay me no mind as I pass. They're too engulfed in the exercises and sequences to notice me. I like it that way. Cheers boom throughout the grounds and into the looming treetops as someone slams another into the ground. Prince Kayd is under an awning near the back of the training grounds, lounging on a makeshift throne. With relentless eyes, he observes each of his men with a cruel examination in his expression. Each guard—except for Halton, who stands just behind the prince—is fighting for his approval. Each one trying to gain his attention with the loudest grunt or the slickest move.

My eyes roll toward the sky before refocusing on my destination. It's only just ahead. Over the hill. I continue walking until—

"Serpent!" His voice stops me in my tracks. He snaps his fingers, the sound somehow traveling across the grounds to me. "Come!" The prince beckons to me with a jut of his head.

The others stop their sparring, all eyes turning to me. My brow creases. Prince Kayd just openly acknowledged me as the killer of his people. Incredulous uncertainty makes my heart thump wildly in my chest. Princess Andrina was so secretive about me. No one—no guard, except for the three who trained me, no servant, no official—knew who I was.

One hesitant step into the training grounds, then another, and another. As the crowd of guards parts for me, my shock dissipates, and my confidence begins to seep through my pores. My shoulders are set, squared and strong. With my chin held high, I command the area without a word. Each elf is looking at nothing but me. Their eyes transfixed on my straight spine and powerful steps. I want them to remember this moment, the moment the Shackled Serpent entered their lives.

Several guards openly gawk at the sight of me, as if I am Death herself. Perhaps, to them, I am. Some glare with eyes as sharp as my knives, fury and disgust contorting their features. If they could, I'm sure they would kill me—just as I did to so many others. I even recognize a few of the guards, whom I've caught watching over me during the days I've been here. Their faces are now frozen in terror as they realize who I am.

Now standing before the prince, I mockingly bow with a glower. "Yes . . . *Your Highness*?" My voice flits upward with scornful sarcasm, that anger I've felt over the days still fresh.

Someone in the crowd growls so deep I almost don't register it. The wind seems to have ceased, and the birds' gleeful chirps are gone. Prince Kayd merely acts unbothered. He picks an invisible speck of dust off the embroidered lapels of his coat and flicks it away, then looks me up and down with distaste.

"You, mortal, are renowned for your abilities with a blade, but your combat skills concern me. It was too easy for my men to take you down when you failed to end my life." His forest-green eyes look at me pointedly. "Spar, Serpent. I want to see what you're capable of."

With a flick of his wrist, he points out a guard and motions him into the middle of the now-dispersing crowd. The others back away, forming a semicircle that gives Kayd and Halton the perfect view of the fight that's about to take place.

My upper lip twitches. I face my opponent, calming the pounding blood traveling through my veins into a steady, serene beat, the same composure I channel on my assignments. He looks young . . . younger than most of the other guards. Possibly a new member of the prince's ranks, if his clenched fists and shifting feet are any indication. He's attempting to hide his terror as I approach, but to no avail. I can see it behind his russet eyes. I can see it trying to twist the muscles in his face just beneath his skin. My sparring partner's facade cracks slightly as soon as I dig my feet into the dirt and lift my fists, ready to pounce.

I let him make the first move. His fist plummets toward my face. I step to the side, and he stumbles forward. His eyes blaze with fury and embarrassment. Despite my pounding heart, I smirk. Red splotches cover his round cheeks. He charges. It takes me a moment to register what is happening, charging so fast I barely see him. Lanky arms wrap around my waist, and he slams me into the ground.

For several agonizing breaths, it's hard to fully fill my lungs with air. My chest burns, and my spine feels like it's cracked in two. I wiggle my toes to make sure I'm okay. The guards around us cheer, excited to see me on my back. My opponent straddles my waist and rams my cheek with his clenched fist. A few more blows to the face before I even register that I've been struck.

With a wicked grin, he lifts his arm into the air and slams his elbow down. I twist my head to the side, avoiding the blow. His bone collides with the hard ground. He hisses in pain, and I use the opportunity to kick him off me.

Scrambling for the upper hand, I crawl toward him and straddle his waist. He's the scrawniest guard that I can see, and he's still better than me despite the training I received from the changeling combat guard. I can't lose. I *can't*.

Roles reversed, I channel all my pride into my fists as they barrel down on him. First, to the throat. Second, to his eye. Third, to his jaw. Over and over again until my knuckles and wrists ache. Finally, I lean down, trying to conceal how tired I am. My breath caresses his face, and he recoils in disgust.

With my forearm pressing firmly into his throat, I whisper, "How does it feel to be beaten by me? Your prince is watching, and here you are, pinned beneath a mortal girl."

The guard thrashes underneath my weight. My straddling thighs squeeze his hips tightly in a vise-like grip, making sure he goes nowhere. Silence surrounds us once more. Slowly, my gaze moves from his red-rimmed eyes up to where Prince Kayd and Halton are observing. I can't decipher what they're thinking.

The prince silently nods at me. I release the pressure against the guard's throat and swing my leg around before standing up. I ignore the throbbing across my cheekbones and muscles. My opponent gets to his feet slowly, bows deeply, and skulks away, immediately blending into the crowd of guards watching me with weary eyes.

The wave of Prince Kayd's hand signals another opponent into the ring. This time, he's larger, more muscular than the first, with jet-black hair to his shoulders and eyes as dark as coal. Rolling his shoulders back and cracking his neck, he readies himself for a fight.

It ends quicker than the previous. I only get one punch in before his knuckles rapidly connect with my gut. Once. Twice. Three times. Burning pain shoots up into my lungs, and I'm stunned by the feeling. In my brief stupor, the guard grips my shoulder and thigh and tosses me to the side, as if I were dirtied scraps of rubbish.

I hit the ground hard—my right side screaming—and roll until I reach the boots of the guards standing by. Many cheer at my loss. Others laugh, clearly pleased at seeing the one they feared only moments ago bruised and beaten.

Rage and embarrassment course through my body, blinding me. With wobbly legs and new determination to wipe the smirks off the elves' faces, I stand up, ready to continue the fight. Instead of the dark-eyed guard, Prince Kayd's right-hand man stands before me. Halton.

"We've seen enough," Halton declares. His hands are firmly clasped behind his back as he stares at me.

My nostrils flare in response. "Fuck that. I'll fight you, then."

I charge.

Before I know it—faster than I'd like to admit—I'm on my back, staring up at the blue Nythfaedell sky. Each shallow breath is laced with shuddered wheezing. My ears are muffled, but I can still hear the other guards whooping and hollering around me.

Halton steps into view, blocking the shining sun that beams down on us. His eyes bore into me as his brown hair falls over his raised eyebrow. He seems amused. "We've seen enough," he repeats.

Fury burns in my eyes. I roll out from under his condescending stare and hop back onto my feet, despite the protests from my aching muscles.

"C'mon, *guard*. I'm not done," I grit out, venom fit for my moniker dripping with each syllable.

Halton blinks, then chuckles deeply, getting back in his sparring stance. "You should just give up, *Serpent*." His voice is a soft coo, a patronizing hoax.

This time, I wait for him to make the first move. Despite giving it my all, I end up pinned beneath him. He hops up, ready to walk away from the fight, but I get back on my feet again. I won't give up. I *can't* give up.

Two more times, I try to win. Two more times, he beats me faster than the last. Not a pebble of sweat is seen on his skin. The echoes of laughter and taunts from the amused guards ring throughout my head. Red seeps into my vision. Automatically, I reclaim my footing and ready myself for another round.

"Enough!" The bellowing voice of Prince Kayd silences the training grounds in an instant. The crowd of guards snap their mouths shut. Halton calmly turns toward the prince and inclines his head slightly. My sharp stare stays trained on the captain for a moment longer before I turn toward Kayd. His eyes are lit with amusement, yet the corners of his lips are angled downward in disappointment.

"I expected more from the one who has taken so many lives. You are feared by all kingdoms and beings, yet you cannot win a simple sparring match—" Kayd interrupts his thoughts with a loud huff, then slowly looks me up and down, taking in all that I am. "Pathetic," he mutters, quietly, but still loudly enough for all to hear. The dozens of guards watching our every move chuckle.

"You obviously do not know what an assassin is, *Your Highness*." I can't stop the words from escaping the barrier of my scowl fast enough. "We don't fight. We slink in the shadows and take the lives of our victims when they least expect it, when they think they're safe."

Chuckles turn into waves of whispers at my blatant disrespect. The prince's features turn sour, his eyes now blazing with a type of anger that makes the hairs on the back of my neck stand tall. Elegantly, the elf lifts himself off his temporary throne. Each step is a dreadful, deep thud in my veins—pounding, pounding, pounding, until he's right in front of me.

A humorless chuckle, then a slap across my face. My cheek stings, and tears threaten to breach my tightly shut eyes. All eyes are on me right now. I can feel every single one of them, especially Halton's.

Do not let them see you cry, Maeve.

Blood begins budding at the corner of my mouth from where one of his rings dug into my skin. Defiantly, my head turns toward him, and my tongue licks at the small amount of crimson before baring my teeth.

"I want my assassin skilled in all things. You will not be captured again, mortal. I will not allow it." A pause. "Halton here is my best fighter. He will oversee your combat training."

It is not a request, I realize. It's a demand. There is no room for argument.

Prince Kayd looks between the two of us. The scowl on Halton's face matches my own . . . but unlike myself, the guard steels away his displeasure and shallowly bows his head toward the prince, accepting his new duty like the good lapdog he is.

I scoff. The thin line of my lips deepens. The prince shoots a dagger-sharp glare in my direction and snarls, "Go, before my patience wears."

Not able to stand being in the presence of Prince Kayd, that unbearable captain of his guard, and the others, I turn heel and trudge off toward the Crystal Lake Garden.

Soon, that temporary peace will be mine.

But before I get there, I hear the prince call out to his guards, "Everyone, line up. Bare palms up. A blood oath is required. Swear you will not speak of that mortal's true identity or face the consequences of your prince."

25

B ANG! BANG! BANG!

A croaking groan vibrates within my throat and rings across the quiet room. I nuzzle into the furs that are draped over my body. Not a moment later, darkness begins to pull me under once again . . .

BangBangBangBangBangBangBang!

My eyes snap open. Irritation pricks at my skin when I hear the gruff grumble of Halton's voice on the other side of the wooden door to my chambers. "Get up, Serpent! Training begins today. Get dressed. Now!"

I don't move from the comfort of my bed. It's still too early for anyone to be woken up. My room is completely cloaked in pitch-black darkness. The back of my hand rubs my closed eyes, and I burrow further into the furs. I don't answer to that creature . . . I don't answer to anyone in this Godsforsaken kingdom. I will get up when I'm ready.

Sleep's grip wraps around my consciousness once again, and I feel my mind drift. My breathing deepens, and my limbs turn heavy . . .

BANG! BANG! BANG! BANG! BANG!

My upper body springs forward into a seated position. The guard strikes the wooden door again with more force. Surely, the entire East Wing is now awake with the amount of noise he's causing.

"If you don't get up this instant, I am going to come in there myself and rip you out of that bed." The cadence in his voice holds threatening authority.

I fling the furs and silks away from my body with a huff of annoyance. The cool air makes me yearn for my bed's warmth as soon as my bare feet touch the wooden floor. Clad only in my sleepwear, I stalk out of my bedchamber and into my sitting area until I reach the door that separates me from the guard.

I rip the door open with a shattering force. Halton's hand halts mid-movement, like he was about to barge in himself. His eyes widen slightly.

"You know . . . most men would like to keep me in bed. Threatening to rip me out of it is not a good look." There's a tinge of teasing as my raspy, slumber-coated voice twines around the snarky words. I place my hand on my right hip in a challenge and size him up, dragging my eyes south, taking in every crease and crevice of his broad body before I casually lift them back up to meet his eyes.

Wide hazel eyes stare at my sleep-crusted lashes, and Halton's face pales faintly. His stunned gaze lasts for no longer than a breath or two before he works to compose himself. With tight jaw muscles and furling fists, he transforms back into the disciplined guard he usually is. The corners of my lips tug upward, and he scoffs in my face, rolling his eyes dramatically before they sharply find their way back to mine.

"So, the dregs of Terakeld do know how to have fun."

My scowl returns, deeper than before. He clicks his tongue, brows furrowing, and his body shudders, as if imagining mortals tumbling into each other's beds disgusts him. The guard's lowered eyes begin traveling up my body at a leisurely pace, just as I did to him before. His eyes glide over my loose silk shorts that stop at the bottom of my ribs and linger on the thin strip of skin peeking out just before the matching loose long sleeve top begins. His irises turn dull, glazing over slightly.

I resist the urge to shift on my feet, suddenly hyperaware of my tangled bedhead. I won't let him rattle me.

Finally, his stare returns to mine. He blinks. No longer does he look dazed, the fog clearing from his eyes. His cold stare returns easily, as if it never went away.

"Get dressed," he says sharply. Then he turns and leaves.

I slam the door behind him. "Ugh!" I stomp toward my bedroom. That elf makes the blood pumping through my veins boil and makes my joints lock up whenever he's near. It startles me . . . that feeling. So intense. So sudden. "That maddening, insolent creature."

The training gear catches my eye immediately, appearing out of nowhere atop my rustled bedding. My upper lip curls. *Magick.* It's a simple tunic, corset belt, pants, boots, and a fur-lined vest with a hood for the cooling weather.

I shouldn't even go. I should leave him there, standing in the middle of that training ground waiting on me—a mortal he detests. I can see his contorted face now when he realizes I'm not coming. The thought makes me snicker, but it quickly dies on my lips.

I don't want to do it, but I *need* this training. Hand-to-hand combat will ensure that I never be put in this situation again. Being captured . . . tortured. *No.* I will not go through that. Not again. With new—albeit unpleasant—determination, I snatch up the black clothing.

He's waiting for me. Slivers of pale pinks and oranges of a new day breach through the tops of the birch trees and gleam against his skin. His hands move swiftly, wrapping his knuckles with a thin white cloth. His face contorts, with brows furrowing and teeth digging into his bottom lip in concentration. Once secured tightly, he cracks his neck and rolls his shoulders, then begins his assault on a sandbag in front of him, held by a sturdy metal stand.

One punch, two punches, a strong slap with his shin. The sandbag stays firm in its spot. Halton starts again. One punch, two punches, a strong slap with his shin. This time, adding a loud hit with his elbow. The guard continues the combination, grunting with each hit and adding a new move with every round.

Watching him move around his target is entrancing. Graceful and fluid, like water dancing along a stream. Still, there is something dangerous and deadly about it, like jagged rocks hidden beneath the waves. There is a certain beauty to it, a beauty that I want. I want to move as he does. I want to be as elegant and lethal as him. And I'll become that . . . and so much more.

"If I get to do that to you, training won't be so bad after all." My words echo against the grounds, disturbing the peaceful early morning quiet.

Halton halts his movements, then turns to look at me. His chest heaves as he catches his breath, with lips slightly parted as he sucks in the crisp autumn air. Beads of sweat glide down his temple onto his neck. A vein pulses against his skin.

He sighs and begins unwrapping his knuckles, throwing the cloth onto the ground at his side. No greeting. Nothing. I'm unsure of what I am supposed to do. So, I stand there, watching him. My training in Phandolus consisted of harsh orders. If I didn't obey, I'd be punished. It was simple. It was routine. I knew what to expect. This, however, is uncharted territory.

"Are you just going to stand there gaping, Serpent?" he grunts out, the second cloth joining the first. He shifts his eyes to me with such speed. I blink at the intensity of it. "Do something."

My jaw falls open. "*Do something?*" An incredulous scoff. "What am I to do, *elf?* You are tasked to teach me. So, teach." My teeth flash as the last syllable buzzes through them.

He sucks in a silent breath as his jaw ticks to the side. His eyes shift, and his shoulders sag.

"Step up to the sandbag," he orders. I do as he says. "Now, I assume you saw the combination I was doing. Do the first two moves. One punch, then follow with two quick jabs." He demonstrates in the air.

One punch. Two quick jabs. Easy.

I raise my clenched fists in front of my face, reel back, and ram my knuckles into the sandbag.

One punch. Two quick jabs.

A cynical huff comes from the guard. "You're sloppy. You have no foundation."

I turn to face him as I shake out my wrists. He leers down at me with his eyebrows arched. The way Halton's looking at me makes me feel incompetent, like I should know how to fight. If I knew how, I wouldn't be trapped in this kingdom to begin with.

"You're still using that same unskilled, clawing-to-survive bullshit you pulled at the trials against those mortal guards. Whoever trained you in Phandolus was hoping you'd fail. We're going back to the basics."

"Oh, you remember me from the trials?" I bite back.

Halton narrows his eyes and turns away from me, walking toward another side of the training grounds. "Come, Serpent. We'll start over here."

The next few hours are spent going over mundane movements I can do in my sleep . . . or, at least movements I *thought* I could do in my sleep. With the amount of corrections Halton issues—a slap to my elbow reminding me to keep it in being the most recent—I'm not so sure anymore. Either way, it's repetitive . . . slow, even. My motions are beginning to lag, going over each one without any thought. Boredom takes over.

Just as the pastel colors in the sky begin to disappear into light blue, Halton picks up those discarded white strips of cloth still on the ground. "We're done for today. You may leave." He dismisses me without a single glance.

My eyes narrow as I watch him bend down and wrap his knuckles once more. As I stand there, watching the movement of his hands, I don't leave. I don't know why. I feel frozen—cemented to the ground as I watch him—steeping in irritation and ire. But I don't move. I simply stare and stare as the elven captain looks over his shoulder and raises his eyebrow.

"Did you need something?" His eyes narrow.

Unbidden, my gut clenches. Shaking my head, I mumble, "No."

Wandering around the elven palace, I try to clear my head after my first training session with the captain of the prince's guard until a low, deep rumble vibrates my abdomen. I clutch it tightly. I haven't eaten anything since last night, and while training this morning was far from grueling, my hunger twists my stomach. A snack will do me well.

Once at the servant entrance to the kitchen, I barge through the door.

"Oh!" The word is nothing more than a surprised breath.

I wasn't expecting to see anyone here this time of day. Usually, the staff has a small break just after lunch. Madam Prea gasps and turns to look at the intruder, purple eyes wide, until she realizes it's me. They ease, her hand coming to rest on her chest.

"You frightened me, girl." She motions me farther into the kitchen.

It's luxurious. I'm filled with awe each time I sneak in here to grab a bite to eat. There are several countertops, three different hearths all made of gold, and a pantry filled to the brim with meats, cheeses, and fruits. The simple basin and counter in my family's cabin is laughable compared to this. These elves have all the luxuries in the world, and they continue to use us for their benefit.

"Wipe that scowl off your face. There's no point in getting worked up over something that will not change," Madam Prea scolds softly, like she can hear the words forming in my mind. Perhaps she can with her magick. "I see it in every single mortal girl who comes through these doors to serve. I understand—"

"No, you don't," I interrupt. She doesn't understand what it is like to live on that soot-covered island. She doesn't know what being ripped away from her family and friends is like.

A defeated sigh, but her eyes remain tender, as if she has had this conversation with others—*her girls*—long before I was born. "Sit, Maeve. Why are you here?"

My mouth opens slightly, unsure of what to say. Why am I here in the kitchen? Or why am I here in Nythfaedell?

She sees my hesitation and rests a delicate hand on my shoulder. "Are you hungry?" Her compassion is astounding. It's hard to show gratitude . . . It's hard to react at all when it's something this unfamiliar. All I can do is nod.

She leads me over to the only clear counter in the room. Ungracefully, I hop on top of it—my heel slamming into the side—as the older elf rummages through the pantry. A moment later, she returns with an apple and a slice of bread in hand. I smile in thanks, then let the silence engulf us.

She's eyeing me. The heat of her gaze sears into my side, searching for any indication of what I'm thinking. Iron walls in my mind and around my heart rise in response. I don't want her to find out who I truly am. I can see the fear and disappointment twisting her kind face already.

"Girl, if you don't stop gnawing away at that lip of yours, you'll chew it right off." Her voice is stern now. That authority I heard my first night is back. "Are you going to tell me the reason you're here?"

Her eyes are expecting, and her lips are pressed together tightly, creating a barely visible line. I huff out a defeated sigh, then bite into the bright red skin of the apple, its juice dribbling down my chin. The wet crunch fills my ears as I mull over what to say.

"It's—" Uncertainty clouds my mind. What will happen if I tell her who I am? What if she reports my secret to the king? My eyes shift up and meet hers. Immediately, I feel better—more relaxed—as soon as I feel the warmth in her gaze.

"Why are you so kind to me?" My words are low and breathy.

Madam Prea's brow scrunches in concern. "Everyone deserves kindness."

She walks over to a basin and begins dunking a handful of mugs and goblets into the soapy water. Never would I have thought an elf would work in the palace. It's a peculiar sight, seeing this ethereal being washing dishes.

"Everyone . . . What about your chambermaids? The conditions they work in . . . They look like they don't receive any kindness. So, why do I deserve it?" I look up at Prea, whose hands paused her washing. "I don't deserve anything. I've done unspeakable things—"

"That's life, girl. We all do things we aren't proud of." She shuts off the water and dries her hand on a green piece of cloth. "You are now a part of Prince Kayd's court, so you get the best we can offer. My girls are given what they need, no more . . . no less."

Madam Prea walks over to me and stands beside my dangling legs. There's pain and sadness in her eyes as she rests her palm atop my knee.

"I hate it here," I whisper, so low that I don't even think I said it out loud. But the way Prea's hand flexes against my knee tells me I did. Her care shines through even more with that simple gesture.

Am I someone who merits such affection? I feel split in half, like I'm two different people. I'm clawing at the person I was before the trials, before I killed those two mortal guards: a powerless girl who could do nothing other than obey or die. And I'm drowning under the person I am after: an assassin who relishes in spilling the blood of anyone who does her and her loved ones wrong.

I don't know which is better. I don't think either is. That darkness that has become so prevalent wraps around me, tighter and tighter. Constricting. I'm lost, just like Madam Prea said. I don't deserve her decency.

"Madam Prea!"

Both our heads snap toward the entrance to the kitchen. Prince Kayd Glyn-vyre barges through the wooden door. Irritation at the ill-timing of his appearance pebbles just beneath my flesh, igniting the lingering ire I felt during training this morning.

"Those incompetent chambermaids of yours—" He abruptly halts as soon as he spots me atop the counter. "Out." His upper lip quivers slightly, bearing a sliver of white teeth.

I brush off his demand with a loud crunch of my apple. My eyes never leave his as I chew on the fruit loudly. A deep growl from the back of his throat reverberates across the kitchen. His lip curls even more.

From the corner of my eye, I notice Madam Prea straighten her spine. "Your Highness, is there a problem with my maids today?" Her question somehow relieves the room of the taut tension between Kayd and me that was ready to snap seconds ago.

"Those mindless, blundering fools cannot do a single thing right. One spilled my tea all over the rug in my parlor. Another had the audacity to approach me without being called upon. And do not get me started on the last." He shivers and rolls his eyes before directing them back to the older elf who remains silent. Her face is puckered and grim. "If they cannot tend to their most simple duties, then they would be better off in the stable, sleeping with the animals. I expect this to never happen again. Fix it, Prea. Or it's your—"

My legs suddenly fling themselves off the counter, interrupting the prince and his infuriating rant.

I turn to the female elf next to me. "Thank you, Madam Prea, for the snack."

Madam Prea's eyes are slightly wider now, looking between me and the fuming elven prince off to the side. *And for your kindness.* She seems to understand. Her eyes soften before bowing her head in return.

Quickly swiveling my body toward Kayd, I stomp right up to him. Each hit of my boots on the floor echoes loudly against the hanging pots and pans. Face-to-face, our noses could touch if I leaned in just a little bit farther.

My voice lowers into a melodic croon, soft enough so Prea doesn't hear. "Remember, *Your Highness*, I know where you sleep at night, and I've been watching your guards. I now know their rotations, their duties, where they sleep, and when they sleep. You best treat your servants well." The threat is there—clear as day, wreathing around each word—and it is deadly.

A scornful chuckle bubbles in the back of his throat. He looks down toward the cuffs of his shirt, adjusting them. Prince Kayd clicks his tongue and slowly slides his eyes up my body. They stop once he meets my stare.

He leans in. His warm breath tickles my ear, and unpleasant bumps form along the nape of my neck. "And remember, *mortal*"—nothing more than a dangerous whisper—"I know where your family is. You best show me some respect."

26

E VERY MUSCLE IN MY body burns, as if poison twists around each cell, acid
pumping through the crevices that hide between my muscles and bones.
My legs are stiff, and my steps are heavy. The bottoms of my boots slosh against
the wet Nythfaedell ground as I rush toward Prince Kayd's training grounds.
Blankets of chilling rain fall from the lightening sky, dousing me from head to
toe. My feet speed up despite my sore body's protest.

"Faster . . ." I mutter to myself. "Shit. I'm so fucked. Halton's going to kill
me."

My chest heaves, and my heart pounds against my rib cage, just as it had done
when I woke up this morning. The lingering remnants of my dream fogged my
vision as I sat in my bed, gripping the bedding beneath me.

Covered in blood, massive flames flared around me. The Phandolus palace
was crumbling ash, pillaged until nothing was left. Behind me, mortals marched,
also covered in gore. To Fiermoor, they were headed. Then to Amphitea. Then
to Nythfaedell. My smile was deranged. I did this. I brought down the kingdoms. For my people. For Mother. For Ottilie.

I blinked away that image and shook my head. When it cleared, I realized how
light it was in my room. Normally, I'm still cloaked in darkness when I wake
for training, the magick lighting in my chambers matching the time outside. I

overslept. I heaved the blankets off me, dressed in the first thing I could grab, and ran out the door.

Halton's going to kill me.

A week has passed since I've begun training with the guard. Two days ago, we finally moved on from basic exercises to actual combat skills. I would rather be doing anything other than spending my early mornings with the irritating elf, but at least it's not just him yelling at me for shifting my weight on the wrong foot or moving my wrist incorrectly now.

I skid to a stop in the center of the training grounds. Halton is standing there, waiting for me. His hair is wet from the rain, and his tunic sticks to his skin, showing off the rivets and valleys of muscle. With crossed arms over his chest and knuckles wrapped in white cloth, he doesn't say a word.

Then, without warning, he lunges at me.

Thinking fast, I try to dodge his jab, but I'm too slow. His fist connects firmly with the top of my abdomen, right below my sternum. My already-weak knees buckle and hit the hard ground. Nausea churns my stomach, and my lungs seize. All the air left my body as soon as his blow made contact with my center.

I stay there, silently hunched over, trying to fill my vacant lungs with the biting wet air, and willing my vision to stop spinning. Tears burn behind my eyes and begin to pebble in the corners. I can't help it. They form just as fast as Halton's punches—too quick to stop, too quick to push away. I feel a few slowly roll down my cheeks before I have the energy to stop more from falling.

"If you're going to waste my time by being late, don't bother showing up." Halton's voice is gruff, like rocks in a can.

Ire pricks along my skin at the sound. I don't respond. I stay looking at the ground, still finding my bearings.

"Get up," he orders. I don't move, my head remaining bowed. "Now, Serpent!"

Every ounce of calm I have disappears without a trace. My head snaps up from where I'm kneeling. My tear-filled eyes meet his, trapping him under my stare. My face feels hot, no doubt red from the aggravation boiling underneath the surface. I feel too much, too *hard*. But this time, I do not care.

My voice is ragged as I yell, "I have a name!"

Birds in a nearby tree fly away, their wings flapping frantically in the wind. Halton's lips part, and his eyes widen before he quickly throws up an invisible wall, masking what truly lies beneath. But I see it. He would've been able to hide the small movement if I weren't already staring at him.

For some reason, it makes me even more annoyed. I can't put my finger on it, why he gets under my skin so much. A grunt slips through my gritted teeth, and I look away from him. The ground of the training area fills my vision once again. His boots come into my view.

I refuse to look up at him, even as I hear the quiet cracks of his kneecaps as he crouches down in front of me. I brace myself for the insults I know will come.

Stupid mortal.

Look at the deadly assassin with tears in her eyes.

Pathetic.

I don't wish for him to see my face when he does.

Moments pass. I can feel his gaze as he stays kneeling in front of me. Strained silence surrounds us, the air thick and heavy with unspoken words. My nails dig into the palms of my hands. He's waiting for something—perhaps for me to look up so he can begin his verbal assault and take in just how hard his words hit.

He sighs, nearly nonexistent, but there, nonetheless. "What's your name?"

The question is soft and unsure. Just from the sound of the words, I can't tell if he's asking because he wants to know or because it will get me off the ground. Did Kayd truly not tell him my name after revealing it for Father's protection? Did the prince disregard me so quickly that he thought no one but him deserved to know?

My eyes shut tightly for five full breaths, trying to calm the churning fire roaring throughout my veins to navigate this new uncertainty. Finally, I look up at him. He's eye level with me now. His hazel irises are swirling around, as if even his elven magick is curious about my answer.

Drops of water drip off rogue strands of dark-brown hair, and a muscle in his glistening jaw feathers. He's all sharp lines and rugged steel. But there—hidden below, barely seeing the light of day—is a soft timidness. It seems to want to push its way through his hard mask but isn't quite strong enough yet. I don't think it will ever be strong enough.

I swallow around nothing, then hoarsely whisper, "Maeve."

My chest tightens and pulls in a way it never has before. His features are set, his muscles as still as stone. Halton—masked underneath the perfect guard—doesn't give anything away.

"My name is Maeve Wyndell."

In response, he nods once and simply repeats it, "Maeve Wyndell."

This morning, I make sure I'm on time. I don't want a repeat of yesterday, realizing I train better when my mind is clear. The rain stopped overnight, and a rare wave of warmer air swept through the elven kingdom, leaving beads of dew along the grass.

Today, I'm the first one here. Halton is nowhere to be found. *Peculiar.* Normally, he arrives at the training grounds with enough time to get a warmup in for himself. Normally, he waits on me.

I'm tempted to walk away and call it a day, especially after the humiliation I felt after I told him my name. It felt too personal, too exposed. Something shifted once I revealed that part of me. Each time I tried to forget it ever happened and focused on a new combat skill, I'd catch his eyes drifting to me, lingering. It irked me, being under his gaze. It made me feel vulnerable. It made me want to hide away from him forever.

Instead—unsure of what to do—I stand in the center of the grounds, unmoving. A few minutes pass of me glancing around before his voice booms from behind. "Hello, Serpent."

I quickly twirl around in alarm, and my face twists itself into a scowl. His easy grin stretches across his face, pleased with himself for using that name instead of my own. Little does he know the knot in my gut uncoils itself, and a weight is lifted off my chest.

Irritating confusion wraps around my mind in response. Just yesterday, I wanted him to know my real name. I screamed at him when he called me Serpent. But now, I relish in the sound of the nickname. It puts distance between us, separates us. To Halton, I should only be the killer I've been made out to be. Only the Serpent.

Halton—oblivious to the relief coursing through me—saunters around where I stand. His gaze travels up and down my body. My jaw clenches tightly.

"Are you a fool, mortal? Why are you just standing there?" Halton's voice is back to that rough grit that sends gooseflesh across my skin.

My mouth opens slightly in confusion at his words. He wasn't here. Does he expect me to spar by myself when he's gone?

"Close your damned mouth." The guard's eyes harden as his gaze drops down to my lips. "You look like a fish." Swiftly, I snap them shut. He continues once he pulls his eyes back to mine. "I expect you to get started on your lesson if I am not here when you arrive."

His breath smells like stale wine. Through his teeth, I can see his tongue is still stained a dark red. Really looking at him now, I notice his disheveled hair, the faint dark circles under his eyes, and several red-and-purple splotches peeking through his tunic near his collarbone.

No wonder he was late.

A flash of red moves in the distance near the palace behind him, and my eyes shift toward it. Under the flickering torches welded onto the exterior of the palace, a beautiful elf watches Halton from afar. A finger is wrapped around what looks like blonde hair, and she's clad only in a silk red robe that doesn't leave much to the imagination. The sultry smile she wears tells me everything I need to know. She's the reason for those marks on his neck, and now, she's seeking a show.

My stomach twists, and something tight and uncomfortable tugs in my chest as I take her in. She's stunning, with her pointed ears and flawless skin. I don't like the way looking at her makes me feel, whatever it is. I want to rid myself of it as soon as I can or bury it deep down until it's a forgotten thing.

Halton notices my eyes shift. "What are you looking . . ." His words trail off as he turns and sees the female in the distance. His throat bobs.

"Looks like you had a fun night, guard." My head turns back to him. My eyebrows raise, and my mouth shifts into a mischievous, teasing smirk.

Halton lets out a deep, threatening growl in response. A warning.

I suppress the chills that dance along my skin at the sound. I laugh at him as he moves his collar to cover the love bites and turns away from me to grab his hand wraps.

Strands of hair fall in my face as I look down at the elven guard. The red markings on his sweat-slicked neck have faded, nothing more than uneven, speckled patches of maroon. A stark difference from just three days ago when I had to endure an entire training session with that blonde female watching nearby.

Halton's wide eyes quickly move from side to side as he takes in my triumphant smile. His brow scrunches in curiosity, and his chest rises and falls beneath my legs. My skills are improving. He's pinned beneath me, proof of how much his lessons help, even though I'll never say such words out loud to him . . . or anyone. I would rather claw out my eardrums than hear him gloat.

"Looks like I've—"

He bucks his hips upward, lifting from his stomach. His legs twist in an expert manner as he flips me over onto my back. His knee lands on my chest, and my eyes bulge before a grimace takes its place. His tongue peeks out beneath his teeth as he smirks down at me.

He was never truly trapped.

I shove at his chest with a loud grunt before he relents and rolls off me. I sit up and get back on my feet.

"That's—" I breathe out deeply, my hands resting atop my bent knees. He hasn't taught me that skill yet. It came so fast, so out of nowhere. "That's not fair."

I want to know how he did it; I want to learn.

"Fighting is rarely ever fair, Serpent," he hums, rolling his wrists out.

"Teach me. I want to know how you did it." My jaw juts out, and I grab the goblet of water resting on a nearby bench and press it to my lips. The cold, refreshing liquid soothes my throat and dribbles down my chin.

Halton doesn't reply. He only watches me while I guzzle down the water. And I watch him. He's unreadable, an enigma. A mystery I can't help but want to unravel.

Smacking my lips together once the goblet is empty, I ask, "Is Halton your real name?"

The guard is taken aback by my question. His mouth opens then closes tightly in a grimace, the corners of his lips pinching together. "It is. Why do you ask?"

I shrug. "I don't know. It just doesn't fit you is all."

"Halton is my only name," the captain of the guard grinds out, his voice strained. "Training is over."

Halton stalks away, leaving me alone.

I finally bested the guard a week ago, using the same move he used on me. It took two days to get the technique right and another three to execute it well enough to beat him. I couldn't help but laugh at the sight of him lying on his back beneath me when I did it. His eyes were wild. His ragged breaths brushing against my skin elated me. It is a memory I hope to lock away forever.

And when I rolled off him, he huffed out a laugh. It took everything in me to not gawk at the sound. Although I could tell he was holding himself back, the sound was nice . . . warm and deep, languid and easy. A sound I wanted to store away as well.

As soon as we got back on our feet, I asked Halton for a day of weapons training to celebrate. That, and to curb my curiosity. I know—or, at least I think I know—that I excelled in weapons during my time in Phandolus, but perhaps that changeling guard was also setting me up to fail just as the combat guard did, according to Halton.

The elf didn't say anything when I asked, but now, as I stand in the middle of the training grounds the next morning, I see him approach with gleaming swords hanging from his side under the setting moon. A breathy laugh escapes the barrier of my lips. He listened. He actually listened. It's difficult to contain the rush of excitement I feel at the sight, my feet bouncing in place, wanting nothing more than to get started.

Halton tosses me one of the sheathed swords as soon as he arrives. My fingers delicately run along the sheath, and my hand firmly grips the pommel, pulling out the exquisite tool. Admiration swells as my eyes widen. I've never seen a weapon so beautiful—elven gold engraved with beautiful vines and flowers along the blade. My reflection looks like it doesn't belong, like I shouldn't be the one to hold such a lovely weapon.

The piercing sound of his sword unsheathing cuts through the air. Looking up, I see him swing. It comes swift and sharp, closing in on my arm. With a startled step back, I raise my own sword and block his blow. As he pushes down against my weapon, I can see his blade is engraved with two mountains, a large snowflake, and what looks like stars. Above that, a stack of letters run down the center of the blade: *N U K O R Y N N. Nukorynn.* I don't know what it means, and before I can ask, the sharp slice of the blades running together pierces the air as Halton steps back.

"Quick reflexes. Good," he muses, circling me. His sword raises at the ready once again.

I match his movements before striking. He parries, then goes on the offensive. Wide slicing arcs, clashing blades, parries and dodges—we move in sync.

The combinations I learned from the changeling weapons guard mixed with the combat moves and strength I've learned from Halton come easily to me.

So, the changeling guard didn't short me. Good to know.

I feel stronger, faster, and confident in my fighting skills. The corners of my lips begin to lift, and by the time I finish a particularly hard move, my smile is full and bright.

"It's good to see you're not completely disappointing," he breathes out. A quick smirk transforms his lips into something playful, something pleasant.

Sweat glistens across the back of my neck. Dribbles of it run down my spine and breach my waistband. I respond with another slice of my blade.

"If you knew how to fight like this, you wouldn't have had to brutally mutilate that mortal guard. The way that guy's head caved in . . ."

My heart begins to pound against my rib cage as I attempt to hold those images at bay. Stepping to the side, I dodge the butt of his sword and use my boot to jab him in the side.

"And those other contenders," Halton breathes heavily, circling me like I'm his prey before charging. "They could've used lessons like this, too. If they did, none of them would have perished." A grunt slips through his lips as I get a quick punch in with the hand not holding my sword. "Especially that first girl. By the end of it, her face didn't look any different from the guard you butchered."

Silence rushes through my ears, only leaving muffled buzzing in its wake. I skid to a stop, planting my feet into the ground and dropping the sword as if it burns.

Ottilie.

"Shit!" Halton yells, his eyes bulging out of his head as his blade swings toward me. I barely register it. He stumbles away from me, boots scuffing the ground before those wide, round eyes flare. "What the fuck, Serpent? You don't just freeze in the middle of a fight. That's how you die."

The guard begins to pace before me, his fingers digging into his hair and tugging at the roots. My throat closes. My once-pounding heart comes to a halt and plummets into my stomach like a boulder falling off a cliff into The Unlighted Sea.

"Are you listening to me?" Halton stops his pacing and steps toward me with wild eyes. I don't move, staring through him like he isn't even there.

The image of that guard flashes before my eyes, but now, all I see is beautiful russet skin beneath the gore and those curls I was always so envious of covered in blood. Bile rises into the back of my mouth. It's getting hard to breathe despite the fresh morning air. My lungs feel like they're constricting around ignited ash, heaving rapidly.

Tears prick at the corners of my eyes. Ottilie died in the most gruesome way possible. She shouldn't have died like that ... She shouldn't have died at all. Ottilie deserved better than anything this Godsforsaken land offered her.

I can feel burning tears begin to fall down my cheek.

Hastily, my body whips around so the elf before me doesn't see how broken I am. I can't stand the thought of him seeing the meek human that's hidden deep beneath the killer inside.

My movement is stopped abruptly by a smoldering, icy touch. The world spins around me before I'm face-to-face with Halton once again. His hand grips around my arm, large fingers flexing against my skin.

Suddenly, light and warmth erupt around me. The presence of Ottilie and Mother. I haven't felt them since that violent dream about the stable boys. I want to sob, knowing that they're here with me again. Their spirits caress against the arm Halton is holding and thrum just below his grip. My muscles tense at the feel of it. The familiarity they provide me mixes with his cold, freezing touch. So utterly different from the warmth of Jerik.

My lips wobble, and my eyes drop to the ground. Teardrops follow, hitting the toes of my boots. Using the deadly point of his sword, the guard brings it up to the bottom of my chin and presses it against my skin until I'm looking into his eyes—eyes that I can't read. Unknown emotions churn throughout the green-and-brown valleys and chasms that make up his irises. Within them is a silent question. It's loud enough to hear despite neither of us opening our mouths.

I'm scared to tell him about her. I'm scared of that vulnerability. The same vulnerability I felt when I told him my name. His thumb glides against the side of my arm, idly tracing soothing lines against my skin. It's a gesture that shocks me and pulls tightly in my chest.

"She was my best friend." My whisper is hoarse. It sounds like gravel is lodged into my vocal cords, disrupting the natural flow of air through my throat. I harshly wipe my tears away with the back of my hand.

The captain is quiet for a moment, his eyes roaming over my face. Surely, he's taking in how weak I am. With the sword still firmly pressed to my chin, he murmurs, "I'm sorry." His voice is soft, genuine. My eyes harden immediately. I don't want his kindness or his pity. His fond chuckle is light, as if he didn't just see my tears soak into the ground. "There's that venomous serpent."

"I hope you're not turning her soft, Halton." The timbre of Prince Kayd's voice cuts through the brisk air. My head turns sharply toward the sound. The tip of Halton's blade knicks my skin, blood pooling at the opening. The prince's eyebrows are raised in question but despite the teasing tone, a biting hard stare—fit for Princess Andrina—sears into the elf next to me. "Her heart is too precious to me when it's icy and black. Do not thaw it out. You're dismissed." The words turn into a menacing growl.

Halton bows deeply. He picks up the sword I dropped and sheaths it as well as his own before leaving the training grounds in silence.

Kayd's eyes follow him until he's gone, then cut to me. "Walk with me, mortal."

27

I DON'T SPEAK. NEITHER does he. The only sound between us is the crunch of gravel underneath our boots as we leisurely stroll across the palace grounds. My eyes drift to the side and watch him carefully. His chin is high, and his shoulders are back, with the regal coat he's donning stretching across them, pulling the seams taut.

"Do you enjoy it here, mortal?" Kayd's eyes gleam as he looks around his kingdom. I can tell he loves it. His pride is clear.

Before I can answer, an older elf with a lavish magenta gown and black hair cascading down her back approaches. A human servant carrying a basket of flowers is on her heels.

"Good morning, Prince Kayd." The female's voice is as soft as butter as she passes us.

Kayd greets her kindly. "Good morning to you, too." His lips turn upward, creating a smile. It's weird seeing something other than a scowl paint his features.

"Good morning, Prince Kayd," the servant squeaks out.

His scowl returns as he turns his head away from the human without a word and continues walking. I watch her shoulders slump as she walks away.

What an ass.

200

Clenching my fists tighter and taking a deep breath, I speed up my steps to catch up with the elven prince.

"Well?" The prince raises his scarred eyebrow.

"Well, what?" I keep my head forward. My eyes roam the open area and snag on a group of elves lounging across a round blanket and watching the sunrise near the edge of the forest.

"Do you enjoy it here in Nythfaedell?"

"It's beautiful here—"

"That doesn't answer my question." He stops walking and turns to me. He looks down his nose, his gaze expectant.

I suck in a breath, and without regret, I answer, "No. This is not my kingdom." The prince's jaw juts out as he contemplates what I'm saying. Nythfaedell is ethereal. It's nice training in the open air instead of the training rooms of Phandolus. It's a relief not being near Andrina, although Kayd isn't much better. But here, in the elven kingdom, I'm without Jerik. "Like I said, it's lovely. Truly the most beautiful out of all the kingdoms . . . and as you know, I've been to them all. But I was not chosen to serve here."

Kayd's jaw tenses. "Yes. Well, you may not have been chosen to serve Nythfaedell initially, but this *is* your kingdom now. You *will* serve it." His nostrils flare slightly. I can see the restraint he's trying to grip onto, like it's slipping through his fingers as each second passes by. "And you will begin now. I have an assignment for you."

That familiar rush of thrilling adrenaline and power courses through my nerves. *Finally.* An assignment. "Great!" The pitch of my voice is slightly higher than normal as I try to rein in my reaction. "Where am I going?"

His face breaks in a wide grin, and he begins laughing, louder and harder than anything I've ever heard from him. The group of elves in the distance glance over at us with quizzical looks pasted onto their faces. With a deep breath in, he calms down just enough to speak. "Oh. Oh no." A small chuckle slips through his quivering brown lips. "You're not leaving this palace. At least not yet. I don't trust you, mortal."

My brows pull together, meeting in the middle, in question. "Okay . . ." I drag out. "So, you want someone in the palace dead?"

Kayd chortles. "There are plenty of people I want dead in this palace, but, no, not this time. You will not be killing anyone on this assignment."

"You *really* must not understand what an assassin does, *Prince*."

The elf takes a menacingly close step in my direction. His hot breath against my face makes me want to recoil, but I don't. The vein in his neck pulses, and his upper lip begins to pull up in a snarl.

He leans closer. "Careful, *mortal*. I would love to rip your entrails out with my bare hands and leave you bleeding out on the grass before your measly heart gives out. But, alas, I have a purpose for you. At least for now." He steps away, and his smile is back with a sinister bite, as if he's imagining when he can bring that threat to fruition.

He begins walking again. I follow, only a step behind.

"You'll be attending my next revel. Dance. Drink. Have a good time. This assignment is vital for the success of your first assassination for the elven kingdom. I need you to be seen with my court, become a part of it. I need people to think that you belong."

My step falters just enough for Prince Kayd to glance over his shoulder and raise his eyebrow. He wants me to . . . party. For an assignment. He must truly be delusional if he thinks I'm going to be doing that. That's not what I do. Revels and pleasantries are not what I'm trained to do.

"I would rather rip out my eyes with my own nails than pretend I'm enjoying the company of the likes of you," I snarl, stopping my steps and crossing my arms over my chest.

"This is not up for negotiation. We came to an agreement. You serve me. I protect your helpless father from the changelings." A pause. He runs those long fingers through his silky strands of hair. "The revel is tonight. If you don't show up, I let Princess Andrina have her way with that sad, old man. Do. You. Understand?"

I refuse to answer. I refuse to speak or move or breathe. He takes my silence as an answer, anyway.

"Good. I expect you to dress appropriately." He slowly takes in my dirtied linen pants and top with a critical sneer. "And be on your best behavior, mortal. I have eyes everywhere. If you so much as think to end the life of one of my courtiers, I will know. And I will kill you."

With that, Prince Kayd walks away from me.

"Why do you really want me to serve you?" I call out to him.

With a brief glance over his shoulder, he says with a grin, "Why not?" Then he leaves the gravel path and strides across the grass. His long, auburn hair blows in the wind, wafting traces of citrus and sandalwood toward me.

Only the elven prince of Nythfaedell can turn the sweetest smells rancid.

28

I CAN'T HELP BUT flinch away from the chambermaid behind me. She's gliding a jewel-encrusted comb through my hair. Each bristle pulls on the knots that formed in the wind on my afternoon walk to the Crystal Lake Garden. My eyes twist shut tightly. I bite down on my inner cheek, trying to keep quiet. I can't handle another apology from the timid girl.

She begins separating my hair into thin strands and curling them around a hot metal rod that was sitting in the hearth. The sensation is strange. A part of me yearns to move away from the scolding instrument. Another part wishes to feel its surface against my scalp. The unbearable pain would be a welcome distraction from the anxious tingle gliding under my skin. I don't want to go to this revel. I don't think I can.

The door to the sitting area bursts open, and my head snaps to the side. I hiss as the hot curling rod grazes over the tip of my ear. The pain is the distraction I hoped it would be. My nerves dissipate for the moment, and before the chambermaid can start apologizing, I meet her eyes in the mirror and smile.

"It's fine," I say softly. Her shoulders sag in relief as I turn toward the door.

Another chambermaid watching the two of us and holding a garment bag stands still at the threshold. She's out of breath, and her braided hair is beginning to fall, with red strands framing her round face.

"My apologies for startling you, Miss Maeve—"

My head shakes at the unnecessary title. "Please, just Maeve."

Her eyes widen, like she's unsure of what to do, like no one has had the decency to talk to her like a person before this.

A moment passes, and she gathers her composure. "Thank you, Miss—thank you, Maeve. I appreciate your kindness. The dress His Highness picked out for you has arrived. When you are ready, I will assist you in putting it on if you wish."

She begins revealing a beautiful, soft, deep green fabric from the gold-and-black bag, then hangs it up atop the partially opened door into my bathroom. She steps back and waits for her turn to help get me ready. It really is a beautiful gown. From the way it hangs, it looks lightweight with a corseted bodice. But I scowl, nonetheless. A gift from the prince that I wish not to accept. His false generosity grates under my skin.

The chambermaid runs her fingers through my curls, breaking them apart and fashioning each strand into the perfect position. She steps away from me with a brilliant smile. Pride swells through her entire being.

"Thank you so much. It's beautiful." I'm being sincere. My hair has never looked so elegant. Her eyes glint in the soft light as she bows before me.

The other chambermaid steps forward, offering her assistance. While I normally don't utilize them for getting dressed, I glance at the gown hanging before me now, the straps and clasps and buttons taunting me like a timid, little girl who has never had to dress herself before.

Gracefully, she comes to my rescue, stepping toward the gown and removing it from its hanger. A grateful smile graces my lips as she begins setting the gown on the floor for me to step into.

Once the last snap is secure, I walk toward the mirror in my bathroom. Both chambermaids give me space to admire myself. One steps away to gather the cooling curling rod, and the other prepares a pile of small golden jewels to attach to the curled strands framing my face.

Standing before me is a woman I've never seen before. The gown's corseted bodice pushes my breasts up in a way that's almost comical. Jewels outlining each crevice of the corset will undoubtedly draw the eyes of the patrons attending the party. Loose, sheer, long sleeves cascade off my shoulders and gather tightly at my wrists. The skirts are simple compared to the rest of the gown. For that, I'm thankful.

I despise the gown, but as I run my fingers through its silky material, I can't help but love it all the same.

"Tonight . . ." I whisper to myself, staring into my reflection. I don't say the rest out loud, not wanting the chambermaids to hear.

Tonight, you need to impress Kayd's court. I know you don't want to, but you will do this. For Ottilie. For Mother. Tonight, you will make your mark on some of the most powerful and cruel creatures in Galfei Thalor. Tonight, you will show them just how sly the Shackled Serpent can be.

Laughter and peculiar upbeat music flitters through the halls outside of the small ballroom deep in the center of the palace. As I approach the double doors, the sounds swell. Sweet scents of lavender and cinnamon swirl around me. My movements halt at the threshold as my gaze sweeps over the room.

The luxury displayed in this single room is astonishing. The amount of golden-covered ornaments and large paintings could cover the cost to refurbish Terakeld in its entirety. My skin crawls at the thought of the elves—all the kingdoms—hoarding this much wealth.

There are less elves in attendance than I expected—only about thirty or so, not including the prince's personal guard—but I assume a prince's court is much smaller than that of a king's.

Elves in grand chiffon gowns and suede suits are lounging across velvet green chaises. Some are gathered around tables of food, drinking goblets of wine, while others are dancing across the small open space in the middle of the room. A small quartet of musicians are settled into the far corner, and a small throne for Prince Kayd is placed on the opposite end, where he's greeting his courtiers with merry smiles.

One step across the threshold and into the ballroom, the doors close behind me. The joyous chatter and music come to a halt. All eyes shift to me. Elves gawk, sneering under their breaths, while disgust twists their features. Many of Prince Kayd's guards line the walls. I recognize the young elf I'd beaten during my first spar. I see the larger raven-black haired guard who beat me right after as well. Although at attention, I can see they're weary of me—the Shackled Serpent—being here.

Standing there alone—clad in a dress I wish I wasn't wearing—I briefly feel as if I'm a minnow in a piranha's territory. That predator inside of me—trained to kill by those she wishes to end—refuses to believe that, refuses to allow the rest of me to believe that. The seconds tick by. A few deep breaths later, my confidence returns.

No. I am *not* the minnow. *I* am the piranha. *I* am the hunter.

My chin raises a fraction higher, and I make my way into the revel.

Prince Kayd approaches and meets me in the center of the room. He's wearing a cream coat with green-and-gold embroidery along its lapels. His pants are a warm brown color that nearly match his glowing skin. Glitter has been dabbed along his cheekbones, and his gold crown and jewelry glint underneath the lit chandelier.

Behind him, Halton stands at attention. An obedient shadow. His guard uniform is gone, and in its place is a casual black tunic with its sleeves rolled up to his elbows and crisp black pants. No jewelry or glitter adorn him, and his hair is mused slightly, as if someone had been running their fingers through the brown locks.

"Serpent." Halton's jaw clicks and tightens as the mumbled word flits between the three of us. His hard eyes are unmoving as he stares at me, refusing to budge an inch, as if he's afraid of what he might see if he looks anywhere other than my coal-lined eyes.

"Guard." I tilt my head to the side.

"I'm happy to see you got my gift," Kayd murmurs as his slender hand stretches out toward me in a graceful swoop, as if it's not the same hand that tortured me for days.

I push down the urge to recoil away from him. Instead, I force my hand out and grasp it, wishing I chose to wear the wrist-length gloves one of the chambermaids had offered me to act as a barrier between his skin and mine.

The prince turns around to face the staring elves, the hand not holding mine stretching out wide. "I know what you're thinking. What is a mortal doing in our court? It's despicable. She doesn't belong. She's tainting the night. She's better off groveling before us. But . . . she is very useful to me, so I expect you to accept her presence. She is one of you now. Understood?"

I look around the ballroom. Few are nodding their heads, accepting that I belong without so much of a fuss. Several continue to stare at their prince and me. I can see the skepticism twining around their thoughts and the disgust they're trying to hide. A handful openly glower at me before turning away, pretending I'm not even here.

"Now, mortal, let's introduce you to my court." Kayd begins to lead me over toward a group of elves picking through platters of fruits and nuts.

The captain takes a step forward to follow us, but Kayd interrupts his movements by waving a flimsy hand over his shoulder. "No need, Halton. Go. Have fun." The elven prince's eyes sweep over a few females who are swooning at the sight of the guard. With a sly wink, Kayd whisks me away.

No longer do I feel like a person. Now, I'm a prized possession as the prince parades me around the room, introducing me to elves I can tell want nothing to do with the mortal who's infiltrated their court.

Kayd never mentions who I am or the reason I'm here. A male behind me whispers to two others and questions whether I'm bedding their prince. Their snickers dance down my neck as they conclude that he would never stoop so low.

What I would give to be in my chambers right now, away from these elves, and enjoying a warm cup of tea from Madam Prea. I wouldn't have to stretch my lips into a fake smile until my cheeks ache. I wouldn't have to pretend that I do not hate these beings. I could be me, no matter how alone I felt.

After the seemingly endless polite pleasantries and promenading, two breathtaking elves with mischievous smiles as wide as their heads greet the prince and me. Kayd rolls his eyes playfully as soon as he spots their lanky forms sauntering toward us.

The similarities between the two are uncanny. It takes me a moment to realize they must be siblings. Both have beautiful light-brown skin that glistens, as if they rolled around in shimmering powder. Their black hair is silky smooth. The male's is short and wavy, whereas the female's silky and straight strands are tied up into a low bun.

As they get closer, I can see the freckles covering their sharp, angular faces, and flashing under the revel's lights are gold jewelry attached to their noses. I've never seen such facial decor. The female's golden hoop resembles a flower and is connected in the middle of her nostrils. The male's jewelry—unlike his sister's—is simple, a plain, thin hoop on the right side of his nose.

"So," the male jests as he takes me in, "this is the mortal that has everyone talking." The smile he sends in my direction is the type that would make anyone dramatically place a hand on their chest and swoon.

"Maeve, meet Niam and Alta Myradove," Prince Kayd remarks. His hands gesture out toward the two. "The first set of elven twins in two hundred thirty rotations and the two biggest pains in my ass." The male—Niam—shoots a smoldering glare at the prince, who chuckles. Actually chuckles.

Before I can utter a word, Alta—clad in a beautiful, golden-yellow gown with a low neckline and a sheer cape attached at her shoulders—swats Kayd's arm, then leans in. She's much stronger than she looks. Her arms squeeze around my body as she pulls me tightly to her chest. She's *hugging* me.

My joints lock up. My arms are pinned to my side, trapped beneath her grip, and my spine is rigid, so much so that an ache forms down the length of my back.

Niam barks out a loud and boisterous laugh when he meets my wide, uncertain eyes. Alta, however, doesn't notice. She pulls away from me, holding me out at an arm's length, and takes me in. I'm used to the languid criticizing leer from others, but Alta's eyes are kind. Radiant tenderness shines behind her gray irises. Weariness immediately prods my mind.

"It is so nice to finally meet you, Maeve. I hope your stay in our home has been accommodating."

I can't stop the incredulous laugh that huffs through my light-pink-tinted lips. Her kind eyes falter for a moment before the crease of her brow furrows in confusion.

The words breach my lips before I can even think to stop them. "If being tortured and tied up for days counts as accommodating, I feel like the guest of honor." I have enough mind to shut my mouth as soon as I finish. I shouldn't have said that. The questions that must be racing around their heads.

The twins blanch at Kayd, who rolls his eyes dramatically, then mumbles about how I tried to kill him.

This time, it's me who blanches at him. My widened eyes stare at the prince, as if he didn't just reveal a part of me he doesn't want the other courtiers to know.

"We want to kill you every day, Kayd." Niam crosses his arms over his chest and gives the foul prince a look full of jest and admiration. "Plus, I wouldn't have expected anything less."

"What—"

"Oh," Niam smirks. "We know who you are."

Alta's head bobs in agreement.

"But I . . ." My words trail off as I look at Prince Kayd once more. He shrugs and takes a plentiful gulp of wine.

"I guess it's best you know who knows." Another gulp, the wine staining his lips. "Niam and Alta, Halton, of course, and my personal guard."

"Speaking of Halton, where is he?" Alta brushes away a strand of hair that's fallen out of her bun.

With a nonchalant shrug of his shoulders, he points behind him, saying, "He's preoccupied."

Alta cranes her neck around me to see. I turn, following her gaze. Lounging on a chaise settled against a wall adorned in gold-and-white wallpaper, a beautiful, copper-haired elf drapes herself over the captain. Her white teeth nip at his neck, her pink tongue dragging over each little bite.

My chest strains like something inside is tugging harshly against it, a taut coil looking to snap. I've never felt anything like it. Not even the thrumming beneath my skin when I'm on an assignment can compare. It's unnerving. It's alarming. Whatever it is, I don't like it.

Even as the others avert their gazes and continue their conversation as if this were a common occurrence, my eyes stay trained on the guard and the stunning female. A breath passes, and I see the muscles beneath his tunic tense before his sensual eyes snap to mine. As that strained sensation becomes even more palpable, I suck in a violent rush of air until my lungs are so full it's painful. His unreadable eyes glint, and a smirk forms as his tongue peeks between his teeth, running slowly along his wine-stained bottom lip.

Scoffing, I roll my eyes and whirl around to face the three elves chatting about something I have no interest in. Alta and Kayd pay no attention to me and the flush that runs along my neck. Niam, however, narrows his eyes as he takes me in.

What is he staring at?

My eyebrow arches, and my eyes harden. His amused smile and quivering bottom lip tells me I'm not as good at hiding my emotions as I once thought.

The elf's lanky hand elegantly extends toward me. "Would you like to dance, Maeve?" Niam's cadence still holds that teasing charm, but there is kindness there. The same kindness I saw from Alta. It makes my gut twist.

Prince Kayd stiffens next to me, his body becoming stick straight and still. I can feel the protest forming on his lips. Before he can interject, I grasp Niam's hand, wanting to get away from the prince. "Lead the way."

As Niam leads me onto the open dance floor, I sneak a glance back at Kayd. Alta is guiding him away toward the table of wines and meads and rubbing soft circles on his back.

Gentle plucks of a violin—the starting notes of another song—pull me back to the elf gripping my hand. He turns me around and bows deeply. I see the female elves around me lowering their heads and curtseying toward their partners. I follow suit, faux confidence guarding myself from the snickers of those eyeing me.

I'm no courtier. I know that, and so do they. I cut my eyes toward a group of elves shielding their mouths with their gloved hands and whispering mocking insults. Sharp as daggers and deadly to their supercilious esteem, the look is enough to silence them, even without them knowing I'm Galfei Thalor's deadly assassin. One's face pales immediately. Another swallows around nothing.

A soft rumble dances around me. Niam's laughing. I can't help but decide it's a nice sound. His arm snakes around my waist, and his other hand wraps around my fingers as he sweeps me away into an elegant dance I don't know. Thankfully, his strong and confident steps conceal what would have been the painful embarrassment of clumsy missteps on stumbling feet.

As he twirls me around the dance floor like a princess I never wanted to be, I take the opportunity of our proximity to look at him. *Really* look at him. His angular eyes are gray, just like his sister's, but they're darker, like storm clouds rolling in before the sky opens. His brown freckles kiss nearly every inch of his face and run down his neck, unlike Alta's, whose merely dust her nose. His features are all sharp edges and masculine slopes, and yet they radiate a comfortable warmth.

"You're beautiful." A flirtatious, sideways grin tugs at the corner of his lips. "Halton doesn't know what he's missing." At that, I purposefully stomp on his foot, then feign a fake smile. He laughs again.

There's something about Niam that's just *easy*. The effortless way he holds himself, like he doesn't have a care in the world. The simple smile that graces his lips as he moves across the dance floor without missing a step. The undemanding kindness he harbors toward me—someone who kills his people.

That kindness . . . I don't trust it.

Somehow, Niam can see right through me. His hand squeezes mine, trying to slow my racing thoughts. I don't like it.

"Relax, Maeve." His breath brushes the curve of my ear before he twirls me.

A few more steps, then another spin, and I begin feeling my tight muscles loosen in his presence despite my mind's protest.

"Oh, good. You're warming up to me." Niam wiggles his eyebrows.

"And what makes you think that?" I say in a deadpan tone.

"Your hands aren't as clammy."

A loud laugh escapes through the barrier of my lips. It's a genuine laugh. A laugh that throws me off-kilter, shocks me to the core.

He continues with a chuckle. "How you humans live like that—*with clammy hands*—I will never know."

My booming laughter dies down into a joyous giggle. Niam's smile radiates around me, and he leads me through a group of courtiers dancing, breaking them apart from each other and sending them a wink. I can't help but chuckle again, regardless of the trepidation I feel at his true motives.

Heat—potent and piercing—slams into my back and runs down my spine. Somehow, I know it's him. Halton staring us down as we dance. However, when Niam twirls me around again to the crescendo of music, that heat disappears, and I can see how preoccupied he is with the redhead. I would have chalked it up to my imagination if not for that heat beginning again. Hotter this time.

Three more spins from Niam. As soon as I get my bearings after he pulls me back into his chest, I notice the deadly glare the prince is shooting our way from over Niam's shoulder. Toward me, mostly. My brow raises in question, and I can practically hear the snarl he releases by the noticeable quiver in his top lip.

"So"—the handsome elf in my arms draws my attention back toward him with a whisper—"the Shackled Serpent. It must have been quite the shock when you were assigned to become a killer." The quiet casualness of his tone feels like a slap to the face. My steps falter, but he conceals it with a flick of his foot and a low dip. The tips of my curled hair touch the floor before he sweeps me back up. "Is it strange being here with us, enjoying the night, and not having to end the life of one of us?"

"Who says I'm not on an assignment right now?" I ask innocently.

Niam immediately stiffens in my arms. "Are you?" His words are clipped, as if they're stuck in his throat, straining to break free.

My laugh rings across the shining, golden chandelier and bounces off the vases full of breathtaking greenery. "No, I'm not. But soon, I will be."

The warm sigh of relief he releases brushes against my shoulder. Gooseflesh erupts in its wake. He smiles back and spins me once more.

Three dances later, Niam comes to a halt, steps away from me, and bows. My chest heaves as I smile at him, unbidden and breathless. Never have I danced so much in my life. My only experience is under the stars of the meadow when Ottilie and I would sneak into the outdoor parties that roughened adults would throw after long days in the fields. We'd dance to the tunes of makeshift lutes and lyres far enough away so they wouldn't see us.

One of Niam's hands remains in mine. He squeezes it as he straightens his body back into an upright position, then he leans in and kisses my cheek. "Maeve, it has been a pleasure." He saunters off into the crowd, leaving me alone on the dance floor.

Don't allow his kind facade to trick you, I silently chide myself as I feel my smile begin to dip into a frown.

Without a thought, my feet guide me away before the next dance begins. Weaving my way through revelers near a table of desserts, a hand grabs onto my arm. The grip is fierce. The pain from short nails digging into my skin causes my muscles to snap back into rigid tension. The hand pivots me around, and I'm left facing a seething Prince of Nythfaedell. No words grace his snarling lips. His eyes burn with a ferocity that makes me bite my tongue.

My feet shuffle against the ground, trying to keep up with the brisk gait of the prince as he drags me out of the ballroom. His unrelenting grip doesn't leave my arm while he weaves us through the palace halls. I don't understand why he's so angry. I did exactly as he asked, carving out a place for myself in his court.

"What is wrong with you?" I grunt.

He doesn't reply, but I can see the way his muscles tighten in his jaw, like he's grinding his molars harshly together.

By the time we arrive at my chambers, I'm demanding he let go of me, making a scene for the few chambermaids who wander the palace halls to hear. He remains deathly quiet, even as he slams the door to my chambers shut, and storms away.

29

I TWIRL AROUND, NEARLY tripping over my feet, as if my body can't control itself. Whiffs of lavender and cinnamon flit around me, and the taste of wine is sweet on my tongue.

I'm back in the small ballroom, back at the revel I could have sworn I was forced to leave. The weight of another's hand is pressed firmly against my lower back as they spin me across the crammed dance floor. Blurs of revelers swirl by.

Niam's boisterous laugh echoes around the ballroom, followed by Alta's sweet giggle. I can't see them. I'm spinning too fast. The room is spinning too fast.

Who am I dancing with?

The twins' voices mix like two distorted ribbons dancing in the air. "We're happy you're here with us, Maeve."

The words echo around the room and reverberate against my skull. I want to believe them. But deep down, a sliver of caution worms its way into my heart.

The music that was once gliding across the glittering, golden room like silk turns shrill and out of tune. Violent plucks of violin strings and sharp blows of a horn make me flinch before the room dramatically darkens. Shadows slither across the walls, and the revelers vanish completely, as if they were never there, leaving no trace behind.

"Well, well, well . . . what do we have here?" A rough voice sends a shiver down my spine. It's filled with a comfort I've been longing for, yet there is something there, something different and stiff.

Turning to my right, I meet his brown eyes. Jerik stands before me. He's here—actually here—in Nythfaedell. My heart swells, and I rush toward him, arms stretched outward, longing to be wrapped around him in a cocoon of safety.

Instead of a warm, welcoming embrace, I'm met with his hard, unrelenting hand. I'm pushed to the side, losing my balance and stumbling to the ground. When I look up at him, what I see sends an icy chill down into my gut. Jerik's eyes are filled with hatred—hatred directed at me.

"Look how pathetic you are. Playing pet with the ones who cause us so much pain . . . our enemy!" He bellows out the words. My body flinches away. His voice strains with rage. "You disgust me. Your mother . . . *Ottilie* would be ashamed of you."

I feel as if a bucket of ice water drenches my very bones. The room spins even faster, making me feel ill. My eyes shudder closed as I claw at the shifting ground beneath me. Searing, hot tears leak through my lashes and run down my cheeks, but when I go to wipe them away, it's as dry as the dusty alleyways in Terakeld during the summer.

It's getting hard to breathe. Each inhale is fast, ragged. In and out. In and out. My lungs constrict. Panic overcomes me. I can't breathe.

Jerik . . . Jerik hates me. He hates—

A wave of pleasure crashes into me. My sharp, constricted breaths transform into sighs—long and lazy and sparked by an insistent buzz washing over me.

Jerik and his cruel words flutter away, disappearing on a gust of wind. No longer do I feel the hard ground underneath me. I feel velvet. My eyes flutter open, languid and dazed. Everything's a blur, but I can tell I'm now sitting on a chaise at the far end of the ballroom.

"You like that, Serpent?" Another voice—just as rough, if not a little bit breathier than Jerik's—caresses my earlobe.

The shadows that twisted sinisterly along the walls are no longer there. Now, everything has an ethereal gleam to it. Flickering candles are soft and slightly out of focus as sparkles dance around the corners of my vision.

Long beige fingers graze over my thighs. Higher and higher, they travel. Nervous jitters jumble in my stomach, and a longing ache sits heavily below that. I mewl at the sensation. Teeth dig into my neck, where my pulse frantically beats. "What other sounds can I extract from that pretty little mouth of yours?"

Warmth replaces the teeth—a tongue, I realize, soothing the bite mark. A breathy gasp I try to hold in escapes. I can feel a smirk forming against my heated skin. Another bite. Another lick. Then a gentle kiss.

Before those fingers apply pressure on where that pulsing ache is strongest between my legs, the excruciatingly soft touch disappears. And as if they belonged to another, those fingers return in a firm and feral grip upon my chin. Twisting my head to the side, I see who they belong to. *Halton.*

His pupils are dilated, his lips are wet, swollen, and red from the attention he's been giving me. He looks as if he is about to come utterly undone. Like I could ask him to do anything at that moment, and he would be at my disposal. The sight shoots a sharp pulse through my veins.

Those fingers begin to trace my jaw until they're wrapped around the nape of my neck, tangling into my hair. The guard leans in, so torturously slow. My eyes flutter closed and—

"Miss Maeve!" A soft voice along with several knocks against my bedroom door pulls me from my dream.

I blink.

Sweat covers my brow. My room—normally so open and inviting—is stifling. Inhaling deeply, I remove myself from my warm, slightly damp bed and open the door that leads to my sitting area. I'm met with a chambermaid with bright eyes, ready for the day.

"Good morning, Miss Maeve. I have a letter from Sir Halton." She extends her nimble arm toward me, and with a quiet "thank you," I grab it and close the door as she turns away. With shaking hands, I unfold the parchment and read.

Training is canceled. Halton is probably still feeling the effects of last night's wine. Or he's wanting more time with the redheaded beauty he spent his night with. That sudden, sharp feeling from last night springs into my chest, but it's quickly diminished by a cold rush of relief. I don't think I can face him after conjuring up his phantom touch in my sleep.

What happened in my dreams last night . . . I don't even want to think about what caused my dream to shift like that.

In my slumber, all I had known was the burning feeling of his lips, his calloused fingers scraping against my inner thigh's soft flesh, and how badly I wanted to feel them elsewhere . . .

No.

Sleep. I need more sleep. It'll be good for me, for my muddled thoughts. I lie back down and nestle under the silk and furs. My body tosses and turns. I can still feel his faux, featherlight graze across my skin.

Close. He was so close.

I squeeze my eyes shut, and with that, I do the same with my thighs. Pulling the furs over my head, I fitfully fall back asleep.

30

I^{T'S BRIGHT BEHIND MY} eyelids. Too bright. Pulling the bedding over my head, I bury myself beneath its warmth.

"Just a few more minutes," I murmur, smacking my lips together and sighing deeply.

A soft knock thuds against the door to my chambers.

With a huff, I pry my heavy eyes open. Still under the silks, I lie in the faux darkness for a moment until another timid knock sounds.

"Maeve?" a faint voice calls out through the doors. The euphonic lilt of it brings back memories of dancing and drinking and laughing last night. I immediately recognize it as Alta's.

Peeking my head out of the covers and blinking my eyes until my vision sharpens, I can tell it's still early. Midmorning, perhaps. Might as well get up. I rise from my bed and pull on a fresh tunic and leather pants before slipping on some boots and venturing out into the sitting area just outside my room.

"Maeve? Are you up?" Alta calls out again, and she knocks once more.

Opening the door, I'm met with a bright smile wrapped in burgundy lips. It's soft, the same smile as last night. I'm immediately on edge.

The elf lets herself into my chambers and falls gracefully onto the chaise before the hearth. Her body shifts against the cushions, writhing around, until she finds the perfect position. Once she's content, she stills and looks up at me with eyes full of mischief.

"I figured you'd be free," Alta's words come out rushed, like it's difficult for her to hold in her obvious excitement.

"And why is that?"

"I saw Halton lounging in Kayd's chambers. I take it training was a no-go this morning after the revel last night. The wine must have rendered him useless." I roll my eyes in response. Her chuckle warms the area around us. "Since you have the day off, would you like to do something?"

I start. I can't say I was expecting that. Something inside me tells me to decline. Why would she want to spend the day with me? Why would I want to spend my day with her? I'm in Nythfaedell to do my job—nothing more, nothing less.

"Please . . ." she whines and tuts her bottom lip out.

A few moments of silence pass, then a soft sigh. "Fine—"

Her squeals of delight pierce the air, ringing in my ears.

A local market I didn't even know was on the outskirts of the palace grounds is bustling with vendors and shoppers alike. Bright-colored tents catch my eye. Carts are full of food, jewelry, and textiles. An elven merchant stationed at one stall is surrounded by children with pointed ears. He spins a stick in what looks like pastel floss until it's covered in fluffy blue-and-pink edible clouds.

"It's practically sugar." Alta leans in toward me as we pass the cheering children. "Do you want one?"

Shaking my head, I respond, "Oh, no, I'm okay."

Alta giggles and begins leading me farther into the market. "It's not that good, anyway."

Music flutters through the tents, and merchants call out to anyone walking by. It's a lively place. I can picture Ottilie bouncing from cart to cart, buying trinkets, and bartering with the cheese merchant. Ottilie would have loved it here in Nythfaedell.

A gentle brush across my wrist replies in confirmation.

As we venture to different stalls, I can't help but notice how kind Alta is to everyone. She seems to know almost all the merchants, and she takes the time to meet those she isn't familiar with. Elves in threadbare pants and tunics approach her just the same as those in luscious suits and gowns. I can tell she loves her people, and they love her.

"I apologize for not introducing myself sooner, Maeve." Alta brushes her fingers along a copper hand mirror placed at the edge of a stall. "I was on the road . . . visiting someone."

I don't understand why she's apologizing. It wouldn't have mattered if she introduced herself earlier or never at all. She's a friend of Kayd, a courtier. I'm an assassin, ready to obey orders.

Glancing away from Alta, I note a handful of elves among a crowd of kind smiles slow their gaits as they notice me. Their brows furrow, and their lips tug tightly. It looks like they're wondering why I'm here. I can't help but wonder the same.

"It's all right," I mumble. "Really."

"No, it's not. If I were here, I would have slapped Kayd for how he treated you." Her brows furrow together before quickly smoothing out. She strolls toward a stand that's selling prepackaged snacks.

Sending Alta a polite smile that doesn't reach my eyes, I follow. I can't help but wonder when the truth will come out—that the warmth and kindness she aims at me is all an act. I'm just waiting for the inevitable punchline.

With a friendly grin, Alta hands over a small pile of golden coins to the merchant and picks out a cream cloth sack holding crackers, meats, and a few different varieties of nuts. She stuffs the goods in a small knapsack that hangs from her hip and turns to me expectantly.

"Okay, now the real fun begins. Maeve, I'm going to show you my favorite place in all of Galfei Thalor." Grabbing my hand, she begins skipping through the market into the forest beyond.

I want to resist. I want to dig my heels into the dirt and refuse to go anywhere with this elf I barely know. This must be a trap, a way to lure me away from the others. A way to show her true colors behind the kindness I don't trust. But my body trails along, obediently following Alta, as if it can't hear my racing thoughts.

Fifteen minutes of navigating the thick, looming forests of Nythfaedell, we arrive at a clearing. Beyond that is a winsome spring tucked away in a secluded nook between the trees. Several clusters of boulders and smaller rocks line sections of the sparkling, clear water. A small waterfall rushing down a larger boulder cascades into the spring's body. The leaves on the trees seem to shimmer in the streams of sunshine.

"Gods . . ." The word slips past my parted lips, awe weaving itself into my breath. My lungs fill up with the fresh forest air, earthy birchwood, and that ethereal scent that only the elves can conjure up. Magick.

I glance at Alta to find that she's already staring at me. Small wrinkles form at the corners of her pointed eyes, her perfect teeth gleaming as her smile grows even bigger.

"Welcome to the Secret Spring!" Her arms extend out wide, showing off the beautiful sight.

"The Secret Spring? So, only you know about it?"

"Well, no. Not really. I'm sure others come here from time to time, but that's what Niam and I have been calling it since we were young. Our mother used to take us here on special occasions. Our village, Lokaep, is just west of here." Her finger points in the direction of what must be her childhood home.

My eyebrows shoot up in question. "You didn't grow up in the palace? From my time in Phandolus, I figured all courtiers do."

Alta's laugh is carefree, but there's a hint of heaviness to it. "No, no . . ." Her voice trails off, and her always-bright smile falters slightly. "We lived with our mother in a quaint, little treehouse. From what I remember, we struggled, *she* struggled. Ma always wanted more for us. She'd say we were destined for greatness. *Elven twins.* She did everything she could to give us a better life . . . and that included forfeiting her parental responsibility and giving us to the crown when we were only ten."

Alta hesitates for only a split second. There's relief twining around the sadness in her eyes. She needs to talk, needs to let it out. My gut sinks as I stare at her, opening herself up to a mortal with blood on her hands. It's then I realize that the kindness I've been so uneasy about . . . it's real, genuine. I feel like I don't deserve it.

"I don't blame her, though. In doing so, Niam and I had the best upbringing offered in our lands. Tutors, tailors, everything you would expect from living in a palace. King and Queen Glynvyre took us in like we were their own. I met my best friends, Kayd and Halton. My childhood was spectacular." A long sigh weighed down by grief.

I remain silent, giving her the time and space to reveal her truth.

"But life without a mother isn't a life anyone should live. Niam and I showed Kayd and Halton the spring just so we could feel closer to her. The longing I felt for Ma was so intense, I decided to finally visit. That's where I was when you were captured. Niam doesn't know I went, but I felt called to see her. I needed to know she was okay without us.

"When I arrived, I found out she died two rotations ago. I just"—the elf's eyes gloss over with unshed tears, glistening in the day's sun—"sat there, weeping on the floor of my old home. She sacrificed everything for us, and I wasn't there when her soul left our world. So, I come here with my new family, carving out pleasant memories in her honor."

Her hand quickly brushes her cheek, stopping an escaped tear from falling farther. A forced laugh and a shake of her head. "My stars, here I am, bringing the mood down. Let's swim—"

"My mother died, too," I blurt out. Alta's eyes grow large. She trusted me with her past, and I can't help but feel compelled to trust her with as much as I'm willing. I can't seem to utter how she died, the words sticking to my tongue, but I can give her something. "She was all things good and pure. Brave. Selfless. Someone who fought for what she believed in. Her name was Livinia, and she inspired many people, including myself. She was my whole world."

The corners of my mouth turn up slightly, forming a soft, understanding smile that doesn't quite reach my eyes. We are one and the same, Alta and I. Two motherless children, trying to find our way in this world. She smiles back and reaches for my hand. The soft squeeze mends something deep within me. What, I'm not sure. But I don't feel so lonely.

"C'mon." Alta gently tugs at my hands and guides us to the edge of the spring.

The surprisingly warm and refreshing water wraps around my limbs as I slowly descend into the natural pool. The surface distorts my figure beneath, shielding off my now near-naked body. Alta and I—stripped down into our underthings—swim freely alongside the gentle ripples.

Diving below, I'm met with an underwater paradise. Small, iridescent fish swim in schools. Cobalt plants sway with the current. Emerald-and-orange creatures with shells on their backs and snapping pinchers crawl along the crevices of stacked rocks, as if they're a miniature castle just for them. It's like a completely different world down here. A peaceful world.

My lungs burn, longing for air, yet I endure the pain. I welcome it. Because, down here, watching each critter and shell and plant move in harmony with the water, I feel free . . . The weight of all my assignments lifts for this moment alone. Only when blackness creeps into the edge of my vision do I push off the sandy spring floor, my head breaching the surface, and my lungs sucking in air once again.

Alta is in the middle of the spring, floating on her back and facing the sky. Her eyes are closed, and a sweet hum accompanies her peaceful smile. "What's Terakeld like?"

"Dirty. Dusty. Dismal." I smile to myself. "But it's home." Treading the water, I begin to make my way toward her.

Alta hums, then pauses before she asks, "Is it true that people get whipped there? For speaking their truths?"

"I—" My mouth closes as I stare at her. I didn't think anyone in the kingdoms knew about the whippings other than the guards stationed in Terakeld. "Do others know that happens?"

Alta's legs dip below the water, and she sits up, treading it. "Kayd told Niam, Halton, and me about it. So, we know. And King Osmar told him." Her voice is soft. Compassion laces each word.

Hearing this, a part of me wants to pull away from her, to not let her kindness get too close. With Madam Prea, it was easier. She reminds me of Mother. There was a pull there that didn't scare me. With Alta, it's unknown. Uncharted territory. How can she be so nice when she's friends with the prince who knows about the whippings and refuses to put an end to it? But deep down, I know I'll be fine if I just give her a chance.

"So, it's true." Alta bores into my eyes, like she can see the sadness in my soul. "I'm sorry."

Boisterous laughter cuts off any reply I may have said. My head whips around toward the direction of the sound. Three figures barge through the tree line. Niam, Prince Kayd, and Halton skid to a stop as soon as they see us.

"What's she doing here?" Kayd shoots a scowl in my direction, then crosses his arms over his chest as his gaze cuts to Alta. "She's not one of us."

"Kayd!" Alta chastises. She turns to me. "I'm so sorry."

"It's fine." I dip my hair back into the water, as if what he said doesn't hold any weight. In truth, it doesn't. "He can seethe and throw a princely tantrum all he wants. It won't change the fact that I'm here, and I don't plan on groveling for forgiveness."

Kayd looks as if steam is about to burst through his nostrils. Niam rolls his eyes at the prince and bounds for the spring, ripping off his clothes in a hurry.

As he jumps off a boulder into the warm water, he yells excitedly, "Maeve, welcome to the Secret Spring!" Breaching the water, his cheeks are puffed out, and he spits water in Alta's face. "You're more than welcome. Don't listen to our grouchy leader."

My giggle carries across the spring. After my day with Alta, I feel more comfortable around Niam now as well. No longer do I see his kindness as conniving. Now—as if my eyes are truly open—I see how sincere he is. Just like his sister.

Kayd scoffs, pulling my attention back to him and the guard who stays unmoving at his side. As the prince begins undressing himself with stiff movements, my eyes shift to Halton. His shoulders are set, and his jaw is clenched. The air between us is taut, heavy.

His unreadable eyes bore into me, almost looking spooked. I can say I feel the same. After my dream last night, I was hoping to go the entire day without running into the captain. My thighs press together under the waves as a tingle runs down my neck and up my legs. Phantom memories.

Niam and Alta's laughter breaks the trance he seems to be in. His upper lip curls slightly, and his eyes turn as cold as his touch. Without another glance in my direction, Halton walks over to where the other males left their clothes and begins undressing himself.

I force myself to look away, dunking my head under the soothing ripples of water. *Don't think about his lips. Don't think about his fingers.*

As I breach the water, drops drip off my lashes, some rolling behind my lash line and blurring my vision. I blink rapidly, the heel of my palms pushing into the sockets. Once clear, I catch my gaze drifting over to Halton. My teeth dig into the inside of my cheek as I slyly take in his broad shoulders and muscular chest. Every inch of him is flawless. No scars, no freckles, just smooth, beige skin and rigid muscles fit for the Gods mortals pray to. Gods who I'm sure don't exist if beings like him do. Before I can take another peek, he's completely submerged in the water.

I push the thoughts away with a shake of my head and swim toward the edge of the spring. As soon as I push my body up and out of the warm water, the cool autumn air chills me. Gooseflesh erupts across every inch of my exposed skin, and a shiver racks through my bones.

Sitting among mine and Alta's discarded clothes is the sack of snacks. Delicately opening it up, I stuff a handful of nuts in my mouth just as Niam swims over to me.

"Hey." He shakes out his dark hair, then smiles when he realizes he got me even more wet. "Where'd you go after our dances? I was looking for you when the party started winding down to say goodnight, but it was like you disappeared."

Another handful of nuts. "Ask your prince."

"Oh, stars," Niam mumbles. I can't help the chuckle that slips out. He turns toward the elven prince, who's on the opposite side of the spring. "Kayd, what did you do?"

The look he gives Niam doesn't hide his confusion. "What are you going on about?" Kayd asks, looking at Halton and Alta, who simply shrug their shoulders.

"Maeve says to ask you why she left the revel early."

If looks could kill, I'd be dead. The way Kayd's dagger-like eyes shoot toward me tells me, at this moment, he wishes he never let me walk out of the palace dungeon alive.

"Her assignment was over." He tilts his head and shrugs.

"What he means to say," I drawl, "is he dragged me back to my chambers and locked me in."

"I didn't lock you in, mortal." Kayd's forest-green eyes roll toward the sky, the sun making them seem lighter than normal, like green quartz. "If you really wanted, you could've snuck back into the revel and danced the night away with Niam."

"And spend the rest of my night in the same room as you?" I bark out a laugh. "No, thank you, Prince."

Alta laughs loudly. "I like you, Maeve. You're sassy. You'll fit in just fine."

"Fit in where?" Halton calls out just before diving into the spring. As he breaches the water, he says, "Hopefully, not with us."

My eyes narrow, and I throw the guard a vicious glare.

Hours pass. The sun begins to dip beyond the trees, the temperature dropping as it sinks. I'm lounging across a flat boulder near the edge of the water. My skin puckers under the cool autumn air, but it's nice, relaxing, even.

Alta and Halton are deep in conversation as they tread water on the other side. Kayd is seated with his feet dangling in the ripples near them. His eyes are closed, and his face is tilted toward the sky. And Niam is boisterous, something I'm learning is common for the elf. Diving into the spring from the highest boulders he can find, seeing how long he can hold his breath, and splashing those of us who don't wish to be splashed.

There's a twinge of envy that twists my gut as I watch him. He seems so carefree, so happy. Sure, his childhood was hard, from what Alta revealed earlier today, but he got out. He was able to have a better life after his mother sacrificed her claim on them.

There is no out for me. In ten rotations, I will be back in Terakeld, working in the fields and holding my tongue.

Niam's laugh floats into the air after dunking Halton under the water. My smile grows. As much as I wish I had a way to change the course of my life, I know I can't. But Niam and Alta . . . I'm happy for them. Surprisingly so. If any elves deserve that second chance, it's the two who have hearts, who somehow care for a mortal like me—dark and undeserving.

Perhaps others are the same. Perhaps not all elves are as vicious as the prince. Perhaps . . . *No.* That's dangerous thinking. Deadly thinking.

They are the exception, not the rule.

Kayd glances over at Niam. More than a few times now, I've caught the prince stealing glimpses of the elf. A large splash toward Alta causes a rare smile to grace the prince's lips before it's replaced with an emotion I can't determine. Something intense, something similar to the look he gave us last night at the revel, but this time . . . not so threatening.

Kayd catches me staring and flashes his teeth at me in a snarl, warding me off from the thoughts undoubtedly swirling around in his head. I merely raise an eyebrow in response before tilting my neck back and relishing in the feel of the crisp evening.

"Are you ready to head out, Maeve?" Turning my head to the side, I see Alta swimming toward me. "I'm starving and definitely don't want to spend my entire evening with this lot." Her thumb jabs behind her toward the three males, who are now making their way over. Niam shoves Halton to the side to get ahead. The guard barely moves, muscles rippling under his wet skin, and shoves him back.

Halton looks away from Niam and toward Alta and me. As his burning stare sears into me, my skin tightens around my bones. I don't think I can stand to be around him for a moment longer. "Yeah, let's get out of here."

My joints crack as I begin to stand. My arms stretch high above my head, and my torso twists. A low whistle prances out of Niam's lips. "I've said it before, and I'll say it again, Maeve. You. Are. Stunning." That flirtatious smile from the revel returns. I chuckle and playfully roll my eyes.

The muscles in Kayd's jaw flutter menacingly. Halton's lips press firmly together, creating a thin white line. His hand flexes at his side beneath the water.

Ringing out my hair and slipping on my clothes, I ignore both of their glares.

As Alta and I cross the spring and step back into the dense Nythfaedell forest, casual farewells are tossed behind our shoulders to the others. Only Niam replies.

31

TRAINING IS BRUTAL THE next morning. Halton's dick attitude is on another level, and it takes all my willpower to not punch him square in that perfect nose of his. The thought of the crunch beneath my knuckles and the mangled cartilage makes the corner of my lips turn upward.

By the time our warmup is completed, we're fully sparring one another. Grunts and snarls fill the empty training grounds.

What is wrong with him? It's like he woke up on the wrong side of the bed and decided to take it out on me simply because I'm the first person he sees each day. With each jab to my ribs and smack to my shoulder, my irritation begins to boil over. I can tell he's baiting me, just waiting for the moment I lose control and snap. I can feel my restraint ticking away as each second passes.

Then he trips me. *Actually trips me.* My palms scrape against the ground, skin shredded from the impact.

"That. Is. It!" The words rip out of my throat as if a clawed, phantom hand reached down and flung them in his direction. I scramble to my feet, stomping until I'm nose-to-nose with the elf. "What is your problem, Halton? Leave your shit off the training grounds!" I scream. My face is red from the air that rushes out with every word.

My chest rises and falls rapidly. The closeness of us doesn't help my breathing. Flashes of that dream—the dream I wish would disappear from my mind—obscure my vision. His eyes go wide at our proximity.

Quickly—almost too quickly to notice—his gaze dips down to my slightly parted lips before snapping back to meet my eyes. What looks like disgust flickers across his features. Betrayal from his eyes. Interesting. I could kiss him right now, grab his face between both of my hands, and crush my lips to his just to spite him. I'd like to make him truly feel that disgust.

Instead, I raise both of my hands to his chest and shove him as hard as I can before marching away from him, putting an abrupt end to our training session.

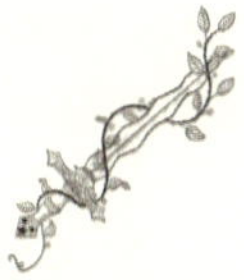

The door to my chamber's sitting area slams shut behind me.

"Agh!" My fingers make their way into my hair, running through each strand and tugging lightly at its roots.

Quiet yelps and frantic footsteps rush out of my bedchamber, scrambling to stand in the doorway. The wide eyes and tense shoulders of three chambermaids greet me. I start at the sight of them, unused to seeing them here this time of day. Usually, I leave for training, and when I come back, my rooms are tidy. Looking at them, I frown, and my heart clenches. Their spines are straight, like soldiers at attention on the battlefield.

I'm the reason they're so startled. *No.* Halton is the reason. *That prick.* He infuriates me, but deep down, I know the truth . . . A truth I refuse to truly face. It's not him that's churning the ire deep within my blood. I'm angry at myself because I wanted him to kiss me . . . not out of spite—but really kiss me. Searing and passionate, even if that passion wasn't one of love.

I hate that I yearn to know what he tastes like. I hate his damn gaze for flickering down to my lips. I hate the way I feel so out of control when he's around. I hate how drawn I am to him. I hate not knowing why that is. I hate him.

Damn him.

I feel ill. Heavy, hot thumps of my heart can be felt in my neck, in the tips of my fingers. The maids stand frozen in their spots, taking in every possible emotion that shudders across my features. I let out a long breath and attempt to give them a warm smile.

"I apologize if I frightened you," I say, with as much gentleness as I can muster. "Please, let me help you with your tasks."

Before I even can finish the sentence, they're already shaking their heads and refusing any kind of help. "Oh. Oh, no, Miss Maeve. We can't allow you to do that. We are here to serve you."

I flinch at the word "serve." No one should have to *serve* me, but I don't want to offend them by insisting.

"All right." My smile grows softer. "At least let me keep you company while you work." At this, they smile and nod before returning to my bedchamber.

Inside, the furs that are normally atop the bed are scattered across the floor. The silks are sprawled haphazardly, with one corner tucked in neatly while the rest are crumpled.

The three maids get back to work. As I watch them—taking pride in their task—I can't help but admire each one. And yet, I don't even know anything about them, who they are.

"What are your names?" The question slips out before I can think better of it.

A brief pause, then they begin talking without worry of troubling the elves they serve. Jasmine, Reeve, and Elia are their names. Jasmine and Elia have one more rotation of servitude. Reeve, who happens to be from the Central District as well, has three. They're kind, and it's nice to see the liveliness lighten up their eyes as I ask them about who they are as people, not as servants. It brings me comfort, and I can tell from their relaxed giggles that they feel the same.

After the bed is made—each pillow placed pristinely against the headboard and the furs shucked neatly across the silks—Jasmine, Reeve, and Elia say their goodbyes and begin exiting my chambers. But before they do, a thought strikes me hard and fast.

"Wait!" I exclaim, stopping them in their tracks.

Bustling around in the vanity obscenely filled to the brim, I find what I'm looking for. In my hand, I hold several brushes and combs. I have more than enough; I don't need them. They're stunned. It's nothing compared to what I truly wish I could give them: their freedom. But it's the only kindness I can offer now.

"I just thought . . ." A hesitant lull. Perhaps this wasn't the right thing to do. I crack my knuckles nervously and continue. "They don't treat you right. I thought this . . ."

Jasmine places a kind hand on my shoulder, halting my rambling. Elia grabs the brushes with a warm and thankful smile. There are enough for any other maid who may want one.

The three of them hug me. Jasmine's arm wraps firmly around my shoulders. Elia is gentle, as if she isn't used to such a gesture. And Reeve crushes me with an unrelenting grip and a laugh as pure as Ottilie's.

Their gratitude echoes in my mind long after they leave.

32

T HE HALLS OF THE elven palace are quiet. A few days of tense training sessions have passed since the not-so-almost kiss. Kicks become harder, punches faster. Halton glares at me when I catch him staring. I glare back. It's been an endless cycle of rigid and straining emotions.

I try not to think about it—*him*—too much. I focus on the good, on the thing that makes my heart swell. Since that day, chambermaids I don't know have come up to me with neat hair and grateful words. They tell me how Elia, Jasmine, and Reeve handed out all the brushes. They tell me how much better they feel when they have a moment to themselves to brush out their hair. I rejoice in their happiness. Small acts of care go a long way, I've learned.

But today, no servants bustle around the golden walkways. All are serving the King of Nythfaedell and his court at the midday meal. I have yet to even see the elven king since arriving in his kingdom. He's aloof, distant . . . as if he doesn't even exist.

My eyes stay alert as I stride through empty halls to Prince Kayd's parlor, where he's requesting my presence. As I approach the extravagant ivory doors, I hear tense voices inside. The discussion sounds serious, dire, even. A few steps more, then the words become clear.

"Unrest is brewing, Kayd," a grim voice—Halton's, by its deep cadence—informs the prince and whomever else is present. "The tension seems to have started in Fiermoor."

Another voice, Niam, adds, "Reports indicate that the Lady of Crullfeld and her followers are unhappy with all elves. The tieflings believe that, since we have magick, we shouldn't participate in the trials. They say it's a luxury we have that they do not."

I silently snort and enter the parlor with a sigh. All talk ceases as soon as I step over the threshold. "Don't stop talking on my behalf."

A thick, auburn eyebrow raises. Kayd isn't impressed by my lack of manners. Halton's face turns to stone-cold granite, his scowl quickly replacing the worry I could hear in his voice just moments before.

Niam pours himself a goblet of wine at a quaint table near the edge of the room. He raises it to me with a friendly wink before plopping down on a chaise next to his sister, whose head rests against her palm. Alta's face shifts from boredom to delight at the sight of me as she waves enthusiastically. I send her a small smile back in return.

My attention returns to the waiting prince. His eyebrow is still raised, the dangerous glint threatening. I know exactly what he wants, and it pains me that I do it. Violently gritting my teeth together, my waist bends my body in half. I bow.

Perhaps this unrest will do my job for me. The elves and tieflings will kill each other and I won't have to bow before the elven prince again. I could return to Terakeld and put this monstrous thing I've become in a grave. *Then* maybe I can be the person Jerik deserves, the person who doesn't feel so much shame.

When I rise, his lips curl up into a smile. I snarl, making sure the others see my disdain. Halton cocks his head in warning, but I roll my eyes defiantly.

"My *dearest* Shackled Serpent," Kayd drawls out leisurely. An exasperated sigh escapes my gritted teeth. Nonetheless, he continues on, as if he heard nothing. "I have my first real assignment for you."

All thoughts of Jerik and the tiefling unrest disappear like smoke on the wind. Finally. *Finally.* My lips curl up, forming a sadistic smile I've channeled from the changeling princess far away. That familiar thrumming deep within my veins pumps through my heart as if this is the sole thing in all the lands that makes me feel alive. For Ottilie. For Mother.

"You will attend another revel tonight. Members of my father's court will be in attendance alongside mine," Kayd explains. "Your target is a nuisance who is causing headaches throughout the palace. I would like him poisoned."

"Sounds fun," I muse, my tongue running across my top teeth.

Kayd's amused chuckle grates at my ears. "It will truly be thrilling, getting to finally see you in your element." He cocks his head toward Alta, who straightens her spine at the look he gives her. "Alta, take our great assassin to the shops. She will need a gown that entices the rogue lord."

The sounds of horse hooves clank against the cobblestone streets as our carriage twines throughout an elven village. Quaint buildings with thatched roofs and round windows pass us by, while elves in day dresses and coats stroll leisurely from shop to shop. The carriage comes to a stop in front of a small store at the end of the village's main street.

Inside, a short elf with wrinkles and a kind smile greets us. Racks of gowns made of silks and felts and feathers are stacked throughout the quaint room.

"You know, I had a really great time with you the other day at the spring," Alta says lightly as she browses the dresses. "It's nice having another female around to hang out with . . . and talk to." The smile she shines my way—the same smile that she sends to Niam, Halton, and even Kayd—sends warmth and affection straight through me.

Quietly, I reply, "It was nice. Even when the others crashed our time together." Alta's chuckle sounds off behind a different rack of gowns off to the side. "It looked like Halton wanted to rip my head off the entire time."

"He normally isn't so serious." Alta's giggle dies down. "Sure, he's all work and no play when he's on duty, but in the spring, he's normally different. You must really get under his skin with all that training you two do."

My eyebrows raise. "So, he doesn't always have a stick up his ass?"

Alta barks out a laugh. "I'm so telling him you said that." A smirk forms across my lips in response. Wiping a joyous tear away from her eye, she shakes her head. "But, no. When I first met him, he was guarded and closed off. I think he was still scared after . . ." Her voice trails off.

Her eyes soften, losing focus, while her fingers dance across a jeweled pink gown.

"Coming to live in the palace was a shock for him. It was very different from his old home. Even with Kayd attached to his hip and Niam and me around after the king and queen took us in a couple of rotations later, he had a hard time acclimating. It took a while for him to warm up to us. But when he did, he really started to come out of his shell. I hope you get to see that side of him one day."

Flashes of Halton's softening eyes and quiet chuckles bombard me. I've seen a sliver of that side of him before he dons his hardened exterior. I can only imagine what he'd truly be like without that mask. "Don't hold your breath," I mumble.

Alta's lips smack together. "Don't say that," she chides. "Like I said, it took a while for Halton to warm up to Niam and I . . . Two rotations to be exact. He'll come around and welcome you with open arms. I know it. It has always just been the four of us. Now—no matter what Kayd and Halton say—I hope to add one more to that . . ."

It's a simple, yet hopeful comment. It makes a pit in my stomach grow. That darkness that resides around my soul pulses, reminding me that I don't deserve friends like the twins. Why would they want to befriend me, anyway? What makes me so special? So, I keep my mouth shut and continue browsing the multiple racks of extravagant gowns.

My palms glide over every stunning piece, relishing in the fabrics. Each gown is unique; not one is the same as another. As the gossamers and velvets glide beneath my touch, I realize I don't truly despise gowns. They're beautiful. They make me *feel* beautiful. What I despise is the life I lived in Terakeld. Resentment rears its ugly head. I hate the luxuries Nythfaedell and the prince offer because I never got that growing up.

An excited squeak on the other side of the shop ricochets across the racks of gowns. I follow the sound of several more squeals. Alta is holding a beautiful blue gown that looks like the meadow's river sparkling in Terakeld's sunlight. Thin sheer mesh sprouts above the neckline that gives off the simple illusion of a heart, creating fake modesty. The mesh glides down and forms simple, long sleeves with hoops ready to hook around Alta's middle fingers. Darker blue fabric shaped like butterflies are sewn into the flowing, floor-length layers of the skirts, looking as if they are about to fly away at a moment's notice.

"It's beautiful," I breathe out. Her gray eyes sparkle at the compliment, and her feet begin dancing around in glee.

"Have you found something you'd like to wear?" The elf walks toward me with her newly found gown draped across her forearm.

I glance at the rack I was flicking through a moment ago. Creams and silvers, sequins and chiffons. "No, I . . ." The words get stuck in my throat. *I have no idea what I'm doing,* I want to say. "I'm sorry."

The apology shocks Alta almost as much as it shocks me. I have no reason to be sorry, yet I said it. Never having had to pick out a gown for myself, I feel like a child. I shut my eyes and release a long exhale.

"I don't know what I'm looking for. I'm way out of my element here." I can feel heat rise up my neck and dust across my nose.

Alta smiles at me kindly. There's no hidden pity or condemnation. "That's okay. May I ask what you feel comfortable wearing?"

Every single racing thought of fabrics and cuts and colors disappears, leaving my mind an empty void. I've never been asked what I'm comfortable wearing . . . or doing, for that matter. I have never been asked to voice what I do and do not want. My hands start to tremble.

The elf notices my reaction and silently consoles me with a kind hand atop my scarred shoulder. My body betrays me and relaxes under her touch.

"The male you're"—she hesitates—"assigned is one of the worst out of all the palace's courtiers. He sees females as property, no matter if they're elf or human. In order to get close, to get his attention, you will need . . . to catch his eye." She worries her teeth over her bottom lip. I can see the sadness and disgust she feels furrowing her brows together.

I nod in understanding. Seduce him. I'll need to seduce this elf in order to get close enough to kill him. Turning toward a rack of red-and-black gowns, I begin sifting through each garment. Alta turns to the rack and begins helping.

A small gasp from Alta pulls my attention away from the sleeveless midnight-black gown I was examining. In Alta's hand is a beautiful deep red—almost blood-colored—dress. It's stunning. And it's perfect

Madam Prea's fingers comb through my hair and fasten it into a graceful, braided coronet with thin pieces of hair framing my face. When she entered my chambers a few hours ago, she said she volunteered to get me ready for tonight's revel so the other chambermaids would have the night off. Just the thought of an elf doing that for mortals makes my heart clench.

"Thank you." Prea breaks the comfortable silence between us as she slips a pin between my braids. My brows push together, and the corners of my mouth turn down. "For the kindness you extended to my girls. They love the brushes."

My face loosens, and I breathe in the warm air of my chambers. "I have plenty to spare."

"You're too kind." After a long pause, she whispers, "Be careful tonight, girl."

"Of what?" My voice is just as quiet as hers.

"Whatever that prince has in store for you."

I think back to the piece of parchment Prince Kayd sent earlier that evening with my victim's name scrawled on it. The piece of parchment that's now nothing but ash in my hearth.

Haryk Morran, the Baron of Orolen.

After placing the last pin in my hair, Prea's hands move to my shoulders, and I turn to face the older elf. "Up. Let's get you dressed."

Pulling me out of the chair, she helps me into my gown. It's nice having Madam Prea get me ready. It's like how Mother used to when I was a child. Her nimble fingers fasten the last of the near-invisible buttons along my lower back. Once she's finished, I stare into the full-length mirror next to the bath.

Deep red vines—covered in tiny silk thorns that shine under the lights—barely cover my breasts and tie together at the nape of my neck. The vines gradually shift into a sheer fabric at my waist and cascade toward the floor in flowing waves. Shimmering fabric so thin, the outline of my legs can be seen through it, and a long slit that nearly reaches my hip bone splits the skirt into two.

It's truly otherworldly, this gown. I look just as deadly as I do desirable. Through the reflection, my gaze connects with Madam Prea's. Her lips are tight, but her eyes are soft and warm.

"You look stunning, girl."

At that, I smile.

33

T HIS BALLROOM IS GRANDER than the one Kayd's court uses. Riches I can't even imagine fill the hallway leading up to it. Solid gold statues loom over passersby, velvet and silk chaises and chairs waiting for exhausted partygoers to collapse onto them. Intricate crystal vases hold pastel flowers dipped in gold flake-filled water. The ballroom's golden-and-ivory double doors take up the entirety of the wall at the end of the walkway, beckoning all to enter with sounds of strings and flutes.

From afar, my vision zeroes in on dozens of gowns twirling together around the dance floor. Flashes of colors glide around one another, creating a rippling rainbow of fabric.

Nerves flit around my stomach like a swarm of butterflies yearning to get out, pushing against my ribs. A sickly feeling deep in my gut roils and threatens to work its way up into my throat. I don't want to attend another revel. Dancing and smiling and pretending to be one of them . . . I'm no courtier. I don't belong. And this time, the king is going to be there.

My steps falter. *The king is going to be there.*

Sweat gathers along my palms, and I stop myself from wiping them on my gown.

Light and warmth engulf me. The presence of Mother and Ottilie immediately makes my nerves disappear, the tense muscles in my shoulders relaxing.

We are here with you, they seem to say.

I nod to myself, agreeing with the spirits. I am the Shackled Serpent, and I will not allow measly gowns and dances to intimidate me. I am the Shackled Serpent, and tonight, I will rid Galfei Thalor of another vile being.

Now thrumming with excitement, I allow my feet to take me closer. A low whistle breaks through the laughter fluttering through the doors. Niam—clad in an embroidered black tunic—waits for me near the entrance. I didn't see him before. His face lights up in delight, and his eyes rake over my body, taking in my scandalous gown multiple times before he meets my eyes. I playfully shove him on the arm. He only laughs, easing the remaining tension in my muscles.

He bends his elbow out to me. An offering. An anchor. I link mine with his and breathe in deeply. "Ready to do this?" Niam's question is just above a whisper, enough for only me to hear over the music.

The deadly mask that I carefully crafted over the months takes its place, shielding myself from those around me. My eyes are sharper, and that sinister smile I learned from Andrina is back. I turn to face Niam's expectant gaze and nod.

He chuckles with a glint in his eye that tells me he doesn't mind ridding the world of this male, either. He says, "Let's go, then, Serpent," as he leads me into the bustling ballroom.

Dozens of elves are present, conversing in smaller groups. I recognize several from the first revel with Prince Kayd's court. They're unsurprised that I'm there. Their blank faces peek over goblets of wine when they see me before they turn toward something else, as if I am nothing to them.

As I descend the few steps leading into the ballroom—Niam tucked tightly into my side—the other elves I don't recognize notice us. A handful of gasps can be heard over the music. Eyes bulge wide, and mouths hang open. Despite their shock, the majority of King Glynvyre's court sends me warm smiles. I'm not sure what to make of that.

We pass three ravishing elves who tilt their chins toward us kindly in greeting before going back to their conversation. Their words carry over to us.

"As I was saying, it's been a little over a month since any reports have come in. Perhaps the Shackled Serpent is dead." One elf pops a cube of cheese into their mouth. Niam's other hand, resting atop my forearm, squeezes my flesh. He heard it, too.

Another shakes his head like that is the most ridiculous thing. "The assassin isn't dead. They're too devious to die. The Serpent is waiting for the perfect opportunity. They'll make themselves known again."

Niam leans his head closer to me as we weave our way through the crowd. He whispers, "You're a legend, Maeve."

Finally taking my eyes off the revel around us, I look up at him. The flickering flames from the chandelier glint against his eyes. "Good." I smile sweetly.

The handsome elf on my arm winks before facing forward once again. Gratitude for Niam swells in my chest. For making it feel like it is only us. For simply being here . . . with me.

I don't notice Niam swiftly leading me toward a giant throne positioned in the back of the ballroom until it's too late. My steps stumble as I see a beautiful, dark-skinned elf with broad shoulders and a gleaming gold crown atop his long auburn hair. *The king.*

"What are you doing, Niam?" I hiss. My unyielding facade remains, but I feel it begin to crack.

His words are just as quiet. His smile never falters. "You, Maeve, need to pay respects to Nythfaedell's ruler. You are one of his guests. It's customary."

My grip on his elbow tightens, but before I can dig my heels into the sparkling marble floor, I'm standing before the king.

King Osmar Glynvyre gazes down at me. Curiosity swirls around his dark-green irises, and there's a splash of confusion there as well. He's the spitting image of Kayd, although more muscular and with a kinder demeanor. There is no snarl along his lips, no menacing glint in his features. Perhaps the king wears a mask just as I do.

At my side, Niam bows deeply for his king. I follow suit, bowing my head, bending at my knee, while my fingers hold out the skirts of my gown. If my curtsy is not up to royal standard, the king doesn't say. Peering through my lashes, I see his gaze rake over us as we hold our poses, lingering on me for a moment longer before simply nodding at the two of us, dismissing us to enjoy the party.

With a grounding hand against the small of my back, Niam ushers me away.

"That was terrifying." My mumbled words carry over the gentle notes of a piano. An amused chuckle is his only response.

Niam leads me over to Prince Kayd, Halton, and Alta, who are gathered together in a far corner of the ballroom. Alta's fingers languidly wrap around a goblet, the wine inside sloshing as she talks animatedly. Kayd laughs boisterously at something she says, and Halton has his hands in his pockets, chiming in on their conversation wherever he can with a rare, easy smile painting his lips.

"Maeve!" Alta wraps her arms around my neck in a welcoming embrace as soon as we approach before holding me at an arm's length. "Oh, I just knew this dress was the right choice! You're a sight to be seen!" Her excited, high-pitched words roll over her tongue quickly.

My smile tugs up, and heat grazes my cheeks. "Thank you."

Turning my attention to the others, I see Halton's gaping eyes narrow as soon as we make eye contact and turn hard. "Serpent," he grumbles quietly.

"Guard." My eyes turn cold in response. Niam's hand stays on my back, soft and reassuring.

Kayd's large hand claps down onto my left shoulder. My skin crawls under his touch. "It's your time to shine, mortal." The prince looks at me with a smile so wide it's alarming. I'm not used to his lips making such a gesture. He's practically bouncing on his toes before he shifts his body, leans in close, and whispers in my ear, "You see that pathetic excuse of a male by the wine table? That's your target."

I follow his gaze.

The elf is shorter than those around him. Rounder, too. He has long wavy brown hair that is tied behind his pointed ears with a strap of leather, and flashy jewelry decorates each of his knuckles. He guzzles down a goblet of wine before shoving it into a human servant's face and demanding she pour him another. Everything about this elf makes that angry flame in my gut flare.

"You will need to look as if you're mingling with others, enjoying the revel, you know. It needs to appear like he isn't your focus." Kayd's hushed voice travels between the five of us. "Dance. Drink. Have fun. But keep your eyes on him."

"I know how to do my job," I bite. His grip on my shoulder tightens harshly, my bones grinding together under his palm. Hate flashes behind my eyes. Ottilie's feather of a touch presses on my heart, trying to calm me down.

Without a word, Niam comes to the rescue before I say something else, whisking me away onto the dance floor.

As soon as we get to the open dance floor, a new song begins. He pulls me close, and we take our first choreographed steps of the night. Niam mutters in my ear, "You shouldn't provoke him like that."

I try to rein in the scoff that escapes my fake grin, but it's too late. "Your prince underestimates me. I'm not stupid."

"He's your prince, too."

A muscle in my jaw feathers. His fingers squeeze onto my back. A playful warning. I scoff again, but it lingers into a breathy chuckle. I was ordered to pretend like I'm having a good time, and with Niam, pretending isn't an issue. He seems to be one of my only true companions in this kingdom . . . besides his sister and Madam Prea.

The sour thoughts of the elven prince disappear when Niam shoots that dazzling smile my way. We dance to two songs, chatting and laughing and . . . having a good time. It's real. No masks, nothing. Just him and me.

Right before the musicians begin their next number, someone cuts in and asks for a dance. I'm unsure if the elf means with me or Niam until his slender hand stretches out toward me with eyes that hold a hint of warmth and curiosity. A farewell kiss on the cheek from Niam. Then I am whisked away in the arms of the stranger.

I don't recognize the elf, so I assume he's a courtier of the king. Ernick—as he introduced himself after asking my name—is kind and polite as we dance, much more pleasant than anyone in Kayd's court. Wisps of short white hair fall into the elf's teal eyes as he spins me away from him, then pulls me back to his chest.

"Thank you for accepting this dance." His breath grazes my face. It smells of mint.

"Of course." I smile at him.

Ernick flicks his wrist and twirls me around again. "I couldn't help my curiosity as soon as you entered the ballroom. A human in the prince's court. Now that's a peculiar sight."

"Isn't it, though?"

The elf sends me a dazzling smile as the last notes of the song hang in the air. He brings me to a stop with a vivacious dip. His grin is contagious, and I don't stop my lips from curling upward, matching his own.

What is happening to me? Will I soon be smiling and befriending all elves? I can already feel my walls lowering in this kingdom. *Not good, Maeve.*

A hand politely grasps onto his right shoulder, pulling both of our gazes toward the intruder. Standing before us is Halton. My mouth hangs open before I remember where I am and who I am supposed to be. As I snap it closed, my dance partner turns to me.

"It was a pleasure to meet you, Maeve." Ernick kisses the top of my hand lightly and leaves me with the guard.

Chilling fingers wrap around my hand as soon as the elf's lips leave my skin, covering the warmth left over. Halton's other hand settles against my lower back. He pulls me close, then we begin stepping in sync to the tune twining around the ballroom. Him leading. Me following.

No words are said. The only sounds between us are heels clicking against the marble floor as others dance by and as the music drowns them out. He's rigid, and his eyes flit around the room, refusing to look at me, as if he's searching for a way out of this dance . . . As if Kayd forced him to in order to keep up the courtier facade.

"You don't *have* to dance with me." My voice is gritty, grinding out through my teeth. Halton's grip on my back tightens ever so slightly, although he doesn't say anything.

In the silence between us, I take the opportunity to really look at him tonight. His sharp cheekbones create shadows beneath them. Unlike most of the other elves in attendance, there are no glitter or jewels decorating his features. He's simple—rugged and raw. So *unelf*-like.

My mouth opens before I think better of it. I close it without saying anything else, but I'm itching to say something, *anything*, to end this strain surrounding us. The tension is so thick it's hard to swallow.

An exasperated sigh. "What is your deal, guard? The least you can do is act like you want to be near me." My words are laced with irritation.

An emotion I can't decipher flits across his features. His eyebrows pull together, and his lips tighten at the corners. Just as he opens his mouth to say some sort of snide remark, I'm sure, a voice interrupts us.

"Mind if I cut in?" Prince Kayd stands between twirling couples, not even waiting for my dance with his guard to end. Kayd's eyes are trained on me.

Halton halts his movements with ease and hesitates for a split second before he steps to the side, giving his prince the room to slide in. I am pulled away not a breath later.

"Couldn't even wait to whisk me away, I see." I shoot a condescending smirk toward the prince.

"Do not insult me, mortal," Kayd scoffs. "I could see your temper was being tested in the presence of my captain. I didn't want your assignment jeopardized because you two could not hide your emotions."

I don't reply. Instead, my gaze stays trained on his, unblinking and unfazed. His grip on my hand tightens before discreetly slipping a small vial of shimmering lilac liquid into my palm. After the last flamboyant twirl in the dance, the elven prince bows to me politely then leads me around the room, personally introducing me to his father's courtiers. I can see the curiosity churning in their minds as we talk idly before Kayd glides me away to another. Like the elf I danced with, they're all kind except for a small handful, and the parade ends at the worst of them all . . . Haryk Morran. My target.

"Lord Morran, I would like to introduce you to Miss Maeve Wyndell, a new member of my court," Kayd projects over the music with perfect pronunciation.

I curtsy before the elf, giving him a generous view of my breasts. Swampy brown eyes immediately lock onto them. Typical. My head stays bowed, but I look up with sultry eyes through my long coal-lined lashes just as his gaze trails up to meet them.

"It's a pleasure to meet you, my lord." I'm all soft curves and batting eyelashes. None of my usual bite can be detected under the pleasant words.

Standing tall once more, I smile sweetly at him. His face lights up with intrigue. Blindly grabbing a goblet from the table behind him, he offers me the drink. I accept before bowing my head to the prince and allowing Haryk Morran's plump hand to drape around my waist and lead me away.

Keeping a conversation going with the elf is easy. All I need to do is stroke his ego, play coy, and appear interested in every word that spills from his mouth.

"You're beautiful . . . *for a mortal.*"

I thank him profusely for such a compliment.

"Prince Kayd is lucky to be fucking such a pretty thing like you."

I force a blush to rise along my cheeks.

"You would look so good serving me."

I bite my bottom lip, then run my tongue along it, pulling his focus toward the motion.

His gravelly, grating voice echoes against my skull, and chills of disgust run down my spine. The lord is none the wiser.

Once my second goblet is finished, I politely excuse myself. I can feel his stare hot on my back as I saunter away, the sway of my hips overexaggerated. It's a long game, and I am willing to play.

Delicately snatching a berry-filled pastry off a serving platter, I stuff it into my mouth and find Alta along the wall on the other side of the ballroom. I smile brightly at her just as she takes a long gulp of wine.

"He's watching you," Alta coos as I approach.

I don't glance behind me. I don't need to. I could feel his gaze burning into my backside the entire way here. "Of course he is." I wink.

The elf chuckles and shakes her head slightly, the glitter sticking to her eyelids and cheekbones shimmering from the movement. "You're good, Maeve . . ."

Tilting my head, I ask, "At what?"

"Deception." Her eyebrows pull together.

It's a simple word—a word I've heard Andrina and Kayd use to describe my work before—but I can't help the way my heart stutters when she says it.

Quickly smoothing the crease in her forehead and forcing out a laugh, Alta runs her hands down the skirts of her beautiful blue gown and changes the subject. She begins telling me all she knows about the others attending the revel. Gossiping, just like how Ottilie used to. Prince Kayd, Niam, a few elves I already forgot, even King Osmar Glynvyre himself. Trivial things. I tune most of it out.

I've never been one for gossip, but I smile politely and nod as if I am listening. Just like my days with Ottilie. Alta and she would have gotten along so well.

Just as Halton's name leaves her nude-painted lips, I softly interrupt her.

"I'm sorry, Alta. I must keep moving. We need to sell the idea that I'm mingling with everyone. No one can know that my sole focus is on that *creep*."

I give her an apologetic smile. In return, hers is big and bright, as if it were made of the stars themselves. She waves goodbye as I walk toward another group of elves.

Truthfully, I could've stayed with Alta a little bit longer, but I didn't want to hear about the guard. I blink away the image of the blonde elf watching our training session and the redhead licking his throat at Kayd's revel. Just the thought makes something strong and unknown simmer deep below—in my gut, in my chest, even in a place I refuse to acknowledge.

Hours pass, and the night grows old. I bounce from one conversation to the other. Always keeping my eye on the baron. After one particularly distasteful joke about the palace's mortal servants from an older male courtier from Kayd's court, I see my opportunity to make my way back to Haryk Morran.

Excusing myself, I glide over to the drink table. I pour two glasses of wine, swiftly dumping the poison in both, then make my way toward the soon-to-be corpse, who is lurking around a table filled with sweets.

The crowd seems to part for me, just like The Unlighted Sea split open when Terakeld rose from its depths. Many of the revelers are swaying and stumbling from the wine and mead they guzzled down throughout the night. Others bid their farewells and trudge out of the ballroom, hanging on one another to relieve their tired feet. The king has already retired for the evening. The rest of my party has as well . . . except for Halton, who has undoubtedly been ordered to keep an eye on me, from the lack of females wrapped around his arms. A few other patrons are passed out on chaises against the walls. It's a pathetic sight, but one that will make my job oh so easy.

The baron is muttering to himself, looking for something along the table. "Those incompetent"—*hiccup*—"mortals. They misplaced my goblet." His harsh words are slightly slurred. The stars align once again.

"I couldn't help but notice you don't have a drink," I coo into his sagging ear.

He turns around, and the fire in his eyes returns as he notices I'm back. He ogles my chest before his gaze rakes down my body. My gut recoils at the look in his eye. I extend the goblet toward him with a seductive smile; he happily takes it from my grasp.

"Would you like to go somewhere quieter?" I bat my lashes. A grotesque grin spreads across his face, nearly reaching his pointed ears, and he leads me out to a secluded balcony adjacent to the ballroom. It's shrouded in the nightly shadows. It's the perfect spot for someone to die.

He goes in for a sloppy kiss, his lips already glistening with saliva. Bile rises to the back of my throat at the thought of letting him touch me like that. I disrupt his line of sight with my goblet.

"A toast first . . . for a fun, *successful* night!" I beam up at him.

Obliging, the elf guzzles down his poisoned wine eagerly. Wiping the drops of red liquid dripping down his chin with the back of his hand, he wraps his other arm around my body and squeezes the soft flesh of my ass, kneading it like dough. My teeth grind together as I let his hands roam. Only a few more moments, and he will drop dead.

You can do this, Maeve. Endure it.

His wet lips nearly graze the side of my neck before a pained gasp escapes, brushing against my skin. He reels back with widened eyes, and his body goes limp. Catching him before the sound of his heavy body hitting the cold, stone ground alarms anyone, I slowly set him down. He's lying on his back, with white foam seeping out of his open mouth. Confusion and fear radiate off his convulsing body.

I don't break eye contact with him. I watch as he takes his last shuddered breath. Then I stare at him for a moment longer before I dump my goblet out over the side of the balcony.

A small closet near the far back corner of the balcony catches my attention. I could easily leave Haryk Morran's body out in the open for palace staff to find, just as I had done on my assignments for the changelings. But something stops me from walking out. I've gone before the king. I've met courtiers who now know my name.

I grip onto the lord's ankles and pull him across the stone floor with barely audible grunts. I prop open the wooden door that leads into a closet full of what looks like cleaning supplies and shove him inside.

After a few attempts, his body folds in on itself as I shut the door behind me and wipe my hands along my skirts, walking back into the revel as if nothing happened.

Halton's brooding figure looms nearby. His arms are crossed, and that ever-present scowl deepens as I approach. "It's done."

He doesn't acknowledge what I just said or what I've done, but there's a fire blazing behind those hazel eyes as he stares at the closet, where the dead lord is, through the cracked ballroom door. A fire that startles me for a moment.

Before I can brush past him, his hand shoots out toward me and grips the top of my arm, with a force that makes me wince, before he briskly walks us both away from the balcony and toward the ballroom's doors.

"What—" I twist my body to the side, trying to escape his hold on me, but he's too strong.

Halton is simmering as we weave through drunken courtiers dancing to pathetic plucks of a cello. It's the first time the icy chill of his touch burns.

Even as we enter the hall and get farther away from the laughter and music of the revel, he doesn't loosen his hold on me. I writhe harder under his fierce grip now, my feet getting tangled in the skirts of my gown, making it hard to fight back. My other fist rams into his arm. Anything to shove him away from me.

"What. Is. Wrong. With. You?" I growl out. Each word is punctuated by a fist connecting to the elf.

"Stop," Halton mutters under his breath as I try to escape once more.

Before I can blink, my back hits a stone wall, and my chest is crushed by his flexing forearm. He pins me beneath his weight in an alcove of spiraling stairs that lead to somewhere I don't know. A small round window provides the only light in the darkened nook. White stones dig into my exposed back.

Fire erupts from his seething eyes as he leans closer and grinds out, "Stop, Serpent. You'll . . . Just *stop*."

A hiss drips from my tongue in response. My breathing comes quickly, as erratic as the flaming blood pulsing through my veins.

The smell of pine and biting spice fill my senses. His labored breath caresses my face. The feeling wraps around my lips in a ghostly, forbidden touch. His teeth are bared, grinding together so harshly I can hear it. He's so close, *too* close. That damned dream flares against my vision again.

My gaze shifts down to his lips. They look so soft. They look . . . My eyes bulge and snap back up to meet his. I seem to stop breathing. I feel stuck in a limbo of uncertainty—not sure whether I want to slap him as hard as I can across his face or crush my wanting lips to his. I need to pull away, but he's right there, open and tempting.

It feels as if we're suspended in time, neither of us moving as we hungrily take in the other. Before I can properly shift through my pacing thoughts, Halton moves, lunging forward, and slamming his lips onto mine.

34

L IPS SLOTTING TOGETHER AS one and teeth clashing for dominance, the kiss is rough and messy and full of unspoken emotions. It's nothing like past kisses I've shared in the shadows of Terakeld. Those were soft . . . caring, even, despite not reciprocating that same emotion toward Drustan. This—this is anything but.

It's fire and ice colliding. His cold lips against the heat of mine, like steam rising from the depths of a frosty hot spring. The stark line that separated the guard and me—the line I refused to cross since that dream—blurs.

What am I doing? What am I *doing*?

My palms reach for his chest. I need to push him away, get him off me. I don't want this. I can't . . .

My fingers betray me, in every sense of the word. My brain screams at them to stop as they fiercely wrap around the thin fabric of his tunic, pulling him closer and deepening the crush of his soft, velvety lips against mine.

A moan. A delicious noise that sticks deep within the back of Halton's throat vibrates against my slightly parted lips and sends a thrilling spark down to the tips of my fingers. The corners of my mouth perk up, smirking against his own. But my tiny victory is short-lived. I gasp as his slender hand wraps around my

256

back and grabs my ass. His strong fingers squeeze it through the sheer fabric of my gown, crumpling it up my backside.

"You like that?" His mumbled words are slurred, running together incoherently. "That foul elf did this to you just moments before you ended him. But you weren't breathing this hard then, were you?" Another squeeze. The grip on my plump flesh is harsh, bruising.

My jaw drops as another gasp breaks through the barrier of my lips. Halton takes the opportunity and slides his tongue along my bottom lip slowly before dipping it past my teeth and allowing it to roam against my own. He tastes like wine with a hint of mint. It's euphoric. I can't stop my barely audible whimper. Now, it's his turn to smirk.

Halton rips his lips from mine and begins traveling his cool touch along my jaw and down my neck. Needy, open-mouthed kisses leave a trail of gooseflesh in its wake. My chest rises and falls in frantic pants. A fire thrums in my veins.

"I hate you," I growl.

His movements halt. Not for long—for a split second at most—as soon as the words leave my mouth, but then the guard quickly begins trailing his lips against my neck again. A breathy chuckle brushes against my pounding pulse point. It's condescending and arrogant, and it makes my gut tighten just a little.

"Your body"—a small bite against my flesh makes a soft moan fall from my panting mouth—"seems to disagree."

I scoff incredulously at the vanity that seems to seep out of his pores as he continues to ravish the section of skin between my neck and collarbone. It's bound to leave a mark, and it pains me to say that I couldn't care less.

The end of my scoff turns into another moan. This time, louder than the first, more crude. The risk of getting caught pounds against my skull for a moment before Halton's other hand begins to massage my scantily clad breast. My head falls back in pleasure, hitting the stone wall behind me with a soft thud. All thoughts of prying eyes vanish.

This—his touch . . . It feels so good. It *shouldn't* feel this good.

Halton's hands begin to roam lower as he slowly falls to his knees. Through his lashes, I can see his pupils are blown. The hazel is almost completely engulfed by black.

Exhilarating power rushes my senses. The guard who has knocked me down countless times is now on his knees for me. A sharp, intense throb shoots down between my legs at the thought. My teeth sink into my lower lip as I gaze down at him. He's looking up at me with heated cheeks, parted lips, and heavy-lidded eyes. I want to sear this moment—the sight of him like this—into my memory forever.

My fingers lightly brush his sharp jawline, tilting his head higher in my direction. My eyes rake down the slope of his neck, and my hand moves to the side until my fingertips graze his plush lips. Opening his mouth for me, I slip two fingers past his lips and hook them against his bottom teeth, prying open his mouth wider. His eyes flash with heat and hate before closing his lips and sucking harshly.

My tongue peeks out and runs across the top row of my teeth as I watch him. That throbbing—the throbbing that seems to pound up from the apex of my thighs to my ears—grows. *Thump. Thump. Thump.* Like a drum pulsing against my blood and calling on my deepest desires.

My thighs shift. They press together subtly, wishing for friction.

Halton's eyes snap down at the movement. Pulling his lips away from my fingers with a wet pop, he leans closer to where I want him most. A deep inhale, his eyes rolling into the back of his head as he does so.

Desperately, he begins gathering the skirts of my gown, balling up the fabric and pushing it toward my waist, until I stand bare before him, underthings forgotten for the night due to the nature of my dress. He moans at the sight and takes another deep inhale before his large hands roughly lift my right leg over his broad shoulder.

"Need to taste you," Halton slurs. His erratic and rapid breaths stroke against the slick pooling before his eyes.

"I—" My words are cut off by his tongue abruptly breaching my folds. All thoughts leave my mind. My mouth hangs open. The feeling leaves me speechless . . . positively drunk on his intoxicating mouth.

His moan is deep and gritty and sends a jolt through my core, lighting my nerve endings aflame. His hands brutally grip onto my hips, pushing me further against the wall and leaving no room for squirming. His assault continues as his nose brushes against the bundle of nerves that no other has bothered to touch before.

At that, I find my voice once again. It arrives in the form of a husky groan deep in the back of my throat as I card my fingers through his brown locks of hair, tugging at his roots, while simultaneously urging him deeper.

"So good . . ." he mumbles against me before his sinful mouth latches onto that pulsing mound again and sucks harshly. I yelp—high-pitched and needy—and it echoes along the alcove walls.

"Stay . . ." A lick. A warning. "Stay quiet, Serpent."

I bite my lip hard enough to draw a few drops of blood. The coppery taste hits my tongue and distracts me, only until I feel Halton's finger begin to push into me. A broken whimper releases at the feeling. My hips buck forward, begging for more.

"Fuck." His voice sounds just as broken as mine, full of savage lust. He adds another finger and locks his lips around my clit once more.

My breaths come faster. Sweat beads across my brow. The deep pulsing that thrums beneath Halton's lips coils into a tight ball, preparing to snap. "Hal—*Please*." That's all I can muster.

His fingers pump in and out with fervor, faster and faster, curving deliciously. The squelch of each thrust mixes with my heavy breathing and the toe-curling slurp of his lips.

"C'mon . . ." he mumbles, brows furrowed in concentration. His cheeks cave in as his lips return to their task, accentuating his sharp facial features.

My legs begin to shake. My fingers tighten in his hair. My hips roll against his fingers and mouth, yearning for more. The coil in my gut tightens. Vulgar curses escape between my clenched teeth, breathy and running together without space in between.

"I-I'm—" A low, needy whine cuts off my words. My eyes shut tightly. My joints lock up, and my knee buckles as the tight aching spring snaps free. My back arches away from the stone wall, and tears threaten to breach my lash line.

Halton's free arm pushes my hips roughly against the wall, making sure I don't collapse. He expertly works me through the pleasure that lights through every nerve within my body. Pleasure that is more intense, more earth-shattering than anything I've ever felt before.

His lips uncurl around my clit, and his fingers begin to slow. I wince as he removes them, then whimper when his tongue swipes upward along my slit for one more taste. Both of our chests heave deeply. I feel lighter, freer in post-climax bliss. A bliss that clouds my judgment because I run my fingers through his hair again before caressing them down his cheeks.

The elf's eyes flutter shut, and his swollen lips perk up into a smile before he wipes his glistening chin with the back of his hand and stands up. However, as soon as our eyes meet, something shifts. Panic begins to roar between us.

Halton's eyes widen. He looks horrified. Without another word, he swiftly turns on his heel and walks away, leaving me with a wrinkled gown and a mess between my legs. As his stride takes him farther and farther into the palace halls, I see his hand—the hand that was inside me mere moments ago—come up and rub the back of his neck before turning a corner and disappearing.

I stand in the alcove, alone and frozen with shock. What did we just do? How did I let that happen? Never again . . .

I steel myself off from my rampant thoughts.

"Just pretend like it never happened, Maeve," I mumble to myself, attempting to smooth out the skirts of the gown. "It's for the best."

With a shaky breath, I exit the dimness of the alcove and begin my walk back to my chambers.

35

T HE MALICIOUS HISS OF Jerik's voice rings against my skull.

You disgust me. You tainted yourself with that elven filth.

You disgust me. You disgust me. You disgust me.

A phantom version of the blond-haired man has haunted my dreams since the revel . . . since the night that line between me and Halton was crossed. Three nights of tossing and turning. Three nights of guilt weighing heavy on my heart. Three nights of wishing we could do it all over again.

Halton has canceled each morning training session since as well. This morning is no different. The letter with the news crumbles easily against my palm as I make a fist.

He's avoiding me. That realization makes something deep inside my chest sink. But I can't blame him. I've been avoiding him, too. I need to work through the contradicting feelings swirling inside me: hatred, hurt, shame, desire, confusion. It's all there. One no more than the other, each simply coexisting.

But now, as I chuck the parchment into the burning hearth of my chambers, I'm angry. I need to spar. I'm itching to get back out there, to burn off all this pent-up steam. Perhaps if I do that, I can actually sift through what I'm feeling.

Hastily slipping on my training attire, trimmed in furs for the colder autumn weather and light dusting of snow that fell overnight, I exit my chambers with determination fueling each step.

Courtiers and servants scuttle past me as I traverse through the halls. Many are whispering to one another. A few are crying.

I see Reeve in the distance, hunched over and murmuring to what looks like a stable boy. I approach the two and send them a small smile before asking, "Reeve, what's going on?"

The chambermaid looks up at me. Her eyes are rimmed in red. "Oh, Maeve!" Her bottom lip quivers. "It's awful. The Baron of Orolen was found dead this morning. People are claiming the Shackled Serpent infiltrated the king's revel a few nights ago and killed him when no one was looking."

My eyes widen, pretending the news is shocking. Another lie to a new companion . . . just like Jerik.

Reeve's arms wrap tightly against my neck and pull me close. "You were there, too. I couldn't imagine anything bad happening to you!" Her wail echoes around us.

Slowly, I wrap my arms around her in return and pat her back. "It's okay, Reeve. I'm fine."

Pulling away from me, she sniffles and runs her hand below her eyes, catching a stray tear. The stable boy wraps his arm around her shoulders and squeezes them softly.

"The kingdoms need to do something about their assassin problem," he grumbles, looking down at Reeve before moving his eyes to mine. "I've heard that pathetic human rebellion is growing because of the serpent's kills. Whoever it is, they're inspiring more and more people to spew lies. It's disgusting."

My heart leaps in my chest, but my face remains glum. More deceit from me to my own.

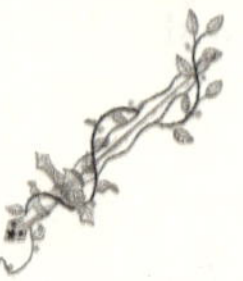

Prince Kayd's guards halt their exercises as soon as I step foot on the training grounds. Some are pinned under others. Some have their swords frozen in the air. Hushed whispers and grumbles can barely be heard over the crunch of my boots, stomping straight for Kayd's throne. Halton stands tall beside him, unwavering under my ferocious and seething glare. The prince's eyebrows raise in amusement. The muscles along Halton's jaw flex as I storm closer.

"So, you're just not going to train me anymore?" I yell at Halton, the words booming against the shields and weapons strewn across the grounds. I take a deep breath to calm myself, then my focus shifts to Kayd. "Give me someone who will."

"You don't give orders." The prince doesn't miss a beat.

My nostrils flare, and my mouth opens to respond. Before I can—

"Show me," Kayd says calmly, despite my demands.

"What?"

"You're my assassin. You're in my court. I would like to see how much you've improved. Halton, spar with my serpent."

The flare in Halton's eyes is quick, almost unnoticeable if I wasn't already looking at him. He bows toward his prince and stalks over to the center of the training grounds, where the other guards clear the same area where we meet every morning. With a tight chest, I meet him there.

We both assume ready positions. A single breath passes before we lunge at the other. With every strike, dodge, and block, I put all my frustration into it. I'm a mirror of him. A direct reflection—moving as if we are one and the same, using what he has taught me, and holding my own. The fight lasts longer than any other during our training sessions. I'm keeping up. I'm going to prove to that horrid prince that I'm the killer he wants.

Halton's pink tongue peeks out between his lips and dabs the corner of his mouth. It's something I've noticed he does when concentrating. I've never thought anything of it. Until now. I can't stop the images of him on his knees and his tongue between my legs from swarming into my mind.

I falter, distracted by the sudden want weighing heavy in my gut. The elf takes the opportunity to bring me to the ground, pinning me down. His forearm pushes down on my heaving chest, his left knee resting between my legs. Halton's eyes dip down, looking at my slightly parted lips. My eyes widen only slightly before a growl rumbles in the back of his throat, and he pushes off me, offering me his hand. I ignore it and get up on my own.

"Tsk, tsk, tsk . . ." Kayd drawls out as he looks down at me, each disappointed sound matching the tap of his ring-clad finger. "I can see you've improved, but you still cannot beat the captain of my guard. A pity." He clicks his tongue, as if that were that.

"She has beaten me before . . . Your Highness." The timbre in Halton's voice is unwavering, confident. My head whips to the side to stare at him. My eyebrows lift, and my mouth hangs open.

"Oh?" The prince questions. "Let's have our little killer show us, then."

The grass—wet from patches of melting ice—scratches against my exposed skin. The outermost layer of my training gear is discarded next to me, the garment contrasting against the speckled white-and-green ground. My joints crack with every shift of my body, and my muscles burn to the touch. After a morning of sparing and defeating each guard Kayd threw my way, relaxing at the Crystal Lake Garden is exactly what I need.

The heat of the sun shines down upon my face. My eyes are closed, but my ears are alert. The sound of the lapping ripples in the water soothes me. I can feel the soft, lulling pull of sleep begin to grip my consciousness . . .

Ice crunches beneath a pair of boots, and my eyes snap open. As I swiftly sit up, the steps come to an abrupt halt. Whipping my head around, I see him. Halton stands just at the entrance of the garden with a tight jaw and wide eyes. Neither of us move. We stare at one another, unsure of what to do or say. We're in uncharted territory, alone together for the first time since the king's revel. It feels as if my lungs collapsed and my heart has plummeted into my stomach.

Releasing a shuddered breath, attempting to calm the nervous pinpricks racing along my skin, I turn back around toward the water. "Are you just going to stand there?" No answer. No movement. I glance back at the guard. He's as still as stone. "You look like a deer who's been caught by a hunter, Halton. Well, then again . . . maybe you have."

An unexpected laugh escapes my lips as he scoffs and begins walking closer to the lake. Keeping a good amount of distance between us, he plops down on the ground and looks out into the water. His muscular arms wrap around his bent knees.

"Did Kayd send you here to keep watch over me?" The hate that is ever present in my soul punctuates each syllable.

"Watch your tone," Halton chides.

I roll my eyes and lay back down. My eyelids flutter shut, and I go back to enjoying the cool breeze brushing against my skin.

Silence fills the void between us until the guard speaks again. "But, no, *Prince* Kayd didn't send me. I like to come here from time to time . . . to think."

The softness of his voice startles me slightly. I turn to the side to face him, the cold grass rubbing against my cheek. "I haven't seen you here before."

"I usually come at night." He continues to look out across the lake. His eyes are distant, yet alert. "It's the only time I can come."

I nod but don't respond. There's a calm quiet that buffers us. A fragile quiet. It feels as if one single word, sigh, or movement will shatter it completely. I continue to gaze at the guard. He's so relaxed. Nothing like I've ever seen from him. His profile shines under the warm sun. He's all sharp edges and clean lines. He's beautiful. All elves are, of course. But Halton . . . he is somehow different, yet the same.

My eyes drift down his nose to the top of his lips. That familiar, dull ache between my thighs makes itself known as I stare at the lips that unwound me that fateful night.

Stop it, Maeve.

Turning away from him to face the gray-blue sky, I try to calm my thoughts. I beg Ottilie and Mother to make themselves known, to distract me from the guard nearby and give me the clarity I need to continue on my path to justice. This time, they don't show up.

Instead, heat brushes against my side, probing at me like it wants my attention—like *he* wants my attention. My skin begins to tighten, and my heart rapidly pounds against my ribs under his stare. I need to get out of here, away from him, but that strange sensation in my chest tugs, calling on me to take a peek.

As soon as I do, I catch the tail end of Halton's movement, turning away from me. He's now staring across the lake again. His lips are pursed, and his brows are furrowed. Something's weighing down on him. A part of me wants to ask him about it. Another part—the part that binds me to Mother, my hatred for the kingdoms—stops me from doing so.

The call of my name rings out between us, severing the trance I was in while looking at the guard. "There you are, girl!" the familiar voice of Madam Prea calls out. "We need to get you ready."

Sitting up now, I look at her and tilt my head in question. "What for?"

"Dinner. King Glynvyre is requesting your presence."

My body locks up, tensing as the words register. Halton begins coughing behind me, clearly taken aback by the news as well.

"What?" The word is barely audible. Madam Prea hears it anyway.

"You heard me, girl. Up!"

The older elf stands at the entrance of the garden in her navy dress and fur pashmina. Her arms are crossed as she waits on me to slowly stand.

I don't know why I do, but I turn and glance back at Halton. He's no longer looking at me as he runs his fingers through his hair with furrowed brows. He seems nervous, unsure.

Same here, guard.

I turn back toward Prea, crossing the Crystal Lake Garden at a snail's pace.

Why would the elven king want to see me?

36

Flickering flames cast shadows against the small dining room walls. Platters of mouthwatering food and goblets of wine and water adorn the wooden table before us. Dinner is intimate, with King Osmar Glynvyre seated at the head of the table in an extravagant chair that's taller than the rest. To his right sits Kayd. Next to the prince sits Halton, who—from what the king told me—has dinner with them most evenings. I'm directly across the captain and an older elf—King Glynvyre's personal advisor—sits next to me. On the opposite side of the king is an empty chair, equally as extravagant as his but smaller.

I don't say much as we eat, only speaking when spoken to. My hands are clammy as I cut into a piece of bread and lather it with butter. Why am I here? In this beautiful gold-and-white jeweled gown, sharing a meal with the most powerful being in the elven kingdom—

"Maeve, yes?" King Glynvyre asks as he pops a cherry tomato into his mouth. I nod with a tentative smile. "Tell me, what were you assigned before Kayd invited you to be in his court?"

My mouth parts as I think of a reply. I know Kayd doesn't want the truth about me to be known to anyone outside his personal guard and friends. I need to think quickly. I can't help the silent breath of relief as the prince inserts himself into the conversation.

"All those mortals from centuries of trials must be merging together for you, Father." His voice is smooth and confident, condescending, if only just a little. "Maeve was chosen as a chambermaid under Madam Prea three rotations ago but has since proven her loyalties to our crown. She has become a fond addition to my court."

The monarch eyes me for a moment longer before nodding his head. "Well," he says, "it's a pleasure to get to know you, Maeve. How has your time been serving Nythfaedell?"

My mask is unwavering tonight. My eyes stay calm, and my smile stays kind, despite the nail-shaped indentations in my palms as anger and anxiety course through my veins. "It is the most hospitable kingdom, from what I've heard, Your Majesty."

Taking a bite out of the roast on my plate, I glare at Kayd before I turn my bright-eyed mask back toward the king, needing to change the topic before I use my etched golden fork to gouge out their eyes. "And the queen, Your Majesty? Since my time here, I have yet to meet her."

The table falls silent. Not a breath can be heard. Melancholy tension thrums between the elves that's so palpable it can be cut with a knife.

"My dear Maeve . . ." The king smiles kindly toward me despite the sadness swirling within his green eyes. "The queen—my lovely Aila—passed nine rotations ago."

"Oh!" I exclaim. "I'm so sorry. I didn't know—"

"No, you wouldn't. This palace has the habit of staying quiet about her, despite my wishes to celebrate her life every day." His sad smile turns downward as he begins stacking vegetables onto a skewer.

I glance around the table. Solemn expressions paint the others' faces. Kayd glares down at his plate, and I can hear his teeth grind together between each bite of food.

Regardless of my hatred toward the kingdoms, of what their trials did, and the blood on my hands, my heart reaches out toward the king. He's hurting. A hurt I could not even comprehend: the loss of his love.

"I lost someone nine rotations ago as well." I'm as surprised by my confession as the rest of the table.

Halton's fork clatters against his plate, piercing through the thick air around us.

"I'm sorry for your loss, Maeve. Do you mind me asking who?" King Glynvyre is so genuine, so unlike his son.

"My mother." Her warm spirit nestles itself against my heart.

The king's auburn hair brushes over his shoulder as he nods with tender eyes. "I'm sure she was a good woman."

"The best." My voice cracks slightly, and I focus back on my plate, finding my food to be very interesting. Being that open with them . . . it scares me. It's different from the camaraderie and trust I've forged with Madam Prea and the twins. This? This is raw—real. This is with someone who rules the elves, who watches under a tent while contenders must face deadly trials. This makes my hands tremble.

Conversations between the king and his advisor start up again, pulling me out of my thoughts. As I look around the small table, my eyes lock onto Halton. Our gazes are unwavering under the other's for only a short while, though it feels like I'm lost in the green-and-brown swirls of his irises for hours. I'm the first to break eye contact.

For the rest of the meal, I contribute to the conversation when appropriate, but don't say much. Moans and sighs of content fill the small dining room as the meal comes to an end. The king waves his hand out in front of him, and the food disappears completely. The wine, however, stays.

"I am retiring for the night. You three, feel free to stay. Drink! Enjoy yourselves!" The king walks around the table and pats both Kayd and Halton on the back, then makes his way to me. "It was a pleasure to meet you, Maeve."

He gently lifts my hand and kisses the top of it. It's not threatening. It doesn't feel like there is an alternative motive to the gesture, just an older elf offering kindness.

As he walks away, I hear him mumble something about being young again. A comment that makes me chuckle. His advisor scrambles after him.

The heavy thud of the doors to the dining room closing is all I need before my smile crumbles. The air turns taut with tension.

"What was *that*, mortal?" Kayd's palms hit the table as he stands up, looming over the wooden barrier between us. His eyes narrow, and his upper lip curls.

Halton stays seated, guzzling down the goblet of wine in his right hand while his left balls into a fist atop the table.

I don't move. Instead, I lean back in my chair and cross my arms over my chest. "What was what, *Prince*?"

He slams his palms against the table harder this time. "How could you be stupid enough to ask about the queen?" Kayd's neck strains, and red tints his skin. He's seething.

"She didn't know," Halton's voice cuts through the room just as I open my mouth to yell back.

Sharply, my eyes cut to the guard. Kayd's does the same. There's a beat of nothing as Halton stares into my eyes before he turns to face his friend, whose mouth is twisted with disbelief. It's like he never would've expected Halton to disagree with him, never would've expected him to defend me.

I never would've expected it myself.

Minutes pass as the silence between the three of us swarms. It's unwavering, unmatched. I watch as Kayd and Halton stare each other down, as if they're communicating without words. I feel like an intruder, like I shouldn't be here as they hash whatever this is out.

The thud of the doors opening and a gasp pulls all three of us out of the tension. Our heads snap toward the sound. Alta and Niam stride through the open door. Both have smiles on their faces. Alta claps her ring-clad hands together while jumping up and down lightly.

"Maeve! I didn't expect you to be here!" she shrieks with excitement and runs over to the table.

"I didn't expect to be here either." I wring my fingers together in my lap.

Niam grabs a goblet of wine from the table and plops down into the chair previously occupied by the king's advisor. His arm drapes around my shoulders as he takes a long gulp. I notice Kayd's eyes lock onto where our bodies connect.

"This is even better." Niam sets the goblet down next to mine. It tilts to the side under an uneven piece of wood. Before it can fall, I catch it. He sends a dazzling smile my way. "Maeve can join us!"

"No!" the elven prince and guard say in unison.

I glower at them both. I don't even know what they're talking about, but the simple fact that they're already dismissing me sets my blood aflame.

"Oh, come on! I've been the only female in the group, surrounded by you three, for so long. I like Maeve. She's my friend." Alta's hopeful expression causes a soft smile to form along my lips. A friend . . . The word is nice to hear. It's even nicer knowing that it's true. "Just because you're the prince, Kayd, doesn't mean you get to dictate our friendships. She's coming."

The finality of her order sends a rush of pride through me. Seeing her stand up to Kayd and make him into the snarling mess he is now brings me an odd sense of joy.

A growl rips from his throat. The same sound—only softer, as if he's trying to hold it in—echoes from Halton. But with a reluctant nod, Kayd agrees.

Alta and Niam's victorious cheers and clinking goblets fill the empty dining room.

Alta's soft, dainty hand—clasped firmly in mine—guides me through the dark, birch forest shrouded by night. The glittering neon bugs and occasional glowing plant lights our way. The gown draping over my figure from dinner is of no help in navigating the terrain. My feet stumble beneath me as I step over logs and avoid hanging branches. How Alta can expertly maneuver the area in her dress is beyond me.

Kayd is in front, leading the pack. As we go on, his walk becomes faster, like he's afraid he'll miss something if he doesn't hurry. Niam and Halton are behind him, leaving Alta and me in the back. The males' laughter flutters between the branches and leaves surrounding us. The sound of Halton's is unrestrained—beautiful, even. It's the first time I've heard him sound so happy and free. I wish he would turn around just so I could steal a glance. I can only imagine what his face—his smile—looks like when that heart-thumping sound breaks through his hard exterior.

Breaching the clearing of trees into the Secret Spring, my feet dig into the earth and come to a halt. My eyes are wide in wonder as I take in the sight before me. The water, plants, bugs, even the rocks, glow under the moonlight. Almost every surface of the spring radiates splashes of bright, luminescent colors. I've never seen anything like it before. It's mesmerizing.

Alta has yet to realize she's no longer holding my hand. Her eyes are trained on the spring, her feet taking her there as if they have a mind of their own.

"What do you think?" Alta turns to her side and realizes I'm not with her. "Maeve?" She stops walking and turns back toward me.

Niam stops undressing once he hears his sister call out my name, like he's frozen in time with only his pants on. Halton and Kayd turn around to look at me, too. I barely notice them. My gaze never leaves the fluorescent world before me.

I shouldn't be here. This otherworldly place doesn't belong to me. It belongs to them. I practically feel the darkness dampening my soul and the blood on my hands tainting the Secret Spring. I'm an intruder, just like I was at dinner. I shouldn't be here.

"It's beautiful, isn't it?" The soft sound of Alta's voice breaks through my thoughts.

Shaking my head languidly, I sweep my gaze over the others still watching me. Niam sends me an encouraging nod before shucking his pants off and wading into the water. Halton looks like he isn't breathing. My eyes meet his. There's something there, something heavy and tense. I can't help the blush that heats up my cheeks under his stare, internally grateful for the neon lights obscuring the colors around us. Quickly—too quickly—Halton's hazel is concealed. His eyes narrow and harden, and he turns away.

Kayd watches his friend retreat to the edge of the spring before tossing his boots behind him and dipping his bare feet into the waves. Turning his attention back to me, the prince briefly looks me up and down with furrowed brows before shaking his head, stripping down, and tackling Niam off a boulder. Halton chuckles at the splash they make.

Finally, I look at the female and can't help but wonder if she knows how little I deserve to be sharing this with them. "This is what you wanted to show me?"

Alta answers, "No." Her smile widens as she glances around the open area. "This is beautiful, yes . . . but this happens every night. It's nothing special. What we're here to see only happens once every rotation."

"What is it?" I internally cringe at the sheer wonder twining around each word.

Alta giggles. A light, friendly giggle. It mixes with the laughs of the others. "You'll just have to wait and find out."

Her smile widens as she wraps her slender hand around mine and pulls me to the others.

As the night grows later, whatever we're here for has yet to happen. From where I'm perched, leaning against a shimmering, mossy tree, I take in the sights around me. Halton and Niam pass the time by jumping off boulders and splashing in the glowing blue water. The way they act is like they're brothers. Born from the same circumstances. Both taken in by the kingdom's king and queen. Both finding themselves and their places in the palace—Niam as a courtier, Halton as the captain of the prince's guard.

I wonder what Halton's life was like before he came to the palace. I wonder if he's from the same village as the twins. I wonder if he misses his home. Stealing a glimpse at the guard, I take in that freeing smile I longed to see earlier on our trek through the forest as he gets out of the water. I don't look for too long, but my chest tightens, and my heart secretly soars at the sight.

Kayd and Alta lay on their backs, with arms crossed behind their heads and feet dangling into the spring. When I asked what they were doing, Alta told me that they're *moonbathing*. Apparently, the moon has mystical rejuvenation properties they want to soak in. I've never heard of such a thing, but it doesn't surprise me that the elves do something so peculiar.

My ears pick up bits and pieces of their conversation. I don't mean to eavesdrop, especially on one of my only friends in this kingdom, but I can't help it. During my initial training in Phandolus, I was taught to always listen, and it's come in handy plenty of times since.

"It's spreading, Kayd," Alta mutters. "My sources say the tieflings have convinced the merfolk to join in their trek to undermine us."

Prince Kayd grunts under his breath. "We'll keep an eye on it. Keep an eye on Terakeld as well. Two rebellions at once . . . Things are changing. *Galfei Thalor* is changing."

Alta tells him that she'll see what she can find out. Before I can hear anything else, a blue butterfly flutters into my line of sight, stealing my attention. It's ethereal, with its halo-like glow and white patterns contrasting the blue . . . the same blue of my beloved satin ribbon that now sits permanently on my vanity.

Tentatively reaching my hand out, the butterfly tickles the tips of my fingers with its antennae, then lands delicately on top of my middle finger. Its beady black eyes peer up at me as if it's staring into my soul . . . My soul that's as dark and inky as its gaze. That doesn't deter it away, though. The small creature stays perched atop my finger, enjoying the autumn breeze.

I don't hear his footsteps until he's already at my side. Halton, with water dripping off his brawny body, leans against the tree with his arms crossed, the side of his body brushing against my own.

"Why are you over here by yourself?" He watches the butterfly inch along my hand. It only flaps its wings curiously at our newest addition. "Do you think you're too good for us elves?"

"I know I'm too good for you." I slyly look up at him from under my lashes. He looks even more stunning than he usually does.

The elf shoots me a glare before it softens, and he breathes out a slight laugh. I can see the reflection of my dress in his gentle eyes. It looks like it's made of starlight itself under the glow. His mouth slightly parts, as if he is about to say something—

"Maeve! Halton! Come on. It's almost time!" Niam calls out across the spring.

I look over at my friend and smile before looking back at the guard, who hasn't moved a muscle. His eyes still bore into me.

"It's hard to stand here, as close as I am, and not kiss you." My breath catches in my throat as his words wash over me. The butterfly flies away hastily like it knows it shouldn't be here for a conversation so secretive, so private.

"They would be horrified if you did." I jut my head in the direction of the others.

"They would." Halton's gaze is fixed on my parted lips.

"You would be horrified if you did," I whisper, startled by how drawn to him I feel. It's something I'm not used to, something that scares me. My heart rams into my rib cage, wishing to be freed. Because if it were, it would willingly leap into Halton's hands without the worry of whether or not he would crush it.

A split-second pause. "I would," he mumbles with a slight nod. His gaze stays where it is.

Niam calls out to us again, this time with more urgency.

"It's a good thing we're being summoned, then, isn't it?" I smirk at the guard, then turn to leave him near the tree.

Kayd narrows his eyes at me as I approach, trepidation twisting his mouth. A beat later, Halton follows. I adjust my gown and sit down on the hard, stone ground next to Niam. Halton sits next to me, careful not to be too close.

I hold my breath for a few moments until I see it. So wondrous and awe-inspiring. Streaks of different colored sparkles dance along the top of the water and flow up into the night sky as if the magick in this spring is being sucked up into the moon and stars. And luminescent creatures begin to appear through the tall forest trees and gather around the spring.

A lavender-and-white fox with five tails and curled ears is the first to reach the water. It bends over the edge and slurps up a few gulps with its plum-colored tongue. Three silver rabbits with antlers and small blue flames erupting from the tips of their ears hop by the fox.

A whoosh of air mere inches above my head pulls my attention toward the sky. Long slinky dragons—the same size as the tattered tabby cat that lounges across the windowsill of the tavern back home—glide above me. There are several of them. Fast streaks of blue, green, purple, and pink fill the sky as their rapid clicking and mewls echo off the tree's trunks. The moon glistens off their scales, creating a rainbow of lights beaming off the boulders.

I laugh as I look around at the others; it's light, but it's real. To my right, the others pay me no mind. Their eyes are glued to the spectacle around them. Awe. Wander. Euphoria. Then, to my left, I'm met with hazel eyes. Halton's unwavering gaze is on me.

"What is this?" My words are no louder than a whisper.

Alta answers for the guard, "The Night of Light." I look past the others at her, and she smiles brightly back at me.

"Halton discovered the phenomenon when we were little," this time, Kayd speaks up. The prince's words are soft. He's not sneering or growling. He's at peace being here with his friends, his family. He cares fiercely for them. I can see it in his eyes when he speaks.

"All four of us snuck out of the palace and came here one night when we were younger, a night this happened to take place. Halton and I were, what, fifteen? You two were sixteen?" The prince directs the question at Niam, who nods in response. "Ever since then, we come back each autumn on the same evening to experience it. Even though it only lasts about ten minutes, it's something we look forward to all rotation long. We're the only ones in Nythfaedell who know about it. Now you do, too."

My heart stutters. *You shouldn't be here*, it seems to say.

Prince Kayd turns toward me and stares for a beat longer, as if he heard what I know to be true, too. He then turns toward a turtle the size of a teacup, with a glowing shell and little wings at the edge of the spring. Its wings flutter in the air as it jumps into the waves, sending little droplets of water near our feet.

I know, I silently tell my heart.

My eyes roam across the magnificent beings once again. The ground rumbles from beneath us, and as if the trees themselves part, a large, two-headed wyrm slithers in the clearing. A few turquoise-and-gray scales are missing along its shimmering side. On the other side of the clearing, the trees seem to do the same. A gold-and-white griffin marches into the area, mindful of the smaller creatures around its paws.

Then, I see it. Straight ahead. A gasp slips through my lips. Slowly exiting the tree line is a beautiful white unicorn. It's *the* unicorn. I can see its horn from here—tattered and torn with deep scratches. I straighten my spine, forcing myself to not run toward it.

"Is that what I think it is?" Niam whispers to no one in particular, awe lacing his question.

"Don't you have eyes?" Alta chides with just as much breathiness.

The unicorn seems to call to me, showing itself because I'm here. I begin to rise to my feet, slowly but without hesitation.

"What are you doing?" the elven prince hisses quietly. "You'll scare it away."

I ignore him. I ignore Niam's hand reaching out to me. I ignore Halton's gaze searing my skin. I ignore all of them.

Weaving my way through the tiny dragons and flying turtles, I steadily approach the unicorn. The other creatures don't even notice as they blissfully drink the water and play with one another.

It observes me with eyes as dark as the soil beneath my feet. They're full of intrigue as I stand only an arm's length away. Jasmine and magick waft from its coat, billowing between us. That's where I first smelled the unique scent. During my trials.

"I found you," I whisper. Its long, coarse lashes blink. A part of me thinks it can understand me. A beat of silence, then I say, "I'm so sorry." My words are broken, holding so much regret and guilt within each of them.

The glow surrounding the spring begins to dim. Animals who were swimming shake their damp fur dry, and those lounging around the water get up. Each one leaving as quickly as the phenomenon came.

The unicorn, however, doesn't move. I don't either as we stare into each other's souls. It seems to see me. Truly *see* me, just like the serpent in the sea.

Like it knows all the heartbreak I've been through. All the anger I hold inside. All the guilt for turning into something that doesn't deserve to be this close to such a pure being. All the hope I hold for Jerik. All the shame I hide for what I did with Halton. All the yearning I still have for him. It sees right through me. It's jarring yet comforting.

Someone . . . *something* finally sees me.

With a shaky inhale, I reach my hand out to the being with bated breath. Its snow-white snout nuzzles into my waiting hand, and I huff out a laugh as a tear glides down my cheek and settles into the corner of my mouth. Its salty taste goes unnoticed.

Too soon, the unicorn lifts its head out of my palm and turns around, entering the tree line once again. My feet are rooted, unmoving as I watch it go.

I don't know how long I stare at the empty spot where it was, my eyes straining to see into the dark forest beyond. Rustling behind me is what pulls me back. Turning to face the others, I see they're all now standing up. Excitement, curiousness, disbelief, and awe stare back at me.

37

Assignments outside of Nythfaedell are finally given to me. The Night of Light bridged something between Prince Kayd and me. The unicorn's trust in me was enough for him. That, or his patience for wreaking havoc on other kingdoms is merely running thin. Lords of Fiermoor, ladies of Amphitea, clergymen, and courtiers . . . I've killed them all under the orders of Prince Kayd and the elven kingdom over the past two weeks.

But I can feel the justice I seek slipping through my blood-coated fingertips. The heart pounding adrenaline that rushes through my veins is nothing more than a distraction now. A distraction as a means to an end, to run from my own thoughts—thoughts that are constantly consumed by *him*.

When I'm slicing my knives across throats and plunging my dagger into chests, I don't think about the way Halton's eyes gleam with intriguing danger or the fluttering feeling I get when I feel his gaze burning into my skin from afar. No thoughts swirl around my head of how much I want him again nor how much I hate him for making me want such a thing.

It's an unusual sensation, wanting to be around someone so badly that it feels like your soul is singing out to their very being. It starts in my chest and seeps into my muscles, nerves, blood—every bit of me—until it's all-consuming.

Trudging back into my bedchambers after an assignment in Phandolus, my body aches for a hot bath. My stinging muscles quiver around my stiff bones. Climbing that jagged mountain just to get to the home of a changeling earl Kayd wanted dead put me in a foul mood. And it has yet to disappear. A bath is, indeed, needed.

Kayd said that the prick deserved it, that it was long overdue. For what? I didn't ask. I didn't care. But from the look on Niam's face, it was something that wasn't worth killing for.

I plop unceremoniously into the waiting water of the steaming bath—thanks to one of Madam Prea's chambermaids who was kind enough to get my rooms ready for my return. I close my eyes with a sigh as the perfumed water's warmth soothes my tired muscles.

Hazel eyes. Brown hair. Beige skin. Sinful lips.

Halton—invading my thoughts once again. A growl—low and galling—rumbles in my chest. I refuse to pine over an elf. It goes against everything I have ever known, everything I am, even though I can feel myself warming up to them. Already feeling like I've lost my true self after the trials, I can't lose the Maeve that was reborn from the blood of others.

I can't . . .

As I sit there—staring blankly into the dirty water—I know all the questions and confusion can wait. Tonight, I rest.

Rest is a luxury I don't get.

Pounding against my door startles me awake. My body jolts into a sitting position, my mind struggling to keep up. It feels sluggish as I try to decipher what's happening.

"What . . ." I croak out.

My eyes try to adjust as I look around my pitch black room. The middle of the night, it seems. It feels as if I went to bed merely hours ago.

The knocking at my chamber door starts up again. This time, it's lighter but still as insistent.

"I'm coming!" My voice bounces against the wall of my bedroom into the sitting area.

The knocking stops in response.

The wooden floor freezes my bare feet as soon as I remove myself from my bed. Immediately wanting to hop back into the warm silks and pillows, I wrap a white fur around my shoulders and trudge to the door.

"Maeve?" a soft voice calls through the wood separating me from the one that woke me up.

A deep, drawn-out sigh slips through my tightly closed lips. "Alta." I swing the door open. "And . . . Niam? What are you two doing here? It's the middle of the night."

My shoulders slump, and a corner of the fur falls from my shoulder. I'm too tired to fix it. The back of my hand rubs my sleep-crusted eyes as I look at the elven twins. Both carry packed bags slung over their shoulders.

"Sorry for waking you, Maeve. Truly." Niam adjusts the part of the fur that fell and secures it tightly around my chest with an apologetic smile. "But we need you to come with us. Overnight, Kayd got reports of a rally against Nythfaedell. He wants the three of us and Halton to go check it out."

Of course.

Opening the door wider, I let the two of them in with a sigh. Niam leans against the door once it's closed as he takes in my chambers with a low whistle. I realize it's the first time he's been here.

"Do you need help packing?" Alta sets down their bags on the chaise.

"No, it's all right." I crinkle my eyebrows together as I walk back to my bedroom and look through my wardrobe, willing the elven magick to conjure up whatever I need. What *do* I need? "Why does Kayd need me to go?"

Niam pushes himself away from the door. His lanky fingers glide over every inch of decor and furniture given to me by his prince before he turns and says, "There's a count of a noble house not far from the rally that Kayd wants taken care of. Two birds, one stone."

I nod. A simple enough explanation. I'll need my gear, then. When I turn toward my bed, it's all there—leathers, boots, holsters, cloak, and corset belt, my favorite knives and dagger, even the sword I rarely use but like to have just in case. It's all waiting for me as if even the magick in the room didn't know the reason I was going until now.

"And why is he making you two go?" I call over my shoulder.

Alta's giggle grows closer. She saunters over to my bed and sits upon the mattress. Niam follows and leans against the doorframe of my room.

"We aren't just the prince's friends lounging around the palace all day, Maeve." Alta flops on her back. Her lips—painted, even this early in the day—pull up into a smirk. "There's a reason why we know the comings and goings of the other kingdoms."

"So . . ." I stuff a black bag down harshly to fit everything I may need before stripping my body of my night clothes and pulling on another pair of fur-lined leather pants, a thick wool tunic, and my cloak. "You're spies?"

Alta's offended gasp pulls my attention away from the stubborn corset clasp I just can't seem to fasten. Her hand is draped over her forehead as if I said the most ridiculous thing.

Niam chuckles at his sister, then comes up behind me to help with the irritating piece of clothing. "Stars, no. But we know where to look for information. Courtiers are charming creatures, and we've had enough practice to know exactly who to charm."

"Sometimes"—Alta shakes her head at Niam—"you can be so dramatic—"

"Like you," I interrupt. Alta scoffs and holds her heart as if I skewered her. My laugh is raspy, laced with the lingering slumber I long for.

Stuffing my feet into a leather pair of boots, I run my fingers through my knotted strands of hair. I use two leather straps to tie it back in messy buns at the nape of my neck and stuff a handful of mint leaves in my mouth to chew. "Okay, then. Let's go."

The Royal Docks are cloaked beneath the deep blue night sky. The large crescent moon lights our path up to a small plain ship nestled between large looming masts and dark-green sails, where Prince Kayd and Halton wait. The prince's arms are crossed over his chest, and Halton's hands are clasped behind his back, a brown knapsack leaning against his boots.

"So nice of you to join us." Kayd unfurls his arms and picks at his spotless nails, inspecting each one with pursed lips and furrowed brows.

I bite down the undoubtedly snide reply that sits on the tip of my tongue.

"She's here now, isn't she?" Niam beats me to it as he strolls past the prince and the captain of his guard, ascends the ramp of the waiting boat, and shakes the hand of the helmsman who will take us across The Unlighted Sea.

"Remember"—Kayd's voice raises slightly so Niam can hear him—"don't draw attention to yourselves. As far as we know, the tieflings don't know we know about the unrest and their schemes. We must keep it that way."

"Got it, Boss." Alta brings two fingers up to her temple and salutes the elven prince, then loops her arm through Halton's, dragging him onto the boat just as he grabs onto his bag.

Following the others, I take a step past the prince before he stops me in my tracks. He holds out a ripped piece of parchment toward me. "Your assignment."

My fingers pluck the paper from his waiting hand. I silently nod at the prince before continuing my trek up the ramp. The cracked wood creaks beneath my boots, but the sound is barely audible beneath the waves crashing against the shell-covered shore.

"Welcome aboard." Awaiting the arrival of his final passenger, the captain of the ship bows his head toward me while offering his hand.

A part of me doesn't want to take it. I can easily get on a boat myself without the help from an elf. That's my bitterness talking. The captain is just doing his job, just like I am. I place my palm in his, and he makes sure I board with ease. His hands are rough and calloused. No doubt from rotations of hard work on the sea.

"Thank you." My voice is quiet but loud enough for him to hear, and he sends me a dazzling smile that stretches across his suntanned skin. His silver hair dances with the wind, and his sepia-colored eyes crinkle at the sides.

"I hope our trek to Fiermoor is comfortable for you. This may not be *The Amithydia* . . ." The captain gestures to the right toward a giant ship with three decks and gleaming portholes along its side. The name of the ship rolls off the elf's tongue in a way it would never for me. It's elven, surely. He gestures to the left toward a smaller but just as grand ship. "Or *The Ryllikaar*, but it's something."

My lips turn up into a soft smile as the helmsman rubs the back of his neck with furrowed eyes as he takes in his ship. I follow his gaze. There's a small deck and an even smaller quarterdeck where the helm proudly sits. The wood of the ship is chipped and worn, and the small sails are white. No trace of Nythfaedell can be seen on this vessel . . . It's used when the elves want to go unseen.

"It's great. Really. What's the name of this one?"

The elf shakes his head. "It doesn't have a name."

My attention shifts back toward the captain, then I smile kindly. "I think you should give it one," I say before bowing my head slightly and walking past him toward the bow of the ship.

No more than ten minutes later, the ship lurches forward and leaves Nythfaedell behind.

The cold autumn air stings my cheeks as I lean against the wooden rail and look across the churning waves. My palms snag against the splintered wood. A hiss slips through my teeth as a chip stabs my skin.

My head snaps toward the sound of a cresting wave crashing against the hull. The sound reminds me of the giant sea serpent I saw from beneath the elven carriage on my way to kill Kayd. I will its shiny scales and silver eyes to appear in the waves again. I want to see the beast swimming openly in the dark depths of The Unlighted Sea. I want to see it soaking in its freedom.

As I search the horizon for any sign of the serpent, silhouettes of tall robust trees against the night sky appear to my left. I immediately recognize the edges of land dropping off steeply into the sea and the abandoned docks. We're passing Derlow Grove, an island that doesn't belong to any of Galfei Thalor's kingdoms. An island that merely exists.

I've had to pass it several times on my way to assignments in Nythfaedell before Princess Andrina ordered me to cross the bridge. From what I've seen, it's all forests and overgrown plants. For all I know, the entire island is deserted.

If we're passing Derlow Grove now, that means . . .

I turn my head to the right. Terakeld. *Home.*

It's nothing more than a sliver of rock in the distance. I can see the rugged edges of the easternmost part of my home and the island where our trials took place. The kingdoms' tents stand stark against the sky. They're nothing but abandoned structures that will stay that way until the next rotation's trials, until the next round of contenders will have to do some vile tasks, like harm an innocent creature or kill one of their own.

My grip on the ship's railing tightens, my nails scratching through the topmost layer of the splintered wood. Alta's flouncy giggle pulls my mind away from the trials. With one last look at my home, I turn toward the sound.

She's standing next to the ship's helm with the captain. Her finger twirls a silky strand of black hair, sending him a dazzling smile that makes him blush. Even under the night sky and the single flickering flame Alta holds with her other hand, I can see his cheeks redden brightly.

"Such a flirt." I can't help the smile that splits my face in two.

I look around for Niam but don't see him anywhere. He must be below deck, catching a few more hours of rest. Something I should be doing as well.

In my search for Niam, my eyes snag on Halton. He's sitting on the steps that lead up to the quarterdeck with his elbows resting atop his knees and his fingers steepled against his mouth. He's staring straight ahead at nothing in particular, like something's on his mind, unfocused eyes and worried lines between his brows.

There's a moment of stillness, a single breath held as I watch him. The way his cheek muscles twitch and his pulse pounds against the side of his neck. That moment of stillness disappears, and I can sense his eyes are about to lock onto mine. It's as if my body is connected to his. I turn back toward the sea before he can.

A minute later, I feel him approaching before I hear him. His attention roams up my spine, the pressure of his gaze increasing the closer he gets. My gut twists, and my chest seizes in response. No footsteps fall against the creaking wood, as if he's a phantom floating toward me. Lighter than the wind itself.

The chill of Halton's body settles into my bones. I smother the shudder dancing just beneath my flesh, trying to rip free. The guard places his hands atop the railing next to me and leans forward. My eyes shift to the side, sneaking a glance at him. He's staring straight ahead, watching the ship pass the final section of earth that makes up Derlow Grove. The muscles that run from the bottom of his jaw, past his pointed ear, and toward his temple flex as he bites down on his teeth. His knuckles turn bone-white and the wood of the rail creaks, his grip tightening as the silence stretches between us.

I know he knows I'm looking at him. I can feel it just as clearly as I can feel the breath filling my lungs.

Look at me, I want to say.

My head seems to fight with my body as I stare at his profile. A deep rumble of need and something more intense courses through my veins and sets my nerves alight. My chest tugs in his direction like it's reaching out, urging me to step closer—like I *need* to be closer. My brain sends waves of guilt through my soul and halts any movement despite my body's protests.

Look at what you've made of me.

As if he can feel me just as much as I feel him, he turns to face me. With his attention locked on mine, it feels like the world around us pauses. The waves' white and frothy crests are frozen. Alta's giggles are silenced. We're in a void. Nothing but us matters.

"Do you have everything set for your assignment?" his voice—raspy and strained—cuts through the cold air.

The sounds of our surroundings flood my senses and fill my ears once again, as if they never stopped. As if they never hung in the air like suspended threads. I know they hadn't, but a part of me wishes they had.

Irritation pricks at my fingertips. Perhaps he couldn't feel that hanging tension as I had. Perhaps I read it wrong. Perhaps there is nothing to read. Of course there's not. There is nothing between us—nothing but ire and some sick sense of masochism.

Shaking my head from the thoughts swirling around, I notice the corner of Halton's mouth perk up slightly, as if pulled by an invisible string. "What?" I ask.

His smirk widens. I want to wipe it clean off his face. "I asked if you have everything ready for your assignment."

The guard has never shown interest in what I do. My brows pull together, and my lips purse. "Do you have a sudden interest in being an assassin, *guard*?"

Halton scoffs, leaning his hips against the rail and waving a hand toward me in dismissal. "How little you think of me, *Serpent*. I could never stoop so low and kill just for the fun of it."

A sharp pounding crashes against my ribs. My heart. Mother's warmth and Ottilie's light twine around it, willing it to calm down. It does, if only just a little. But their presence doesn't stop my anger from stoking the flames in my gut.

"You don't get to tell me why I do what I do." The words are a dangerous growl, vibrating within the depths of my chest.

Halton blinks. Then his eyes soften as the words leave my lips. It makes that fire flare even more. Turning away from the elven guard and The Unlighted Sea, I stalk off and make my way below deck.

Tucked into a forest full of tall trees with charcoal-colored trunks and no leaves on sharp branches, the inn is dull and dingy beneath the midmorning sun. The wooden door is damp and warped, matching the exterior.

"You'd think Kayd would be able to make sure our accommodations were up to par," Alta hums as she takes the steps up the creaking and cracked porch toward the front entrance. She adjusts her cloak, the hood sitting atop her head hiding her ears. The others do the same.

"We're not to draw attention to ourselves. Remember, Alta?" Halton chides, though I don't look at him. Instead, I turn in a circle, taking in my surroundings before I leave for my assignment.

The inn is in a minuscule forest town on the outskirts of Holmfirth, a tiefling village that prides itself on providing the royal family its lumber. The count—my next target—calls Holmfirth his home. His estate shouldn't be hard to find. Scribbled on the parchment tucked into my pocket is the description of it and where he's likely to be.

"Through the blocks of inns and shops and into the forest," I mutter. That seems like the best route to get there. I'll leave as soon as we get our lodging.

Turning back toward the inn's entrance, I realize I'm now alone. The others are no longer there. I can see Halton through a grime-coated window talking to a large tiefling behind a desk. The guard's eyes are set firm, and his fingers clench into a fist at his side.

With a sigh, I enter the inn. Mildew and stale ale swarm my nostrils. My nose crinkles on its own. To my right, leftover revelers are strewn across tables in the inn's tavern. Snores and tired moans leave their open lips. One tiefling with maroon skin opens their glassy eyes and looks at me before falling back to sleep.

"We don't have any rooms left."

I'm pulled away from the fly-covered tavern and turn toward the voice. The tiefling at the front desk leans back in his chair and crosses his hairy arms against his chest. He sucks on a tooth as he looks the others up and down.

I make my way over to them. I catch the tiefling's attention, and he sneers at me.

"We were assured that there were rooms available before we made the journey here." Halton's words are clipped, irritated.

"Why don't you mortals run off now. Like I said"—he glares at each of us in the eye—"there are no rooms."

Niam steps up next to Halton, placing a hand on the guard's shoulder with a peculiar look before addressing the inn worker. "My good sir, I think we got off on the wrong foot. You see, we need a room. Two, preferably, but we'll take one. And by the looks of it, the state of this place needs an upgrade."

The elf reaches into his bag and pulls out a velvet pouch, dropping it on the table with a thud. The tieflings eyebrows raise in interest, and he slowly grabs the pouch to inspect. As soon as it's open, his black eyes widen. His mouth opens and closes, and he looks up at Niam with intrigue before reaching beneath the desk and pulling out a single onyx stone key.

"Looks like a room just became available." The tiefling pockets the coins and hands Niam the key, who simply nods and turns toward the stairs leading up to the rooms.

As we follow him, he leans over to me and whispers, "I told you, we know how to charm." Then he winks at me before finding our room.

It's small and cramped, but large enough for two dust-covered beds and a small table. An even smaller bathroom with a barrel-sized tub is off to the side. Alta sets her bag atop the bed farthest from the door, and Halton sets his on the other. A brief moment of panic rushes over me. Niam seems to notice and picks for me, placing his bag next to Halton's.

The elves remove their hoods and gather around the small table. Halton unravels a detailed map of Fiermoor and begins debriefing the others about what he knows of the rally.

I lay out all my weapons atop mine and Alta's bed and clean them as I listen.

"Kayd's source says the rally is supposed to take place this evening in front of a Spiicrete pottery shop in the town's square." Halton points at a few locations on the map. "Tieflings and humans alike are expected to attend, so we'll need to wear our hoods."

Tossing the cloth I was cleaning my weapons with to the side, I stand and sheath each one. The slice of my blades drowns out whatever else is being said at the table.

My feet take me to the window, and I pry it open. Without looking behind me toward the others, I announce, "I'll be back," then jump through the opening onto the rocky Fiermoor ground.

38

GOING UNNOTICED IN THIS no-name town is easy. Killing the count of Holmfirth was even easier.

Thunder rumbles above me, and raindrops sizzle against the ground as I slink through the town's center. For midafternoon, it's dark outside. Clutching my hood tighter around my head, I slip past a group of tieflings hammering together a makeshift stage in the open area between several shops before rounding a corner.

Just as the sky opens even more and the rain pounds harder toward the earth, I enter the inn. No one is stationed at the front desk, but loud chatter and singing fills the area. In the tavern, the revelers are now awake and are already guzzling down goblets of wine and mead. That maroon-skinned tiefling is on top of the bar, pouring plum-colored liquid down one female's cleavage as another male slurps it up against her corset.

Disgusting.

Lowering my head and climbing the stairs, no one pays me any mind. I trudge through the halls of the inn's upper level until I reach our room's door. I don't mean to open it as quietly as I do, but no one notices me at first.

Alta is getting ready for the rally, tying her hair up into a cascading waterfall of silky black strands. Niam is lounging across his and Halton's bed, with his

294

head perched atop a pillow and his hands resting on his stomach. And Halton sits at the table, hunched over the map and other scattered pieces of parchment that weren't there when I left.

As I close the door—just as silently as I opened it—Halton speaks without lifting his head. "Welcome back."

"Thanks. Killing for the fun of it is my favorite way to start my day." My voice is low enough for only the guard to hear, though I see Niam open an eye and peek as I remove my hood. Halton's body tenses at my words, but I turn away from him as a gasp cuts through the room.

Alta stands stock-still with wide eyes, alarm and unease lacing her gray irises. Her open-mouthed stare roams my face. I sigh. The count's sticky blood still covers my skin. That pesky artery just had to soak me in his gore as soon as I wretched the knife from the side of his neck.

The way she's staring at me . . . I hate it.

"I need a bath," I declare before swiftly rushing toward the bathroom and locking the door behind me.

There's a beat of silence before I hear Alta ask, "Is . . . is she okay?" Her voice is muffled behind the wooden door.

A loud sigh and the creak of a bed screeches in response. "She just killed someone, Alta." *Niam.* "What do you expect? Sunshine and fairy dust?"

"Be quiet. Both of you." Halton's gruff voice interrupts any reply Alta might have had. "Focus on our mission."

Silence is the twins' only response.

Leaning my head against the door, I inhale and exhale long drawn-out breaths.

In and out. In and out.

The anger I felt on the ship with Halton is still brewing, twisting around my darkened soul that I wish was lighter. And seeing Alta look at me like that, like I really am the monster I try to hide, makes it worse. I sit in that internal darkness for a moment longer before filling up the bath.

Our wool hoods cover us from the misty drizzle that flutters down from the evening sky. Niam, Alta, Halton, and I walk through the crowd. It's bigger than I was anticipating, full of tieflings and mortal servants heading toward the rally.

As we round a corner and see the now-complete stage, Halton turns to each of us. "Blend in. Stay hidden. Do what you must to not draw any attention to yourselves. And keep your ears open. Any information you can get is valuable."

Niam nods and weaves through the waiting crowd close to the makeshift stage. I see him nod to some and smile at others as he settles into easy conversation with a mortal holding a coat nearby. Courtiers and their charm.

Just as I'm about to turn around, Alta's voice stops me. "Be careful, Maeve," she whispers.

I send her a thankful smile. "You too." I glance at Halton and nod curtly. "Guard."

The way he looks at me makes my skin tighten. His lower lip twitches, as if he wants to say what he always says back—*Serpent*. But it's too dangerous to utter such a name. Instead, his eyes roam my face before he places his hand on Alta's back, saying, "Come, Alta," and guiding her away.

I watch the two of them settle into the crowd on the far side of the town's center before my feet take me toward the back. Sticking to the shadows, to the place where I'm most comfortable.

Easy conversations swirl around me while we wait for the rally to start. Tieflings who traveled from Holmfirth and other surrounding villages are dressed in lush suits and gowns, mingling within groups. I notice our inn's front desk worker near the middle of the crowd, talking animatedly with his hands and howling at something someone else says.

The chatter slows down into quiet murmurs, then whispers, until the crowd is completely silent. A beautiful tiefling with light-red—almost pink—skin, plum corkscrew horns, and a gown that screams of wealth ascends the stairs of the stage, followed by three others: two burly tiefling males and an emerald-haired woman with a clipboard held toward her chest. Gaping slits in her neck quiver against her bronze skin. A mermaid.

"Welcome!" The tiefling female spreads her arms out wide, addressing the crowd. "You know why we are here, and you know what we want! The elves are selfish beings. Their greed needs to be diminished!"

The crowd cheers wildly. A few tieflings in front of me look around, nodding at anyone they see and patting each other on the backs.

The female continues. "Nythfaedell thinks they can have both servants and their magick tricks. They are *wrong*!"

"Yeah!" someone near the front yells. The leaders on the stage smile down at the crowd.

This time, one of the males speaks up. "The elves do not deserve to participate in the trials. And we will make sure they don't! Our movement is growing. Soon, all of Galfei Thalor will rally behind us, and when that happens, we will forcibly take Nythfaedell's servants away. We will ban them from ever taking contenders. We will make sure they feel the isolation their greedy asses deserve."

"Fuck the elves!" yells someone in the back near me.

More cheers.

A deep roar breaks through the applause. Then someone screams a guttural "fuck you" before shoving someone else to the side.

Standing on the tips of my toes, I peer into the crowd. The same maroon tiefling from the inn's tavern sways on his large feet before punching someone wearing a hood. A mortal.

"Elven spy—" His words are slurred, and the end of his accusation is interrupted by a deep grunt.

The mortal man tackles the tiefling onto the ground—only possible due to how drunk the creature is—and they knock down another rallygoer. Soon, the entire crowd is shoving each other as tieflings pummel and bash anyone nearby and as mortals fight back.

It's an all-out brawl. It's chaos.

I quickly lose sight of the others. The fight started near Alta and Halton, but the swarm of beings makes it hard to see. Niam is lost on the other side of the town's square.

The crowd surges around me. Large tieflings press into me, making it hard to breathe.

I need to get out of here.

"Maeve!" Someone screams my name . . . my real name. "Maeve!" It's Halton. His voice is raspy and raw.

My head swivels around, trying to find where he is.

"Maeve!" he yells again, screaming it as if he cares.

A large elbow slams into my chest. I fall, my back hitting the damp, stone ground. Before a heeled boot crushes me, I roll onto my hands and knees. Each time I'm close to gaining my footing again, I'm shoved back down. It's utter madness.

Inch by inch, I crawl through tiefling and mortal legs alike. Inch by inch, I shift with the crowd, dodging kicks and falling bodies. Finally, I breach the outer lines of the brawl and stand. My eyes shift back and forth over the fighting.

Where are the others?

Suddenly, large unrelenting hands grab me from behind and drag me away.

39

MY BACK SLAMS AGAINST the side of one of the surrounding shops. Sharp bricks dig into my flesh and a heavy arm pushes against my chest. My vision blurs. Nothing more than a figure surrounded by darkness stands before me.

"Elf bitch." The pure hate in that voice sends a cold chill down my spine.

Blinking my eyes rapidly, I will my vision to clear. As soon as it does, I'm met with dark-blue eyes and ivory skin. A large, muscular, mortal man pins me down.

"Your kind is the cause of all of this. *Greedy Bastards.*"

I buck my hips and twist my shoulders, anything to get free. His arm pushes into my lungs harder, making it hard to breathe, and he rips the hood off my head with his other hand.

Something flashes in his eyes as he takes in my rounded ears. Fueled by his adrenaline from the brawl, he doesn't release me. A sneer lifts his upper lip as his leer roams up and down my body. He's looking for a fight.

"What are you? A rebel or loyalist?"

The question stops my heart in its tracks, and my gut sinks as if it's made of lead. I don't reply.

He takes my silence as an answer—an answer he dislikes. The man's features twist, contorting into harsh lines and tight muscles. There's a fury behind his eyes, fueled by fidelity and hatred. I can't help but recoil as far away from him as I can. It's a look that will haunt me forever.

Piercing pain erupts across the back of my skull. My head throbs as I feel warm liquid trickle down my neck and spine, and the world spins around me.

Did he . . . Did he just . . .

I can't conjure up a single coherent thought. Nausea roils just beneath my sternum, and acid travels up my throat, sitting at the base of my tongue. Before I can swallow it down, the man wraps his hands around my throat and squeezes.

Air from my lungs is cut off completely. I can feel the muscles beneath his harsh fingers twitch. Black spots dance around my vision, and my limbs begin to tingle as I claw at his straining arms.

I'm going to die.

A brush of wind flutters around my fingers digging into his flesh. *Mother and Ottilie.*

I fight even harder now that they're here with me. My nails tear open his skin. Blood seeps from the cuts on his forearms and drips onto the ground of the alley he shoved me in. I fight and fight and fight until I begin to feel my heartbeat slow.

I'm going to die.

My now numb arms fall to my side. My fingers twitch and rub against one of the knives strapped to my thigh.

Another brush from Mother and Ottilie. Their warmth and light glides between my fingers, nudging me against the knife again.

Fight, they silently urge. *Fight until you're free. Fight until you're safe. Fight, Maeve.*

My fingers twitch again.

Fight, fight, fight.

Gathering all the dwindling strength I have left in my body, I grip onto one of the knives and reel my arm up and out. The blade slides through his temple like butter, and his skull crunches slightly under the pressure.

I pull the knife out, the nauseating squelch making me flinch, and the man's body slumps to the ground. Staring at the mortal as his life leaves his eyes, my chest rises rapidly, trying to get as much air into my body. My throat is raw, stinging with every inhale. Bringing my fingers to my neck, I wince as pain shoots through my muscles as soon as they brush my skin.

I almost died. I—

My heavy breaths turn crazed. No longer am I only sucking in the air that was stolen from me. Now, my shattered lungs heave with panic. I can't help the way my hands begin to shake and the way my joints lock up.

It was terrifying, knowing I could cease to exist right then and there. Is that how every one of my victims felt as their blood trickled out of their bodies? Is that how those mortal guards felt during the trials, when my ax connected with flesh and that helm bashed through bone?

The gaping hole in the man's skull mocks me as I stare at him. Waves of blood seep down the side of his face and pool around him.

It's too much. It's . . .

The next thing I know, I'm running. Running away from the deserted alley, where the man's body lays lifeless. I run, not back toward the inn but through the forest of ash-colored trees. I run over roots and around boulders. I run without a destination in mind. I run to get away.

I run and run and run until I reach a secluded clearing in the middle of the forest and fall to my knees. Sobs rip from the depths of my chest. A guttural sound that doesn't sound human leaves my trembling lips. Wet, salty tracks cascade down my cheeks, and snot drips and gathers at the peak of my top lip.

I killed him. I killed another mortal.

Tremors beneath my skin vibrate, and my heart speeds up.

I almost died. And I killed him. Just as he was about to kill me.

Kill or be kil—No. *No more excuses.*

I killed a man. *I* did that. One more mortal to add to the growing list.

Through the tears gathering along my lash line, waiting to drop, that dream of slaughtered stable boys flashes across my blurry vision. The puddles of blood sticking to the hay on the ground, their lifeless bodies scattered around.

Violently shaking my head, I push the images from my mind. Unlike those initial moments after that dream, I don't feel calm. I don't feel as if I could mow down anyone in my path. I feel panic, disgust, guilt.

My time with Alta and Niam and Prea . . . even Halton, has softened a part of me that I haven't felt since I last saw Jerik, when we spent a few peaceful moments at the creek on the outskirts of Phandolus's palace grounds.

"No more mortals," I vow. "Never again will I cut the string of life for another human."

Three mortal deaths are too many.

Hurried footsteps pound against the rocky forest floor. With a thrashing heart and trembling limbs, I spin around and point the knife still coated in the man's blood toward the direction of the sound.

The blade shakes violently in my hand as I come face-to-face with Niam. He stands on the edge of the clearing with wide eyes and his hands raised, stopping just before his face. It takes me a few heartbeats to realize it's him. When I do, I drop the knife as if it's scalding hot, the clank of the blade echoing around us as I stare at him with fear-stricken eyes and a wobbling lower lip.

His eyes travel down to my neck. He doesn't say anything, but his lips tighten. Finger-shaped bruises are most likely forming across my skin. Without a word, he slowly approaches, then sits next to me.

Silence swarms us for long moments. There are no expectations attached to it. Niam's simply here. With me. For me. He's whatever I need at this moment.

The back of my hand wipes my eyes. I sniffle.

"You should be afraid of me." My words are a mumbled mess of raging emotions.

"I'm not." From the corner of my eye, I see Niam turn his head to look at me. His eyes roam down the side of my face. "I could never be—"

"I killed someone tonight."

"You've killed plenty of beings before, Maeve."

My heart clenches at the statement. For the first time, the truth about the blood on my hands hurts.

"I-I almost died tonight, Niam. Just a few more seconds, and I would have . . . I got a glimpse of what every single one of my victims feels before they take their last breath. I was terrified. I still am. I never want to feel like that again. Not even the days I was tortured by Kayd—when I thought I wouldn't survive another maiming—compare to how it felt as my heart slowed under that mortal's hands. I never want to inflict that upon anyone again." A ragged inhale.

A single tear rolls down my damp cheeks. The terror I felt as my life slowly began to slip away slices through my chest, making me relive it all over again. A terror that will forever stain my already-spoiled soul.

"But there's this darkness in me. A darkness that feeds off the carnage I bring down upon the kingdoms . . . upon my own people. A darkness that surrounds me no matter how much I will it away. I . . . I think it will always be a part of me. I will always be a murderer, no matter my reasoning. So, yes, Niam. You should be afraid of me."

Another tear follows the first as I turn to look at him.

With bright, focused eyes and unwavering resolve, the elf grabs my hand and squeezes it. "I'm not."

I can feel the muscles in my chin begin to crumble around the surety of his words. Digging my teeth into my bottom lip, I try to stop it from wobbling.

He squeezes my hand again. "Do you want me to heal your neck?" Niam asks, his voice as soft as his hands in mine.

"No." I shut my eyes and shake my head. "Not tonight. I want to remember."

He whispers a soft "okay" before he tugs on my hand and pulls me toward the earth with him. Niam's arms wrap around my shoulder, and my back rests atop the hard ground as we lay in silence, staring at the night sky. Bright orbs of sparkling light reflect against the moon's light. Like diamonds in the dark waves of the sea.

Niam turns his head to me. I can feel his gaze against the side of my face. "You may feel like you're drowning or suffocating in that darkness surrounding you, Maeve, but you aren't. Not truly. Just like the stars above, your light still shines, no matter how dim it may be."

"I don't think that's true." The words stick to my tongue. It feels heavy with emotion.

"It is. Souls have light within them. Even when it doesn't seem like there is. And the stars above are created from that light." Niam pauses for a moment. "My ma is up there."

My head pivots to the side, staring at the elf beside me. He's now staring up at the twinkling stars. His eyes are glossy as the corners of his lips turn upward in a sad smile.

"Alta thinks she's protecting me by not telling me where she went a couple months back, but I know. I couldn't understand why she wouldn't take me to see her, too. I was so distressed those initial days she was gone. Halton stayed with me in my chambers, comforted me, even when Kayd sent word that you were captured. He delayed his duty for me."

Now, Niam's lip begins to wobble. I slide closer to him and lay my head on his chest, trying to give as much comfort as I can. His grip around my shoulders tightens.

"When Alta came back, I just *knew* Ma was gone. She shuts me out any time I try to ask her about it. All—all she's doing is holding in that grief, not letting me share the burden of it. It's lonely. For her. And for me." Niam wraps his other arm around me, a hug we both need. A stray tear drips onto my hairline and rolls down my forehead. "But Ma's in a better place. A place where all elves end up, shining their light down upon those still here."

"Do you think some of those stars are human souls?" My words are barely above a whisper, cracking under scattered vowels, as my mind drifts to Mother and Ottilie.

"Yes." His warm breath brushes against the crown of my head. I tilt my head to look at him. His gray eyes twinkle under the starlight as they roam the skies.

"Really?"

"Really." A light brush of their presence drifts up my arm.

Rooted to the forest floor, we watch the night sky change as the minutes tick by. Stars and stardust shift. Thin clouds travel past the moon. It must be past midnight by now.

"We should probably head back." Niam breaks the comfortable silence we fell into after we spent the last hour talking about easy things, things that relieved us from the heaviness we feel.

I nod and sit up from the ashen floor, relieving his chest from my weight. He sits up, too, and holds his hand out to me once he gets his footing.

"Let's go, Serpent. The others are probably worried."

And as we both begin to make our way toward the edge of the forest, something stops me. A feeling of knowing and accepting. Turning around, I look back up into the sky. A new star blinks into existence. The man I killed.

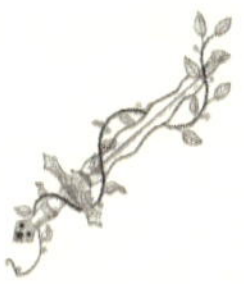

"Where have you been?" Halton's voice cuts through our room at the inn as soon as we open the door.

The guard twirls around from the window he's staring out—ready to berate me—but suddenly halts. His gaze dips down toward my neck, and something snaps from deep within him. A fire flares behind his widened eyes. His shoulders tense, and his fists curl.

"Who did that to you?" The question is no more than a low, dangerous rumble in his chest.

"Oh, stars!" Alta gasps a second later, noticing the bruises littering my skin. She rushes toward me and wraps her arms around my body. I appreciate the warmth she tries to give, but I can't seem to relax in her embrace. Not when Halton looks like he could rip the world in two.

"It's fine, brother." Niam approaches the guard and pats him on the shoulder. It does little to calm him down.

Halton shrugs off his friend's hand and strides toward Alta and me. His eyes never leave mine, and mine never leave his. He's a looming presence in front of me, anger and something else radiating off him.

Alta unravels her arms from around my back and holds me out at an arm's length. My eyes—still glued to Halton—finally move to her as she asks if I need anything.

I open my mouth to say something, but nothing comes. Instead, I close my mouth and think about what I want, what I *need*.

I need companionship, but I don't want to burden Alta, or even Halton, the same way I burdened Niam in the forest. I need to bathe and wipe off the events of the night. I need to be alone.

"I just want to go to bed." My voice sounds distant, like it belongs to someone else. It's been an exhausting day. Tiredness seeps into my muscles and grips tightly.

"Okay." Alta lets go of my arms and nods. "Yeah."

I shimmy past her and Halton. Both stand there a moment longer before shaking themselves out of whatever trance held them there.

Sliding into mine and Alta's bed, I nestle under the furs and close my eyes, ignoring the dust and grime coating my dirty skin. I hear the others move around the room in silence before I feel the mattress dip. Alta slides in next to me.

"Good night, Maeve," she whispers, her breath brushing my back.

I don't reply.

I hear someone blow out the candles burning in the room and slide into the bed I'm facing. I feel him then. Halton's gaze roams over my face as he lies no more than a few feet away.

He knows something's wrong. I can tell. A sudden, almost overbearing pull to open my eyes overcomes me. It begs for me to let him in on what's plaguing my mind. It begs me to open my soul to him, sharing all the feelings that reel inside me.

I squeeze my eyes shut tighter, pretending to sleep, until it finally pulls me under.

40

C OARSE BRUSH BRISTLES COMB through my hair as Madam Prea hums delicately behind me. Her nimble fingers trail the brush, ensuring no knots remain.

I bask in her calming presence. When I get back from my *trips*, we spend the following day together and simply talk. It's become somewhat of a ritual for us. Sometimes, we sit on the furs strewn across the floor, basking in the warmth of the hearth. Other times, we have lunch together. Today, however, Prea insisted on combing my hair—an act I've learned calms her when something heavy is on her mind. I can't help but wonder what it is.

Alta decided to join us today. She's lounging across the sitting room chair she's turned away from the hearth to face us, her knees draping over one arm and her hair cascading down the other.

"After hours of seething and worrying, here comes Niam and Maeve bursting through the door." Alta recounts parts of our trip to Prea as she kicks her hanging legs out one at a time, her sock-covered feet hitting the side of the chair each time they swing back in. "It was such a relief. But I've never seen Halton so angry before."

I don't want to relive what happened in Fiermoor. Despite the lack of bruises around my neck—thanks to Niam healing them on the ship back to Nythfaedell yesterday—I can still feel the terror I felt when my life almost left my body. I can still feel the haunting disgust I felt as I killed him.

"Madam Prea?" I interrupt. She hums in response. "What was it like growing up here in Nythfaedell?"

I want to change the subject, but I'm also genuinely curious. She has become a rock for me in this kingdom, and I'd like to know more about her. Her hands pause their movements, hovering over my scalp.

"There's not much to it. I was born in a nearby village nearly five hundred rotations ago." I whip my head around and gape at her. She only rolls her bright purple eyes and smacks my shoulder playfully. "Not a word, girl. Remember, respect your elders."

Her mature laugh twines around mine and Alta's, dancing together with companionship in the quiet room.

She continues. "My family was poor. My mother and father needed help. So, I applied to work here for extra wages. The newly crowned King Osmar and Queen Aila welcomed me with open arms, and I have been serving here since."

"Did you always watch over the human maids? Or did you do something else?" I can't help but ask.

She smiles. There is a sadness and longing along her features. "I was Queen Aila's personal chambermaid. I did everything for her. Got her dressed, held the flowers she picked in the gardens, you name it. I even helped deliver Prince Kayd when he was born."

My lips are moving before my brain can process it. "Has he always been so vile?"

Madam Prea's body shifts, her muscles tightening. She glances at Alta, who's already looking at her with a smirk.

"I'm a courtier, Madam Prea," Alta hums and sits up, digging her elbows on her knees and resting her chin in her waiting palms. "I know how to keep my lips sealed when I need to. Go on. I'd love to hear what you truly think."

The older elf shakes her head and huffs out a laugh. The tension in her body releases with that single gesture. "No, no. He used to be a kind boy. Someone I was confident would rule our land with care."

Prea's voice lowers slightly. "But Prince Kayd turned sour when the queen—his mother—died. He was only fifteen—so young . . . especially for an elf. It darkened his heart. And Lady Alta"—she nods toward my friend—"can attest to this. He blames the human chambermaids who tended to her while she was ill, but no amount of healing would have stopped what happened . . ." Madam Prea's words trail off as she loses herself to her thoughts.

Alta nods in agreement. Her lips are turned downward, and her eyebrows are pulled together.

Gently, still looking up at the older female, I bring her back. "What *did* happen, Prea?"

A long shaky sigh cuts through the silence between the three of us. "Queen Aila came down with a rare illness. She was weak. Her beautiful skin turned dull, and her hair thinned. The only way to cure it was with our elven magick . . . and the pollen of a rare flower found only in Phandolus. The *changelings* wouldn't allow our people to cross their borders to get the thing our queen needed most." There's a bite in her tone, something I rarely hear from her.

"He blames the chambermaids? But it wasn't their fault," I voice, with a frown deepening the lines on my face. "The changelings are the ones who—"

"Anger and sorrow make even the strongest of us blind, girl," Madam Prea interrupts, and something deep down twinges at her words. Before I can think about it too much, the older elf continues. "Queen Aila was graceful, even in her death. When she realized we were unable to get the pollen, she accepted her fate and urged the king to not retaliate, not wanting a war to start on her behalf. She knew her husband would take care of their son, the kingdom, their servants, and anyone who crossed his path."

Prea smiles fondly at the thought. "The king and queen were always so kind to their servants, to me. Now . . . Now, the future of Nythfaedell hangs in the balance. I'm afraid of what the prince will do once his rule begins. That anger and hatred and blame he feels toward mortals for his mother's death has spread throughout the palace and into several parts of our kingdom—"

The wooden door bangs loudly against the wall, cutting off our conversation. Alta yelps and braces her hand against her chest. I jump up, getting my footing, before whipping my body around to face the intruder. Halton stands at the threshold of my chambers. His brown hair is disheveled, like he's been running his fingers through it, and his jaw is set with determination.

His eyes glide over the three of us before he juts his head toward the hallway, silently ordering Alta and Prea to leave. There is no emotion on his face, as if he's steeled himself off before barging in.

"You really know how to ruin a mood, you know that, Halton?" Alta sighs and stands up from the chair. She comes over and hugs me gently. "Don't forget about tomorrow, Maeve. Niam and I will meet you in our chambers in the morning before we go to the market."

I smile at her and nod. Just as she passes Halton, Alta mockingly bows at him with a chortle, then leaves my chambers.

Madam Prea follows after I thank her for the company and hug her tightly. She leaves without so much as a glance toward the guard.

Halton shuts the door behind the elf and pointedly looks at me with a raised eyebrow.

"What?" I snap. "They're my friends."

There's a moment—so fast I almost miss it—where Halton's hardened mask slips. A second of something that looks like remorse flashes across his features before he returns to the mean, stone-like guard I've learned to tolerate.

"I didn't know someone like you could have friends." His lips curl up into a smirk. He's hit his mark, and he knows it.

My fists curl at my sides, the tips of my fingers tingle with a deep hunger to wipe that smug look off his handsome face.

My eyes roll toward the ceiling, and I cross my arms over my chest. A tired—so, so tired—sigh. "What do you want, Halton?"

"You." That single smooth word surprises me. It lights up my nerve endings. My throat turns barren, and my body tenses. A rigid stillness that would rival Halton's stick-straight back when he's on duty.

It seems that it surprises him, too, like he didn't mean to say it. His eyes are slightly rounder now, and I notice his fingers flex at his side before he inhales deeply and approaches me.

"You will be the end of me. You know that, Serpent?" Halton's voice is gruff, as if he's trying to rein himself in, trying to rid himself of the conflicting emotions I see swirling behind those hazel eyes. But his body doesn't seem to listen as his steps continue toward me. "These months spent with you have been some of the worst I have ever lived. Seeing you all the time and not being able to do anything about it. Knowing you're . . . Did you know, after you told me your name, I drank myself stupid that night? I bedded another just to stop my mind from thinking of it."

Then he says my name. *Maeve*, not Serpent. It comes out as a longing sigh, like a praise on those sinful lips I catch myself staring at.

His eyes glaze over as they roam my face. He continues as if in a trance. "I canceled training the morning after that first revel because I couldn't stop the images of you laughing in Niam's arms from entering my head. The way you looked in that dress . . . I pumped myself dry as I imagined ripping it off with my bare hands. I couldn't face you after that. When I finally got to taste you, I barely survived. You're addicting and everything I imagined you'd be. And when I saw you approach that unicorn, my world stopped. A mortal living in a fantasy world. So natural . . . So beautiful . . ."

Now, standing inches away from me—close enough to feel his rugged breaths brush against my lips—his chest rapidly rises and falls, matching my own. That ever-present pull from within thrums rapidly as I stare into his unfocused eyes. It's hard to ignore. It feels like I can't live without being in his presence.

"Do you touch yourself thinking about me the same way I do?" The words are mumbled, as if he doesn't even realize he's saying them. The heat of his gaze trails down my neck and lingers on my heaving chest and hot, blushing skin. His throat bobs.

A whimper slips through my lips, and his eyes snap up and lock on mine.

With a single blink, the glossy film that glazed over his features suddenly disappears. In its place is that cold, hard leer that I've grown used to.

"Show me." His demand is rough and shoots a ribbon of fire and ice through my veins.

"What?" I whisper, eyes wide.

"Let. Me see. You touch. Yourself. Just like you do when you're alone at night." And that look he gives me—wild and alluring—it's a look I want to be the reason for over and over again.

Sucking in a sharp breath to calm my heartbeat—to no avail—and running my tongue along my bottom lip, I walk past him. My arm brushes against his, featherlight and searing all at once. I shouldn't allow this to happen. Or *anything*, for that matter. What transpired between us the night of the king's revel was a mistake.

A mistake, I growl internally.

My mind is screaming at me to end this, to throw him out of my chambers and slam the door in his face. But my body is already thrumming with that familiar, intoxicating pulse at the apex of my thighs and that peculiar tug in the center of my chest. I can't seem to stop my feet from bringing me to the chaise before the hearth. The perfect spot to put on a show for the eager elven captain. Halton follows, his footsteps echoing mine.

I turn and face his waiting gaze. Gulping down the saliva that has pooled into the back of my throat and keeping my eyes on him, I bring my nimble fingers to the front of my pants. His darken as he watches me slowly unfasten each clasp. It's torture for him. I can see it in his eyes. A measured, buzzing type of torture as he watches each of my slow movements.

My hands are clammy from the nerves. Never have I done something like this . . . touching myself as someone watches. It's appalling and exhilarating all at once.

My slick palms run down the sides of my legs as I push my pants toward the ground. Stepping out of the garment, I then lift my tunic over my head. Clad only in my underthings—black and lacy and something I would normally never wear if it weren't for the chambermaids taking my dirty clothes to get washed earlier this morning—I stand before Halton, whose eyes are wide and burning with an emotion I can't quite read. An emotion that scares me a little.

As I sit down onto the plush chaise, our eye contact doesn't waver. A sliver of Halton's tongue peeks through his lips, wetting them in a way that makes my breath catch in my throat. My hands shake as I grant my fingers permission to graze across my skin. They roam up my body, dancing over my ribs and brushing my outstretched neck. Knowing he's watching my every move stirs a dull hum beneath each ghost-like touch.

My left hand caresses my clothed breast. My eyes flutter closed, and my breaths turn shallow as I palm and pinch and knead my flesh. Heat—hotter than the sun's rays in summer—rises to the edges of my skin, turning it red with want and desire. My right hand inches up my thigh. Before I reach the black lace, my hand travels back down toward my knee. An impatient huff from Halton hisses through the air. Chills seep down my spine from that sound alone.

My fingers work their way up my thighs once more—slowly and seductively—and my legs spread open slightly wider. One sharp twirl around that glorious sweet spot has my back arching off the lush cushions. The friction from the lace is too much and not enough already. A volcano erupting, a stream of water trickling away. After a few more circles, I finally dip my fingers under the fabric and sigh at the feeling.

A single finger swipes up and down and dips in just enough to pull a whimper from the back of my throat. Halton lets out a deep growl and takes a step closer.

My finger moves back to the pulsing bundle of nerves, drawing tight circles around it.

There's a shift in the air around us. My movements become erratic, clawing at my breast and plunging my fingers deep into my core as my palm presses down on my mound. Sweat beads along my collar bones as soft moans echo off the walls. More constant and full of need. I can hear Halton closer now than before. His feet shift. The sound of fabric and buckles hitting the floor mingles with our heavy breathing.

"Fuck . . ." His sigh is broken, wrecked beyond belief.

I open my eyes partially and see him standing there completely naked, gingerly stroking his cock with his hand. His eyes stay trained on my hand under the lace. His teeth dig into his bottom lip. The sight makes my heart stutter. If I thought he was beautiful before, he's otherworldly now.

Muscles flex beneath his flawless beige skin. The divots defining each one glistens under his sweat and the fire's bright flames. "That's a good girl."

A needy mewl dances through my parted lips, bringing his gaze to mine. That single look sends a jolt through my spine and down into my core.

Coolness erupts across my skin as he places his pointer finger on my ankle. Slowly, he drags it up my leg. His light touch makes me squirm. The trail halts at the top of my thighs. Then his fingers leave my skin completely before his hand grips mine and pulls it away from the place I yearn to be touched the most.

Before I can complain, his palm cups my center roughly. "Mine," he growls. He slaps his fingers sharply against it once, then hooks his fingers around the lace and pulls it down. The cool air hits the slick that has begun to gather, and the warmth of the fire soothes my chills. "There she is," he mumbles, licking his lips and dragging that wicked finger through my folds. His other hand grips onto my breast band and rips it from my chest.

My stomach twists. I want him . . . I *need* him. That fire roaring deep in my gut intensifies, that pulling becoming erratic. Sitting up, I paw at the elf standing over me. His eyes glint at how needy I am. I don't even care.

Roughly, Halton picks up my body and flips me onto my stomach as if I were a rag doll. No warning. No kind words. A wanton moan slips through the cracks. He grips onto my hips and lifts my ass into the air, pushing my chest down against the chaise cushions and burying his tongue between my legs.

The euphoric feeling of his mouth is short-lived, no longer feeling his breath against me. I whine—*actually whine*—at the loss until I feel the tip of his erection press against where I want him most.

"*Please . . .*" I wiggle my ass against him, craving what he has to offer.

A harsh slap. My flesh stings, and my clit aches at the sensation. We groan in unison. Halton's fingers dig into my hips, bruising my skin, before he slams into me with a fierceness that steals the breath right out of my lungs.

The guard's thrusts are relentless, pounding deeper into me than anyone else has before. With each plunge, my moans become louder and louder, feeling every ridge and vein along his shaft. He hisses and grunts, noises that increase the ache burning deep down. I grip the cushions beneath my body, and my knuckles turn bone-white as he plunges into me. Skin slapping against skin. Sweat smearing between our bodies. Another slap to my ass, and I clench around his length. My limbs begin to shake.

With a cruel grip, Halton hoists me up onto my knees so that my back rests against his chest. His left hand wraps around my throat, but he pauses. Sheathed inside me, unmoving, he glides his fingers across my pulsing veins and muscles, where purple bruises were scattered across my neck only yesterday.

Flashes from the alley with that man should be sending alarm bells across my nervous system. I should be scared. With him—for reasons unknown to me—there is no fear. I feel safe. Lifting my hand to his, I place his palm against my throat once more and squeeze.

"Please . . ." I whimper. "It's okay."

This time, he squeezes down on his own. It sends a jolt through my body, my head lulling back against his shoulder. His punishing and cruel thrusts start again, so unlike the way he touched my neck not more than a few breaths ago.

His other hand twines around my hip and brutally rubs my clit, causing me to scream. The hand around my throat presses harder.

"Come for me, Serpent," Halton pants with uneven, rigid breaths.

The tip of his cock hits a sweet spot inside me with each erratic thrust. My body screams—screams for him and only him. I can feel I'm close to relishing in my rapturous release. A few more harsh, fast rubs against my sensitive bundle and another tight squeeze against my windpipe send me over the edge.

"Halton!" My voice is a high-pitched drawl. The knot building deep in my core breaks, flooding all my senses with nothing but heart-stopping pleasure. My body shakes, and my breath gets stuck in my throat.

Halton bites my neck to mask his husky groan without compromising the speed of his hips snapping into mine. He's unyielding. Several more thrusts, his bruising grip returning to my hip, then he rips himself out of me and roughly pushes me back onto my stomach.

"Shit!" he gasps before I feel the splatter of his warm release on my lower back. I clench around nothing at the feeling. My limp body slumps against the cushions. I feel Halton get up from the chaise and walk away.

My chest unwillingly clenches.

What we just did . . .

Shutting my eyes tightly, I try to calm myself. I urge my heart to settle down. I stomp away my racing thoughts.

It's not like I haven't bedded someone before. It's not like my virtue is lost to an elf.

It's not a big deal, I tell myself. Even as I think those words, I know they're false.

Much to my surprise, Halton returns after a long moment and begins to clean the mess on my back and between my legs with a damp piece of cloth. That simple gesture makes my heart pound and gut churn. It's kind and caring and something I don't want to think too deeply about.

Finding my strength once he's done, I sit back up. He begins to gather his clothes and pulls his pants back on.

"Oh, Kayd called for you," he says, nonchalantly, albeit still out of breath. "One of our newer guards challenged you to a spar. He thinks he can beat you despite my training."

My head snaps to him. Scrambling off the chaise, I shoot him a disbelieving look. "Why didn't you say anything?" The words rush out as I begin to dress in my discarded clothes.

He shrugs. "I got distracted." He looks at me longingly. I can't keep the creeping blush from running across my cheeks. "I'm hurt you're itching to get away from me so quickly," he says with a smirk, but there's a soft vulnerability behind the words.

My movements slow as I look at him. Arrogance and softness are fighting a battle just under his skin. I want to go to him and hug him or kiss him or fuck him again. It's too much right now. It might always be too much. Instead, I shrug and run my fingers through my hair. "Nothing—not even you, *guard*—can compete with the thrill of beating the shit out of an elf in front of their prince."

"Your prince," Halton chides with a look that gives me chills.

Rolling my eyes, I lace up my boots, then make my way to the training grounds—leaving the elf, who just once again ruined me, half-dressed in my chambers.

41

I SHOULD TELL THEM.

I wring my fingers together, pressing down on the bruises littering my knuckles after sparring with that young guard yesterday. We went three rounds, and I beat him each time.

Falling into step between Niam and Alta, we walk along a gravel path through the palace grounds toward the market. The twins talk animatedly—arms swinging and smiles wide.

"I still need to find a dress, Niam!" Alta lifts the skirts of her gown and hops over a groove in the pathway with a soft grunt. "Dressing for a ball isn't as easy when you're a female. All *you* really have to do is find a nice coat. I need to find a gown, shoes to match, accessories—"

"I have to find all that, too!" Niam runs his finger through his dark wavy locks.

A short, loud chortle bursts through the barrier of Alta's navy-stained lips. "I can't wait to see what gown you choose for yourself."

Niam reaches around me and shoves Alta's shoulders. She stumbles to the side, and his laugh dances around the three of us.

I should tell them.

I can still feel the aftermath from Halton's cock between my legs. With each step, a dull soreness throbs at the apex of my thighs. Bruises scatter my hips from his unrelenting grip—bruises a part of me wants to wear with pride.

I trust the twins. I know I do.

I should tell them.

But I don't know if I'm ready to talk about crossing that line with the captain. I don't know if I'm ready to face it myself.

A loud bray in the distance shakes off my troubled thoughts. To my left, mortal stable boys guide a group of steeds toward a barricaded field. Courtiers stand at the iron gates, waiting for their riding session.

As I watch each servant assist waiting lords and ladies, a certain blond-haired, brown-eyed man comes to mind. If I close my eyes, I could imagine Jerik being here in Nythfaedell. He'd help a blushing lady up onto her ride with a friendly smirk. He'd live in the elven palace and spend his evenings with me and the twins. He'd come with us to the Secret Spring and watch The Night of Light.

His life in Phandolus—of cells and beatings—would cease to exist. I wonder how he's doing and if he misses me just as much as I miss him. Another thought pops into existence. A thought I don't want to know the answer to . . . I wonder how he would react if I told him about what I've done with the elven captain.

After our tumble on the chaise in my sitting room, I told myself I would never cross that line with Halton again.

That was nearly a week ago, and since then, I realized I'm not a good listener.

There's something intoxicating about him, something deep-rooted that makes him irresistible in my eyes. Our training sessions usually end in tangled limbs and steamy kisses. Frantic trysts in shadowed nooks throughout the palace, and secret looks only meant for one another have become second nature. Like we're meant to be doing such a thing.

Usually, I'm the one to initiate it. His cold, hard demeanor stays intact for longer and longer each time, like he's fighting against the want I know is raging in his chest. Like he's fighting a piece of himself. But every time, he relents. And when he does so, it's rapturous, like the Gods open up the sky and sing for us as our bodies connect. Euphoric. Earth-shattering. Soul-swelling—

"Oh!" The breathy gasp escapes my parted lips as Halton deeply thrusts into me one last time before releasing himself onto my stomach.

My attention never leaves him as he rolls off me and lays naked against the hides on his sitting room floor. I swipe my finger across his warm release—the only thing warm about him it seems—and as he turns to face me, I wrap my lips around it and suck it clean.

A deep growl rumbles from his chest as he watches. The fire from his hearth reflects dangerously against his eyes, and drops of glistening sweat slide down the rivets of his muscles. The side of my mouth lifts, smirking as I sit up and begin to pull my discarded tunic over my head. He watches me with an intensity that's jarring, boring into my soul.

Just as I stand and pull my pants over my hips, his voice breaks through the taut silence between us. "You don't have to go, you know."

I look down at him with a raised brow. Never has he suggested I stay after bedding me.

"I don't want all the other females to see you leave. It might make them jealous." Halton winks at me, his grin shining through his usually hardened facade.

"Oh, is that so?" I muse. Sitting back down on the sweat-soaked fur I was lying on, I cross my ankles together and pull my knees to my chest.

"Most definitely." The guard props himself on an elbow and pulls a discarded length of silk across his lower half. "My reputation would be in shambles."

My laugh is unexpected, light and easy and fluttering across the empty room. His chuckle—more reserved, but still lighter than any other time with me—dances with mine. The sound dies from my lips as I look at him. He's breathtaking.

Even when he's grinding his teeth and flexing his jaw muscles, he's something to look at. But moments like this—when he doesn't have that invisible weight closing him off—is when he's the most ethereal.

It makes me want to learn every part of him.

"Tell me about yourself," I say quietly. His gaze turns intense and locks onto mine. "I mean, I'd like to think I know you pretty well"—my eyes shift down to the tented silk covering his naked body—"but I don't truly *know* you, do I?"

He doesn't say anything for a few heartbeats. His features are unreadable. Then he sucks on a tooth and shrugs. "There's not much to tell. I came to the palace when I was seven, leaving my family behind. I haven't looked back since."

"You don't miss them?" The question leaves my lips before I can reel it back. Just because we're fucking, doesn't mean I have the right to prod into his past. By the guarded look on his face, he thinks the same.

"Do you?" he bites back.

I don't hesitate. "Every day."

An emotion flashes across his features for half a breath before it's gone. I look down at my crossed knees as the elf sits up fully and crosses his own, the light of the fire flickering across his bare chest.

He lets out a deep sigh. "On the ship to Fiermoor, when you told me that I didn't have the right to tell you why you kill . . ." His words trail off into silence. Another deep sigh as he runs his hand down his face. "Is it for them? Your family?"

A long drawn-out quiet stretches between us. I can feel his attention roaming across my body, looking for a way into my mind. A part of me doesn't want to answer. Why should I reveal the deepest part of me when he hides so much in return?

"I'm sorry," he blurts out. "You don't have to tell me any—"

"Part of it is because of my family. My mother, mostly." The words crack in the quiet.

"And the other part?" Halton chances with another prodding question. That tightness in my chest pulls ever so slightly, urging me to open up to the guard. I press my lips closed tightly. My molars push down against one another at the sensation. "It's for her, isn't it? Your friend from the trials."

"I don't know what it is, but every time I want to omit the truth from you, something in me yanks so hard it's nearly impossible." A defeated laugh. Finally, I look back up at him. His eyes are rounder, the whites around the hazel more visible. "Why is that?"

Halton swallows down against nothing and slowly shakes his head. "I . . . don't know."

Silence engulfs us once again. It's not uncomfortable, but it's tense. Minutes tick by.

It's too hot in here. Suffocating, really. I should never have breached into uncharted territory. Our personal lives have nothing to do with the trysts we partake in. Moving forward with him on a level deeper than physical pleasure is reckless.

"I should go." I push up from the floor and slip on my boots.

He nods in response and lets me leave.

Luxurious silk bedding rubs against my bare legs. Shifting from my side to my back, I gaze up at the darkened wood ceiling and dim iron chandelier hanging above. My fingers run along the seams of the oversized linen tunic draped over my upper body, and I gnaw at my bottom lip, deep in thought.

The soft patter of rain against a small circular window above the bed is the only sound in the room. *His room—his bed.*

I turn my head to the left. Muscular bare limbs are tangled between furs and silks, the sweat drying along each crevice under the cool air. Halton—the elf who consumes all my thoughts, my entire being, if I'm being truthful—sleeps soundly next to me.

I told myself I would never stay after bedding the guard, that I wouldn't be reckless. I told myself it was fine when I started lingering only days after our tryst before his hearth. Now, here I am, staying the night.

My heart thumps wildly against my chest as I stare at the elf. I catch myself smiling at him. His lashes flutter peacefully. There's not a worry in the world marring his features. Content, relaxed.

He trusts me. The realization slams into my chest like a pile of bricks. He trusts me . . . He isn't afraid of me and my bloody past. Tears prick at my lash line. They appear so fast that I don't even have time to wipe away a wayward drop before it rolls onto the bed. Someone in this Godsforsaken world isn't afraid of me . . .

Oh Gods, I care for him.

Acid rises into the back of my throat. I swallow down on it, forcing my breathing to calm. This . . . I cannot be feeling this way about the guard. It's petrifying. It's *wrong*.

Mother's warmth and Ottilie's light travel up my side and nestle into the crook of my neck, pulsing lightly against my skin.

Guilt presses down on my chest. The two most important people in my life thrum against the feeling. I should be wreaking havoc on this kingdom and all others.

For Mother. For Ottilie.

The justice I seek will not come from rolling in bed with an elf.

I look at Halton again. My heartbeat picks up, mixing with the shame I feel. It's intense, ancient. A line between his brows appears, and his eyes unconsciously close tighter, creating wrinkles along the thin skin there. I wonder what he's dreaming about.

Feeling the insistent pull toward him, I lean over and kiss the line away.

Pressure against my throat cuts off my air. I choke on nothing. I claw at nothing. No one is before me, and yet I still feel him. I still hear him.

Rebel or loyalist?

My heartbeat slows, and just as my final breath leaves my lips, I shoot up in bed. Sweat pebbles at my hairline and runs down my spine. Halton's tunic is twisted around my torso, and my fingers are locked within his silk sheets.

It takes me a moment to remember where I am. Halton's chambers, that's right. The magick-infused room is lighter now. Early morning, most likely. However, I'm alone. The side Halton slept on is empty.

"Okay." I run my hands over my face and through my knotted hair. "Calm down before he gets back. Everything is fine. That human is gone. You killed him, and now he's in the sky with all the other souls. You're fine."

As I sit in the silence, evening out my breathing, I hear muffled voices on the other side of the bedroom's closed door. One of the voices grows in volume. It's Prince Kayd.

"That's impossible—"

A loud shush—from Halton, I presume. Then, quietly, the prince seethes. "She's here?"

Getting out of bed, I tiptoe toward the wooden door. The wood doesn't creak. I silently thank the changeling guard for my stealth training.

The elves have resorted to whispers now. Even with my ear pressed to the door, I can barely make out what they're saying.

"I've never ... such a thing ..." is all I can pick up before I hear the door leading out of Halton's chambers open and close behind the prince.

"Serpent." Kayd corners me just as I'm about to spend the afternoon at the Crystal Lake Garden. His voice is gruff, his eyes narrow.

"Yes, Prince." My right eyebrow raises as I stare at him.

I can see his temper already fraying in my presence. His brown skin grows darker, and deep shades of red run up his neck and over his cheeks.

"It seems the captain of my guard is distracted lately. I will not stand for that." The elven prince adjusts the collar of his coat, looking bored. "Stay away from him. If you would like to train, you can train with my entire guard. No more one-on-one sessions. Do you understand?"

I scoff and roll my eyes toward the overcast sky. Of course. Despite my softening feelings toward a handful of the elves, I am still their property, *owned* by them and their prince. My freedom is gone, no matter how comfortable this prison is. Now, *my* temper is beginning to fray.

Opening my mouth to give the prince a piece of my mind, I don't get the chance before he cuts me off. "If you care about him, you'll stay away."

That bored expression is gone. His eyes are sharp, peering down into my soul. The way he's looking at me ... I've never seen him look at anyone else like this. It's unnerving.

I straighten my shoulders and lift my chin. Faux confidence. "Who says I do?"

A sad smile laces with pity and another emotion I can't quite place. "I can see it in your eyes, mortal. Nothing good will come from one of us bedding your kind."

42

THE LACES OF MY boots tighten with each pull. An annoyed huff escapes my gritted teeth as I pull on them once more. A new assignment came this morning, right on the heels of Kayd's warning. The elven prince says this is my most important kill yet.

Lady Evelaide of Crullfeld, the leader of the tiefling rebellion, will be dead tomorrow evening by the Shackled Serpent's hand.

Like Niam said before, *"two birds, one stone."* Cut the head off the snake and watch the rebellion burn while keeping the mortal assassin away from his captain.

The door to my chambers creaks open. Just as I secure a wool cloak over my concealed weapons, Madam Prea sticks her head in before fully stepping over the threshold and closing the door behind her. "Good, you're still here. I have a message from the prince."

My eyebrows lift, unsure why he sent Prea instead of a note. She seems to sense my question.

"He didn't want to miss you. So, instead of writing it out and sending another maid to deliver it to you, he sent me."

"Okay . . ." I nod and tie the top half of my hair up with a leather strap.

Prea studies me as if she's seeing me for the first time. The corners of her lips tighten, and the lines around her eyes deepen. "Prince Kayd says to make sure she feels it."

My fingers pause mid-tie. A dull hum buzzes in my ears as a void surrounds us. I don't move. I don't say anything. I simply stare and stare at the older elf.

"You're it, aren't you? The Shackled Serpent."

A wave of shame washes over me. Never did I want Prea to find out who I really am. I didn't want to disappoint her, and by the look in her eyes, I have.

Nodding, I open my mouth to say something, anything that could make this better. But before I can, Prea speaks up again as she runs her hands down the skirts of her gray gown. "That's the darkness I felt when you first arrived." Her voice is low. "We—the kingdoms, I mean—we made you into a killer. I'm so sorry."

"What? No." Small strands of hair fall around my face as I shake my head adamantly. I take a step toward her with my hands out. "*You* have no reason to be sorry. I do what I'm told. I don't have the luxury to refuse. That's just the way the world works."

Madam Prea looks as if she's about to cry. It makes my heart clench. "I do have a reason to be sorry, girl. We *all* do." She slumps down upon the chaise.

I timidly sit next to her. She stares into the flames within the hearth for a long while before turning her piercing purple gaze on me. It's laced with a deep sadness I can't comprehend.

"If it weren't for that dreaded war and the selfishness of the kingdoms' rulers, you wouldn't be feeling the weight of the blood soaking your hands."

Confusion washes over me. "I don't . . . I don't understand what you're trying to say. I'm an assassin because that's what the kingdom who chose me at the trials wanted. And the trials are a result of the Last War that started because of mortal mutiny. When the kingdoms came together to put an end to it, a group of mortals wanted to thank them for giving our kind a home, a purpose—"

Madam Prea's eyes bulge in horror, and her jaw drops like a fish out of water. "Is that what you're taught? Is that the story your so-called Elders tell you?"

Dread fills my entire being. My nerves crackle, and my muscles tense, bracing myself for what Prea is about to say. A reveal that will upheave everything I've ever known. A truth I don't know I'm ready for.

The elf's long lashes flutter closed. She lowers her chin to her chest and exhales loudly. "The Last War wasn't because mortals decided to rise up against the kingdoms." Prea's words are slow, and her voice is soft, making sure I hear everything she's saying. "Nythfaedell declared war on Phandolus because there were reports of changelings capturing the mortals in their kingdom, locking them up, and forcing them to do labor. Nythfaedell and all elves thought it was wrong and wanted to stop it. However, Amphitea and Fiermoor saw how much the changeling kingdom was thriving with the free labor. So, they sided with them."

My fingers curl into the plush cushion beneath me, my knuckles turning whiter than Princess Andrina's hair. I feel the sorrow behind Prea's gaze linger there for a moment before continuing.

"After several battles in Nythfaedell, Phandolus and their allies secured their victory. The elves lost, and as a result, our livelihoods were threatened. The other kingdoms gave King Osmar's father, King Dryden Glynvyre, an ultimatum: join this new way of life—a life where humans serve—or the elven kingdom would fall.

"Reluctantly, the elves agreed. So, Terakeld rose from the depths of the sea, and the trials were created—not by humans who wanted to show their appreciation, but by the kingdoms, so they would have slaves serving them." Prea's warm hand wraps around mine. Her thumb rubs circles into my flesh. "So, yes, Maeve. I am sorry for turning you into a killer. We all should be sorry."

The world tilts around me. The flame in the hearth seeps out onto the floor, and the furniture around me blurs. Slowly—so slowly—everything spins, and flashes of the ceiling mural in the changeling palace interrupt my vision.

Changelings, merfolk, and tieflings celebrating in victory. Golden weapons scattered on the ground showing the elves' defeat. The truth was right there in front of me.

I need to get out of here.

"Thank you, Madam Prea." The words are strained, clipped. "For telling me the truth."

Abruptly standing up, I rush out of my chambers.

I stalk the Lady of Crullfeld through the slate-covered halls of her manor into her chambers like a ghost. The tiefling's sharp, light-red shoulders are relaxed, and her onyx-painted nails run over small trinkets lining shelves mounted to the wall.

She has no idea she's about to die.

I reach down toward my thigh holster and pluck a knife between my fingers. My steps falter as soon as the cold weapon touches my skin. The same weapon I used when I killed that mortal man in this kingdom.

My throat constricts, making it hard to breathe, as if his phantom hands are wrapping around my neck at this very moment. The same terror that shot through my veins that night barrels into me again. It's blinding.

I bite the inside of my cheek, willing away the reaction my body is having from the memory. Blood pools along my tongue, and the pain grounds me.

This tiefling will feel that way soon. As my knife rips into her skin. As her breaths slow. As the light leaves her eyes.

And I will be the cause of that. Just as Andrina and Kayd wanted.

I'm merely a pawn in the kingdoms' game. A game that began more than a thousand rotations ago. A single burning flame flickers in my soul.

The truth of it all rings through my skull and pounds against my bones. The Last War as I knew it was a lie. Everything was a lie. The Elders killed my mother just to hide within the lie they and the kingdoms spun, to hide in their clean clothes behind the faux power they hold. Dozens of other mortals—*rebels*—died trying to get others to open their eyes.

And Ottilie . . . She died because people were too afraid to speak up, because *I* was too afraid to speak up.

A biting pain shoots through my temple and into my fingertips. I collapse to the floor. My brain rattles against my skull, and my vision blurs. I feel like I'm going to vomit. Warm liquid drips down my cheek and onto the floor.

Lady Evelaide peers down at me. A bronze-and-maroon crystal vase is raised above her head, ready to strike again. *Spiicrete.*

Her manicured hand rams down toward me at an alarming pace. It's merely a blur.

But my instincts kick in automatically, like my body knows that I'll die if I don't do anything. I free myself from her path and disarm her with a move Halton taught me not long ago.

Ending it quickly, my knife punctures the side of her neck, severing an artery.

She bleeds out without a sound, and I retch onto the floor.

43

M Y TRUDGING STEPS ECHO off the pristine elven palace walls. Each stomp is a reminder that I'm alive. Hurt and tired and still reeling from the truth, but alive. The gash on my temple throbs, and crusted blood sticks to my face.

After killing the rebel leader a day ago, I raced toward the coast, where a kind helmsman waited for me. Before I could clean myself on the journey back to Nythfaedell, my world turned black, pulling me under from the pain in my skull.

Now, as I enter Prince Kayd's parlor, I ignore the searing stares directed at me. I ignore the prince and his captain—as well as Niam and Alta—completely. Instead, walking straight to the ever-stocked side table and pouring myself a generous goblet of wine. I need a drink.

I guzzle it down in one go before pouring another and collapsing into one of the plush chairs facing the elven prince's throne. Looking up, I'm met with narrowed, forest-green eyes. Kayd stares at me in silence. A swift glance at the others, and all I see are wide, worried eyes.

I roll my eyes. "It's done," I say gruffly and chug the wine. Red droplets run down my neck into my tunic.

Alta sets a course straight for me. Niam and Halton soon follow.

"Oh, Maeve!" My friend kneels next to me and inspects my head. "Are you all right?"

Waving my hand through the air, I shrug off her concern. "It's nothing severe. I'm fine."

Niam perches next to me on the chair's arm and lightly rests his hand on my temple, healing my wound without being asked. The familiar tingling sensation returns for a split second before vanishing once again.

"There you go," he mumbles, his friendly smile gleaming under the flickering candles strewn throughout the room.

Halton stops in front of us, not coming any closer than he needs to. He's standing stick straight with wide eyes as he takes me in. His jaw clenches like he wants to say something but doesn't. The corners of my mouth lift quickly. A soft smile toward the guard. Something bright glints across his eyes before it's gone in a heartbeat.

"Good. Now that you're healed," Prince Kayd begins with a bored tone, "I have another job for you."

Halton's head whips around to look at the prince, and his nostrils flare. "Kayd, she just got back."

Alta nods, agreeing with the guard, before she sends a sharp look toward the prince. "And she was hurt. Let her rest. Then she can do whatever job you need of her," the female adds.

Pushing myself up to a standing position, I ignore the other's protests. "I'm fine." I politely brush off Niam's hand that rests on my shoulder. "Who is it?" I simply ask.

"Oh, no. This is a different kind of assignment." Kayd grins brightly, mischief in his eyes.

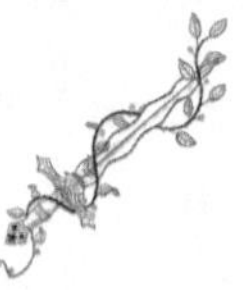

The twins and I approach the waiting carriage parked outside of the palace.

"That stubborn prince! The nerve he has to use Maeve like this!" Alta rants loudly, the volume raising with each word.

"I can hear you," Kayd calls out from the stairs that lead into the palace's entrance.

Alta sends him a crude hand gesture as she climbs into the golden cart. "I was hoping you would!"

"Alta . . ." Niam chides just as the prince barks out a loud laugh and blows her a kiss.

Once Alta and Niam are settled, I climb in after them. Glancing back at the palace, my eyes lock onto Halton. With his hands clasped behind his back, he's every bit the stoic guard I first met. But now, I know better. I can see the writhing emotions swirling around his features. That hardened mask is slowly slipping away, revealing more inside.

Kayd glances at his friend before glowering at me. A slow blink, then I turn away from his piercing stare. The carriage door shutting behind me, we begin our journey.

Inside the ornate carriage, Alta's grumbling continues, as if she has the attention of the entire court. "You were hurt, Maeve. The fact that he didn't even let you rest before ushering you off to the shops . . . it's disgusting!"

"Alta—" Niam chides her again.

His sister snaps back immediately. "Oh, shut it, Niam. The only reason you're not more upset is because you think Kayd can do no wrong. You've been in love with him since we were children!"

Alta snaps her mouth closed, her gloved hand shooting toward her mouth.

Niam pales. His eyes bulge, and I can see his hands begin to shake.

"Niam . . ." His sister clings onto his hands, pulling them to her chest. "Niam, I am so sorry. I didn't mean to say anything out loud."

Niam's dark-gray eyes swell. Tears gather at his lash line like a storm cloud trying not to release its rain. He opens his mouth to say something, but nothing comes out.

"Hey . . ." I lean toward him, placing my hands over his and Alta's. "There's nothing to be ashamed of. This doesn't change anything. Not our friendship. Not who you are as a person. Okay?"

Niam nods. A few drops fall from his eyes, and I wipe them with my thumb.

"Besides," I say, dipping my head lower so I can meet his downcast stare, "I'm confident he feels the same."

Solemnly, he shakes his head, as if anything of the sort could be true. "Doubtful."

I barely hear him say it. How could he think so lowly of himself? Anyone would be lucky to have him as a partner.

Alta's hands slip from underneath mine and begin to rub his back. I squeeze Niam's palms, sending as much care as I can. "Say that to the murderous stare *His Highness* gives me anytime we touch. You should have seen his face when you and I were dancing together at that first revel."

Niam's throat bobs in thought.

"I told you so," Alta whispers, leaning in toward her brother with a smile tugging at her lips.

The silky-smooth fabrics of purples and teals and reds brush lightly against my skin as my fingers gracefully glide over the gowns hanging in the shop. It feels as if I was just here, preparing for my first Nythfaedell kill.

Alta is humming quietly to herself as she browses the selection near me. Niam, immediately going to a smaller room in the back of the shop that I hadn't noticed before, peruses the men's section.

"So . . ." I drawl, taking a navy-blue gown off the rack and inspecting it. "What's this ball Kayd mentioned?"

I recall Alta and Niam discussing attire on our way to the market not long ago, but I didn't think I'd attend. Why would I in the first place?

Alta's squeal in response brings out a chuckle from the depths of my throat. She bounces on the balls of her feet in excitement. "Oh! The Autumnal Ball is a *huge* deal within the kingdoms to celebrate the last night before winter." Her wide smile is almost contagious. "It's the one night the kingdoms truly feel at peace with one another and can enjoy themselves."

"Oh?" My hand pauses at a green two-piece gown with jeweled flowers along the skirts. "Where in all of Galfei Thalor could that happen? If the ball is held in one of the kingdoms, wouldn't that have some sort of sway on the night?"

Alta turns to me with kind eyes, holding up a light-pink dress with puff sleeves. I shake my head, rejecting the piece. She places it back on the rack and says, "It takes place in Derlow Grove."

The little island I would pass on my assignments. I thought it was abandoned.

"It's neutral ground," Alta continues. "All the past treaties between kingdoms were signed there. There is a castle in the middle of the forest where it takes place, and the most important beings in each kingdom's court attend unless they can't for one reason or another. It's a celebration that many would kill for. You're lucky you get to go."

I can't help but wrinkle my brows together. "But why? Why does Kayd want me to attend?" If not to take the life of someone attending, then what? I'm beginning to think he truly doesn't know what an assassin does.

"My only guess is because he's vain and wants to show *you*"—she silently mouths the words *the Shackled Serpent* before continuing—"off."

I scoff. "That's arrogant of him."

With a dramatic roll of her eyes and a heavy sigh, Alta replies, "What's new? I told him he's being reckless. Surely, it's best to keep you hidden. But he's set in his decision to reveal the truth in front of—"

The bell above the door to the shop dings. Two older elves enter and, upon seeing Alta and me, approach us. I recognize them as courtiers of the king.

"Hello, Lady Alta. Miss Maeve," one says, dipping her head toward us. We say our hellos before they glide off to a few racks in the middle of the shop with more modest cuts.

"As I was saying . . ." My ears perk up at the elves' hushed conversation. Alta's browsing hands pause, too. More and more, I'm appreciating the art of being a courtier. If I didn't want to be pummeled by my friend, I'd call her a spy once more.

"Riots are popping up all over Fiermoor and Amphitea. It's getting bad, *violent*. Many are saying it's because a tiefling lady was found dead in her manor. Some say her head was cut clean off," one of the courtiers whispers.

The other gasps in response. Alta whips her gaze to me. A question lies within the look. Shaking my head, I reassure her, and her shoulders relax as the two elves decide to browse another section on the other side of the shop.

There's a lull between Alta and me. She presses her lips together and continues to browse. Then she whispers, "Do you enjoy it?"

"Enjoy what?" I turn to look at her. Her eyes are glued to a teal feather corset.

"Killing," she states simply, finally allowing her gaze to connect with mine. "Do you enjoy killing?"

I blanch. My mouth opens wide in shock at the question.

"Why would you ask me that?" The words come out in a whisper, falling off the tip of my tongue. Hurt twines around each letter.

"I don't know . . . It's just . . . I can't . . ." Alta stumbles over her words. Her nails rake down her scalp as she blows out a long breath. Her voice dips lower now. "You just looked so terrifying when you came back to the inn before the rally. I haven't been able to stop thinking about it. You, covered in blood. And before you poisoned Lord Morran . . . you were so nonchalant. Like it wasn't a big deal. Like you revel in the blood you spill. I just don't get it."

I can feel the line between my brows deepen as she looks at me.

"The trials—*the kingdoms*—took everything from me. Don't I deserve to get justice?" My lower lip wobbles.

"Justice and revenge are two different things, Maeve." Alta rubs her left palm against her right arm.

"I know that." Clipped words.

"Do you?" Sadness—*pity*—contorts her lips, twisting them into a pout.

I feel myself begin to retreat away from my friend. Tears prick at the corners of my eyes, and I look away quickly, suddenly interested in gowns I've already mentally rejected.

"Maeve . . ." Alta takes a step toward me. My muscles tense in response. Her hitched breath lets me know she noticed. "I'm sorry. I'm sorry for doubting you. You've become so important to me in such a short amount of time. You're one of my best friends, Maeve. Please." Another step toward me. "I'm just not used to so much death. Forgive me. Please?"

Finally looking back into her eyes, I study her, then send her a watery smile and a short nod. Alta pulls me into her chest, wrapping her arms around me tightly. "I promise never to doubt you again. I know the real you. I *know* you."

She lets go and sends me a genuine smile before starting to look for a dress again.

I know she means well, but my heart aches. Alta—even if it was just in that moment—thought so low of me. Before she came into my life, I basked in the blood I've spilled, but now . . . No. I hesitated before killing Lady Evelaide of Crullfeld. I hated killing that mortal man. I've changed. I could never hurt her or Niam or Halton . . . or even Kayd.

I turn back around toward the gowns that seem to have lost their vibrancy.

It's all okay, Maeve, I tell myself. *Hide your true feelings, just like you had to pretend to love the kingdoms back home. There's no difference in doing so now. Everything is* fine.

Alta's gasp disrupts my somber thoughts. She found the perfect gown for the ball.

44

A WEEK AFTER KILLING Lady Evelaide of Crullfeld tensions are still high throughout Galfei Thalor. Whispers of burning villages and deadly mobs in both Fiermoor and Amphitea almost distracted the kingdoms' nobility from the Autumnal Ball.

Almost.

Each royal house held a vote a few days ago and decided to go forward with the celebration. "*They said it's important to show unity during trying times like this,*" Prince Kayd had mocked.

And now, as soon as I step into that ball, all of Galfei Thalor will know who I am, what I've done. The journey from our court's chambers inside the ancient Derlow Grove castle to the party feels like a lifetime. Even longer than the ship ride to the island. My heels click against the stone, echoing in my ear drums and matching the beat of my pounding heart.

I'm shaking, terrified to be laid out bare for the others to see. No longer will I just be the scary story told at revels and in cells. I will be real. I will be tangible. They will now have a face to go with the name, and all because Prince Kayd wills it.

340

With his arm twined around mine, Kayd leads me through the corridors. Halton trails behind us. My steps falter, and the prince brings me to a stop, unlaces his arm with mine, and turns toward me.

"Lock up those measly nerves, Serpent. We're here to put on a show." He glares down at me.

As I leer back at the prince, a soothing chill runs up my arm. Halton steps closer to me—a move that doesn't go unnoticed by the prince—and grazes his hand against my lower back. A gesture of comfort I'm incredibly thankful for.

My heart clenches when I feel that familiar warmth and light press into the iciness of Halton's hand. The three of them together—Mother, Ottilie, and Halton—comforting me in any way they can.

Kayd stares at the captain's arm for a moment longer before gliding his narrowed eyes up to mine. "Lock it up, mortal, and channel the bloodthirsty killer I know you are."

He holds out his bent elbow for me again. I place my hand in the crook of his arm, and we continue on our way.

Grand double doors carved with mythical creatures, like satyrs, nymphs, and fairies, greet us. They're closed, but the heavy stone doesn't stop the fun melody of strings and percussion from fluttering through before switching to something darker. It's light enough to still dance to, but I can't help but think the musicians know the Shackled Serpent is about to enter.

A deep inhale, and I slide that iron, scaled mask over my features.

Just as I let out a long, silent breath, two doormen open the doors for us, and we stride into the ballroom.

"Prince Kayd Glynvyre," one of the doormen announces to those in attendance as he looks down at his scroll of attendees, "and his guest, Miss Maeve Wyndell, Galfei Thalor's Sh—"

The word dies on his tongue, and he gapes at us, terror twining around his features.

"Go on," Kayd growls at the mortal servant, who's eyeing me up and down.

Clearing his throat, the doorman tries again. "And his guest, Miss Maeve Wyndell, Galfei Thalor's Shackled Serpent."

Several gasps pierce the air of the ballroom. Despite all eyes on me, I cross the threshold with grace and confidence, with my head held high and my lips curling into a sinister smirk. Descending the massive staircase leading into the room, I meet every staring eye and whispering tongue head-on while taking in the ballroom. It's massive, with gray stone walls and winding vines bordering the large windows. Tall ceilings are covered in ancient artwork, and crystal chandeliers hang just below. It's enchanting.

My gown swishes against my legs with each step I descend. The black chiffon skirts are beautiful but do not draw the eye of the ball's attendees. Each gaze locks onto the tight bodice and pointed shoulder pads that connect to a sheer cape. Both are bedecked in snakeskin, the scales glistening under the candelabras and chandeliers. With each movement of my body, black transforms into silver. Silver transforms into black. I am the Shackled Serpent, morphing in front of their eyes.

Raising my brow at the group of partygoers, I take the last step onto the shiny marble floor, and they seem to pale. Even the skin of the changelings turn whiter than before.

Beside me, anticipation and pride ooze off Kayd in waves. A cruel smile morphs across his features, and his chest puffs out beneath his coat. I can't help but wonder if Kayd would have brought me if the king were here. Instead, he's exploiting his father's wish to have the prince represent the elves at the ball.

"What are we waiting for?" The elven prince raises his free arm into the air and turns around in a circle. "Let the debauchery continue!"

Whispers echo across the room before attendees gulp down goblets of whatever their drink of choice is. The orchestra seated on a second-floor balcony hesitantly begins again, and dancers slowly take their places on the open floor. Even then, I can tell they're weary still, stealing glances at the three of us every so often.

The coolness of Halton's body seeps into my back as he stands at attention. Closer than is appropriate for a guard. No one seems to notice but me. I lean back slightly, grasping at the comfort he provides.

I look up at Kayd, whose eyes are trained on something in the distance. Following his gaze through a sea of purples, emeralds, teals, and golds, I'm met with icy blue. *Princess Andrina.* Her gaze is firm as her face twists in rage. Fire behind her dagger-like stare burns a hole through the dancing crowd.

My heartbeat increases. Each thump is faster than the next. I don't let her pick up on it. My eyes nonchalantly swoosh away from her, as if she isn't worth my time. I can imagine the smoke coming out of her ears at the thought of a mortal brushing her off with not even a glimpse of fear. Much to my surprise, my gaze connects with wide brown eyes next to her.

Jerik. Jerik Flint, here, at the Autumnal Ball. Jerik Flint, dressed in a navy-blue-and-silver coat with snowflake embroidery on its breast and a sword at his side. Jerik Flint, handing Andrina a silver goblet with his head respectfully bowed. Jerik Flint, here. What is he doing here?

The gasp that escapes my quickly fading smirk is loud enough to pull the attention of the elven prince and the captain of his guard. Halton steps up to me, now shoulder-to-shoulder. I can see his stone-hard face flitting between me and where my eyes lay.

Kayd raises an alarmed eyebrow at me, then ushers me over to a beverage table. A large group of the patrons disperse as we near. "What is it?" Kayd demands. His eyes are hard as they bore into me.

Halton reaches for a goblet and hands it to me. A grateful smile graces my lips before sighing, long and weary.

"Nothing . . . It's—it's just . . . someone is here that I wasn't expecting to see," I say, only loudly enough to be heard over the sound of strings playing.

"Who is he?" Halton's voice is gruff. He's staring daggers into the back of Jerik's head, the muscles in his jaw flexing, and his nostrils flaring. If looks could kill . . .

Kayd follows his best friend's leer before turning back to me. "I see you have a thing for guards."

The scoff that rips out of my throat is sharp, deadly. Halton gives his prince a look I've never seen him send to his friend. A warning.

"We shared a cell together in Phandolus. We . . . bonded a lot during that time. He was sentenced to a servitude in the stable, but, obviously, that's changed since I left. I'm happy for him. He endured a lot that he didn't deserve at the hands of the other stable boys . . ." The words trail off.

My eyes glaze over at the memories that flood back to the front of my mind. Memories that seem so long ago, a lifetime ago. The hardships he faced. The warmth he poured into me just from his hugs. His understanding when I opened up to him. The yearning I felt as I contemplated pressing my lips to his.

Wisps of white clear my thoughts. Andrina leans into Jerik. Her lips graze against the shell of his ear as she whispers to him. His brown eyes bulge wider before bowing his head to his princess and saying something back.

"It will be nice to catch up with him," I hum. My voice sounds distant.

"You'll have plenty of time to do that later," the elven prince interrupts. "Now, we must show the Shackled Serpent off. A dance, my lady?"

Kayd whisks me away onto the dance floor. The others leave a wide berth between us. His eyes brighten when he notices. "How does it feel?"

I look up at him and tilt my head slightly. "How does what feel?"

"Being the most infamous predator in this room."

The prince dips me low before pulling me back to his chest and smiling maniacally.

Rolling my eyes, I don't answer. He chuckles at that.

For the next two songs, we don't talk. He's too busy soaking it in. Whomever holds the Shackled Serpent's leash is one of the most powerful beings in Galfei Thalor, and he's proudly basking in that title.

I don't mind the silence between us. It gives my mind time to wander, focusing elsewhere—on brown eyes and blonde hair.

"My turn." Warm fingers dance along my arm. To my left, Niam bows deeply, then winks.

Kayd stiffens. I wouldn't have noticed if I wasn't already in his arms. "Of course," Kayd grinds out between his teeth, though his smile is unfaltering.

Before Niam can whisk me away, I ask, "If you can, Prince, will you send Halton my way? I'd like a dance with him as well."

I don't miss the way Kayd's jaw tightens, but any reservations or care I may have had are thrown away as Niam swings me around and flings me into step.

"You're a menace," he whispers, gliding me through throngs of dancers.

"So are you." I send him a playful glare before lowering my voice. "Do you want His Highness to murder me out of jealousy?"

Niam's honey-colored lips tighten. I lower my eyes to catch his gaze. "You know you can talk to me, right? About anything. I would never judge you."

"I know," he mumbles before twirling me out and pulling me back into his chest, continuing the dance.

After a handful of minutes, the music crescendos with a clash of powerful notes, and Niam dips me deeply with a laugh. Mine echoes his as he pulls me back up.

"Thank you for the dance, Miss Maeve." He kisses my cheek just as my chest tugs harshly.

He's here.

"Thank you, Lord Niam." I send him a loving smile and turn toward Halton.

He's standing tall with relaxed shoulders and a smile that makes my stomach flutter. "I heard I was being called upon."

He reaches his hand out toward me. I clasp it with one hand and wave goodbye to Niam with the other. Then we're off. The glares and scared whispers of the others on the dance floor go ignored as he spins me around with ease. This dance is so different from the first we shared. No longer is he stiff and silent. The hardness melts away as he takes me in with roaming eyes and an easy grin.

"You're staring, Serpent," he muses and tightens his hold around my waist.

"So are you, guard."

His chuckle sends a pleasant shiver down my spine.

Four songs fly by. Four dances with him and his devastating touch. It doesn't seem like enough. I could dance with him until my toes bleed, and it would still never be enough.

The ending notes of our last dance ring across the ballroom, and the guard bows, bringing my hand to his lips. His eyes lock onto mine. "A dance with Death herself," he murmurs against my skin, "is even more radiant than the stars above."

My flesh puckers under his touch, his kiss leaving pinpricks in its wake as he turns and walks away toward his prince. Hiding my smile and the blush I feel beginning to dust across my cheeks, I glide off the dance floor.

"Hello? Maeve?" Alta waves her perfectly manicured hand in front of my face. "Did you hear me?"

Nearly dropping my goblet of rose-colored wine at the interruption, I shake my head free from all thoughts of Halton and Jerik and the kingdoms knowing who I am.

Once I get my bearings, I send my friend an apologetic smile. "I'm sorry. My mind was elsewhere. What were you saying?"

She huffs out through her nose and playfully rolls her eyes. "I *said* . . . who is the guy that hasn't stopped staring at you since you arrived?"

I follow her gaze and am met with those large, brown eyes. Jerik looks my way for a split second before turning around and replying to whatever was said to him by another Phandolus guard.

"An old friend," I simply say.

"He's cute," she coos as she takes him in.

I chortle. "You think everyone is cute."

Jerik nods at the guard who was talking to him and turns around. I watch him walk toward a stained-glass door on the opposite side of the ballroom and slip through it, leaving it slightly opened.

He wants me to follow.

My attention shifts to Princess Andrina, who's dancing with a tall muscular changeling. This is it.

"I haven't had a chance to catch up with him." I look at Alta, who already has a knowing look on her face.

"Go on, Maeve. Make sure you tell him all about me." With delicate hands, she ushers me forward, and I slip through the open door out toward the Derlow Grove gardens.

Small sparkling lights are threaded through tree branches and around massive stone columns lining the outdoor walkways. The cold air is fresh, burning my lungs in a way that feels light and free.

Jerik is leaning against a stone railing, overlooking a maze of flowering shrubs. I don't think he notices me yet. It gives me a moment to admire him.

No longer are bruises splattered across his pale skin. He's more muscular, broader under his clothes. His face is fuller, and his trimmed beard casts a shadow under the light. His time as a royal guard has done him well. He looks good, healthy.

"Hi, stranger." I say the very words I uttered when I last visited him at the stable. The smile that can be heard in each syllable widens when he turns around to face me.

His lips turn upward, and his eyes soften as he takes me in.

"Maeve." It's a sigh laced with relief and something I can't quite put my finger on. I rush forward and pull him into my chest, wrapping my arms around his neck and refusing to let go. Here he is, in my arms once again. I've missed him so much.

But this hug feels different from the last one we shared. *I* feel different. No longer am I contemplating kissing him. No longer do I yearn to feel his lips on me and his arms around me while I sleep.

I feel . . . content. Content being here in his arms. Content knowing that those dreams of a life with him after servitude *were* created out of shared trauma and convenience. Content with friendship.

"I-I am so happy to see you," I say, pulling back from him and staring into his doe-like eyes.

As I take one step away from him to get a better look, Jerik scratches the back of his neck. A blush turns his cheeks pink, and a shy smile graces his lips. Lips that are no longer cracked.

After a breath, his eyes bore into me, becoming sharp and clear, as if he's looking at me—*really* looking at me for the first time. "Why didn't you tell me?" His words rasp out through his teeth as his eyebrows furrow together.

I frown as I take him in. "I . . . Jerik, I couldn't. They threatened . . ." I let out a deep, defeated sigh. "I wish I could have. I'm sorry."

How can I express the sorrow I feel for lying to him? I can't. No words can do that.

Shaking my head at myself, I link my arm with his and walk a little farther away from the ball. When we come to a stop, I glance at him through the corner of my eye. He's different now. Something has changed since I left.

"Jerik . . ." He turns to me when I say his name, his soft smile aimed at me. "I'm so proud of you." Just as fast as it came, his smile crumbles. Looking anywhere but at me, I see something break inside him. "I never deserved a friend like you, always so kind and true. While I was darkening my soul in the blood of others, you kept my light from fading. I owe so much to you."

His forehead wrinkles, and his frown deepens. Something heavy weighs down on his heart. I can tell. The silence between us grows, suffocating me as it constricts around my lungs.

"But," I exclaim with a self-deprecating chuckle, "enough about me, and all my wrongdoings. What about you? I'm so happy to see you're doing well. Congrats on the new servitude position!"

His frown inches up. Not quite a smile but lighter than before. "It's definitely a lot better than shoveling horse shit," he chuckles. I join in, our light, airy laughs fluttering in the cold breeze.

"How did your servitude assignment get switched? That's pretty rare, isn't it?" In fact, I've never heard of that happening before.

Jerik huffs out a laugh. "Yeah, it is. Her Highness approached me in my cell before I had to head out to the stable a few months ago, asking me a bunch of questions. In exchange for answers, she said I'd never have to work in the stable again." He shrugs, his hand rubbing the back of his neck.

"Wow, I never thought she could be so generous," I muse with a teasing smile.

Jerik's jaw twitches, and his back goes rigid. A move so subtle I wouldn't have noticed if I wasn't already studying him. "Your time spent with the elves has clouded your vision, Maeve. The changelings have always been generous, taking us in, and providing for us while we do our duty."

I almost laugh. *Almost.* The bubble of giggles dies in the back of my throat when I realize how serious he is. Things really have changed since I left. The chuckle that breaks the barrier of my lips is forced now, unsure of how to proceed.

Several beats of silence hang between us. Then I ask the question that's burning against my skull. "C'mon, Jerik, amuse an old friend. What information did you have that Andrina didn't?"

The words weigh heavy in my gut. The facade—a facade I never had to wear in front of him before—remains friendly. Inside, however, there's whirling anxiety and dread. Something is off. Something is wrong between us. It was supposed to be easy with him.

A shudder flutters over his features, and his throat bobs slightly. For a second, I think that's remorse but then I blink, and it's gone, as if I imagined it. There's only cold, hard resolve.

"Information you provided, Maeve. The rebellion. How there are more people who think like them . . . like *you*." His voice slithers out of him as if *he* were the Shackled Serpent. The hiss is full of disdain.

I take a step back. "What?"

He mimics me, taking a step forward. "*That* really piqued her interest. She thought she knew everything about you. Imagine her surprise when I told her about your mother."

Another step back, but he pounces. Searing hot pain erupts just below my ribs. It's a pain so unbearable that no sound leaves my throat as my head slowly looks down. Wedged deep into my skin is a silver-and-cobalt dagger. Jerik's hand is wrapped so tightly around the hilt that the bones of his knuckles protrude against his skin. With rigid movements, I look back up at him. My mouth hangs open in pain and betrayal. How—how *could* he?

"Jerik—" A pained gasp rips from my throat as he twists the dagger into my flesh then pulls it out roughly. A panicked look flashes across his face before he wills it away, quickly covering it up.

My limbs give out from underneath me. I stumble into his rigid, warm body, gripping his arms desperately. My eyes are wide now, heartbroken from what he did and ashamed for trusting him so blindly.

As if I were nothing more than the dust gathering in our old cell, Jerik shakes me off. A loud thump echoes around us as my body hits the floor.

He leans over me as blood begins painting the cobblestones. "I told you I'd do anything to get a better servitude assignment. Princess Andrina sends her regards."

45

M Y MIND IS STILL—A blank canvas—as I blink away the blur in my vision and stare at the twinkling lights above me. It's peaceful. It's silent. It's like the world around me paused, and I'm drifting in an abyss, suspended in time itself. As if my consciousness is hiding the truth from right in front of me.

Then a dull, insistent pulse presses against my skull. I concentrate on it, dissecting it, trying to decipher what it is. Breaking through, it crashes around me. Pain. Confusion. Hurt.

I feel the very essence of my life slowly seeping out of me. Pain ricochets just below my ribs. Warmth oozes out of me, a river of blood draining into the rivets of the stones beneath my body.

Flashes of deceptive brown eyes pierce my soul.

Jerik.

How could he do this to me? After all those nights spent in his arms in our cell . . . After all our whispered conversations and quiet dreams. *How could he do this?*

My gut churns and turns to lead. My dying heart beats harder than ever before, like it's clutching around what little life remains before it slips away forever. The same terror from that night in Fiermoor rips through bones and flesh. Terror of death I've inflicted upon dozens of others before.

Perhaps I deserve this fate. A life for all the lives I've taken. My blood is merely a token for all the blood I've spilled.

I blink, and the lights soften, each bulb out of focus.

My heart doesn't beat as hard anymore. A serenity engulfs me. My life for theirs. Yes . . .

Soon, I will be with Mother and Ottilie. Another star to add to the night sky.

Mother, I'll be with you soon. Ottilie, you won't be alone any longer.

Mother and Ottilie. Mother and Ottilie. Mother and . . . Father. Father. Arden. Alta. Niam. Halton. Kayd—even Kayd.

No. I can't die. I don't want to die.

I need to live. I need to see Father and Arden again. I need to hug Alta and thank her for the kindness she's extended to me. I need to prove to Niam that his truth is beautiful. I need to tell Halton how I feel . . . how he makes me feel.

A dreadful, frigid cold seeps into my bones. My breath turns ragged, panicked.

Faint footsteps in the distance echo against the walkway pillars. I can't tell where they're coming from or where they're going. I can't tell how far away they are. But they're there.

"Help . . ." The word is nothing more than a weak wheeze, no louder than a whisper. My eyes struggle to stay open.

The footsteps don't stop.

Another quiet "help" squeaks through my now-chattering lips.

A pause in the stranger's gait before they take another step.

"No. Please. Don't leave," I want to yell, but nothing comes out.

Taking a deep breath, ice and fire fill my constricting lungs, and I put all my dwindling energy into my cracked, dying voice. Only one word comes out. The most important word. "Help . . ."

The footsteps halt. A long moment passes, and I call out once again. The stranger's shoes pound against the stone ground, picking up speed. Louder and louder, the steps become. Closer and closer. I feel hope wedge itself into my chest. My head droops to the side. I blink my eyes, hoping to see my savior appear.

Instead, my consciousness seeps into a deep, dark void slowly consuming me. My body begins to convulse, the shivers overcoming me as my body temperature drops drastically. The pain begins to fade . . .

"Serpent!" I know that voice. I know it. I . . . I just can't place who it belongs to. I'm entirely numb, my body going into shock. A familiar icy touch brings me back enough to just barely open my eyes.

Black seeps around the edges of my vision, and the figure kneeling before me is blurry. His panicked breath grazes against my clammy skin. My eyes shut again.

"Maeve . . ." Their voice is a rasp, broken between shards of terror. "Open your eyes, Maeve. Please!"

They place their hands against my cheeks. Cold—too cold on my searing skin. My heavy lids open for a brief moment before closing again.

"Maeve!"

I hold onto that voice, anchoring myself to it and using it as the strength I need to blink my eyes open again. I blink and blink and blink until the person before me sharpens. I'm met with terrified hazel eyes. *Halton.*

My lips lift at the sight of him. The guard—*my guard*—is with me in my final moments.

I open my mouth to say something, anything, but words don't form. Warm, sticky liquid dribbles down my chin and beneath my gown.

"No. No, no, no, nonono." His words run together. I can't tell if it's him or if it's my muddled brain squishing each syllable, making them one. His icy fingers brush over my side, my blood coating his skin. "Fuck!"

Halton's arms shimmy beneath my body and scoop me up against his chest. My body jerks against him. He's running, I think.

The elf's breaths are fast. In between each inhale and exhale, he mumbles reassuring nothings into my ear.

I've got you.

You're going to be okay.

Don't let this be the thing that kills you, Serpent.

You are strong. You will make it. I've got you.

His words are a conviction of confidence, filling my dying vessel with hopeful strength. I believe him wholeheartedly.

That is, until the hallucinations begin. From the blood loss, I'm sure. Or perhaps, Jerik's blade was dipped in poison. The lines of reality and fantasy blur together as my vision spins. White bleeds into brown. Icy blue flickers and flashes against hazel.

"You're not . . . Where is . . ." My words slur together. It's getting harder and harder to form coherent thoughts.

Where white once was, brown returns. Beige fingers glide against my cheek, and hazel eyes peer down at me. *Halton.*

Darkness seeps in, and I succumb, feeling no more pain.

46

P AIN. NOT THE SEARING hot pain of phantom claws digging into my side that I vaguely remember. This is a dull pain—deep beneath my flesh, behind my very bones.

I squeeze my eyes tighter as a flood of events slams into me.

Derlow Grove. That's where I am . . . or was. A party—the Autumnal Ball. Jerik. Pain, so much pain. *How could he?*

Muted laughter and music can be heard in the distance; the ball is still going on. Voices—two male voices—are closer. Their words are hushed, the sentences frantic. They sound familiar, but I can't quite place where I have heard them before.

"Did she see anyth . . ."

My ears strain to hear what they're saying.

I grit my teeth. It's so hard, too hard.

"It's like . . ." The second voice. "Couldn't control . . ."

"That has never happened bef—"

My eyebrows knit together. A grunt escapes the back of my throat as that dull, aching pain sharpens when I shift my body to face the two deep in discussion. The talking ceases.

Slowly opening my eyes, the figures come into view. Halton and Kayd. The captain rushes toward me, falling onto his knees next to the bed I'm resting in. I'm in bed . . .

I glance around the room I'm in. A large window with torn curtains. Strips of said curtains in a bloody pile in the corner. A single bed with black bedding. A large desk with a golden sword and leather bag filled with clothes strewn atop it. Most definitely not the chambers Alta and I were assigned.

I try to sit up even more, but a tunic I wasn't wearing before snags from the movement. It's black and oversized. I inhale deeply. It smells like Halton. Pine and spice. I'm in his temporary chambers.

Looking back at him, worry creases his brows. His hand tenderly reaches up and tucks an unruly strand of hair behind my ear before cupping my cheek, his cool thumb swiping over the scar just below my eye.

"Do you—" His words are clipped as if he's having trouble forming them. "Do you remember what happened?"

I glance behind Halton for a split second. Kayd stands stiffly behind him. His eyes hold something soft and curious as he takes us in. Shifting my attention back to the guard, I gaze into those enchanting hazel irises, now swirling with emotions I can't place, and my tears form automatically. They burn the back of my eyes, but I force them not to fall.

I nod. My own words sticking on my tongue.

"Okay . . . Okay," he coos. His thumb continues the soft, short trail along the side of my face. Warmth spreads beneath my cheeks. *Safe.* "I won't ask you to recount it now, but we need to know exactly what happened when you're ready to talk. But you're healed. Kayd used his magick to save you. You're going to be okay, Serpent. You're okay."

My head whips toward the stoic prince. A wave of nausea washes over me from the fast movement before settling in my gut. *Still weak, got it.*

Gratitude worms its way into my chest. "Thank you, Kayd," I croak out, my voice gravelly from lack of use.

His plump, brown lips curve up into a smile. There's a kindness there I'm not used to. He nods at me and sneaks a worried glance at his friend before taking his leave.

Halton's thumb, absentmindedly tracing my features, begins to lull me to sleep. My eyes flutter shut. "You're okay." His soft words caress my flushed skin and seep into my heart.

I'm okay. I'm okay.

Flashes—fast flashes under my eyelids of things I can't comprehend. They startle me, scare me, even. I think I was poisoned, just like the merfolk queen's advisor. Those hallucinations . . .

A gasp blows through my closed lips, and chills erupt across my body, confusion etching itself across my features.

"What's wrong?" Halton asks, urgency lacing each word.

"When . . ." I trail off, trying to gather my jumbled thoughts. "I-I swear I saw something. It doesn't make sense. It . . . I know what I saw, though." My face twists as I try to recall what now plagues my mind. "You . . . were you, but you also . . . weren't."

Halton's hand slides from my face down to the bed, and his mouth opens and closes, fishing for a response but unable to find one. He stammers over his words. So unlike him, it makes me nervous. *Unsafe.*

"Halton . . . what is it?" My voice is strained.

He squeezes my hand. "It must've been the blood loss." It's unconvincing. A lie. Something taut in my chest seizes.

"No. Don't do that. Don't lie to me, Halton. I'm not . . ." My voice, barely audible, cracks. "I'm not *unwell.*"

The elf visibly flinches at the sound of my voice. His head droops, with the tip of his chin almost touching his chest, which rapidly begins to rise and fall as he stares at our connected hands. Twisting his eyes shut, he lets out a long and dreadful breath.

"No. No, you're not. I-I haven't been completely honest with you, Serpent. I am . . . not who I say I am." The elven guard sounds remorseful.

The tone of his voice knots my stomach into a tangled mess. *Unsafe.*

My heart turns to stone, heavy and weighted with dread, and my nerve endings spark to life. "Halton . . . What . . . do you mean?" I don't think I want to know the answer. I don't want to know the truth. I want to live in this blissful, *easy* world we created—filled with heated trysts and tender moments.

His gaze travels up my tense body and settles on my face. It sears into me, my chest tugging harshly. "I'm no elf. My eyes are not hazel. My hair is not brown. I'm from Phandolus . . . I-I'm a changeling."

"What?" I whisper. The knot in my stomach twists tighter and tighter until the pain drowns out the nausea threatening to spill. *A changeling.*

My very existence rattles, threatening to shatter under the truth. I finally felt like I was coming to terms with my feelings for the *elven* guard. I like him . . . I wanted to be with him. He made me feel things I never felt before . . . and now, I feel like a fool. Just as I did at the trials.

He's a changeling. The same creatures who tainted my soul and made me a killer. It hurts. Too much to comprehend, but what hurts the most . . .

My body moves on its own accord, shame and embarrassment propelling me forward. Silks and furs tangle between my flailing limbs, and my vision blurs from the sudden movement. I launch myself out of the bed, nails on display and screams ripping from my throat, thrashing against my raw vocal cords.

The icy cold of his hands seeps deep into my bones, gripping tightly around my wrists. I recoil at the feeling. Instead of the exhilarating steam I once felt when his skin touched mine, it now burns me with frostbite.

"You lied." My voice is hoarse and shattered. My breaths become erratic, but my body stills in his grasp. A salty tang drips onto my cracked lips. Tears.

With all my strength, I shove him off me and back away from the impostor I was so close to giving my heart to.

"You lied!" I scream again. A torrent of tears cascades down my cheeks, and tremors rack throughout my body. "You lied. You lied . . . I thought . . ."

Shaking my head violently, I take another step away from him, my feet stumbling over one another. The more distance, the better. Another step. I need to get away from him. Then I turn and beeline toward the door.

"Wait!" Halton shouts, distress lacing that one word. "Please, Serpent. Please. Don't leave . . . Don't leave me, Maeve. You're—"

"I'm what?" I yell, spinning around to face the guard again, with my arms stretched out wide.

Halton looks scared. His eyes are gaping, nearly out of his skull. His lip trembles. His hands flex at his sides. "Y-You're my—"

"What, Halton?"

"You're my mate!" The words ricochet through the chamber and hang between us.

Halton's heavy breaths sound shattered as he stares at me with wide eyes. That tugging in my chest that I've felt since arriving in Nythfaedell pulls tightly, harshly, as if it's yanking me forward toward him.

Mate. What does that even mean? I've heard it before. I remember hearing it . . . but where?

With a shaky breath, I stare at the guard in front of me. His hand reaches forward, reaching toward me. I have to get out of here. I can't be bothered with a term I don't understand. I'm trying to wrap my head around the fact that he isn't who he said he was.

Still drowsy from my brush with death, I messily turn around. Before I stumble out of the room, I see Halton's face fall. Hurt flickers across his features.

And as I stumble through the castle's hall, all I hear are the calls of my name . . . my real name.

The dark shadows of the Derlow Grove gardens conceal me from prying eyes as I run through the shrub maze and toward the dark forest beyond. Once I breach the clearing of tall trees, nymphs and satyrs scatter, hiding from the mortal who disturbed their night.

When my frozen feet can't take another step, I fall to my knees, not caring about the light dusting of snow stinging my bare legs or the cold chilling me to my bones. Nothing compares to the sharp, insistent tugging in my chest that is now strained, like something inside has cracked.

A sob—loud and messy—shatters through the silent forest. Hot tears slip down my face and over my neck. Hyperventilating wheezes accompany my cries.

I'm breaking. I'm losing myself. The cracks in my soul become chasms, void of absolutely anything light and lively.

Despite knowing from the beginning that nothing would come from mine and Halton's trysts simply because of who we are, it hurts. It hurts to breathe. It hurts to think. Everything hurts. Because a secret part of me wanted it, wished for something real to blossom between us.

A deep, silent realization hits me so hard I feel as if my lungs collapsed into nothing but dust. A realization I don't want to acknowledge . . .

Oh Gods.

I suck as much frigid air into my heaving lungs as I can. One gulp. Two gulps. It's too much.

My hands fly to my chest, and I begin clawing at the linen tunic draping over my body. I feel like I'm choking, suffocating underneath the lurking serpent. Pieces of fabric rip in two, falling onto the white forest floor. I rip away more and more until I'm in nothing but tattered shreds of black barely covering my body. Stripping myself from the killer within.

It's useless, a meek voice prods into the back of my skull.

"I know," I whisper, letting the last strip of tunic fall from my fingers.

You are *a killer. Your story is one of darkness, no matter how much light surrounds you.*

I wipe my wet cheeks dry before slumping forward and gripping onto the snow underneath me. My shins are numb now, but I welcome the sharp pinch of cold on my palms. I try to catch my breath and clear my thoughts.

Once I do, I feel them. Mother's warmth swirls around my body. Ottilie's light penetrates my chest. I break down again, crying even harder than before.

PART III:
A SYMBOL

47

"**O**PEN THE DOOR, GIRL!**"** Madam Prea's voice carries through the wood separating us as she knocks violently against it.

I haven't left my chambers since we returned from the Autumnal Ball. That was days ago. I'm rotting away, lying in an all-consuming void spurred on by the whirlwind that is my mind.

Jerik's blade slicing through my flesh. Icy blue leaking into Halton's beautiful hazel eyes. That word . . . *mate*.

My thoughts don't cease, no matter how badly I wish them to.

Another sharp knock makes me flinch.

"If you don't open this door . . ." Prea trails off. It's the same voice she used when we were in the kitchen, and she caught one of her chambermaids sneaking off to visit the stable before finishing her work. Stern and caring.

With a low sigh, I pull myself out of bed and answer the door.

I open the wooden barrier and am met with a scowl, but as soon as Prea takes me in, her features turn soft. Sharp edges are replaced by soft curves. Furrowed brows are smoothed out.

There's pity there, too. I must look like a mess.

The elf enters my chambers and leads me over to the chaise after closing the door behind us. As I sit there, I watch her begin to tidy up my rooms.

365

"*Stars*, girl," she whispers.

Bending over, Madam Prea begins to pick up pieces of a decorative plate. I shattered it against the wall the day we got back and haven't had the courage to pick the shards up yet. Broken pieces scattered just like the broken pieces of myself.

I stay silent for a long while, watching Prea clean up the mess I made. If only she could clean up the mess I've become since learning the truth.

"That's why you don't like him. Halton, I mean." My words are raw, having not used my voice in days.

Madam Prea pauses her movements. She approaches me, as if I'm the white unicorn in the Nythfaedell forest, before sitting down on the nearby chair.

Smoothing her palms over her skirts, she looks down. "It's not that I don't like Halton specifically . . ." She worries her bottom lip between her teeth, the lines deepening around her eyes. "It's hard to accept someone who came from a kingdom that caused us so much pain. I'm trying to be better. Really, I am. But sometimes, all I see is Queen Aila, lying sick in bed, when I look at him."

"Why didn't you tell me?" I can't help but ask.

Madam Prea looks up from her lap and smiles sadly. "It's not my story to tell."

Silence looms over us as I let that sink in. It was Halton's story to tell, yet he never said anything to me. That strained churning in my chest makes itself known again.

As I wring my fingers together, a question slips through my lips before I can stop them. "Do—do you think the universe fights for souls to be together?"

Prea eyes me curiously, then nods. "If the souls are meant to be, then, yes."

I bob my head in response, my mind drifting to that word. It's been haunting me since Halton blurted it out in his moment of desperation. It's completely unknown to me. No humans I've come across have used that word. Wife, husband, lover . . . but never *mate*.

"What's a mate?" It comes out as a whisper, and I brace myself for another truth to be revealed.

Prea's spine straightens, causing her to loom over me. Her jaw drops, and her eyes widen. "Where did you hear that word?" Barely any sound is attached to her question, the words drifting silently off her lips.

"Um . . ." Suddenly, I feel like I'm a child explaining myself. It feels like I shouldn't reveal what was said to me, but then I look into Prea's gaping purple eyes and see it. Shock. Concern. Care. I go forward with answering her. "When I found out the truth about Halton, I tried to leave, and he told me that I'm his mate. I . . . I didn't understand what he meant, and at the time, I didn't care because all I felt was anger from his lies. But that word has been gnawing at me nonstop since. It's like—"

"A pulsing ache in your chest? Like a rope tugging you toward him, connecting you to him?" Madam Prea interrupts.

"Yes," I breathe out.

With a solemn nod of her head, Madam Prea grabs my hand and squeezes it. "Being someone's mate is . . . It's like two halves of a whole, connected through a bond stronger than anything you can imagine. You are Halton's other half. His soul sings to you, and yours sings to him. You just didn't understand the feeling of it."

My heart thumps wildly in my chest as her words sink in.

"Truthfully," Prea continues, "I've never heard of a mating bond happening with a mortal. Perhaps you're the first. Perhaps you're not. But that doesn't matter. The universe deemed you two the perfect pair. For one reason or another, he and you are one, connected together for eternity."

My stomach knots, twisting and turning around this new information. I don't like it. I always felt drawn to Halton, my body reacting in ways it never has before. But before now, it felt like a gradual shift. A choice. Now faced with the truth, I know I never had such a luxury. He was chosen for me by some unknown force. No choice . . . just like everything else in my life.

Prea squeezes my hand again and droops her head to meet my gaze. "I can see you working through it, and I can see that darkness swirling around you as you fall into a pit of anger and sadness. The only way to heal the pain you're feeling is by facing it head-on."

"I don't know if I'm strong enough to do that." A lone tear rolls down my cheek just as that tug—*that bond*—yanks harshly in my chest.

"You are the strongest person I know." The elf wraps her arms around me and pulls me into a warm, comforting hug. "I've known that since the day I first met you, covered in blood and bruises. Face your pain. Face the darkest parts of you. You yearn for freedom, Maeve Wyndell, but you will never truly be free until all of you is."

I barge into Halton's chambers and pause as I take in the state of it. Only a handful of candles are lit. Clothes are strewn across the floor of his sitting room. Dust motes swirl in the air and cover his normally pristine shelves.

Halton snaps his head up at the sound of my entrance. He's sitting at his desk with several documents scattered across it. His hair is disheveled. His eyes are glassy with dark circles underneath. He looks as I probably do—tired and heartbroken.

Immediately standing up, he strides toward me, but I stop him with my raised hand.

"When—when did you find out I was your . . . mate?" I ask, choking on that word. My attention never leaves him. I want to see his genuine reaction before his normally stony facade covers it up.

Much to my surprise, he's open, vulnerable. No hint of his mask is in sight.

"I felt it the moment my eyes met yours. When I handed you Nythfaedell's trial." He stares into my aching, twitching soul. As if he feels it himself, his gaze darts down to my chest before sliding back up to my face.

My hands fist around nothing.

Halton knew the entire time he's known me and didn't think to mention it. This is my life, too. I deserve to have a say in it.

"Why—" My voice cracks. I feel the sting of tears forming behind my eyes. Angry tears. "Why didn't you tell me?"

The elf—*changeling*—takes another step toward me.

"I wanted to. Trust me, I yearned to tell you as soon as I felt the bond snap into place, but I couldn't. Interrupting the trials is considered treason—an act of war against the other kingdoms. I wanted so badly to take you away from the horrors you faced that night."

Halton begins pacing and running his fingers through his faux brown hair. "And when you were chosen by the changelings—by my . . . kind—I decided to let it go. I hoped you would do your time and live a fulfilling life. Perhaps find a nice man and marry him in Terakeld. I was okay with that because you would be happy.

"And then you got captured. My mate was here in Nythfaedell with me. It felt as if the stars couldn't handle us being away from each other and guided you here. I wanted to tell you as soon as I got you alone, but I remember . . ." Halton pauses and swallows around nothing, his throat bobbing up and down. "I remember the way you scrambled away from me when I untied you from that horrid chair Kayd forced you in. The fear in your eyes . . . I couldn't handle you ever looking at me like that."

Halton's hand clutches at his chest as he takes in a shattered breath. Tears pebble against the corners of his eyes as he silently remembers that moment. A moment I thought nothing of, but now . . . I remember the way his gaze peered down at me with hardened features as he took in my injuries. I remember the way he barked at Kayd for torturing me. I remember the way his hands shook as he got close enough to untie me.

"I never wanted you to fear me"—Halton interrupts my thoughts—"but I could handle it if you hated me. Hate is easier. Easier than fear, easier than . . . Just *easier*. So, I made sure you grew to hate me. But—*fuck, Serpent*—it was so hard. Each moment I spent with you, I wanted to know you. I wanted to have you in any way you would let me . . . I'm—I'm so sorry. I should have told you. I regret not telling you . . . about *everything*."

I can't handle this. I can't . . .

I'm not as strong as Prea thinks I am.

Turning heel, I swiftly exit Halton's chamber without a word.

Be strong, I tell myself as I march through the halls of the elven palace toward Prince Kayd's training grounds the next day. *Be strong enough today.*

It's the first day in weeks without snow, and it looks like everyone in Kayd's court is celebrating. A crowd of courtiers lounging on furs and cushions stacked atop wooden landings around the grounds cheer as I approach. Clinking sloshing goblets and stuffing their faces with fruits and nuts, they watch sparring matches between guards. Prince Kayd sits atop his makeshift throne. His legs are crossed, and his hand drapes over the armrest, lazily gripping onto a bushel of red berries. Halton stands beside him like he always does. As if he can feel my presence—with this *bond*, I'm sure he can—his heated stare snaps to me, burning into my skin. Fire beneath flesh.

My heart clenches at the sight of him. My mind shifts to the moment he handed me Nythfaedell's trial. The way his eyes flashed and his nostrils flared . . . At the time, I thought it was disgust twisting his features, but now . . .

Shaking my head to clear my thoughts, I notice the twins are there as well, each sitting in smaller seats on either side of the prince. It's my first time seeing them since leaving the Autumnal Ball. The sail back to the elven kingdom was spent avoiding them all behind a locked door beneath the deck. I want to run to them. Cry and scream and demand why they didn't tell me when they must've known. *They didn't tell me.* My gut twists at the thought.

Silently, I approach the prince and his most-trusted council—his friends, *my friends.* I stand to the right of the prince, mirroring Halton's position.

"Yes, mortal?" Prince Kayd muses. His eyes stay trained on the entertainment.

From the corner of my eye, I see Alta twist her head toward me, surprised I'm here. Niam does the same. Their eyes bulge, and I notice how their bodies strain, as if they're dying to rush forward and smother me in hugs.

I don't look at them. I don't acknowledge them. *They must've known.*

One thing at a time, Maeve.

"I need to go to Phandolus." My voice is hard.

Prince Kayd finally looks my way. His eyes bore into me, the heat of his gaze burning my body. "And why is that?"

"I . . ." I trail off before regaining my composure. "I need to pay a visit to an old friend of mine."

Kayd thinks this over, dramatically running his slender finger over his chin . . . drawing out his decision. "Are you going to kill him?"

How narrow-minded the prince is. Sure, I could kill the man who held me tight at night, then stabbed me when it was convenient for him. It would be easy, but my sights aren't set on Jerik. If only Kayd knew who I was really going to visit. The one who started it all.

Andrina is *mine.* I'm going to face her and all she did to me. Cutting the head of the snake clean off.

What Prince Kayd doesn't know won't hurt him.

"I haven't decided yet." I shrug my left shoulder.

A curious hum, almost appreciative. "You will not be able to cross the bridge." The others try to interrupt him—to stop him from even considering my request—but much to my delight, he ignores them. "You will need to travel to the changeling kingdom another way."

I nod swiftly, and without paying mind to the others, I leave the prince's landing. As I step down the wooden stairs to head back to the palace, my ears pick up at the sound of a meek voice. "Is Maeve all right? Did something happen?"

Alta's quiet and sad questions drift off behind me.

48

D ELICATE WAVES ON A secluded sliver of the Nythfaedell shore run over my boots. The sand beneath shifts with each movement, lulling me into a state of quiet content as I wait for him. He should be here by now.

The message Prince Kayd sent not long after my request to leave for Phandolus said to meet him here just after midday. Supposedly, he has a way to get me across The Unlighted Sea quickly.

As if conjuring him up from my thoughts alone, his lazy footsteps approach. As he comes to my side, I look at him. No pleasantries are shared, not even a subtle nod. His eyes are trained on the horizon, where the gray winter sky meets the inky black depths of the sea. Leisurely held in his hand is a golden flute.

Without a word, he brings the instrument to his pursed lips and begins playing. The light, yet strange, notes twine into the air. Nothing happens at first. The sea is still, the once-thrumming waves now looking like liquid glass. The air is quiet, the wind coming to a halt, as if the flute demanded it.

Then ripples in the water begin to emerge in the distance. Closer and closer, they draw near. And then I see it. Swimming toward us, I come face-to-face with a giant serpent. That same giant serpent I saw all those months ago, when I was still under the thumb of Princess Andrina. It's even more magnificent up close.

Dark-green scales—nearly as black as the void in my chest—sheen under the sun, with purple reflecting against the light.

"How?" I breathe, disbelief contorting my features.

Kayd is silent for a long while, staring longingly at the creature. Then he answers, "Before the Last War, elves lived among mystical creatures, in unity . . . including the great giant serpents. These creatures used to live on land, but they left. The Last War devastated Nythfaedell. My father says it took hundreds of rotations of recovery."

The beast looks at me with curious silver eyes before its attention rests on Kayd, whose eyes gloss over. "However, during that time, all the creatures that roamed openly across the kingdom went into hiding. Most found refuge in the forest, like the ones we see during The Night of Light. The serpents, however, went to the sea. While they're in the merfolk's domain now, the connection we share with them is eternal.

"My music drew it here, and my magick will tether it to you," he explains without breaking eye contact with the snake. It slithers closer to us. "You can ride the creature across the sea, and it will wait for you near the changeling shores until you are ready to come back."

He's so certain I will come back. No threats. Nothing to bind me to this land. If I wanted, I could easily find my way to Terakeld, be done with him and that lying changeling once and for all. But I won't. Deep down in the pits of my soul, I know I have found a home in Nythfaedell and the prince's court.

Slowly, with tentative steps, I approach the serpent. My hand stretches toward its triangular head. Its pitch-black tongue slithers from out of its lips, regarding me with unblinking eyes. It doesn't spook. It looks calm, like it's accepted its fate—simply a means of transportation for a mortal.

I suddenly whip my head toward Kayd. "It will not be tethered to me forever, right? It will be free once I'm done?"

A sense of realization hits Kayd at my question. I can see it in how he looks at me, *really* looks at me. The wild serpent and his serpent are one and the same.

Both looking for freedom. He nods, his fixed gaze penetrating my soul. "Yes, it will be free."

Good. I nod toward the prince, a minuscule smile brushing against my lips—a token of thanks—then mount the slimy back of the serpent. Its scales dig into my thighs. Musk and salt waft into my nostrils as I lean forward and dig my hands into the rivets between each scale. The beast is serene as I do so. With a tight grip, we take off across The Unlighted Sea.

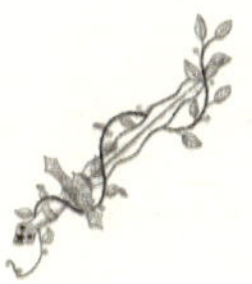

The serpent drops me off near a cluster of boulders on Phandolus's rocky shore. Cold mist sprays into the stale, briny winter air, coating my dry lips. The roar of the surge falls in line with the beat of my heart; a death song sung for what's to come.

Andrina is *mine*.

Slipping off the serpent's back, my hair is knotted, and my clothes stick to my skin, soaked from the journey here. No words can describe what I felt while riding the serpent across The Unlighted Sea.

Exhilarating. Terrifying. Freeing. Those don't even begin to scratch the surface. My heart pounded against my rib cage from the beast's swift moments. My throat is now raw from the shrill laughs I couldn't contain as we glided through the waves.

It blinks at me. Its tongue tastes the air. The serpent's thin lips lift into what looks like a smile. One and the same. That's what we are.

"I'll be back soon," I state. It nods its large head, salt crusting between each scale the longer it stays above the waves. It understands me. One and the same. "And then you will be free to roam the seas."

One last look at the creature, then I make the trek up the shoreline. Rutherglen—the small beach village I first stepped foot in all those months ago—is different from how I remember it. Several windows are boarded up. No children are playing tag. No music flutters through the streets. There's a chilling bleakness that makes my gut twist and the hairs on my arms rise. I wonder what happened.

I tug my cloak around my damp clothes and keep my head down as I continue toward the looming pine tree forest.

Creeping through darkened corners and alleyways, I hear two changelings talking on a bench near the center of the village while watching the sunset. "Things can finally start getting back to normal now that the vile assassin is dead. No more hiding in our homes at night. No more looking over our shoulders."

My steps falter, but not enough to draw any attention.

Proud grins split the two females' faces in half. "I heard Princess Andrina was the one to kill the Serpent. How brave she is!" One changeling claps her fur-lined gloves together in giddy excitement.

The other nods, but her smirk dims. With an unimpressed scowl, she mutters, "But now that *Maeve* girl is a martyr."

The sound of my name makes me freeze. I knew what the consequences of going with Kayd's plan and attending the ball would be, but having my name spoken by changelings who didn't attend makes a shiver run down my spine.

"Her name is becoming a dangerous whisper in the wind for all mortal rebels. The Terakeld rebellion is growing, Gemma. It's bigger than ever before. I even heard there were riots. Apparently, the Towne Hall, where their leaders are located, was ransacked. Thankfully, they all survived. And hopefully soon, they can squash the traitors."

I stand still, silently cloaked in a corner's shadow, as I take in what the changeling said. A surge of pride rushes through me. They're fighting back. Perhaps change isn't as useless as I previously thought while watching whippings in Towne Square.

Then a thought pierces that pride. *Father.* My heartbeat picks up just a hair as I imagine him amid the unrest. I hope he's okay. I hope Ms. Beverlye is looking out for him. I hope—

Oh, Gods. Ms. Beverlye is a loyalist. How will she react when she finds out I'm the one who was terrorizing the kingdoms? Surely, she wouldn't take it out on him. Surely . . .

I need to keep moving. I can't be caught. Sending a silent prayer for my father's safety to the Gods I don't believe in, I continue past the two changelings and enter the forest.

Infiltrating the changeling palace is simple. So easy, it's laughable. I know the layout all too well. I know where the best corners to hide are, the corners where the darkest shadows rest—unmoving voids that swallow all light. I know the easiest routes into the palace and each plausible exit. Every guard is stationed in the exact same spots since I last stepped foot on this property. No changes in their rotations. No added security. It's an insult, really.

That, and with the night sky covering the palace in a dark blanket . . . Too easy,

My eyes zero in on a lower-level window that leads into the hallway near the servants' cells. My old home. I can't help but think about Jerik and our nights spent together. I assume he's far away from chains, since he's a part of the princess's personal guard. I wonder if Andrina put him in my old chambers just to spite me.

Shaking my head free from those intruding thoughts, I climb through the open archway. My feet land silently against the black-and-white marble floor, and I tiptoe toward the foyer and Andrina's chambers.

Thankfully, the palace is quiet, empty. The royals and courtiers—even their guards, by the looks of it—have all gone to bed, comfortable with false security. They think I'm dead.

I ascend the massive staircase that leads to Andrina's wing. At the top is the family portrait. A quick glance at the royal family, then I trek on.

My steps are nearly silent as I approach Princess Andrina's chambers. No guards in sight.

My hand reaches toward the glinting door handle.

Soon, I will face her. Soon, I will kill her.

Before my fingers reach their destination, I stop, arm paused midair. My heart thumps wildly, and my throat turns dry as flashes of all the lives I've taken barrel into my vision. The mortal guards during the trials. The mortal man in the Fiermoor alley. Even those that died on my assignments—dozens of elves, changelings, tieflings, and merfolk.

Prea said I won't be free until I face all the darkness swirling inside of me . . . But if I do this—if I kill the Princess of Phandolus—aren't I giving into it?

I stare at my hand, willing it to grasp onto the handle and do what I came here to do. It doesn't move.

Nothing will change the fact that I'm the Shackled Serpent. Killing Andrina won't change what I've done.

Unwanted tears gather at my lash line, and my hand trembles. But as I stand here, I know it's not from fear. I was an angry mortal, a motherless child who lost her best friend and left her home. I was given knives and daggers, and I told myself I was using them for good. I lost myself under the blood I shed, but I want her back. I want to rid myself of the resentment and anger that's constantly bubbling under my skin. I want to be strong enough to fight for myself. *I want to be free.*

It's time to move forward.

Without another thought, I turn away. Away from Andrina. Away from this palace. Away from the revenge I sought. Yes, revenge. It was never justice, no matter how many times I told myself it was.

A smile graces my lips as I leave that darkness behind . . . in the place that started it all.

49

T HE NYTHFAEDELL SHORE COMES into view, glittering under the new day's sun, and I see her standing there.

Alta's black hair billows in the wind. Her fingers twist around one another in front of her apricot-colored dress, and she shifts from foot to foot while watching me ride the giant serpent toward her. Her eyes never leave me. Questions swirl around the light gray as they sear into my soul. My heart shudders at the sight.

With a long sigh, I dismount the creature as it comes to a stop a few feet away from the elf. Running my palms firmly against its scales, I walk around its body and kneel in the shallow water. The cold sea air goes unnoticed while I gaze into the beast's eyes.

"You're free now." I lean my forehead between its eyes, feeling its tongue slither out and tickle my cheek in response.

Stepping back, I watch the serpent turn around and dive back into the depths of The Unlighted Sea until I no longer see the ripples left in its wake.

Long moments pass before I move. Swiftly turning heel, I stride back toward the elven palace, past Alta without a word. Sparing the life of the one being who made me into a killer was enough for one day. I don't want to face something, *someone* else right now.

"Maeve!" Alta's frantic voice grips my heart and squeezes. "Maeve, wait!"

I can hear her fast footfalls chasing after me. Closer and closer until I feel her arms grip my shoulders, and she spins me around to face her. Her wide eyes are full of hurt. Guilt sinks deep into my gut.

"What did I do?" Her perfectly nude-tinted nails dig into my arms, desperately. Unshed silver tears pebble in the corners of her eyes. "Why won't you talk to me? Please, Maeve. Just *talk* to me."

I open my mouth, but no words come out. Burning tears spring behind my lashes. Alta's gaze flicks from side to side, taking in my features. I try again, opening my mouth. A breath later, the question I've been wondering for days—since the Autumnal Ball—comes out quietly, so quietly that I'm surprised she hears it. "Did you know?"

Alta's eyebrows furrow, and her lips turn down. "Did I know what?"

My throat clenches as I try to stop the sob that's waiting to burst through. Several tears fall down my cheeks instead. "Halton . . . What he is? What I am to him?"

Alta's fingers delicately wipe away each rolling tear from my cheeks. Speaking as softly as possible, Alta bends her head to gaze into my downcast eyes. "Halton's truth . . . If it was *my* truth, I wouldn't want anyone else to reveal it other than me."

"Are you a changeling, too?" I sniffle.

"Stars, no," Alta giggles before her face turns serious once more. "I figured Halton would tell you in his own time. It took him two rotations to reveal that part of him to Niam and me. I'm sorry if not telling you makes me a terrible friend. You've become so dear to me, Maeve, in such a short amount of time, and I don't want this to come between us."

I stay quiet for a moment, letting the frigid sea breeze fill the silence between us before I whisper, "Alta, him and I . . . We . . ." I stop for a moment, unsure of what to say. My brows furrow together, and I bite my bottom lip, willing the tears to stop. They don't, so I start again. "I've given my body to someone before. But . . . I-I gave Halton a part of me that I've never given anyone else. I don't even think he knows he was holding my heart—my trust—in his palm. I never told him. I was too scared."

Alta's eyes widen, and she crushes me into her chest. Hidden against her chest, I let free the sob I was holding on to. It tears through my throat—gutted and broken.

"But who—" I cry. "Who I gave it to was a lie."

I feel her head tilt down toward me. Looking back up at my friend, I watch her stare run over my face with what looks like worry. "What did you mean when you asked if I knew what you are to him?"

A shuddered inhale. "I'm his . . . mate."

Alta—the rock, the anchor in my time of despair—breaks. Her hand flies to her open mouth, and the tears she's been holding back breach her lash line. No sound escapes into the air as her lips mouth, "What?"

"He told me at the Autumnal Ball when I was trying to leave after . . . finding out what he really is." I reach for her hand that's slack at her side. I feel the need to comfort her despite everything—Halton, my decision to turn away from Andrina, and this helpless feeling of not knowing what's next now that I'm finding the light in my soul again. "Apparently, he's known this entire time."

"What?" she repeats more forcefully. Harshly wiping the tears from her face, her eyes harden. "Being mated is one of the most beautiful things that can happen to someone . . . and that stupid male kept it from you!" I'm surprised by how angry she is. Red creeps up her light-brown neck and settles on her cheeks. "I'm going to kill him."

50

M Y STEPS ECHO IN the palace halls as I make my way toward Kayd's parlor after being summoned. It's been three days since I've left behind Andrina and opened up to Alta. I feel lighter now, not dragged down by anger. It's still there, though, pulsing remnants of tainted darkness swirling around my being.

One step at a time.

Yelling pulls my attention toward a closed wooden door. Halton's door. Slowing my steps, I recognize the voice. It's Alta.

"Why would you keep something so important from her?"

My eyes widen. I've never heard Alta so angry.

"I—"

"No. No excuses," she cuts off Halton. "Even if you thought for some stars-forsaken reason it was a good idea, it wasn't. You're an idiot, Halton!"

Despite everything, I feel for him. The ache in my chest is proof of that, but I can't help the chuckle that slides through my grinning teeth as I continue down the hall. Alta's an incredible and fierce friend. I'm truly thankful to have her by my side.

Entering the prince's parlor, no one else is here except Kayd, who's standing near the warmth of the hearth. His arms are clasped behind his back, his shoulders are tense, and he's staring intently at the flames. Light and shadows flicker across his face. Looking at him now, I realize this room is more than just a place to meet with his court and give orders to his assassin. I think it's like a sanctuary for him. Somewhere he can think. Somewhere he can relax. Somewhere he can spend time with his chosen family.

He doesn't even realize I've arrived until I'm standing right next to him. My eyes stay trained on the fire, but I can see him start slightly from the corner of my eye.

"You cannot be sneaking up on me like that, mortal," he mumbles, turning to face me now.

I meet his gaze and give him an amused grin. "Isn't that what you captured me for? To sneak around for you?" My eyebrow raises in question.

Prince Kayd chuckles—the sound vibrating from deep within his chest—and shakes his head, turning his attention back to the hearth. A beat later, I see his brows pull together as if something is weighing heavy on his shoulders. It's a sight I never thought I'd see.

"Kayd?" I ask. "Why did you call me here?"

This seems to pull him out of whatever thoughts are rolling through that princely head of his. He pulls his eyes back to mine. Still, the prince doesn't move as he gathers his thoughts. "War has been declared, Maeve." His voice is grave.

My world comes to a grinding halt. Time stops. Dust hangs in the air. Stagnant flames settle in the hearth. The blood in my veins freezes over.

"What?" A whisper.

"Phandolus created the declaration against us for being in possession of the Shackled Serpent. Fiermoor and Amphitea signed on quickly after, seeing it as an opportunity to bring Nythfaedell down. Looks like their little rebellion reached the ears of the tiefling and merfolk royal houses soon after you killed Lady Evelaide."

My lungs constrict around nothing, and my breathing turns rugged. While Amphitea and Fiermoor signed the declaration merely to go against the elves, Phandolus—the ones who created the feared assassin, *me*—is using said assassin as a means for war. *A war.* There hasn't been war in Galfei Thalor for over one thousand rotations.

If I had only done things differently, this wouldn't be happening. If I had done something more in the other trials to make them pick me instead. If I didn't get so angry at what the mortal guard said about Mother, I might not have caught Andrina's eyes. If I didn't kill in the first place.

Kill or be killed.

Father and Arden with bloody, torn throats pop into my head, and my throat closes.

Kill or be killed.

The soft brush of Ottilie's light and Mother's warmth dance along my cheek.

Kill or be killed.

Kayd places his warm hand on my scarred shoulder. It's a kind gesture. Something rare for the prince when it comes to me. "I wanted to tell you first before the others—"

"It's my fault." I cut him off. My hands begin to shake. Guilt weighs down against my chest, overpowering Mother and Ottilie's presence.

"No." Kayd's warm hand squeezes my flesh, accentuating what he's trying to say. "It's my fault. If I wasn't so blind, I wouldn't have revealed who you truly are."

"Yeah . . . why did you do that?"

With a breathy laugh and a shake of his head, Kayd rolls his eyes. "I wanted to wipe Andrina's smug smile off her face. I seared the moment she realized you were with me at the Autumnal Ball into my memory. That's all I ever wanted. A little payback for the things she's done in the past. She deserves at least that much."

Kayd pauses. His eyes drop focus for a moment, lost in thought.

"Kayd?" I question hesitantly.

My voice knocks him out of the trance as his stare bores into me. "You know, when I first made that deal with you—to leash the Shackled Serpent—it was simply because I wanted power. I tortured you to get that power because I didn't care who you were or what happened to you to make you so angry. You were nothing to me." The elven prince pauses, his throat bobbing up and down. "But now . . . Now, you are everything to me because you are everything to *him*."

My throat closes, and my mouth parts. Kayd stares at me with seriousness.

"Halton is my best friend. We've been through everything together. Did you know he gave me this scar?" Kayd points toward his left eyebrow and the white line that separates it into two. A mirthful smile tugs at the corner of his mouth as he recounts a day long ago. "We were fifteen. It was right after my mother . . . I was hurting. I was angry. And I wanted to spar. So, we did. It was sloppy and messy, and the only thing I saw was red. That is, until actual red clouded my vision.

"I didn't time my steps correctly—a stupid mistake. Halton's sword snagged my eyebrow, and it snapped me out of whatever rage-filled trance I was in. I could've healed it afterwards, but I chose not to. It grounds me. *He* grounded me. Halton . . . he's one of the good ones. And you, mortal, make him happy . . . Although, I don't see why." A sly, teasing smirk tugs at his features.

My eyes water slightly before I'm barreling toward the elven prince. Instead of beating him to a pulp like I always fantasized about, my arms wrap around his neck and pull him tightly against me. He's stiff under my hug—arms hanging at his sides—but I don't care.

"Are you done?" he questions in a deadpan voice, prompting me to push him away with a huff.

"Prick," I giggle. A bark of a laugh from the prince—loud and free—as he playfully shoves me aside. My smile fades slightly. "Did you know I was his mate?"

Prince Kayd's eyes soften as he nods. "Yes. I went to visit him one morning and realized you were sleeping in his chambers. He tried to play it off"—Kayd chuckles to himself—"but I can read him like a book. That's when he told me."

I hum and nod along with him. "Is that why you forbade me to see him?"

A grimace twists his lips. "Yes. You—you must understand . . . A mortal being mated, it's unheard of. I did it to protect him. That didn't stop him, though. Just the way he looked at you. I knew nothing would keep the two of you away from each other for long."

Prince Kayd turns back toward the roaring hearth fire. "You should give him a chance. He's . . . a mess. You're good at hiding it, but I can tell you are, too. That's what the bond does—it connects you in ways you never thought possible."

My chest seizes, tugging persistently at the prince's words. "Are you . . ." I'm unsure if it's appropriate to ask. It's personal, but my mouth keeps moving, ignoring my brain from stopping it. "Are you mated? You sound like you know from experience."

Kayd chuckles and shakes his head. "No, but my parents were. My mother's death . . . My father said it felt like his soul was ripping in two." His distant voice picks up, stronger and higher in pitch, changing the subject. "But even if you and Halton weren't mates, there's an impending war. It might be good to clear the air before then."

"You should take your own advice, Prince." I cock my eyebrow.

His face twists in confusion. He looks lost, unsure. "What do you mean?"

Shrugging my shoulder, I muse, "Like you said, Kayd, a war is coming, and you still can't tell Niam how you feel."

The prince's eyes bulge. His mouth opens and closes like a fish out of water. Fear overcomes him, radiating off the prince in searing ripples. To my surprise, he doesn't deny it.

"He likes you, too, you know. Just tell him." Giving Kayd a warm smile, I can see the relief travel through his body. His muscles relax slightly, and his brows smooth. The elven prince returns a smile of his own. That panic in his forest-green eyes turns into hope.

Someone behind us clears their throat. Prince Kayd and I spin around quickly. Madam Prea stands at the open parlor door.

The glare Prince Kayd sends me speaks for itself: *You're an assassin. You should have heard her approach.*

I shoot him an ugly face back.

"I'm sorry to interrupt, Your Highness. King Osmar would like to see Maeve. Right away."

Kayd and I both start at the request. What in the world would the elven king want with me? The prince is back to his normal, rigid self, with eyes set and jaw clenched. Sweat begins to pool along my palms, but I walk toward the older elf with my shoulders back. Kayd is a step behind mine, following my path toward Prea. However, her wrinkled pale hand halts the prince in his stride.

"I'm sorry, Your Highness. The king has requested to speak with Maeve . . . alone."

What—

My steps halt, and I twirl around toward Kayd, nearly slamming into his chest. My eyes are wide, and my gut knots, making me feel sick. A moment of horror passes between us before the prince expertly melts his surprise into a serene expression.

Nodding his head at Madam Prea's statement but never moving his eyes from mine, he says, "As His Majesty wishes."

51

T HOSE GRAND GOLDEN DOUBLE doors—the same doors I've avoided since the night I was captured—loom before me. I fiddle with the seam of my tunic, and the rough, calloused tips of my fingers rub against the fabric.

"You'll be fine, girl," Madam Prea mumbles quietly next to me. She places a reassuring hand on my arm before pushing open the doors and announcing my presence to the king.

One step across the threshold, and the doors shut behind me. The thud echoes across the chambers, rattling my bones. The grand sitting area has multiple chairs and chaises, a dark wooden desk that has vines and flowers carved into it, and elven gold. Tons of it. Furniture. Art. Sconces. It's blinding, but there is still a sense of comfort within these walls. It smells like cinnamon and vanilla with a hint of flowers, as if Queen Aila Glynvyre never left this world or her husband's side. It's a home—lived in and loved in.

A luxuriously massive bed sits in the middle of a connecting room. Through the arched doorway, I see him. King Osmar sits against the elegant headboard, covered in silks and furs. He looks frail from where I'm standing, so unlike the king I've spoken to before.

"Come in, Maeve," the king speaks out. Although, his voice sounds different—raspy and wet.

My feet begin to move, bringing me to the entry of his bedroom. My stomach drops at the sight I'm met with. Not only does the elven king look frail, but he looks old and withered. Sick. His beautiful brown skin is ashen. No longer does he sit tall and proud. Now, he slumps with eyes so dull his normally vibrant green irises can barely be seen. Despite his wilted state, his smile remains the same . . . kind and real.

He motions me closer. "Come and sit." His veins are blue and purple, each branch stark against the paper-thin skin of his hand. His wrists shake as if he doesn't have control over them. It's heartbreaking to see.

I sit gingerly on the edge of his bed, facing him with furrowed brows. "Are you okay?" The question comes out just above a whisper, my voice cracking throughout each word.

He laughs. It's weaker than what I've heard before, but it's there. "I'm ill, my dear." He shifts his body, his joints groaning and creaking from the movement. As he does so, watery coughs erupt from his throat, and a slight wheeze can be heard through his chest. "I feel my time here is coming to a close, and then I can finally be reunited with my Aila."

"What—what do you mean? How did this happen? It's all so sudden."

"No, Maeve, I've been ill for a while now." A sad smile, his lips stretching over frail, porcelain teeth. "It has just been hidden in plain sight. A glamour shielding me from all except those of my choosing. Only my advisor, Madam Prea, and now you have seen me without the magick."

"Me?" I ask. King Osmar nods. "Why—Wait. Kayd doesn't know?" I blurt out, eyes gaping.

"No. My son . . ." An uneven, rugged sigh. *Heartache.* "I'm afraid of what will come when I die. Kayd's misplaced hatred for humans has spread through-out my kingdom, transforming it into something elves never stood for. It's like the very virus in my body. Attacking and killing the goodness that once prevailed in our kingdom. Several elves now hate mortals just as much as the other kingdoms. It's disheartening to see. We never wanted servants, you see.

And when we were forced to get them, we treated them well. My Aila and I have always treated them well, but I'm afraid of how he'll treat them once he's king."

Before today, I would have agreed with King Osmar without even thinking, but I think Prince Kayd could change. I think he *is* changing to some extent. But his hatred is like poison, already infecting this kingdom and turning it into something akin to Phandolus.

I think of the cold cell I woke up in after the trials. I think of the way the chain and shackle rubbed my skin raw. I think of the bruises littering Jerik's skin. I think of the matted hair and cowering shoulders of Reeve, Jasmine, and Elia.

"Why don't you claim more mortals at the trials, then?" I lean forward toward the sickly male before me. "If you took more in, then they would have better lives here. At least better than in the other kingdoms. It can't only be because the other kingdoms don't think you need them."

King Osmar's white-and-auburn eyebrow raises as he studies me. "My son really does keep his closest court members informed, doesn't he?"

Stupid. I'm so stupid for letting that slip. I smile sheepishly toward the king as he looks at me even closer now, folding his weak hands across his lap.

"But no, that's not the reason. When the Last War ended, the trials were created as genuine tests. Each kingdom was looking for something different depending on what servitude position they needed filled, whether it be strength for soldiers or grit for field workers or compassion for those who helped healers and worked with animals."

The king's clouded eyes stay trained on me. Like he's searching for something as he tells this tale.

"Around two hundred rotations ago, the royal houses of the other kingdoms decided they didn't care who they got. So long as they got servants, they were happy. They started making the trials as dangerous or entertaining as possible. Nythfaedell never did that, much to Kayd's disdain. This rotation, we wanted to test the contenders' character. The creatures the contenders faced are naturally docile. Extracting the item from them doesn't hurt.

"Those who faltered at the idea of harming a helpless being passed the first carefully curated test. Only one contender passed the second test. The first girl. She chose to make a healing potion, but she died during the changelings' ghastly combat trial. You and every other contender made poison."

My eyes snap up toward him, and my jaw drops.

"Yes, I remember you from this rotation's trials. So, that leads me to my question, Maeve. I have brought you here to show you my true self. Now, will you show me yours?"

The king looks at me expectantly. I stammer over my words. "I-I don't understand."

He only smiles warmly and leans forward just a little before he explains himself. "I know my son, and he would never have a mortal in his court. Who are you really to him?"

A dribble of sweat slides down my spine. My teeth trap my bottom lip, chewing it softly. I can't tell him. I don't want the kind king to know what I really am. A monster cloaked in darkness and disguised in ballgowns. A monster that's trying to be better.

The way King Osmar is looking at me—with those soft, caring eyes—I know he wants the truth before he goes. A last wish.

"I . . ." A long inhale releases through my nose. An equally long exhale out my mouth. I look down at the golden embroidered silk bedding beneath me. "I'm the Shackled Serpent. I was tasked to kill your son and the captain of his guard but was captured. I've been doing Prince Kayd's bidding ever since."

The words come out fast, muddled together in one long breath. That way, the dying king couldn't interrupt and I wouldn't lose my courage. Sneaking a peek back at his face, I see his weak gaze bore into me. My soul cowers away. But then the corner of his chapped lips tilts upward, and his frail hand reaches toward me, clasping mine with his.

"I had a feeling. You, my dear, have evidently caused a rift in the world as we know it."

"King Glynvyre," I tighten my hold on his hand, "I am so sorry for every-thing. For all the lives I've taken. For the blood that will permanently stain my hands. For the war that will only end in more death—"

"You know about the declaration? My son really does keep his court in-formed." The king sits back against the headrest of his bed again. He sucks on his bottom lip. A move I noticed during the dinner I shared with him, a move he does when he's thinking. "Huh."

"I believe I'm the only one who knows at the moment," I say quietly. "He told me right before you requested my presence."

The king nods. "A war is not ideal, but we can use this as an opportunity to fix what our ancestors did more than a thousand rotations ago. I have hope that after all the fighting and death and grief, our world will be better," King Osmar Glynvyre declares. "And you, dear Maeve, will make sure that happens."

A huffed laugh dances off my lips. The elven king is nothing what I imagined he'd be . . . and I am nothing like he expected.

A king afraid of the fall of his empire from anger and hatred. A mortal full of anger and hatred and trained to kill. Nothing alike, yet both dreamers. Dreamers who want a better world. In this moment, we are connected, bound together by our unadulterated hope that Galfei Thalor will be alright.

52

"HISTORY IS REPEATING ITSELF. War is upon us!" King Glynvyre's voice booms across the massive gold-and-ivory throne room. Green banners at each corner of the room seem to shudder at his words. He's cloaked under his glamour again, standing tall and proud before guards, courtiers, and a handful of commoners all tightly packed into the room.

Hushed, anxious murmurs erupt from the crowd. Feet begin to shift and worried eyes flit across each face in attendance. "One-thousand-twenty-seven rotations ago, we stood up for humans. *All* humans. And we will continue to do so. Today, we stand by Maeve Wyndell"—the king gestures toward me—"Galfei Thalor's Shackled Serpent."

Audible gasps ricochet across the throne room. My eyes shift near the front to Ernick, the elf I danced with at the king's revel, whose eyebrows raise in shock. Next to him is a courtier—an elf in the king's court, who I realize didn't attend the Autumnal Ball. He sneers up at me as I stand next to Prince Kayd. "The rumors were true . . ." His eyes rake down my body as his lips curl. "*Look at her.*"

I flinch under his scrutiny. Halton—on the other side of the elven prince—stiffens at the courtier's words. My heart seizes at his minuscule movement. It's hard having him so close, and yet I can't seem to even look at him. I want to. My soul yearns to, but I'm scared and stubborn and need time. So, instead, I stay looking ahead, ignoring the eyes meant only for me in a sea of judgment.

Thankfully, Kayd sends a glare toward the courtier, who promptly closes his leering mouth. It doesn't stop his—or others'—dagger-like gaze from penetrating me to my very core.

"Now," King Osmar demands the attention of the crowd once again, "we all know this war was bound to happen. The other kingdoms are merely using this human as a means to start it . . . using her like generations of humans were used before."

Some elves with soft, regretful eyes nod at the king's words. One female places her palm against her chest and sighs sorrowfully. Seeing them makes hope bloom in my soul. But then, I see the others. Several—including the male who sneered at me—grimace at what King Osmar said. They're the ones who've been poisoned by Kayd's hate. Hate that I can see is beginning to dim, whether the prince likes it or not.

"Galfei Thalor's kingdoms," the elven king continues, "us included, forced her to become a killer. All the blood she has shed over the last several months stains our hands as well. Our world is changing, and that is because of the Shackled Serpent. Through this war, we have a chance to right the wrong that took place after the Last War. We as a people—as the elves of Nythfaedell—will make sure that change—*positive change*—is seen across the lands!"

Out of respect for the king, the crowd claps and cheers. But I see it. The way many of them glance at me. The uncertainty they hide under pleasant masks.

My truth is out. It's been confirmed for the residents in this palace and surrounding villages. I am the Shackled Serpent, and this war is my fault.

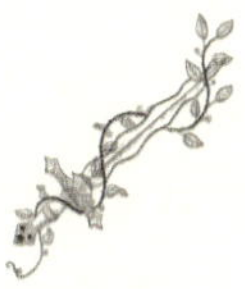

In the days following King Glynvyre's announcement, there's been a shift in the palace. Tension twists throughout the hallways, pulsing against the warm, ever-present ribbon of magick—competing with it. I feel that strain rising and rising, nearly at its boiling point, ready to snap.

Guards openly sneer at me. Courtiers whisper viciously in concealed groups as I walk past. Mortal servants—chambermaids I considered friends, like Reeve and Jasmine—avoid me at all costs.

They hate me. All of them.

After a nice, quiet dinner with Madam Prea in a secluded part of the kitchen, I wind my way through the hallways toward my chambers before an arm loops around mine.

"Why am I the last to know?"

I spin around and come face-to-face with Niam. His dark eyebrow is raised, and there's a smirk plastered across his face.

"Know what?" I playfully roll my eyes.

Yanking my arm, Niam pulls me into a stone alcove with winding stairs. The same alcove where Halton and I first kissed—first crossed that line after the prince's revel. I feel heat graze my skin, and my chest tightens at the thought.

"That Halton is your—"

"Don't say it." A hiss.

"Don't say what?" Alta pokes her head around the corner.

Niam and I jump back, startled by her sudden appearance. Her light giggle bounces around us as she steps into the alcove.

"That Halton is Maeve's—"

"Niam!" I press my palm to his mouth. I can feel his smile against my skin, and he presses a light kiss to my palm with a wink. Turning toward Alta, I narrow my eyes. "It appears everyone knows now."

Alta's eyes flicker, and she steps closer to Niam and me. "I'm sorry, Maeve. He wouldn't stop bugging me about why you were distancing yourself. I swear on the stars I didn't give any details."

"So"—Niam bumps me with his hip—"give me the details."

I lean against the stone wall and slide down it, letting out a deep sigh. Alta and Niam follow, squishing me between them.

"He's my mate. He knew the whole time and didn't tell me. Not much else to tell."

"He knew?" Niam's spine goes rigid. "I'm going to kill him!"

Like sister, like brother.

My arm shoots out across his chest just as he moves, most likely getting ready to spring onto his feet and march all the way to wherever Halton is now.

"I already chewed him out, brother. Enough for the both of us," Alta hums and leans her head against my shoulder.

"I've . . . been distant because I'm trying to process it all." Tilting my head, I rest my cheek against Alta's hairline. "I don't really know how to feel. I have this undeniable urge to see him . . . *be with him*, but I'm scared of what it all means."

A lone tear rolls down my cheek, and Niam gently wipes it away before wrapping his arm around my waist. Bright, shimmering stars sparkle above us, shining through the alcove window.

"My mother would know what to do." Biting my lip to stop it from wobbling, I take in the millions of souls in the sky. "Ottilie would, too."

"Who's Ottilie?" Alta asks quietly. "I've heard you mention her, but you've never told me about her."

Her light twines around my heart. It makes me smile.

"She was my best friend. She died during this rotation's trials. She was the only one out of nine contenders who was *good* enough to be chosen to serve

Nythfaedell. It makes sense, though. She was always so happy and positive. She cared for everyone she came across."

I tell them stories about Ottilie—our time spent in the meadow, pretending we were merfolk in the river, how her smile and laughter would brighten the darkest of days. I love the way sharing her with them makes me feel.

"You would have loved her. You both would have," I finish.

"She sounds amazing," Niam whispers.

"She was." The words crack against my tongue.

An hour of sitting in each other's company passes before I stretch my back and bid the twins a good night. I feel lighter now, having spent that time with them. Freer. Another little sliver of darkness disappearing from my soul.

Just as I'm turning the corner of the alcove, I hear Alta's quiet voice break the silence between the siblings. "Niam, I have something to tell you. It's about Ma."

"I know, Alta," Niam murmurs. "I know."

Bang! Bang! Bang! A loud, insistent knock rattles against the door to my chambers.

"Alta!" I yell across the sitting area, placing my pointer finger against the page I'm reading in a book I found nestled on a shelf in Niam's chambers. "I'm not in the mood to hang out tonight!"

A gravelly huff slips through the crack between the floor and the door. "Not Alta, and as much as I wish I could dance around the palace with no *real* responsibilities, I can't. Open up, mortal. It's *dire!*"

Kayd.

He bangs against the door a few more times. Whatever it is, it's urgent.

Closing the book, I hurry over to the door and swing it open. As soon as I come face-to-face with the elven prince, his fingers wrap around my wrist, and he pulls me out of my chambers, leaving my door ajar.

"You need to come with me right now."

The way his voice is strained. The way his grip is like a vise around my arm. Something is wrong. It scares me. Immediately, my mind goes to Halton. Did something happen to him? I would've felt something through our bond if something did. Or so I'm told.

"What's going on?" I ask, worry lacing my words.

The elven prince doesn't answer as he drags me out of the palace doors and onto the snow-covered ground. His steps are fast, unfaltering. It's hard to keep up, my toes clipping his heels. I can barely register where he's taking me.

"Kayd! Tell me what's happening. What's wrong?"

I'm met with more silence.

My wrist aches under his grip. My lungs burn from the cold air. He won't stop. He won't let go. Panic begins to bubble into a silent roar deep in my chest, making my gut churn with dread.

"Kayd!" I rip my hand out of his hold. "If you don't tell me what's happening, I swear, Kayd . . . What is going on?"

He stops walking and turns around to face me. His broad body looms closely enough to block wherever he was taking me. Gone are his contorted features. All signs of stress and panic evaporated. Now, he smiles at me—wide and proud—with mischief in his eyes.

"This." His left arm swoops forward as he steps to the side and gestures to the scene behind him.

Halton stands atop a sage-green blanket near a secluded part of the banks of the Crystal Lake Garden. Small platters of food are laid out across it, and orbs of floating lights surround him, casting him in a beautiful, warm glow. Snow falls gracefully from the sky but doesn't touch him or the blanket, as if Kayd himself is using his magick to shield the area. In the guard's hand is a bouquet of glowing, iridescent flowers.

From where I stand, I can see Halton's face relax as he takes me in. Hope, vulnerability, uncertainty, and fear flicker against the shadows along his features. Kayd's warm hand gently rests along the small of my back, and he leans in and whispers, "Hear him out."

My voice is equally as quiet as I stare at the guard—*my mate*. "What if I'm not strong enough to do that yet?"

A tender squeeze of his hand. "You are. You're the Shackled Serpent. You can do anything."

53

P RINCE KAYD'S WARMTH LEAVES my side, and his footfalls retreat. Muffled by the insistent buzzing in my ears, I barely hear the crunch of snow under his boots. The cold that was once stinging my skin now goes unnoticed. My focus is entirely trained on Halton.

Nerves rage against every inch of my being. Tremors vibrate beneath my flesh, and my heart pounds against my ribcage. My heart yearns to run up to him and pull him close to my chest, but my head begs me to turn away.

A breath to calm my racing heart. Another to conceal the fear and longing deep within my gut. I take my first tentative step toward him. Then another. Before I know it, I step into the magick bubble surrounding him. The chill from the snow seeps out of my body as I stand face-to-face with the elf—*the changeling*—who lied to me.

"Tell me. Tell me everything." My voice is calm, the opposite of every other emotion that pounds against my chest. At the nape of my neck, I feel Mother and Ottilie. A quiet, soothing brush of wind lets me know they're here.

Halton's mouth opens, but no words come out. He tries again. Nothing.

"Tell me!" My scream tears through my throat. Anger boils deep within my gut. Fear cements itself around my heart. Sorrow twists around my veins.

Tears spring to the back of my eyes and fall before I can stop them. My bottom lip trembles, and my hands shake. Halton's eyes are wide. Sadness, heartbreak at the sight of me.

The volume of my voice drops to a whisper. Any louder, and the words would crack. "That tightly wound cord—that tug, *the bond...*" I shove my hand against my chest as I stare at the now blurry figure in front me. "Whenever I feel it, I feel like I can't live without you. But I *will* if I need to. So, tell me, guard. Who are you? *Really?*"

With a shaky exhale, Halton nods and lowers himself onto the blanket, placing the flowers meant for me to the side. "Sit. Please, Maeve."

Quickly wiping the wet tracks from my cheeks, I drop to my knees and sit across from him.

A long sigh—trembling and weak—then he begins his story. "The first seven rotations of my life were fine. Great, even. Phandolus was an incredible home to me. I had it easier than most, being born into the royal family—"

Coughs rack through my body, and my jaw falls open.

"The queen never got over the loss of her son." The changeling guard's words barrel into me. Halton was the second baby in the family portrait.

The corners of his lips curve upward for a split second, amusement lighting his features before he contains it and continues. "I lived with my mother and father . . . and my twin sister, Andrina . . ." He pauses, allowing this to sink in, and gauges me wearily.

When I don't say anything else, he wrings his fingers together and tenses his jaw before starting again.

"I loved the outdoors. Running around the lush Phandolus pine woods and trying my hardest to make it to the closest mountain before getting caught by the guards my parents insisted watch over me. I never did."

He chuckles. Despite the ragged emotions caving in around me, I smile at the sound of his laugh. A sound I've loved since the first time I heard it.

"One day—not long after mine and Andrina's seventh birthday—I was play-ing with her in the woods . . . only about a mile outside the palace grounds. It was something we would do from time to time. I-I just didn't know this time would be different. I was climbing onto this dead tree stump near a ravine when Andrina suggested we play hide-and-seek. She said I could count first, and she would hide. I happily agreed because she never let me go first.

"As soon as I closed my eyes, she came up behind me and . . . pushed me off the stump. My body was flung down the cliff. I-I remember the feeling of the sharp, jagged edges of each rock digging into my skin. My chin . . . was sliced open by a particularly large boulder, and I broke my foot.

"I remember trying to stand but quickly realized I couldn't. I was bloodied and bruised and broken. I called up to my sister, asking for help. Asking for *her* to help. I yelled at her to get our parents. The way she stared at me . . . Thinking about it now makes me sick, but at the time, I didn't notice. She just stared and stared. No emotion. Nothing. She just . . . turned around and left me."

My breath hitches in the back of my throat, and my heart shatters against my ribs. Andrina left him . . . He was a *child. She* was a child when she walked away. And then she asked me to finish the job, sending me here to kill not only the elven prince but her brother, who somehow survived.

Halton clears his throat, trying to hide his pain from reliving this moment again. Pain I feel in my chest as if it were my own. I want to tell him he doesn't have to continue. Before I can, more words slip past his gritted teeth.

"I thought . . . I thought she went to get our parents, but . . . they never showed. The sun seemed to set quicker that day, like Phandolus knew its prince was about to die. The darkness of the wild forests surrounded me, and I . . . I was so scared."

Halton's hands clutched in his lap begin to tremble. As if it were instinct, I reach over and wrap my fingers around his. His shoulders relax slightly at the touch, and a small elated huff releases from his lungs. His flesh is frigid under my touch. The same cold that seeps out of Andrina. It should make me recoil, but knowing it's him, I don't. It's comforting. *It's Halton.*

"I-I remember curling up into a tight little ball on the damp soil and counting the stars. I don't know why I did that, but each number that left my mouth . . . the higher and higher I got . . . the less afraid I was."

Halton shifts uncomfortably as his tongue peeks out from the corner of his mouth. I can see the misty start of tears beginning to form across his eyes. I squeeze his hand. His fingers squeeze back, clutching onto me desperately.

"Luckily, for me," he continues after a moment, "a group of elven thieves found me. They were trekking through the ravine, cloaked by the dark night, with jewels and treasures they stole from the palace—my home. One of them noticed me, and as soon as they saw my dirt-covered garments and the royal crest atop my breast, they decided to take me with them. As some sort of ransom, perhaps.

"Before I knew it, I was pushed to my knees in front of King Osmar and Queen Aila . . . along with a portion of the stolen riches. I think they thought that if they presented the royal family with riches and the Prince of Phandolus, they'd be rewarded. King Osmar sent them away with nothing but hefty fines for crossing into changeling territory illegally."

My thumb begins to trace small circles along his hand as I scoot closer. I hate that he's reliving this for me.

Looking back up at me, his red-rimmed eyes flash with emotion as his lip wobbles. Clearing his throat, he says, "I remember the look Queen Aila gave me. It was a look of second chances. The way her hazel eyes bore into me, like she could see into my soul. At that moment, I knew I would be okay if she had any say in it. King Osmar was just as kind, and they took me in as soon as I explained what happened. They gave me a new home. They allowed me to play and train with their son. They saved me. The elves—who I was taught to think were my enemies—saved me. That day, I shifted into the elf you see now, so no one—no elves or changelings—would know my true identity. And since then, I've only ever been that elf."

Halton's attention bores into mine. Scared. Ashamed. Unshed tears pool just beneath his lash line.

"You . . ." The words stick to my tongue. "You said Queen Aila had hazel eyes. Is that why you have hazel eyes?"

His lips pull up in the corners. His smile is soft, reminiscent. Nodding his head, a tear finally falls. "Yes. She was like a mother to me. When she passed, I swear a part of me died, too."

"And everything else?" I can't help but ask. "The hair, the skin . . ."

"Truthfully?" he asks, and I nod. "It was merely the first thing that came to my adolescent mind. I think one of the thieves who took me had this skin tone. And I couldn't tell you where the brown hair came from, but it stuck."

He chuckles. My light giggle follows suit, dancing under the snowy night. The way he's looking at me now. That strained rope in my chest pulls so hard it makes me gasp.

"Serpent." The nickname he always used to call me sounds different now. *He* sounds different, broken. But there's a softness to the word now. A term of endearment I'm surprisingly okay with. "I'm so incredibly sorry."

"Don't—" I squeeze his hand tightly and stare into his open soul, his soul he bares for me and only me. What he went through—that betrayal from his own blood—no one should have to endure such a thing. "Don't apologize. You do not need to. I understand . . . I understand now. You've had to lie and hide your whole life. *It's not fair.*" The last three words are merely a broken whisper.

Halton leans forward and tucks a stray piece of hair behind my ear. I lean forward and wipe a wayward tear gliding down his nose. As I pull my hand back into my lap, I pause.

There's a question I need to ask. A question I've been mulling over since I found out the truth. A question that I've asked before, but something inside me screams to ask it again. "Is Halton your real name?"

"To me, it is. I've been called Halton for most of my life. Since that first day I shifted seventeen rotations ago. But no"—he shakes his head—"it's not my real name."

"And what name is?"

He hesitates, but not because he doesn't want to tell me. I can see the emotion in his eyes. I can feel those same emotions in my chest. He's nervous about uttering the name of his old self. "Amsden. Amsden Verral."

"Amsden," I repeat. It's only a whisper, but something shifts as soon as it falls off my lips. The bond flares, tightening around my lungs and searing itself into my soul. Our gasps—loud and surprised—pierce the warm, magicked air.

"Say it again." His usually smooth tenor sounds wrecked, his chest rising and falling rapidly.

"Amsden," I coo. The name feels *right*. It's light on my tongue and drips languidly off my smiling lips.

His eyes squeeze shut. "No one has called me that since I was taken. I never wanted anyone to call me that again . . ." His eyes snap open—watery and full of emotion. "Until now."

I say his name again. Each syllable opens up a small part of me and trickles of light pour into me, like my body—my entire being—knows this is right. It's waves crashing against the shore. It's the sound of the Moon Elm Tree swaying in the breeze. It's euphoria surrounding The Night of Light. *Amsden . . .*

Bringing his palm up to cup my cheek, Halton—no, not Halton, *Amsden*—leans in. He gives me ample time to back away. Nothing in all of Galfei Thalor would make me do such a thing.

His chilly lips lightly brush against mine, a touch that's barely even there, before pressing them firmly. It sucks the breath right out of my lungs. It's all-consuming. My soul sings in response. It feels like magick erupting all around us, as if the trees are singing and the stars are dancing.

As he pulls away, I chase his plush lips until I can no longer reach. I open my eyes, adoration wafting off him in waves. "I hate you," I say. It's a whisper.

His chuckle makes my skin pucker. "No, you don't. Not really," he says with a smile.

I shake my head, a grin pulling against my lips. "No, not really."

Our lips meet again. This kiss is passionate, filled with the longing we felt when we were away from each other. Our teeth clash, and our tongues wrestle together. It's everything I've silently dreamed of since the Autumnal Ball—since I kicked him out of my life.

Amsden begins to lean over me, lowering me onto the plush blanket. My hand rests against his chest, stopping him halfway down. His body stiffens under my touch. Worry gnaws away at his features as he looks away.

Shuffling back up until I'm upright again, I whisper, "I want to see you . . . I want to see all of you, Amsden. The *real* you."

His eyes snap back to me, widening at my request. They're filled with shock and worry. Fear—so much fear is buried underneath him. A child left for dead by his sister. A child alone in a new kingdom.

His slender hands begin to shake at his sides, and his bottom lip wobbles. "If I do . . ." It's a scared whisper, cracking with so much vulnerability, so much weight. "Please—please don't leave me."

I don't know what to say, so I kiss him once again. All my emotions—everything I can offer—flows from me to him. Anger for what happened to him, sorrow for the boy prince who died seventeen rotations ago, longing for his touch, lust, and love—so much love. It's all there in the firm press of our lips.

As I pull away, his shaky breath hits my lips, and the shift begins. Slowly, gray-white leaks into the beige skin I've learned to love. His brown hair disappears as strands of snow white take its place. Much to my delight, it stays the same length and style. A cut so handsome that I couldn't help but notice even as I was tied to a chair. Hazel irises turn ice blue—darker than Andrina's pale, nearly white. His sharp facial features round out slightly, and his frame becomes broader than what I'm used to. The shift is a gradual, easy flow, like snow melting away as the earth warms during spring.

A jagged scar, even paler than the rest of his flesh, adorns his chin. It takes me a moment to realize it's what is left from that fateful day. The day Amsden became no more, when Halton was born. His entire body is trembling. Vulnerability shines through those foreign, yet familiar, eyes. He's breathtaking. A phantom prince.

My hand—still resting on his chest—presses firmly above his heart. "Mine." My other hand reaches toward his ghostly face—olive dark against white. My thumb traces his cheekbones, wiping away a lone tear that breaches his lash line. "You are mine, Amsden," I breathe, "as I am yours."

Frigid lips crash into mine. His fingers trace up the side of my throat and wrap around the back of my head, gripping onto my hair as he pours all he is into it. Fire and ice, as we once were . . . as we still are.

I move my lips against his with as much passion as I can muster. Blissful moments pass before his mouth traces along my jaw and travels down to my collarbone. Pounding violently against my ribs, my heart races as his lips lower and his hands begin to untie the leather straps at the front of my tunic. His movements are slow, unrushed as he begins to undress me.

My top is shucked over my head and tossed to the side. His wandering hands fall to my leather pants. Adoration shines brightly in his eyes as they roam over my body. And while I gaze into those icy blues, I know what I want to do. I want . . . No, I *need* to show him just how much he means to me despite everything that happened.

My hand softly covers his, halting his work on my bottoms. Amsden looks up at me, confusion clouding his features. I kiss him swiftly on the cheek before adjusting my weight and pushing him onto his back.

"I want to make you feel good, Amsden. Will you let me do that?" My voice is seductive, laced with devotion. For him. Only him.

The guard's mouth drops open slightly. Words do not come. He simply nods.

A swift kiss to his bottom lip as I reach for the bottom of his tunic, pulling it over his head. His torso—more muscular as a changeling—makes my mouth go dry. I need to taste him. I lick and bite and kiss down his chest until my lips reach the top of his pants. I can't help my smirk as Amsden writhes beneath my touch. The sounds of his stifled groans ring around the warm bubble that shields us from the snow.

Everything blurs by the time my tongue licks a long, slow strip from the base of his cock to the tip. I don't remember taking his pants off. I don't remember seeing his length spring free. My need to pleasure him—*to love him*—clouds my mind. As if time itself skipped forward.

"Shit . . ." he groans as I lick him once again before suckling the salty tip. The taste of him—something so utterly *him*—makes my mouth salivate. His bone-white fingers push into my hair and wrap themselves around the roots, pulling lightly.

My moan is loud, embarrassingly so. His entire body stiffens from the vibrations. I take the opportunity to lower my mouth as far as I can. When he hits the back of my throat, I hold him there, my nostrils flaring and tears prickling against my eyes.

A beat of stillness. His hand lightly holds my nose against his white curls before I move back up his length and repeat. Picking up the pace, he begins to squirm under the heat of my mouth. Filthy curses leave his lips, spurring me on. My thighs clench together as that familiar throbbing makes itself known. A feeling only he can elicit.

Soon, it becomes too much for him, and he's pulling me off, a string of saliva connecting my swollen bottom lip to his leaking tip. He growls at the sight. Dragging my body up, he captures my messy lips with his. His tongue glides across mine, the taste of him still lingering in my mouth.

Carefully, he flips me around. The way he's handling me . . . it's nothing like before, nothing I've ever experienced with him. Gone is the harsh pulling and pushing of our bodies. Slow passion replaces it.

His white hair falls into his eyes as he stares down at me and smiles. It's a smile so real and true it makes my heart swell in size. Nimbly, he finishes what he started and removes my pants. The icy wake left behind from his fingertips leaves chills across my flesh.

"I need you. I need all of you," he mumbles desperately as he positions himself between my bare legs, with his arm propping his body above mine near my head. Ice blue and white swirl around his eyes. "You steady me and stir me all at once."

Placing an open-mouthed kiss to the puckered burn scar on my right shoulder, Amsden slowly pushes his length into me. It's a new sensation—a slow, leisurely glide against my walls—and I can't stop the sob that pushes through my parted lips. Tears pool in my eyes before slowly falling down my cheeks.

I'm whole. Truly and utterly whole.

"Shhh . . . I've got you, Maeve." I whimper at the sound of my name. "I feel it, too."

Unshed silver lines Amsden's eyes as he deeply thrusts into me. My legs wrap around his waist, urging each thrust as deep as it can go. The feeling . . . It's so different from anything I have ever felt before. Our unhurried movements become one just as our souls do. A beautiful love affair.

A deep vibration thrums just below my sweat-slicked skin. Amsden's thrusts quicken without losing his depth, and his other hand slips between our bodies and rubs that sensitive, aching bundle. Short high-pitched mewls echo around us and mix with his heavy breathing.

"Amsden," I moan. "I-I'm going . . ."

"Let go for me, Serpent," he growls. I clench around him.

His fingers circle my clit, and his thrusts hit a spot so deep within me a guttural groan rips from my throat as that tightly wound spring snaps free, engulfing my body in blissful euphoria stronger than anything I've felt in my life. Thick hot tears roll down my neck as he mumbles encouraging words and works me through my pleasure.

Amsden's movement continues—just as deep and just as slow—before I come down. Light tingles flutter under my skin, and my limbs hang limply at my side. And the feel of him, pushing and pulling within me, makes me see white.

Not long after, his thrusts begin to stutter, his rhythm faltering as he gets close. My sensitive core is screaming, but I push it away. His eyes are closed, squeezing tightly as he chases his release. My fingers move to cup his face, gliding against his slick skin.

"My guard. My *changeling* guard . . . *My mate*," I coo. A whimper flies through his gritted teeth. "Look at me, Amsden."

Bright blue eyes meet mine as he pushes deep into me and stills. I feel his length pulse. His rigid breaths brush against my lips as he fills me.

A smile stretches across his face as he brushes a few strands of hair stuck to my forehead.

I can't help the giggle that flutters from my lips. After a beat, he joins in.

The green blanket is soft against my exposed legs as I lay on my stomach and stare at the changeling next to me. Amsden—clad only in his pants—gazes up at the starry night above us. One arm is draped behind his head. The other stretches toward me and plays with the fabric of my tunic. His chest glistens under the floating lights and the gathering snow reflects against his white skin.

He's breathtaking. I could lose all track of time simply taking him in. I would forfeit everything just to stay here and admire such a sweet creature. Grabbing his hand, I bring it up to my lips and gently kiss his fingertips. A gentle touch for each.

He shifts his head and gazes at me for a moment before fully turning onto his side and propping his head up upon his hand. The way he's looking at me . . .

would have once made me want to shy away from him. But now, I relish in it. He's seen me—all of me—just as I've seen him.

"I love you, Maeve Wyndell."

His declaration rings throughout my entire being. I hesitate. I don't *want* to hesitate. I can *feel* the love I have for him . . . I *know* I love him. I realized it as soon as I broke down in the forest of Derlow Grove. But the words won't come out. I'm scared. If I say it, I feel like it will all be ripped away from me, just like everything else that's good in my life. Mother. Ottilie. I can't lose him, too.

His smile doesn't drop. If anything, it widens. "You don't have to say anything, my beautiful serpent. I just want you to know how I feel."

I smile back just as color begins to seep into his skin, beige replacing white. The tips of his ears begin to point. Icy blue disappears behind hazel.

"Wait," I blurt out. Amsden's brows shoot upward in question. The shift halts halfway. "Can you wait just a little longer?" My voice is meek—embarrassed, even. He smiles as his elven form drains away once again.

And as I stare into his piercing blue eyes, I know—deep in my heart, down the ever-present cord in my chest that connects him to me—that I could never love someone more than the changeling guard next to me.

54

FOR THE FIRST TIME in months—*in rotations*—I feel . . . happy. A happiness full of fluttering stomachs and unrestrained smiles. A happiness I don't shy away from. A happiness I'm not used to.

I always thought I didn't deserve feeling this way after Mother. And after Ottilie, I never truly wanted to. Even with the hope of a false future with Jerik, I knew the emptiness I feel from their absence would always linger, and I welcomed that.

But as fate would have it, I've felt utterly whole during the three weeks following mine and Amsden's night in the Crystal Lake Garden. Having Amsden as a mate . . . It's euphoric. It's unrestrained and free.

Soaking in the hot water of my bath after a particularly heated afternoon tryst only moments ago, my blissful smile drops. Amsden's arms tighten around my waist and pull me even closer against his naked chest, as if he felt the shift in me.

"What's on your mind, Serpent?" His breath brushes against the shell of my ear before he presses his lips just below it.

I weave my fingers through his. The cold touch of his hand is like a spark against my nerves under the hot water. "Madam Prea told me I have to face everything—all parts of me—in order to truly feel free. There's one thing that

412

still haunts me, and I feel like sharing it with you—with my mate—will allow me to rid myself of the burden that plagues me."

Another kiss down my neck. A tight squeeze around my waist. "I hope you know I will happily bear any burden you face. You can tell me anything."

"I know," I sigh, my muscles relaxing in his hold. The water lapping over the edges of the bath fills the silent lull in conversation. Opening my mouth, I try to speak. Nothing comes out. Another squeeze from his muscular arm. A deep inhale. "When we were in Fiermoor, when the brawl broke out at the rally, I got dragged into an alley by a mortal man."

Amsden tenses under me. My thumb rubs across his hand.

"He thought I was an elf . . . and when he realized I wasn't, that didn't stop him. He attacked me. I . . . almost died. I-I was so scared, Amsden. That feeling . . . knowing I would no longer exist, still haunts me. Sometimes, I wake up in the middle of the night without any breath in my lungs, like that man is lurking in the shadows, waiting to finish what he started."

Large hands peel me off the chilly chest I nestled against and turn me around. Brown brows furrow deeply as he stares into my soul.

"If I was there . . . If I saw . . ." he begins, shaking his head and tilting his chin down. "That entire village would be nothing but smoldering ash."

I feel tremors underneath his skin. Barely felt, but they're there. His hands dig into my flesh, shaking under the rage brewing deep within him. My fingers graze across his cheek and over his nose. "I know, Amsden. I know."

Facing him now, I try to continue, but I cower underneath that burrowed shame I've felt for weeks. Amsden notices, the anger dissipating from his pores in an instant.

"No. No, don't do that. Don't hide from me." He pulls me toward his chest and hugs me tightly, then whispers, "Put the weight of your burden on my shoulders."

"I'm—" My throat closes tightly, grappling around the words I don't want to say. I try again. "I'm . . . I'm ashamed."

Amsden leans back and raises his eyebrow in question.

"I'm ashamed because he asked me if I was a rebel or kingdom loyalist, and I didn't—*couldn't*—answer. I'm ashamed because, for my whole life, I criticized the kingdoms and the injustices humans faced, but when the time to claim my stance came . . . I froze. I'm ashamed because my mother—*the first mortal rebel*—was whipped to death nine rotations ago, standing up for her truth, and I couldn't even proudly say that I stand with her. What kind of daughter does that make me?"

Amsden's eyes are lined with unshed tears. He leans forward and kisses my forehead before resting it against his. "It makes you human, Maeve." His faux hazel eyes burn into mine. "Beautifully and utterly human. You have nothing to be ashamed of. I'm sorry you feel like that, and I'm sorry I wasn't there for you when you needed me. But I'm here now, and I will make sure you never feel that way again. Okay?"

A stray tear falls down my cheek as I nod. His thumb is quick to swipe it away.

"Good," he mumbles before pressing his lips to mine. His kisses trail over my lips, across my cheeks, up my nose, and against my eyes. "My Serpent. My love. My human. My mate. I love you."

Nimble fingers dance down my neck, my skin tightening under his touch. They stall near my breasts, featherlight touches teasing my flesh.

"Amsden . . ." The word is nothing but breath against his jaw.

"Let me take care of you." His right thumb brushes over my nipple. It hardens at the sensation. "I will always take care of—"

A knock at the bathing chamber door interrupts him. His fingers stop their movements.

"Miss Maeve!" A timid call of my name. A chambermaid. "There is a letter for you."

"Just slide it under the door, please," I yell over my shoulder. My voice breathier than normal.

"Yes, my lady." A piece of parchment folded three times and sealed with a forest-green-and-gold circle of wax I know too well skids across the floor.

Amsden grunts under his breath at the sight. "He couldn't have waited fifteen minutes?"

With a giggle, I peck my guard's cheek and step out of the bath. Frothy water splashes over the sides, wetting the floor, and floral soaps and citrusy perfumes fill the air.

I place my hands into a small cutout trimmed with elven gold in the wall near the basin. The water droplets on my skin evaporate as soon as my hands enter the magickal nook. With dry hands now, I pick up the letter. My eyes scan the words elegantly written, then look up at my mate.

"Kayd is summoning us. Now."

Amsden and I enter the prince's parlor hand in hand. The room is nearly full. Kayd's personal guard and a handful of courtiers are scattered throughout. Kayd is on his throne, and Niam and Alta are draped over the velvet chaise.

Alta gives the two of us a warm, happy grin as we make our way through the crowd and stand against the wall near the throne. Eyes—so many sneers—shift to us. A few scoffs can be heard piercing through the quiet. Amsden ignores them and casually throws his arm over my shoulder before Kayd begins addressing the room.

"The changeling, merfolk, and tiefling armies have arrived on the shores of Nythfaedell. They are currently marching inland toward the palace grounds. Surrounding villages have been evacuated. We can expect the battle to commence at dawn."

Silence. No one utters a word as the weight of the situation suffocates the room. It's here. War has finally reached us. I begin to shake. Amsden can feel it against his body. His arm squeezes around me tightly. *Everything will be okay*, he says with that gesture alone. The bond tugs in response.

Nearby, I hear low, mumbled words deep in the crowd. A guard with slate-colored hair leans over to another, muttering something below his breath. Kayd hears it, too.

"Fletcher, isn't it?" the prince inquires, sharply, as he stares down the guard. The elf starts now that all eyes are on him, his back going rigid and his eyes bulging out. "You seem to have an opinion on the matter. Go on. Won't you be so kind and share with everyone?"

The guard's eyes grow impossibly wider. A beat. No one talks. No one moves, except for Kayd, who leans over his knees and juts his head to the side.

The guard straightens his shoulders and meets his prince's gaze before nodding once. "I was saying, Your Highness, that *mortal*," the guard spits out with venom dripping off his tongue as his head snaps in my direction, then points at me, "is the reason we are now at war. We should just give her over to the changelings and let them do what they wish to her. She is not worth it—"

"That *mortal*," Amsden cuts him off with a deadly growl as he steps toward the guard, his arm falling from my shoulders, "is my *mate*." Loud gasps cut through the tense room. His body is taut with fury next to mine. Eyes blazing as sharp as daggers in the direction of the guard. "If you say another word about her, I will rip your tongue out before sending you to the gallows."

Protests erupt from the back of the parlor. Whispers and murmurs bounce against the walls. Several heads turn toward me and Amsden.

"All right, all right!" Kayd's voice booms over everyone else's. He stands from his throne and looks down his nose at his court. As soon as it quiets down, he turns his attention toward the guard in question. "You heard him. Sir Halton here is the captain of my personal guard. He's in charge of my troops, in charge of *you*. If I were you, I'd take his threat seriously. You are dismissed. All of you.

"My court, I advise that you stay in your chambers until further notice. As for my men, your king and I will meet you in the armory to administer weapons and armor before dawn. From there, we will march to the fields on the edge of the palace grounds, where you will wait for your final orders. Go." Kayd's voice leaves no room for arguments.

My feet move on their own. I begin to walk toward the entrance of the parlor when Amsden's hand wraps around my wrist, stopping my retreat. I look up at him in confusion.

"You're one of us, Maeve," Prince Kayd says lightly behind Amsden, leaving the confines of his throne and plopping down onto the chaise between Niam and Alta. "You're family now. You stay."

Family. I look around at the four of them, four beings I once thought I despised. Tears prick the corners of my eyes. Amsden guides me over to a now-vacant, oversized chair and sits me down before leaning against its arm.

"There is something else, though. I waited for the others to leave . . . for Maeve's sake." Kayd's words are grave. My muscles tense. The others look toward the elven prince in confusion. Staring solely at me now, he continues. "The Elders of Terakeld sent a proclamation of support for Phandolus and the other kingdoms in the war against us . . . with an amendment that Maeve is to be captured and taken back to Terakeld to be punished. Amphitea and Fiermoor happily agreed. Phandolus also agreed, under false pretenses; they still think that guard killed her during the Autumnal Ball."

My world stops. Kayd's words are suspended in the air. Niam and Alta's horrified expressions are frozen. Amsden's bark of protest hangs off his lips.

Punished.

I know the truth behind that single word. Like Mother, I'll be whipped—most likely to death—in front of my people. In front of Father.

Harsh, rapid breaths rip from my lungs. It hurts to breathe. It hurts . . . Heat rises against my skin, my body becoming flushed.

Punished.

Punished.

Punished.

Whipped.

"Maeve . . ." The voice is nothing more than an echo ringing against my eardrums. "Serpent!" It's loud this time, stern. The voice breaks through whatever trance overtook me, and now, I can't hold back the deep-rooted sorrow boiling deep within my gut. With my head bowed, hot tears fall from my eyes and sear into my skin, sizzling under the heat of their stares.

Amsden's right hand slides up my shoulder and rests against the side of my neck. Without lifting his touch, he moves in front of me, kneeling on the ground as his left hand cups my cheek and lifts my head to face him and only him.

I can't focus.

Whipped.

My gaze shifts around in panic.

Whipped.

"Eyes on me, Serpent," he coos, the calm in his voice attempting to soothe me. Finally, my eyes land on his—soft and comforting. I lose my voice for a moment, opening and closing my mouth, but no sound seems to form. "Keep those pretty eyes on me. I won't let anything happen to you." With languid strokes of his thumb across the side of my throat, his palm catches the tears that fall.

"A death worthy of a monster like me." My voice is nothing more than a whisper.

"No." That single word weaves into my veins, toward my heart. It's absolute, unbreakable. The grip on my cheek tightens, his other hand following suit and cupping the other. "That unicorn—the embodiment of purity, of hope—would not have allowed a monster to share such a special moment with it. A monster would not have given those chambermaids brushes when she didn't need to. A monster would not have fought so fiercely to protect and honor those she loves. My serpent, my Maeve, my mate . . . you are *no* monster."

Calloused fingers wipe away my falling tears, brushing the raised skin on my scar. Amsden kisses my forehead. His hands move to mine as he pulls me out of the chair and squeezes me tightly against his chest. I sob and sob and sob. His tunic turns wet, but his grip remains steady, unrelenting. "You are no monster," he repeats against my hair over and over like a chant.

You are no monster.

Warmth wraps around me then. Bodies press against Amsden and me, arms wrapping tightly around our bodies. We're engulfed from all sides. Alta hugs me firmly from behind, her slim frame covering my back. Niam wraps his arms around Amsden and me, his caring eyes looking down on me as I cry. And Kayd stands close to my other side. His warm hand rests on my scarred shoulder, squeezing it comfortingly.

55

TEARS DRY, WINE IS poured, and day turns to dusk.

The five of us a family, no matter how odd we may seem. A family with an assassin who's learning to live, a prince whose heart is growing, rare twins who care for others more than themselves, and a hardened guard who's not what he seems. A family who spends our last night together before a looming war begins on our doorstep.

Boisterous laughter fills the room. My lips tip upward into a smile as I take in the scene. All eyes are on Alta as she waves her hands animatedly in the air. The wine in her goblet spills over the sides onto the nice chair she's occupying.

"And Maeve, listen to this. This is the best part!" A hiccup interrupts her thoughts, and she giggles meekly. "Halton tackled Kayd down a hill into a muddy creek just to stop him from being the first to jump in the river!"

I chortle and glance at my mate, who punches Kayd in the arm and laughs so freely that the rope in my chest pulses with affection.

"And I still managed to get there first." Kayd punches Halton back and saunters over to the chaise where Niam sits cross-legged.

Plopping down next to him, Kayd's arm wraps around Niam's shoulders and tugs him close to his chest.

"Disgusting." Alta winks at the two of them. Red tints Niam's cheeks, but he's beaming brighter than the Nythfaedell stars. The prince's green eyes meet mine, and his smile doesn't waver as he nods subtly in my direction. "Now that all of you are all loved up, each of you better spend the next however many revels helping me find my better half."

"You're too much of a flirt to settle down, Alta." Kayd rolls his eyes, and the female sticks her tongue out at him in response.

Glancing up at my mate, I'm met with bright, hazel eyes. Amsden's already looking at me. The smile that graces his lip and shows off his white teeth holds so much emotion in it. All aimed at me.

"I'd like to say a few things," the guard says loudly enough for the others to hear. As Alta, Niam, and Kayd's attention shift to us, Amsden breaks our eye contact and turns to look at the others. "Tomorrow will be a day that will go down in Galfei Thalor history. The day a mortal"—his hand reaches out to me—"changes the course of our world. The day Nythfaedell stands by her side and fights for what's right. No matter what happens tomorrow, this moment right here, right now, will live in our hearts until the end of our days."

He scans each of our faces, soaking in this time with his family before everything changes.

"I am grateful to my sister for pushing me down that cliff because, if it wasn't for her, I would have never met any of you. Alta"—Amsden turns his attention to the female's wide eyes—"you inspire me to be better at everything I put my mind to. We could all learn to have a more positive outlook on our lives . . . and have a heart as caring as yours. Thank you for always being a light in our often-moody group."

Chuckles flit across the parlor. Alta blushes.

"Niam, your kindness will lead this kingdom to great things. You have taught me to expand my heart, and for that"—he glances at me—"I can never repay you. You will change lives. I know you already have."

Niam sends a dazzling smile—wide and unrestrained—toward the guard. Kayd rubs Niam's shoulder, pride shining through the prince's eyes.

Amsden's stare shifts to Kayd. "My dear friend . . . my brother. You saved my life. I have never known a friendship that runs as deeply as ours, and I know I would have died long ago if it weren't for you and your family. Thank you—for everything."

Kayd bows his head to the guard.

"And my venomous serpent . . ." His hazel eyes bore into me. A few laughs from the others flutter around us. "You are the best thing to happen to this kingdom, to us. To me. You are the strength that holds us together. You are the humanity that differentiates us from the others. All of Galfei Thalor is better off because you are here."

My eyes water, and I smile at him. His cold lips connect with my cheeks before turning back to the group and lifting his goblet into the air. We all follow suit.

"To fighting those who stand between us and a new era. We will bring change to our lands. We will fight for those who do not have a say. We will make this world better for all, no matter how long and how many battles we must face. To Maeve!"

"To change!" Kayd chimes in.

"And mortals!" Niam cheers.

"And wine!" Alta giggles.

"And family!" I smile, and a single teardrop falls to the floor.

With hearts bursting full of life, we clink our goblets together, wine spilling on the rug beneath us.

"Oops . . . Sorry, Your Highness!" Alta chirps.

Lying in the dark, silk-covered bed, my fingers trace over Amsden's bare chest. Moonlight filters in through the small circular window above us. White ripples against beige. His elf form is present more often than not. It's a part of him now, and although I know the truth, he will never give it up. He shouldn't have to.

A low, deep hum vibrates beneath his chest—the only sound in his silent room as the two of us simply bask in the warmth of the crumpled bedding. It's comfortable. It's perfect. He's perfect.

Idly moving my fingers across his skin, the weight of what tomorrow will bring clouds my thoughts. I may be a killer, but I am not a soldier. There will be death, more death than I ever wanted to bestow upon these lands. Amsden and Kayd could cease to exist after the battle is over. Even Niam and Alta—while not fighting—will be near the battlefield, ready at a moment's notice to help the injured. They could get hurt. They could . . . I don't even want to think about it.

Hopefully, soon, all of this will be over. To think it all started with the ring of a bell at the trials.

"Do you think she'd be proud of me?" I whisper hoarsely. Tucking my chin into his chest, I nestle against his cool presence. "My mother, I mean."

He's quiet for a moment before he inhales my scent and kisses my hairline. "I'm not sure she'd love the idea of you letting a changeling fuck you silly."

I slap his chest, and his head tilts back, laughing loudly. The joyous sound slithers across my skin and seeps into my soul. Looking back down at me, Amsden leans down and presses his lips to mine. He whispers, "She would, Maeve. I can imagine the smile on her face as she watches you change the world that she stood defiantly against all those rotations before. Your mother would be so proud of you. And so would Ottilie. And Queen Aila."

"And your mother?" I ask timidly. "Your birth mother, that is."

Her haunted look as she stared up at the family portrait flashes in my mind.

A muscle in Amsden's jaw feathers as he thinks it over. "She . . . I don't know. I really don't know the Queen of Phandolus. I barely remembered what she looked like until I attended my first trials with Kayd six rotations ago and saw her sitting under the changeling tent. I'd like to think she would be proud as well, but even if she wasn't, it doesn't matter. I am proud of you, and I know the most important people in your life and mine would be proud, too."

The image of the grieving queen in my mind fades away like mist on a gust of wind. All that's left is the family portrait. Of Amsden as a baby, so innocent and unsuspecting of the life he'll live. In the memory of the painting, something snags at my attention. A small symbol embroidered on the white fur wrapped around him. Two jagged mountains in front of a large pointed snowflake with a crown of stars.

That symbol flashes again, repeating itself as I think back on everything that has happened since the trials. Carved into the wardrobe in my Phandolus chambers. Faintly etched into Amsden's sword . . . A symbol of Phandolus, of the royal changeling family.

The truth has always been there, plain as day, if I looked closely enough. My changeling prince, my elven guard.

"That word on your sword . . . *Nukorynn*," I speak into the quiet room, stumbling over the syllables of the name. He turns his head to face me, but my eyes are distant. Too-fast thoughts bang against my skull. "What does it mean?"

He shifts, and his brows crease. "When did you—"

"The day we decided to train with weapons," I mutter, bringing my gaze back onto his.

His chuckle fills the air, lightening the heavy thoughts weighing on my mind. "Only you, Serpent, would take notice of such a small thing."

My eyes roll into the back of my head, and I shove him with my shoulder. There's a pregnant pause. His jaw twitches as he looks away from me and mulls over whether he will tell me. "You don't have to—"

"It's elven . . . for 'nobody.'" The word is a breath, desolation lacing around it like an ominous storm cloud. *Nobody*. My lips move on their own accord, forming an upside-down crescent moon.

"Amsden." His eyes squeeze shut, as if he is in pain, then turns to face me once again. "You are not nobody. You are the Prince of Phandolus, who has been through much more than anyone should. You are the captain of the elven prince's forces, who fights for those around you. You are a friend and a lover. You are vexing and kind, and you give me butterflies every single time your beautiful hazel—or sometimes-blue—eyes meet mine. You are *you*. You are *my mate*. You are *somebody*."

A pink blush glides over his fair cheeks. His ethereal eyes—always so guarded and plagued by his past—are having trouble staying locked on mine. Bashful and hesitant.

"You know," I continue, "my brother, Arden, taught me how to survive when our mother died. Your sister taught me how to kill when I had nothing but an unyielding thirst for revenge. But you . . . you have taught me how to love."

My throat bobs. Suddenly, it feels like sandpaper, dry and barren, as I attempt to say what I've always known. "I love you." Resolute and unwavering. His mouth parts slightly at my admission. "I love you as Halton. I love you as Amsden. I love all of you. You are mine . . . and I am yours."

Two tears fall down his cheeks and neck, pooling into the divot of his collarbones. He is the one who's crying, yet my cheeks are being enveloped in his embrace. Cool knuckles brush across my cheekbones and fingers swipe against my lips. He's comforting me, like he knows just how hard it was for me to say that. He always knows what I'm thinking, what I'm feeling. He has always known me . . . the *real* me.

I lean into his touch, and our lips slot together in a kiss that's full of all our love.

Love. For we have only and always loved each other. Just as fate carved it into our destiny long ago.

The night before the end of the world as we know it is spent making love. Beautiful love that sends tremors deep into the universe, shaking it to its core. The last peaceful night before the storm.

56

MY FINGERS TWITCH AT my side, trembling under the nerves slicing through my body. My left hand is clasped in Amsden's, and my right is wrapped around a steel ax, the weapon I chose this morning in a room full of anxious soldiers awaiting orders.

An ax. The weapon that began it all and the weapon that will end it all. No more servitude. No more assassinations. No more anger.

Hundreds of elven guards and soldiers are lined up, ready for battle. The empty, sloped hill—normally covered in green grass and flowers—is blanketed in snow. The sun has yet to wake, but the flickering torches surrounding the battlefield give off enough light. Puffs of fog leave our mouths as we nervously wait . . . and wait . . . and wait.

Each fighter is in gleaming gold armor with dark-green accents. All except me. Untrained with the heavy weight of armor, Kayd and King Osmar gifted me an elven gold breastplate dipped in melted black steel with carved scales, as well as matching vambraces. I didn't want to accept it. How could I when I feel like I'm the reason we're about to fight to the death? They wouldn't hear it, practically shoving the sleek protection in my arms before patting the backs of their men.

The two royals are in front of their ranks, atop blond stallions, who are also covered in that shiny golden armor. They seem to be the only royals on the battlefield with their men unless I just can't see the warrior tiefling monarchs among their ranks.

The king's glamour is intact. He looks fierce and strong and healthy. No longer do his hands shake. His back is straight, and his chin is held high. I asked—*begged*—that he stay in bed today when I got him alone before the march here, but he merely shook his head and flashed me a kind, kingly smile.

"No leader is truly a leader if they do not fight with their men, Maeve" is all he said, before squeezing my shoulder and striding off to the stable.

Kayd's ferocious, vicious eyes scan the horizon, where the changeling, merfolk, and tiefling armies are lined up, ready for slaughter. A mix of silver, bronze, and Spiicrete armor-clad warriors await their orders.

Several tents surround the edges of the battlefield. Some are made up of plain white canvas, a place for elven healers to tend to the wounded, while others are bright, festive colors. Those tents are filled with spectating changeling, tiefling, and merfolk royals and courtiers dressed in lavish gowns, as if this war is something to celebrate. Their laughs dance along the cold winter air. Their clinking goblets ringing out is a slap to the face, stinging more than the biting wind.

A gentle squeeze around my hand pulls me back. I look up at Amsden, those same beautiful hazel eyes I saw beneath his helm at the trials study me. A swirl of emotions flicker across his features. He should be with his king and prince, leading his men to victory. Instead, he's here, with me . . . lined up like every other common soldier. *For me.* My hand squeezes his back.

"When all of this is over, I'm going to make you my wife, Maeve Wyndell, and I'm going to spend the rest of my days loving you." His mumble is low enough so only I can hear.

I look back at him with widened, teary eyes. My heart thumps loudly in my chest.

"Okay, Serpent?" His thumb rubs the top of my hand lovingly.

I nod, my throat drying up faster than a creek in the summer season, but I force the words out anyway. "Okay . . . *guard*."

His smile takes my breath away. The bond in my chest tugs and pulls toward him fiercely. I take a step to the side, and my arm rubs against his, his cold seeping into my clothes.

A horn—loud and low—bellows across the battlefield. The enemy is ready and waiting. Fists and weapons clang against their armor. Fierce battle cries to intimidate our forces.

"The course of history changes right here, right now!" King Osmar yells out to us, his soldiers. His voice is strong and loud. The stallion beneath him shifts on its feet as its master addresses us. "Today, we fight for mortals who were disregarded and demeaned for hundreds of rotations! Today, we fight to defend our home and our values! For Nythfaedell!"

"For Nythfaedell!" Deep, roaring yells sound off around me. Then a horn cries just behind us.

Shouts and howls erupt around me, and soldiers run past, following their charging prince and king. A golden wave of armor slams into a shore of enemies. I don't move. I can't. My feet stay planted into the snow-covered soil, refusing to run into the carnage that is bound to happen. My heart feels like it will break through my chest, and my hands shake uncontrollably.

Amsden—always my rock—stays with me. His grip is firm around my fingers, his gaze unfaltering. "You can do this, Serpent," he encourages. Love and pride and confidence in me lace his words.

I know I need to move. I need to fight. But my body refuses. "I can't—"

"Yes, you can. You will fight because you *need* to fight. You need to be on that battlefield more than any of us. For your people. *For you.* Because we will win this war, and when we do, we will change this world. Do you understand?"

I nod silently, my lower lip wobbling as I try to bury the trembling in my body deep down. Amsden sheaths his sword quickly and lifts his helm just over his nose, his other hand never leaving my grip. Crashing his lips to mine, I feel everything he longs to say in that single kiss. It's a promise for us right now at this moment. It's a promise for our future together as lovers, as husband and wife, as mates.

"Good." Amsden pulls his helm back on and grabs his sword. "Now go show them who the *real* Shackled Serpent is."

A quick squeeze of his hand, then he's pulling me with him. I'm running hand in hand with my lover into the storm. Swords clash around us. Blood splatters onto our skin. We swing together, moving as one, until we're forced to separate. Although Amsden's firm grip on my hand relents, I feel his eyes stay on me as I fight off hordes of soldiers. Several from all three opposing kingdoms notice my scale-covered breastplate and charge toward me. A large amount of changelings in silver armor go after my mate. Orders from Andrina, most likely.

An ember of fury sparks in my gut at the thought. His own sister—*his twin*. I tear down soldier after soldier after soldier. And as I do that, despite fighting off enemies of his own, Amsden's hot gaze never leaves me, and the pull in my chest intensifies.

My mate. My mate. My mate.

As if he were next to me, as if he hears the pounding chant of my soul, a reply echoes in my mind. Faint and far away, but it's all the same. *My lovely mate*, he seems to say back.

I exhale happily—a quick huff—just as a tiefling runs at me. Spinning around with ease, I swing my ax's blade through his wide red neck, then come face-to-face with . . .

"Drustan." The tiefling's severed head falls to the ground with a thud, but I don't look down at it. My eyes are trained on the man standing before me now, staring into those murky eyes I once gazed into while he thrusted into me. Now, those eyes are full of hatred.

"Maeve." Drustan's teeth grind together, like it pains him to say the name he once moaned out.

"I see you did become a soldier after all," I say, giving myself time. I step to the side. He mimics my movement. His copper armor reveals that he was chosen to serve Amphitea and the merfolk. But his blade, it's Spiicrete. The tieflings and merfolk working together to take down the elven kingdom.

"Drustan . . . I don't want to hurt you." He barks out a laugh, a sound so grotesque and vicious it makes me shiver. "Please. Walk away. I don't want to hurt another mortal—"

"Look around, Maeve!" he screams. Disgust and rage seep out of his pores. "You already have. We're dying because of *you*. *You* are the cause of this war. *You* attacked the kingdoms. *You* just couldn't deal with the death of your mother, so you cut down *innocent* beings. *You* are a disgrace."

Innocent? I know the deception in the kingdoms runs deep but *innocent*?

Drustan lunges at me. His sword is raised, and a snarl rips from his throat. He wants to see me dead. I sidestep his move and block his blow. He attacks again and again.

"Please, Drustan. Stop!" I beg, barely blocking a blow that would've severed my hand.

"Did your victims beg you to stop as you ended their lives?" he mocks, upper lip curling and teeth flashing.

I can't kill a mortal. I can't . . . Not after everything.

Several fast blows from his sword. I block every single one . . . until I don't. The Spiicrete slices into my thigh, leaving a gash gushing a river of blood. I hiss. He won't let up. He won't stop. His loyalty for the kingdoms won't let him stop. It's deep-rooted, never wavering.

Dread cements itself into my stomach. This is just like the trials.

Kill or be killed.

I unleash the serpent within, and before I know it, he is on the ground, bleeding from the gaping hole in his gut. Staring down at him, I freeze. I didn't mean to cut him so deeply, so fatally. I only wanted to wound him enough to get him to relent. Blood gurgles in the back of his throat as he stares up at me.

There is no fear in his features. Only anger. Fury toward the woman he used to bed.

I stumble back, away from his bleeding body, yet my eyes stay trained on him. Four mortals. I've now killed four mortals. I feel ill at the thought that he'll never see his family again.

"Maeve . . . dear."

The call of my name is faint, nothing more than a whisper fluttering on the cold winter wind.

"Maeve . . ."

Ripping my eyes away from Drustan, I whip my head around toward the direction the sound came. An early morning ray of sun glints off a piece of gold. Squinting at it, I see it's shaped like vines or branches. *Branches . . .* My heart drops. It's a crown. It's the king.

I sprint toward King Osmar and heave off several bodies strewn on top and around him. I fall to the ground as I take him in.

"My dear . . ." Blood pours from his mouth as he talks.

I frantically look around. We need a healer. Where are Niam and Alta? In my search, my eyes catch Kayd's. Horror spreads through his features as he realizes who I'm with. After kicking his current opponent—a young merman—to the side, he rushes toward us. As he does, King Osmar's glamour disappears.

"Father!" Kayd cries out, dropping to his knees and taking in the withered version of the man he knew. "Father, what's happening? What's—No. Please don't." His voice breaks, and his chest heaves.

A shuddering breath falls from the king's split lips as he reaches out to clasp his frail hand around Kayd's. "It's my time, son. I have been yearning to be with your mother for a long time, and now, I'll finally get to see her again." He inhales shakily.

Large teardrops drip out of the corner of Kayd's eyes. Mine are misty, with tears welling along my lashes.

"No more hatred, Kayd, okay? You, as king, with the help of my dear Maeve, here," he grabs my hand, "will fight to make things right again. I have faith in that."

A loud, shrill noise pierces the air. The fighting around us ceases as soldiers and guards and healers look around trying to figure out what or, more importantly, who it is. The tail end of the noise echoes around the battlefield before another long shrill bellows out again.

"Stars," Prince Kayd breathes out with awe twirling around the word.

My head follows his and the king's gazes, and the breath is knocked out of my lungs at the sight.

Cresting a hill in the near distance is a group of maybe fifty or so mortals. Each one holds elven gold swords high above their heads, except for their leader. In front, the woman who sobbed when Mother died, raises a black handmade flag. Embroidered in the center is a green snake.

My jaw hangs open, and tears gather behind my eyes. The mortal rebellion—the movement Mother started—is here, fighting for their freedom. With war cries ripping from their throats, they charge.

"They believe in you and the future you dream of, Maeve. As do I. Mortals don't deserve the life we gave them. They were more than happy to answer my call for aid and board *The Hathil* to fight for that very future," the king rasps out.

Kayd turns his gaze toward his father. His eyes are wrinkled together. "*The Hathil*? We don't have a ship named that."

King Osmar weakly laughs before it turns into wet coughs. "We do now, son. I named it after your assassin, after all."

Turning back toward the elven king, I whisper, "What does *hathil* mean?"

The king squeezes my hand as firmly as he can and smiles despite the blood leaking out. "Hope."

A sob bubbles up my throat and escapes my tightly pressed lips.

The king continues after a few moments of rugged breaths. I can see him struggling to breathe, to talk. "Despite the outcome of this war, we have won. For we have hope. Now go. Fight. Fight for what's right."

King Osmar Glynvyre smiles at the both of us as best as he can before his body goes limp and his eyes lose all life. Prince Kayd bows over his father's body and wails.

57

"**K**AYD, GET UP. YOU need to get up!"

Minutes—precious minutes that could mean life or death—passed before we were noticed. Soldiers from all three kingdoms charged at us. I jumped up, ready to fight them off.

That was seven kills ago. I swing my ax at an oncoming changeling soldier, shielding the prince's grieving form.

"Kayd! Now!" My booming voice startles him.

He sluggishly removes himself from his father's limp body. Wiping his red-rimmed eyes, he looks up at me. So much heartbreak. So much despair.

"Fight, Prince. Don't let your father's dying wish die with him."

Something snaps in him. Something so raw, his demeanor changes completely. A determined nod from Kayd, and before I know it, he's swinging his sword at our enemies. This time, however, guttural screams of fury and agony rip from his throat as he kills each one.

Down and down, limp bodies fall. My heart shatters as I watch him fight. A swift shake of my head, and I'm moving once again. Back-to-back, Prince Kayd and I fight as one, until flesh and blood stain the snow and seep into the soil.

435

When there's a lull in attackers, I face the prince. "Will you be okay?" My voice is soft, treading around the obvious. He's not fine. Not even close, but he must be. For him. For his father. For his kingdom. For all of us.

The smile he sends my way breaks my heart. It's full of sorrow. "Go, mortal. I'll be here with him. Find me when this is over."

A single nod, and I'm running into the throng of fighting. Dodging blades and leaping over dead bodies, I make my way toward the woman I yearn to know and the group of rebels surrounding her.

My gaze shifts to the side, making sure no more oncoming attackers are nearby. Suddenly, my eyes lock onto *him*. Jerik Flint.

He pales when he sees me, his movements coming to a halt. Standing in place as still as stone, horror contorts his entire being. His legs quiver, and his hands shake.

"You're alive . . ." his shattered voice carries on a gust of wind, as if the universe wants me to hear the mortified way he says it despite the distance between us.

That small flare of anger brews brighter as I look at the man who nearly killed me. I take a few steps in his direction, my ax dragging against the ground, dirt and snow churning under the blade. Jerik backs away slowly.

A pounding against my skull makes my steps falter—deep and forceful. A reminder. The vow I made in that bare-branched forest in Fiermoor repeats itself over and over like a chant.

No more mortals.

No more mortals.

No more mortals.

Drustan was an accident.

I channel the feeling I had when I turned my back away from Phandolus for the last time—lighter, freer. I want to feel that again. I want to completely rid myself of the darkness that I know still silently lurks.

Only a few steps away from Jerik now, I know I won't hurt him. Physically, that is. But I want to scare him. I want him to feel the fear I felt when I thought I was about to die. I want him to remember what he did to me, to stew in the decision he made.

He's stuck in place, as if his feet are cemented into the ground. Once I'm nose-to-nose with him, I smile. It's a sickly sweet smile that makes Jerik visibly shiver.

"You do not deserve to meet an end as quick as death, Jerik. You will spend your days in fear, constantly looking over your shoulder because, one day, I will kill you." An empty threat. I know it just as clearly as I know Amsden is my mate. *No more mortals.* "It may be tomorrow or months from now or even several rotations in the future. You won't know when I'll strike. You won't know, and it will eat you alive. So, here's some advice from the girl you wrapped your arms around every night for a month: learn how to sleep with one eye open."

The sound of trickling liquid fills the space between us. Looking down at his shaking legs, I notice one of his dark-blue pant legs getting darker. Jerik Flint is pissing himself . . . from fear of me.

My gut sinks. Perhaps I went too far.

I need to center myself again, remember what I'm fighting for. Remember the darkness I left at Andrina's threshold and banish it away from my soul.

I don't say anything as the wet spot grows larger. Then I run my eyes over his body until our gazes are locked. "Goodbye, Jerik."

I walk away from the future I thought I wanted.

Stepping over dead, bloodied bodies and making sure I avoid the guts and gore strewn across the ground, I look around the battlefield. Half of the field is on the ground bleeding out or being carried away to various healing tents. So much death, so much hurt.

Royals and courtiers in tents nearby are chatting among themselves, nibbling on bread and guzzling down wine. They don't blink an eye at the bloodshed being spilled at their feet.

I am not a monster, I sternly tell myself, *but they are.*

A whip of snow-white hair in the wind catches my eye. Andrina sits atop a throne in front of two larger ones in a blue luxurious tent to my left, gleefully watching the carnage.

Her high-pitched, honey-coated laugh stabs me in my chest. She's as beautiful as ever. The voice in my head that talked me out of truly harming Jerik is quiet now. That flare of fury erupts in a swift explosion as I watch her brush her long white hair away from her shoulder and nibble on a piece of jam-covered bread.

There's a reason I turned around and didn't kill Princess Andrina in Phandolus. I thought it was because I was shedding my skin and ridding myself of the monster she's turned me into. But as I look at her now, I know the universe knew what she's turned me into is nothing compared to what she has done to Amsden. She tried to kill her brother—*my mate.*

My grip tightens on the wooden handle of my ax.

The serenity I felt while walking away from her chambers disappeared the moment I learned the truth of what she did. I thought I walked away for myself, but it was really fate sparing her life for what she did to me so I could take it for what she did to him.

That deep, simmering rage boils higher and higher, like a cauldron overflowing. My boots stomp toward her. The snow crunching beneath each step sounds like bones shattering after a hit to the jaw. My hands adjust their grip on my ax, and we lock eyes.

Hers widen. I can see the whites of her knuckles as she clenches the arms of her throne. A thrill runs down my spine. I'm coming for her, and she knows it.

There's a sharp yell to my right. "Serpent! Don't!"

Twisting my head, I lock eyes with Amsden, and the bond in my soul stretches taut, begging me to go to him. He's fighting off a group of tieflings. In a single move, he plunges his bare fist into the chest of one soldier and rips their spine clean out. A deadly wolf mutilating its prey.

His helm is gone, and his lovely face is drenched, sweat rolling down his temple and splatters of blood across his chin. His eyes, however, don't even meet his opponents. They stay trained on me.

This is for you, Amsden. For what she did to you all those rotations ago.

I try to convey that in the look I give him. His mouth parts, and he shakes his head.

This is for you.

With a deep breath, I turn back toward the princess and stalk toward her a few steps more.

"Maeve!" The sound of my real name halts my movements. Red boiling rage fills my vision as I stand still, staring at the princess. I can vaguely hear the clashing of steel against elven gold against Spiicrete. I can barely hear the thuds of bodies falling around me. "Maeve!" he calls out again.

My head snaps toward Amsden. He's done fighting off his attackers and is now making his way toward me, his desperate footfalls picking up speed trying to get to me. The rage I feel clears like early morning fog dissipating as midday rolls around. He's shaking his head, begging me to not go down this path.

You are not a monster, his words echo in my mind.

What am I doing? So easily, I fell back into my old, fury-filled, hateful ways. All that anger bubbling over until I couldn't recognize myself any longer. And, like always, Amsden pulls me out of it, grounding me.

I turn away from Andrina, turn away from that miserable, hateful life and begin running toward my mate.

Get to him, Maeve. He is your rock. He is your tether to all things good.

I have tunnel vision for him. Nothing around me—not the battle, not the princess—matters.

A scream pierces the air once I'm close. Guttural and raw. I don't realize it's my own until I feel my throat tearing apart under the sound. It burns so intensely it feels like my vocal cords are ripping to shreds.

Standing before me is Amsden, eyes wide, and a Spiicrete blade through his chest. He stumbles forward, the sword sliding out of his elven gold armor-covered body with a nauseating squelch as if he were butter. His heavy body collapses into my arms. Time snags. Blood seeps out of the center of his chest and soaks through my measly armor and tunic beneath. It's warm and sticky. Bile shoots into the back of my throat at the feel of it.

Amsden's weight pulls both of us to the ground.

"No. No, no, no, nononononono," I sob. Gently laying him onto his back, I press my shaking hands to his chest and apply pressure to the wound. It's no use. His blood seeps through my fingers. "No. Please, Gods no. I just got you back! Help!"

He looks up at me with eyes full of love and adoration. His cold hand struggles to lift, but when he finds his strength, he cups my cheek, wiping away the tears beginning to fall.

"Don't cry," he says. Amsden's voice catches, and his breathing sounds gargled, wet as his gore seeps into his open lungs. I sob harder, and my body begins to shake. The light in my soul dims. This can't be it. He can't . . . "It's okay. It's okay," he hushes.

It's getting harder for him to breathe. Each exhale comes out slower and slower. Shattered. He sounds like King Osmar only moments before. He coughs up blood, droplets splattering against his neck and cheek. "Will you . . . will you look into my eyes—my real eyes—one last time?"

A sob rips from deep within my chest, but I nod. Tears run out of the corner of his red-rimmed lash line as he shifts. White engulfs him. His muscles stretch against his gold armor. Beautiful. He is so beautiful as elf and changeling. Those bright blue eyes stare at me. He looks scared, yet there is a sense of peace framing his features.

"Don't leave me. Don't leave me, Amsden. I can't do this without you." The words come out between my sobs. The bond tugs violently in my chest, grasping at his life force . . . begging him to not leave me. "Don't go where I cannot follow."

"I'll look for you in every lifetime, my venomous serpent," Amsden breathes out. "I love you. I will always love you." A deep, tattered inhale, then his chest slows. One last tear slips through his lashes. His hand falls from my face. And he's gone.

My heart—now mended together after all these months—rips in two. The cord in my chest that connects him to me for eternity snaps. A serrated knife plunging into my ribs. A predator clawing at my soul. The other half of my being, gone forever.

It's a pain I would never wish upon anyone, not even my worst enemy.

Forever broken. A wound that will never heal.

I scream. I scream until my face is red. I scream until my throat is raw. The sounds of clashing weapons come to a halt as my heartbreak and pain pierce the battlefield. It's completely silent other than my wails. "No! No. You can't leave me! You can't leave me! Kayd! Niam! Alta! Anyone! Help! Help him!"

I'm hysterical. I can barely breathe.

Fast, panic-stricken footsteps bound toward me not a minute later. It's Niam. He dodges bodies scattered across the battlefield, jumping over discarded weapons, and pushing through those standing by to watch.

The elf's stormy-gray eyes fill with horror as he stands above Amsden and me. Tears slip out and fall into the red-painted snow. Silently, he kneels next to me.

"Bring him back," I whisper. "Niam, bring him back!" My scream—aimed at my friend—makes him flinch. And yet, he does nothing. Why won't he do something?

His head moves from side to side as he stares at the lifeless changeling body in my arms. His eyes are vacant. "I-I can't, Maeve. We can heal, but we can't bring someone back." He sniffles back tears dripping out of his nose, and his lips wobble. His voice catches in the back of his throat. "He's gone."

The tug in my chest—frantically searching for its other half—falls limp at his words.

Loud gasps and cries sound off from behind us, along with several hurried steps. Before I can even look at who's approaching, I'm shoved to the side by strong bone-white hands. The King and Queen of Phandolus scoop up their son's body and hug him to their chests. Numbness creeps along every inch of my body as I stare at the monarchs.

I try to reach out to him. I try to expand our bond to wherever his soul may be now. I don't feel anything. Nothing stares back at me. Nothing. I am nothing. My love is gone. And his murderer still stands before me.

The changeling queen's wails begin to drown out around me. Black boots shift in the corner of my eyes. Slowly, I lift my gaze to Amsden's killer. There is no life behind my glare. I died when this soldier plunged that forsaken Spiicrete sword through his chest.

I am nothing. Rage erupts from the deepest part of my being.

"Maeve!" Niam cries out as I grab *Nukorynn* from where it fell out of Amsden's limp hands and swing upward.

The killer blocks my blow. I go for his throat. Another block. I swing and swing and swing in hopes of spilling the blood of the man who spilled Amsden's. Another block and another block, he stumbles away. It's like he's not even trying.

I vaguely hear the call of my name, desperate to pull me away from the blood I seek. But it goes unnoticed underneath the raging, frantic heartbeat pulsing in my ears. If I could, I would rip his throat to shreds with my bare hands.

My sword arcs into the air before it plummets down toward his face. He stumbles back and, in that moment—so fast, I nearly missed it—a rusted chain glinting catches my eye. It looks familiar. Why does that look so familiar?

It hits me then.

A gasp leaves my lips, and I stagger backward as *Nukorynn* clatters to the ground. The necklace that hangs out of the top of his armor sends me reeling.

Memories flash through my mind. That necklace. I know that necklace. It's the same as . . .

I finally look at Amsden's killer properly.

No.

"Arden?"

58

M Y BROTHER, MY LOVELY and caring brother—who, from what I can see, is a general or some high-ranking officer in the Fiermoor army—killed the best part of me. The only good part of me. My mate.

I step back away from him even more. The world beneath my feet begins to spin. He reaches out to me. My body flinches away, but he doesn't retreat. His strong hands wrap around my arms and hold me upright.

He killed him. Arden killed Amsden. And I . . . almost killed Arden.

"Maeve," he whispers. There is pain in his eyes. I can't tell if it's because of who I am and why he's fighting or because of the tears streaming down my reddened face. I don't have the courage to ask.

He killed him. *No.*

Arden was only following orders. Arden is fighting in a war that I caused. Arden didn't mean to kill my love. There's no way he would have known. He didn't mean to. He didn't . . .

"I—" My words lodge themselves into my throat. I'm sorry. I'm angry. I'm broken. I'm not okay. *I'm the Shackled Serpent.*

"I know." My brother pulls me in close to his chest, engulfing me under the heat radiating off his body. "I saw you at the trials. I . . . The grief I felt when you had to kill those guards. The anger I felt when I saw the changelings pick you . . . I'm sorry. I'm so sorry."

Sobs rack through me, making my body convulse violently. His arms squeeze me tighter as he shushes me calmly and runs his blood-stained hands through my hair.

"Grab his body," a deep voice orders behind us. My body stiffens under my brother's embrace, and I peel myself away from him, turning around to face the crowd that has gathered.

Prince Kayd, Niam, and Alta are all huddled around Amsden on one side. The changeling king and queen are kneeling on the other. Princess Andrina stands just behind them.

I growl at the changeling king. "Do not touch him."

I go ignored. As two changeling guards approach and lean down toward Amsden's lifeless body, I scream again, lunging at them. "I said do not touch him!"

A stunned gasp comes from the changeling queen dressed in a silver gown and a fur wrap. She looks me up and down—covered in blood and dirt—with a sneer.

"Father!" Andrina screams, shielding herself behind her mourning parents. "That's the Shackled Serpent! Amsden wouldn't have died if this war never happened. She is the cause for my dear, long-lost brother's death!"

Her white finger jabs toward me, accentuating her point. My brother stiffens behind me and steps closer to me, but my glare zeroes in on the vile princess. Despite the tears that continue to cascade down my dirtied face, I laugh.

"Sure, let's talk about who's at fault, Andrina. *You* chose me in this rotation's trials. *You* trained me to become an assassin. *You* had me kill for you."

"What is she talking about, dearest?" the King of Phandolus questions with furrowed brows and a deep frown.

Andrina's voice hitches. "Look at her! She's unwell! She's making things up!"

Ignoring the princess for a moment, I turn to the king and queen. "You really don't remember me, do you? It wasn't that long ago when you pitted me against mortal guards and forced me to kill them. Do you truly not care about mortals enough to not remember the servants you acquire?"

The changeling royals open their mouths, their jaws hanging open, but I don't give them room to respond. My leer cuts to Andrina again. "But there's more. Princess, would you like to tell the rest of the story? Or shall I?"

Andrina steps forward, still protected by her parents. Her jaw twitches, and her fists curl.

"No? Okay. *You*, Andrina, sent me to Nythfaedell to kill Prince Kayd and the captain of his personal guard. *You* found out from your spies that your brother disguised himself as an elf, and *you* wanted to fix what you started seventeen rotations ago when you pushed *my mate* off that cliff."

Gasps echo through the crowd, reaching the frozen soldiers and courtiers on the sidelines. Widened eyes of horror and sorrow zero in on me.

"Oh Gods," I hear Arden mutter behind me. "He was your . . . I-I didn't know."

Andrina's eyes bulge. Pure, unadulterated horror swirls around her. Her secret is out.

"You're his . . . mate?" The queen whimpers and looks up at me with glassy eyes. Her lips quiver, and her gloved hand moves to cover her slackened mouth.

"Yes." My features are hard as I channel my changeling guard and address her. "Amsden Verral, your missing son and the Prince of Phandolus, is my mate," I growl. "Did you know he waited for you—*his parents*—to come and get him? He was scared and cold and *broken*, and he waited and waited and waited to be saved by you, but you never came. You left him. So, I will tell you one more time . . . Do. Not. Touch. Him."

Agony twists the queen's face, like she was the one who was stabbed through the chest, as she turns toward Andrina. Disgust twines around her heartbreak as she stares at her daughter. It's like she doesn't even recognize the princess who stands before her.

"You—you told us he was captured. You said you ran after him despite the darkness of night. You said you—you came straight to us. You . . ." She turns to me, her voice raising in hysteria, her body quaking. "We searched for him! We searched and searched, but it was like he vanished. And then we mourned him. He . . . We loved him! He needs to come home with us. He needs a proper burial."

Kayd stands up now, his eyes red from the loss of his father and brother. "And he will get one, Your Majesty. But Phandolus stopped being his home when he was betrayed by his kin." The queen begins to wail again, her face buried in her hands. "And for what? One can only assume power or leverage." The elven prince stares daggers into Andrina. She sputters slightly and slowly attempts to back away before her back hits the hard chests of a group of changeling guards. "I do not care to hear Princess Andrina's motives, but his home is Nythfaedell. And we will lay him to rest and honor him as our own."

The King of Phandolus is red in the face, glaring at his daughter. With disgust, he orders his guards to take her away. As shackles—the same kind of shackles I once wore in that cold, wet Phandolus cell—are placed upon the princess's wrists, she whines and wails and begins to cry.

Fighting against the strength of the guards, her eyes snap to me. "I will kill you, Maeve Wyndell! I will hunt you down, and you will regret ever crossing me! I deserve to rule Phandolus, and I will! Mark my words!"

The queen's muffled sobs become stronger. The king guards his emotions and steels himself off before turning toward Kayd. "I understand my son spent most of his life in your home. I understand that he should be given a burial by those who were there for him all this time. But please, young man, now that you will have to step into your role as King of Nythfaedell much earlier than you anticipated, I ask your permission to allow my wife and I there when you do."

The changeling king's eyes water as he stares at Kayd, whose eyes are wide as he looks toward Niam and Alta before settling on me. He stares into my soul, asking me if I'm okay with that. A part of me wants to refuse King Verral's wish. But then mother settles into my heart.

A parent who has lost a child should be there, Maeve, she seems to say.

She's right. I know she is. I think deep down, Amsden would have wanted them there, too.

I nod at Kayd. He gives me a small smile, then turns toward the king before nodding toward him.

The merfolk queen and the king and queen of the tieflings step forward, breaching the surrounding crowd. "The kingdoms' rulers must meet." The tiefling king speaks in a low voice. Spots of dark red blood splatter his face, nearly blending into his skin.

With relief relaxing his taut shoulders, King Verral nods. "There is no true victor in this war, and the motives behind it were"—he looks in the direction the guards took his daughter—"lies. We must discuss our next course of action."

Kayd lets out a shaky exhale before turning his undivided attention to his best friend. Kneeling, he places a soft kiss on Amsden's forehead, wipes away his tears and despair, and stands up, following the others.

As onlookers begin to disperse, I fall to my knees next to Amsden's cold, dead body. Niam and Alta scoot close, huddling around me. I can hear their voices as they mumble kind, loving words. I can feel their touch as they wrap their arms around me, holding me close to their warmth. But everything . . . All of it doesn't matter. I am nothing but a shell.

Arden stays with me, even when Niam and Alta are called on to help with the wounded. He stays with me as tears flow down my contorted face. He stays with me when I feel a slab of cement wrap around my heart and when my soul crumbles into ash. He doesn't leave his spot behind my slumped figure. Always looking out for me, ever since we were little.

I am nothing. I am nothing. I am nothing.

I don't know how much time has passed when someone silently hands Arden a torch. Hours, it seems, as the sky grows dark and night approaches. The light from the torch's flame flickers shadows across Amsden's still body. He's gone. Nothing matters. I am nothing.

As my thumb rubs circles across his cold, unmoving hand, footsteps approach. They're soft but certain. I don't look up at the intruder.

"Serpent." My eyes squeeze shut tightly. More tears fall as memories of Amsden calling me that name rush through my mind. I don't move an inch. "Maeve, you have to get up. We need to take his body."

Finally, movement. My head begins to violently shake back and forth. "No." My voice is hoarse.

The intruder bends his knees, crouching in front of me. I finally look at him. It's Kayd. A single tear rolls down his cheek. "We have to move him. We need to send him off."

I know we have to, but I don't want to be without him. If I could, I would stay right here, by his side, and let the freezing snow swallow me whole. Die from the ice. Pretend he's wrapping his frigid arms around me and merely fall asleep. There is no moving on after him. Death would be better than to live such a lonely life.

I bite my lower lip and nod but stay unmoving. Two elven guards remove his body from the cold, snow-covered ground, and I bury my head in my hands as they walk off.

"Why? Why did it have to be him?" My voice is broken, hollow with grief.

"Fate is a cruel thing. But, Maeve, he would not want you to cave in on yourself. Not because of him. If he were here, he would tell you to pick yourself up, be that stubborn, irritating mortal he loved, and make this shithole of a world better for everyone."

"But he *isn't* here." The words crack weakly against my tongue.

"No, he's not. So, make sure his death is not in vain." I look at the soon-to-be elven king and feel Mother and Ottilie. Their presences wrap around me in a hug.

I am proud of you, Maeve. I always have been, Mother says, her warmth pulsing through my veins.

Ottilie's light seeps into my bones. *Be happy, Wyndell. After all you've been through, be happy.*

Hot teardrops fall down my cheeks. I once thought they showed themselves to me when I was losing sight of what I wanted . . . revenge. I thought they were reminding me to stay on track. But now, I realize they were merely reminding me that they'll always be with me through everything. No matter what.

Like a splash of cold water, I feel something else. Cool yet comforting, thrumming with love. It pulls at my chest and fills a void in my soul. It's Amsden.

A sob barrels out of my chest at the feel of him. It feels like home.

I will always be with you, he seems to say as his presence nestles next to my heart. Looking up at the night sky, I see a new star—brighter than the rest—shining down on me. *Live, my serpent, my Maeve, my mate. Live.*

Kayd turns around and looks up at the sky. A breathy, broken laugh slips through the barrier of his lips. And just below Amsden's soul in the sky, a white figure breaches the forest tree line. The unicorn stands tall, staring only at me. *Hathil. Hope.*

Kayd looks back down at me with silver lining his eyes. I nod. An answer. A step toward hope. The elf's hand reaches out to me. "Let's get started, Serpent."

PART IV:
A SURVIVOR

EPILOGUE

1.5 ROTATIONS AFTER THE BATTLE OF SERPENT HILL

COMFORTING. THAT'S THE BEST way to describe the silence that wholly surrounds me. It's a silence that never leaves, a silence that resides deep in my chest.

Stop being so dramatic, my love. A soft brush of cool air glides down my neck and nudges at my pulse point. I can't help my smile from twisting across my face.

Birds hidden from the sweltering summer sun in nearby trees chirp. I'm back in Terakeld, the first but not the last home I've ever known. Sitting on the newly laid grass in front of my old family home, I bask in the quiet moments in my life.

It's a nice change of pace after nearly a full rotation of royal negotiations and massive life changes. A treaty was signed by all four kingdoms, and the trials were officially banned. Mortals can now roam the kingdoms, just as we did more than a thousand rotations ago. What I would have given to have Amsden by my side when it was declared.

But it wasn't easy getting to that point. Kingdom loyalists fought back, teaming up with many kingdom leaders. Riots erupted across the lands. Villages were pillaged and left in embers. When their efforts didn't stop the treaty for change, several loyalists moved to other kingdoms, and mortal ambassadors were sent to live in each royal palace to make sure what started the Last War doesn't happen again.

Princess Andrina was exiled by her family. It's said that she was sent to the farthest corner of Galfei Thalor. A desolate island that isn't even on our maps. An icy prison she is unable to leave for the rest of her days.

I also heard Jerik decided to stay in Phandolus. I try not to keep tabs on him, but knowing how many times he locks and double locks his doors and windows at night sends a sly thrill down my spine.

Arden chose to stay in Fiermoor to continue leading the tiefling soldiers. Something about a nice chambermaid he met during his second rotation as a servant. They now have a spire home in a village near the palace. He writes every week, keeping me updated on his life. It's comforting knowing how happy he is.

High-pitched laughter floats through the clean alleys and wraps around my heart. Children—mortals, elves, changelings, tieflings, and little merfolk younglings who fall behind on their wobbly legs—are running around, weaving in and out between homes and playing tag. Loud hammering mixes with their giggles. Builders from the best lumber and textile shops in all the kingdoms are hammering new panels on houses and painting unwarped doors.

In the distance, my father is gardening with Ms. Beverlye, who's beginning to warm up to me again. He seems to feel my gaze upon him because he finally looks me in the eye. A faint smile graces his chapped lips. He's getting better. It's going to take a long while before he's back to his old self—if he ever does—but it feels as if I finally have a sliver of the father that disappeared all those rotations ago. My lower lip quivers slightly as I watch him.

Next to me lies Alta. Lounging on her back, she soaks up the sun in her extravagant two-piece set, her midriff catching the eye of many who walk by. Several of which send me weary glances, still unsure of how to act around the Shackled Serpent. The elf glances over at the group of mortals and grins widely, sizing up her prey, and basking in the attention.

She truly does thrive here. If she could do away with the luxury of the elven palace and the Secret Spring, I'd like to think she'd move here permanently. Her month-long visits will just have to do instead.

My eyes shift to the space between my best friend and me. Wrapped in that beloved sage-green blanket sits a little girl with olive skin and a worn stone-blue silk ribbon sitting atop her snow-white hair. My daughter, Aila Ottilie Livinia Verral. Named after the mother figure in her father's life, as well as the best childhood friend and mother of her mother. At only eight months old, she's already a force to be reckoned with . . . just like Amsden. Her eyes—one gray-green and one icy blue—follow the older children as they play. They're alight with wonder and mischief, something I feel she gets from me.

Looking down at this pure little girl, my eyes mist over. I used to secretly imagine starting a family with Amsden during those weeks between our night in the Crystal Lake Garden and the battle. But in each of those dreams, I wasn't alone. I had my mate by my side. So, when I found out I was with child a couple months after the battle, I was terrified. Utterly broken. In a world so unstable and new, I didn't know if raising a child was the right thing to do. Let alone doing it by myself. It was something I wasn't sure I was ready for. But my family—new and old—gave me the support and strength I needed.

Amsden would have loved her. He *does* love her. Sometimes, I catch her giggling and swatting at her arm or leg or belly. I like to think it's him—his cold, comforting presence—brushing against his daughter.

My guard's legacy lives on through her. There are even reports of other children being born from love as pure as mine and Amsden's . . . children just like Aila.

A new world. A new future.

A high-pitched, delighted squeal escapes her little pink lips. Her tiny arms reach out, and her hands wiggle, as if she wants to grab something. I look up and see who she now wants. The newly mated Kings of Nythfaedell, King

Kayd Glynvyre and King Consort Niam Myradove Glynvyre, approach us with warm, loving smiles.

Before I can even stand to greet them, Kayd is already bending down and scooping Aila into his arms. His smile is infectious as he lightly kisses the top of her head.

"I'm glad to see who takes priority now. Kayd, you shouldn't have favorites," Alta chides with a teasing smirk, while hugging her brother tightly. The king and I embrace each other as tightly as we can without squishing the little girl. Then I move over to Niam, who picks me up and spins me around, our laughs twining together. I've missed them both so much. Months without seeing them is far too long.

"I'm the king. I can have a favorite if I'd like. And how could this little one not be mine?" Kayd chortles.

My heart swells and breaks simultaneously. Aila will not grow up with a father. She won't get to experience all the love he would have given her. But my little girl has them, a support system that would do absolutely anything for her in this new, uncharted world of ours.

After a few hours of relaxing in my father's yard, we all bid farewell to him before making the trek to my home.

"Let's take the long route," Kayd suggests, propping Aila on his hip and reaching his hand out toward Niam, who takes it with a twinkle in his eye. "I want to see our progress."

The elven king went above and beyond to champion the improvements of Terakeld. He hums in approval at the patches of grass and newly planted trees. He inspects the wells and checks each brick and wooden board on every building he passes.

Once in Towne Square, my throat closes. Emotions barrel through my chest. As if she felt my shift, Alta weaves her fingers through mine.

Towne Hall—where the Elders once ruled—is in the process of being torn down. Pathways are being created, and flowers are being planted throughout the area. The fountain has a new addition now. A human statue, taking its place next to the changeling, elf, tiefling, and merman. And covering the whipping post are memorials full of lit candles and family tokens for those who died during past trials or their servitude.

I walk toward the memorial for Mother that Father and I erected together. It's a large, simple bowl with items she loved or would have loved if she were still here. Kayd and Niam stand back with Aila. Alta stands by me, squeezing my hand.

"There was a time when I thought you could never be proud of the life I was living. I know now how wrong I was." I wipe a stray tear that drips from my lashes. "I get thanked a lot for the change I created. But it was never me that changed this world. It was you. I wish you could see the impact you made."

Bending down, I pull a black piece of cloth from the leather bag slung across my shoulder and unfold it. A green embroidered snake stares back at me as I place it in the bowl. The rebel flag is back where it belongs, with the true heart of the rebellion.

"She's seen it, and she *would* be so proud of you," a soft, lilting voice sounds off behind me.

Standing up, I turn toward the direction of the voice. I'm met with the woman who knew my mother probably more than anyone else. Her friend. Her follower. Her successor. Hardened determination no longer clouds her green-blue eyes as it had before. Now, they're soft—warm and relieved—as she looks at me.

"Livinia started the change little by little, and you helped finish it. You have her spirit and her heart. You're so much like her." A smile forms on her chapped lips as her gaze shifts across my features. "Whenever you're ready, I have some stories about your mother I think you'd like."

My throat closes, and my heart squeezes tightly. Nodding, I whisper, "I'd like that a lot."

"Good." Her smile doesn't waver as she begins to walk away.

"Wait!" I stop her before she can fully turn around. "What's your name?"

"Lyra. I look forward to speaking more with you, Maeve Wyndell." Her voice catches on a swift gust of wind that feels like Mother's warm presence. Lyra's eyes flutter closed as if she is thinking the same. Then, she turns around and walks toward the market.

Alta squeezes my hand when we can no longer see Lyra in the distance and guides us toward the other side of the whipping post. There, a small painting of Ottilie sits atop a metal stand. Flowers—rich in color, just like her personality—surround it. Her mother and father stand nearby, nodding at me as I approach her memorial.

"Ottilie, I miss you every day. You are the light I needed when I was suffocating in darkness. You are the light the world needed in its darkest time. Sometimes, I wish I could go back and trade places with you." A shuddering breath escapes my lungs. "You deserved to see the kingdoms. You deserved to live in Nythfaedell and experience The Night of Light. You deserved so much more than what you got. I love you. More than words can say."

Digging through my bag, I pull out what Kayd acquired for me a few months ago. A yellow silk ribbon to match the blue one she gave me in the meadow. I tie the ribbon around the corner of the frame, then stand to leave.

Wiping my eyes, I approach the others, and they engulf me in a tight hug before we continue our path.

As the sun dips down toward the horizon, my home comes into view. Sitting next to the rushing river and Moon Elm tree, my home—much bigger than anything I ever dreamed of—is now a silhouette against the sky.

"Ah, home sweet home," Alta sighs. She skips up the wooden stairs connected to the wraparound porch.

Sometimes, I feel like it's too big, but when I watch my friends—my *family*—barge through the door with my daughter wrapped in their arms, I understand why Kayd insisted on paying for the extra rooms. This home is not only mine. It's *ours*.

With a wave of Kayd's hand, supper appears atop the dining room table.

"Show off," Niam mumbles before kissing his mate's cheek.

Supper is lively as it always is with the elves. Wine is guzzled, and food is shared. Joyous laughter and little shrieks from Aila fill the space, bouncing off the walls and rattling off the furniture. But soon, it turns into yawns.

Alta is the first to retreat to her room, followed closely by Niam. Soon, it's only Kayd and I sitting on the forest-green velvet chaise and a very tired Aila, who is struggling to keep her eyes open.

"I should get to sleep, too," I mumble, standing up and looking at the king. As I sat in that cell—tied up and tortured—I never would have thought the elf I believed was so sadistic would be one of my closest friends. "It's way past this little one's bedtime." Lifting my daughter off Kayd's lap, he stands with me and walks me to my room.

"Niam and I must leave before dawn tomorrow. We simply came to see how you and our princess were doing." *Our princess.* My heart swells. "But we'll be back for an Alta-length stay soon," Kayd muses, and I snicker in response.

"Or, if you're up for it . . . you know you and Aila are always welcome in the palace. Your chambers are still yours, and we've added a nursery, as well. Plus, Madam Prea misses you. She brings you up nearly every day. And don't even get me started on how much she gushes about the little one. I swear, she delivers our girl, and now she's turned into a softy."

"She's always been a softy," I laugh. "You just never got to see it."

"Yes, well . . ." Kayd purses his lips together. "It could be a nice vacation for you. And it'll give me the chance to show my niece exactly what she's missing out on. By the time I'm done with her, she'll be begging to live in a golden palace, just as she should."

My eyes dramatically roll into the back of my head, and a playful chuckle slips through my smile. "You know Amsden wouldn't have wanted that for her."

Kayd smiles softly with a sad gleam in his eyes as they trail to a portrait of Amsden he commissioned as a housewarming gift, as if the house itself wasn't enough. "I know."

"But"—I turn to face him fully—"when she's older, I want to show her, her father's home. His *real* home."

King Kayd beams. He can barely hold his excitement. "She would love seeing The Night of Light. And I can teach her how to ride. And—" Aila, now half asleep, squirms in my arms from his rising voice. Mouthing a silent sorry, he sends me a sly wink. "Good night, Serpent. I look forward to doing all of that and more with the two of you." He turns toward the room Niam entered not too long ago.

"Good night, *Prince*," I call over my shoulder. He tilts his head back and laughs from deep within his stomach. I smile broadly at the sound.

Finally, I reside for the night. I enter my room—large and mostly empty—and gently place my sleeping daughter into the cradle next to the bed. Soft snores come from the blanket-wrapped bundle.

Smiling down at her, I whisper, "Your father and I love you so much, Aila Ottilie."

Then, as I slide under the cold, pale blue silks—a lovely color that's a mix of Ottilie's ribbon and Amsden's eyes—my body finally relaxes, engulfed by cool darkness. The feeling reminds me of his touch. Cold and safe. Reaching over, my hand grazes against his side of the bed. The side that should've been his.

A cool ribbon of wind twines up my arm and settles near my heart. My lips tug into a smile, and a few silent tears fall. That lingering thread of darkness creeps into my chest. It happens at times, usually when I think about the life I should've had with Amsden at my side. But now, there is always light ready to combat it.

I'm finally free.

When my eyes are too heavy to keep open, I sleep and dream of my mate . . . the changeling guard I once believed to be a monster and who made me more human than ever before.

461

ACKNOWLEDGEMENTS

As I sit here and stare at my screen, it's hard to put into words what I'm feeling right now. Elation. Relief. Anxiety. Fear. Appreciation. Gratitude. Words can be difficult—even for writers—but I will try my best to properly express how thankful I am to the people who made this book possible.

To Stevi, my amazing editor, The Shackled Serpent as we know it wouldn't be here today if it weren't for you. You transformed my story, taking my messy early draft and guiding me through ways to make it better. You refined it. You understood my vision and helped me figure out how I wanted to translate that onto paper. You found plot holes and brainstormed ways to fix them. You sent praise and suggestions and kept me focused. Your endless amount of support during the editing process is so appreciated. You made a difficult task feel like a breeze. Thank you for believing in me, my characters, and my story.

To my proofreaders, Samantha and Susan, who are both rockstars! Thank you for being so attentive and caring when it came to my book. You caught the little things that I never noticed. Samantha, thank you for taking the time to teach me all you know. When I had any questions (and there were a lot of them), you jumped at the opportunity to share your knowledge. Because of you, I now know so much more about writing and grammar. I truly appreciate it. And Susan, wow! First of all, thank you for working with me to create the perfect blurb. I loved collaborating with you until we got it right. Second, thank you for also working so diligently and making sure The Shackled Serpent was ready to publish. I appreciate you so much!

To Rena, my cover designer and illustrator, you are incredible! Despite only reading snippets, you easily transformed the world I created from words into art. The cover is everything I dreamed it would be. And the interior illustrations, including the beautiful map of Galfei Thalor, are to die for! I'm so thankful for you and all your hard work!

To Tasha, you were the first person I worked with on this book, and I'm so thankful I found you. I wasn't even done with my first draft when I reached out and asked about character art, and you didn't even hesitate to answer the call. You took my jumbled descriptions and created masterpieces. Maeve, Amsden, Kayd, Niam, Alta, Jerik, and Andrina all have been brought to life because of you. Thank you!

To Kelsey, my writing buddy, who should honestly get a collaboration credit on this book. You truly saved me during this entire process. Thank you for staying up late with me so I could bounce ideas off of you. Thank you for reading through my dozens of texts and picking apart good ideas from the bad. Thank you for always being there for me when I didn't know what to do or thought I couldn't do it.

To Mikayla, Bri, Lexi, and Liv, what would I do without you? You are my best friends and my biggest cheerleaders. You have been nothing but supportive during this entire journey, and I don't think I would've come this far if it wasn't for you all. Thank you for letting me gush about new scenes I randomly thought of in the shower. Thank you for being so enthusiastic about it all, even when reading isn't your favorite (I'm looking at you Mik lol). Thank you, thank you, thank you. I love you all so much!

To my family, who always checked in on me and asked how the book was coming along, I appreciate every one of you fiercely. Even from afar, I could feel all the support you were giving me. It means more than you know.

And to my husband, John, I love you and all that you've done for me and The Shackled Serpent. You encouraged me to write the story of my heart even when I didn't know if it was the best thing to do. You acted out fight scenes with me just so I could get them right. You cheered me on when I felt like I was on top of the world, and you let me vent when I was feeling down. Thank you eternally for all the love, support, and donations ;) I love you.

IMMERSE YOURSELF IN THE WORLD OF

The Shackled Serpent

LISTEN TO THE OFFICIAL PLAYLIST NOW!

MEET THE CHARACTERS

Sir Halton
Amsden Verral
Kayde Glynvyre
Nian + Alla Myradove
Jerik Flint
Andriaa Verral

About the Author

K.M. Lister is a native Texan who spent her childhood imagining stories and scenarios any chance she got—on the playground, in the shower, under the covers when she was supposed to be sleeping...you name it. She studied Communications and Media Studies at Texas A&M University—Corpus Christi and went into the journalism field soon after graduation. While writing news scripts, her mind always drifted to the endless amounts of stories that filled her heart. Thus, The Shackled Serpent was born. As a lover of angst, Kaci hopes her stories speak to her readers while bringing out emotions that might be hard to swallow.

Be sure to follow K.M. on her social media for any writing news.

@earthtokace

kmlister.com